AWAKENED

VAMPIRE AWAKENINGS
BOOK 1

BRENDA K DAVIES

Awakened
Vampire Awakenings Book 1
Copyright © 2012 Brenda K. Davies

Warning: All rights reserved. The unauthorized reproduction or distribution of this copyrighted work, in whole or part, in any form by any electronic, mechanical, or other means, is illegal and forbidden, without the written permission of the author.

This is a work of fiction. Characters, settings, names, and occurrences are a product of the author's imagination and bear no resemblance to any actual person, living or dead, places or settings, and/or occurrences. Any incidences of resemblance are purely coincidental.

Cover Art and Design: Christian Bentulan
Formatting: Jamie Davis

CHAPTER ONE

Shoving a loose strand of her blonde hair aside, Sera balanced the books in her arms as she searched for her keys. Finally locating them in her cluttered pocket, she pulled them free and slid them into the lock. Bumping the door open with her hip, she muttered a curse as the force of it knocked her precariously balanced books free.

Impatiently kicking them into the room, Sera slammed the door shut. Scooping everything up, she dumped the pile onto her neatly made bed. Her gaze drifted to her roommate's side of the room. She had to suppress a groan as she took in the disaster area. They had only been back for two weeks, and Kathleen had already managed to make a complete mess of things. Then again, Kathleen had made a mess on her first day back.

Pillows, sheets, and blankets cascaded off her bed and spilled onto the hardwood floor. Her desk overflowed with papers, books, garbage, pens, and markers. Sera had no idea how Kathleen managed to find anything in the clutter, let alone accomplish any studying. A poster of a rock band was peeling off the wall above her desk, and the one over her bed was torn and wrinkled. The garbage can next to her bed overflowed with wadded up papers.

Sera gathered her books and moved toward her desk. Unlike Kathleen, her desk was perfectly neat, with everything in its proper place, and her books sorted in alphabetical order. Kathleen said she was too uptight, while Sera thought Kathleen was a complete slob.

The door suddenly burst open. Sera jumped and stifled a frightened cry as it bounced against the wall with a resounding thud. It swung back rapidly, just missing Kathleen as she came bounding into the room. Sera shook her head in disbelief; Kathleen had the energy, and sometimes the capability, of causing the destruction of a tornado. However, unlike a tornado, Kathleen never intended to harm anyone or anything. Sometimes, it just worked out that way.

Sera, who had always been reserved, had been more than a little wary of Kathleen when they were thrust together freshman year. Sera's concerns about having a horrifying roommate seemed to have come true when she'd first met Kathleen. Kathleen arrived at the college two days before Sera and made her stake on the room first. It was trashed by the time Sera stepped through the door. She'd been horrified by the mess in the room, and certain she'd gotten the roommate from Hell.

However, the short, gregarious blonde standing in the middle of the mess didn't give her time to be appalled for long. Kathleen had rushed over and hugged her, squealing with enthusiasm about how much fun they were going to have. Sera had been astonished by the embrace and more than a little afraid of the energy Kathleen exuded.

Then, as she had come to know Kathleen, and started to become accustomed to her overwhelming ability to make everyone around her happier, Sera became incredibly grateful the college threw them together. Kathleen helped ease Sera's fears about being away at school with her own excitement about being there. She also could make friends with an ease Sera still found astonishing.

The thing that amazed Sera most was Kathleen actually liked her too. Kathleen was outgoing, bubbly, full of fun and adventure. Sera was reserved, scared of new things, and shy but for some reason, Kathleen was willing to put up with her introverted ways and be her friend anyway. Sera thought it was because Kathleen found her to be a challenge she planned to master. She had been determined to help Sera be more outgoing, and over the past three years, she succeeded in many ways.

"Hey, sweetie!" Kathleen called, throwing her bag and notebooks on the floor. "I had such a long day! What about you?"

"Long," Sera agreed, slumping onto her bed.

"Uh-oh, I know that look! What's wrong?"

Sera looked up at Kathleen's short figure. She was a little plump, but most of her weight rested in her overwhelming chest. She wore a body-hugging white tank top that stretched provocatively over her large breasts. Pulled into a ponytail, the end of her short blonde hair bobbed against her neck. Her sky blue eyes always sparkled mischievously. Her nose was small and pert, with a slight slope at the end of it. Her pristine plum lipstick contrasted prettily with her fair skin.

"Just beat," Sera finally replied. "Glad it's the weekend."

"Oh yeah! There's a party at Omega house tonight; we have to go!"

"I don't know," she replied, standing up and moving to the window.

"Oh, don't you dare do this to me!" Kathleen cried, dramatically throwing herself on the bed. "I'm not going to spend another semester dragging you out. It's the end of September, and you haven't been to any parties yet. We've been back for three weeks already. You're going willingly, and you're going to have a good time! I mean it, Sera."

Sera knew it was pointless to argue with her, Kathleen almost always got her way. She was tired and didn't feel like going to a party, but it would do her good to get out of their room and see people she hadn't seen since before summer break. Besides, she wasn't in the mood to clean Kathleen's mess tonight, and she knew she would if she stayed here.

"You're right," she relented.

Kathleen grinned as she bounced eagerly on the balls of her feet. "Honey, I'm always right! You should know that by now."

Sera laughed, some of the tension of the week finally easing. Kathleen always made her feel better. "Omega huh?"

"They're always good for a few laughs," Kathleen replied with a giggle. "Now, come on. It starts at seven, so that means I only have three hours to get ready. You have to help me. Then, of course, I'm going to help you."

Sera walked over to Kathleen's overflowing closet. Clothes were falling off the hangers, laying on the floor, and spilling out the door. She didn't know why Kathleen even bothered to unpack, she couldn't find anything in this mess, and her stuff was neater when it was in boxes and suitcases.

"What are we going to wear?" Kathleen pondered while tapping her finger on her lip as she perused the mess before her.

Sera sighed in resignation, but Kathleen chose to ignore it as she pawed her way through the mess. Kathleen was always trying to dress her up. Sometimes she permitted it, other times she put her foot down. She was not the type to put on an abundance of makeup or skimpy clothes. She preferred to dress down and fade into the background.

"You're going to look spectacular!" Kathleen cried as she pulled clothes from the closet and tossed them across the floor.

Sera pulled self-consciously at her clothes as she followed Kathleen toward the frat house. She felt awkward in the midnight blue, midriff-bearing shirt hugging her upper body. The short black skirt covered her to mid-thigh, but the slit on the right side rose another two inches. Kathleen had bought the outfit without trying it on, and to her dismay, discovered it didn't fit her. At least, that's what Kathleen told Sera, but Sera didn't believe her for a minute. It was a little too coincidental it fit Sera perfectly.

"Stop that," Kathleen said, slapping her hand away. "You look fantastic!"

"I feel uncomfortable."

"Get used to it. I've been trying for three years to get you to be more sociable and outgoing. This is our final year together, and I'm going to succeed."

Sera shot her a scowl as she followed Kathleen up the stairs of the frat house. They passed by a group of men sitting on the stairs, leering at them. One let out a low, appreciative whistle to the enjoyment of his friends. Sera fretted with her hair, anxiously shoving it behind her ear as she tried to ignore them.

They made their way past another group of guys in the doorway smiling at them. Sera averted her gaze; her skin was already beginning to crawl with discomfort. Alcohol was being passed around, and a cup of draft was shoved into her hand. She sipped at it before placing it on one of the speakers blaring music. Kathleen led the way through the crowded foyer and toward a side room. The decrepit, ugly furniture had been shoved against the dirty white walls to create dance space. Dancing couples and groups of friends packed the area. People laughed and shouted to be heard over the pounding music. It was enough to give her a headache.

"Hey!"

Sera looked up as Michelle appeared at her side. "Hey," she replied cheerfully, happy to find another friendly face in the crowd.

Michelle flashed a dazzling grin as she turned to survey the cluttered room. Her short black dress clung to every one of her slender curves. Her auburn hair had been pulled into an elegant French twist accentuating her long neck and the delicate sweep of her high cheekbones. She wore little makeup, but she didn't need much to illuminate her refined features and startling beauty. Her deep, mahogany eyes slanted at a provocative, almost feline, angle.

Where Kathleen exuded energy, Michelle radiated a cool, poised elegance. During Sera's second semester of school, she and Michelle had been paired as lab partners. It took them a while to get to know one another, but once they had, they'd hit it off. They had more in common than Sera did with Kathleen, and she found Michelle's friendship a pleasant break from Kathleen's tremendous excitement. It was good for Sera to have a chance to slow down and talk to someone a little more like her.

Michelle's gaze returned to Sera; her eyes swept disdainfully over her. Her thin lips, her only flaw to perfection, were pursed. Her long, slender nose scrunched distastefully. "You look nice," Michelle finally stated.

"Thank you," Sera replied, feeling even more uncomfortable under Michelle's scrutinizing stare.

"She looks wonderful!" Kathleen butted in; her voice tinged with aggravation.

Michelle turned her cool eyes to Kathleen; her gaze became even more disapproving. "I suppose you dressed her," she drawled.

Kathleen's eyes narrowed. Sera shook her head at the

hostility between her two best friends. Usually, when one was around, the other wasn't. However, when they were together, it took all she had to stop them from bickering.

"Of course," Kathleen said. "Someone has to teach her how to live life."

"And that's going to be you?" Michelle retorted.

Kathleen's shoulders thrust back as she prepared herself for battle. Sera looped her arm through Kathleen's, knowing it was time to separate the two. "I'll see you in a little bit, Michelle," she said as she pulled Kathleen toward the dance floor.

"I don't know why you put up with that bitch," Kathleen muttered.

"Michelle's not that bad; you just never gave her a chance."

"Oh, I gave her a chance, and then I realized the stick shoved up her ass is never going to come out."

"Kathleen," she groaned.

"It's true; you need better taste in friends. But oh well, let's dance."

Sera didn't have time to protest as Kathleen pulled her onto the dance floor. She found herself instantly swept up in the music and the mood. Another drink was thrust into her hand, and she decided to keep this one.

She danced for almost an hour before making her way out of the packed room. She grabbed another drink to wet her parched throat as she wound through the crowd toward the front door. Michelle was standing by the door, talking and laughing with two guys who were openly leering at her. Sera paused, not wanting to go near the guys, but the idea of fresh air was too tempting for her to refuse. She made her way toward them.

"Hey," she said, stopping beside Michelle. "Having fun yet?"

"Oh yeah," Michelle drawled, her voice dripping with sarcasm. "You?"

"Actually, yes."

Disapproval flashed through Michelle's eyes as she turned back to the two guys. Sera glanced at them, unable to stop her sneer of revulsion as they openly ogled her. Michelle looked at them disdainfully as she took a sip of beer. "Who's your friend?" the taller of the two asked, his eyes rapidly scanning Sera from head to toe then back up again.

"This is Serendipity," Michelle replied, the annoyance apparent in her voice.

"Huh?" he asked stupidly.

"Serendipity, but everyone calls me Sera," Sera replied.

"Pretty," he drawled, "Suits you."

Sera's face scrunched in distaste. He continued to leer at her, refusing to acknowledge her obvious revulsion. Unwillingly, she began to fiddle with her shirt again. A flash of satisfaction flitted across Michelle's face as she noted Sera's discomfort. A wave of resentment washed over her as she purposely made her hands still. No matter how close they were, Sera would never be able to get used to Michelle's attitude of superiority.

"Well, I'll see you later," Sera said coldly.

"Where are you going?" Michelle asked.

"Outside for some air."

The house had suddenly become overwhelmingly hot and noisy. If she didn't get out soon, she would melt or her head would explode. Fresh air was just what she needed to calm the growing tension inside her.

She hastily moved past the small group, making sure not to touch the guys as she headed out the door. Rapidly descending the steps, Sera strolled onto the front lawn. People were scattered across the grass, drinks in hand, laughing and dancing as they drunkenly stumbled around. Some had gathered beneath the trees to talk, while others were making out under them and on the lawn. One indiscreet couple was having sex next to the small rock wall.

Sera sat on the edge of the lawn, stretching her long legs. Tilting her head back, she admired the stars shining in the clear night sky. It had grown cooler, but summer was fighting to hang on for a little longer. She smiled as the alcohol seeped further into her bloodstream and warmed her from the inside out. The sky blurred for a second, before coming back into place. Laughing from the effects of the few drinks she'd had, she propped her head on her arms and relished in the cold air against her warm skin.

LIAM PUSHED his way through the people gathered on the stairs, ignoring their indignant looks and muttered words. He wasn't really in the mood for a party, but it had been a long week, and he needed to relieve some stress. Not to mention there would be plenty of girls here tonight.

"Hey, it's about time you got here."

He glanced up as Mike appeared beside him. Mike's light, sandy blond hair was tousled and wet with sweat as it curled in tendrils around his flushed, broad face. Mike had already been on the dance floor and had at least a few drinks in him as his clear blue eyes were bright with merriment. At an inch taller than Liam, and broader in the shoulders and chest, Mike was built like a linebacker and the star player on the football team. In many ways, he was the classic jock, except he was far from stupid. Mike often saw more than most people did.

He thrust a plastic cup of beer into Liam's hand. "Thanks," Liam muttered as he surveyed the crowd.

The house was already packed with people; the party in full swing as music blared from the speakers. It was going to be an interesting night, he realized as his gaze settled upon Michelle. She stood in the doorway talking to two guys he didn't know; both were admiring all her openly displayed charms. She laughed loudly, her head tilting back as she stroked one's arm flirtatiously.

Liam paid her no more attention as he turned to survey the rest of the room. "There are plenty of girls here tonight," Mike said. "Easy pickings."

"Hmm."

Mike laughed and slapped him solidly on the back. Liam scowled as beer sloshed onto his hand. He wiped at it absently before draining the rest of the cup. He tossed it over the banister on top of the overflowing garbage can. "Want another?"

"Yeah."

Liam stepped off the last stair as Mike led the way to the keg by the door. His gaze drifted back to Michelle. She was still standing in the doorway, but there was another girl with her now. Liam frowned as he paused to study the new addition. She was small, and delicate, with a petite frame emphasized by the body-hugging clothes she wore. Her breasts were high and full, a little more than a handful. Her waist was no more than an open hand width, her hips small and round. Despite her tiny appearance, her legs were amazingly long. In the short skirt she wore, he was able to admire the elegant curve of her calves and lower thighs.

He tore his gaze away from her legs as a familiar tightening began filling his groin. Her long, golden hair fell freely over her shoulders to spill down her back in thick, cascading waves. Her nose was small and narrow with a small slope at the end of it. He couldn't see her eyes, but he imagined they were as spectacular as the rest of her. Her mouth was full and an enticing dark, rose red color. A mouth designed for kissing, he decided.

"Who's that?"

Mike lifted his head from the keg. "Where?" he inquired as he thrust another beer into Liam's hand.

"The girl with Michelle, who is she?"

Mike's gaze followed his. He chuckled under his breath as he smiled. "That, my friend, is Serendipity, or Sera. Forget it, you'll never get close to her."

Liam raised an inquiring eyebrow as he took a sip of beer. "Really?"

"Yep. No one ever has."

He shot Mike a questioning look. "No one?" he asked in disbelief. The girl was beautiful; he highly doubted she had any problem attracting men. Even now, there were a bunch of guys hovering around her like moths to a flame.

Mike turned to him, his cornflower blue eyes intense. "As far as I know, she's never dated anyone on campus, and I've never seen her with a guy."

"But she comes to frat parties?"

"She comes with her roommate, and she leaves with her roommate, or by herself."

"Is she a lesbian?" He certainly hoped not, but it was a possibility.

"Never heard or saw anything like that either. Leave her be, Liam."

His brow furrowed as he turned to stare at Mike in disbelief. "Why, because she turned you down?" he quipped.

"I've never tried."

Liam laughed as he shook his head. "Yeah right. I know you, and there's no way you wouldn't try with someone like her!"

Mike bent to refill his cup. "Seriously, I haven't."

Liam stared at him in astonishment. He knew Mike as well as he knew himself, and he knew he intended to try with her. He didn't believe Mike for one second. Mike took hold of his cup and bent to refill it. "Why not?"

Mike shoved the cup back into Liam's hand. "I don't know. I mean she's hot, don't get me wrong, but..."

"But what?"

He ran a hand through his disheveled hair. "I don't know. We had Trig together last year; she helped me out a lot. I couldn't have passed the class without her, you know how I am with math, but there's something about her..." his voice trailed off as he frowned thoughtfully.

Liam sensed there was more, that Mike had used his incredible powers of deduction on the girl and hadn't liked what he'd discovered. "What about her?" Liam prodded.

Mike's frown deepened as he turned troubled eyes to Liam. "Honestly, it's almost as if she's scared of something. The few times I accidentally touched her, she would get this look on her face that, well... it just wasn't normal, wasn't right. I didn't want to scare her even more by making a pass at her. Plus..." Mike broke off, his brow furrowed as he stared at Sera and Michelle.

"Plus what?" Liam prodded.

Mike took a sip of beer. "I don't know; there's something about her, something I can't put my finger on or describe. Something different."

Liam couldn't believe one word he was hearing. Mike usually didn't care about a girl one way or another. No matter what. The fact he'd restrained himself from going after someone was astounding, but to hear him talk about her as if he genuinely liked her was an absolute miracle.

"Are you okay, Mike? Are you sick or something?"

Mike's frown disappeared as he grinned merrily. "No, I'm not. Trust me when you get close enough you'll see it, and you'll understand."

Liam turned to look at her. "Who said I was going to get close enough?"

Mike laughed. "I think you should leave her be, but I know

you, you'll be heading in that direction. For now though, let's see what other options we have available to us tonight. You're going to need them."

Liam didn't think he would need any other options. He had marked his conquest for the night, and he was going to have her, but it never hurt to look. "Sounds good to me."

Liam watched as she slipped out the door. He almost went after her but decided against it. She would be back; of that he was certain. When she came back, he would make his presence known. Until then, he decided to give her time alone and to inspect the rest of the women available for another night.

He followed Mike onto the crowded dance floor, instantly finding himself swamped by a group of girls who made it quite obvious he could have whatever he wanted from them. He tried to focus his attention on them, but his thoughts kept wandering to Sera, and when she would return.

CHAPTER TWO

"Here you are!" Sera looked up as Kathleen stumbled toward her. Beer splashed out of her cup, splattering on the ground. "Whatcha doing out here?"

"Just getting some air."

"Hmm, it does feel nice. Having fun?"

"Yeah, you?"

"Of course, but I got to show you something."

"Now?"

"Yup, get up!" She pulled on Sera's arm, spilling more of her drink onto her hand and down her arm. "Come on, Sera!"

"Can't it wait?" Sera protested, not ready to go plunging back into the house.

"No way! Come on!"

She jerked one more time, and Sera reluctantly climbed to her feet. "This had better be good," she mumbled, wiping absently at the back of her skirt.

"Oh, it is." Kathleen hurried back toward the house, tugging Sera behind her. "They're having fun!" she cried as they passed the couple by the wall. "Get a room!"

Sera laughed and climbed the stairs to the door. She plunged back into the house, allowing Kathleen to drag her toward the dance floor. The music pounded around her, vibrating the floor of the house, and hammering into her head. She instantly wished she were back outside where it was peaceful and refreshing.

"Look!" Kathleen yelled.

Sera looked around the crowded mass. "Where!" she yelled back.

"Over there!" Kathleen pointed.

Sera looked at the group of girls gathered in the back, but she saw nothing unusual about them. She was about to give up, thinking Kathleen was losing it, when she spotted Michelle. She stood amongst the group, a sweet smile on her usually composed face.

Sera was briefly perplexed by Michelle's actions. She was never so openly flirtatious, or seemingly carefree. Then the group parted to reveal a young man in their midst. He was leaning casually against the wall; his arms crossed over his chest as he smiled at the girls surrounding him. He was by far the most gorgeous man she'd ever seen. Her heart began to pound rapidly in her chest as everything around her seemed to freeze. The noise was gone; the room seemed to cease moving. He became the only thing she could see and feel.

She had the overwhelming urge to cross the room to him, but she couldn't get her legs to move. They were riveted to the floor where she stood in shock. Gradually, the girls surrounding him came back into focus. The music filtered back into her startled mind, and the room once again swarmed with people.

She watched the girls in amazement as they flirted outrageously, and overtly grazed against him with their bodies. He could have his pick of any of them, even Michelle, who was usually too condescending to even think about picking a guy up at a party. Sera glanced back at Kathleen, who wore the same starry-eyed expression she was certain had been on her own face seconds before.

She looked back to find the strange guy staring raptly at her. She was unable to break free of his intense gaze as his eyes locked on hers. The room seemed to disappear again as he smiled and bowed his head to her. She swallowed heavily and managed a small smile in return before the group enveloped him once again. Sera felt as if she had just broken free of a trance. She took a startled step back, bumping roughly into the doorjamb. Kathleen turned to her and grasped her arm in a bruising grip.

"Isn't he hot?" she cried.

"Who is he?" Sera managed around the lump in her throat.

"I don't know. He just transferred here this semester. I can't get close enough to talk to him and find out anything."

Sera looked back at the group surrounding him, blocking him from view. She felt a startling sense of loss that completely confused her. She didn't know anything about him, not even his name. She was acting like a silly fool. She was acting like one of the girls crowding around him.

She wasn't acting like herself.

"Come on," Kathleen said, her voice filled with determination.

"What, where?" Sera gasped as Kathleen dragged her toward the dance floor.

She didn't have time to offer more of a protest as Kathleen plunged into the crowd. "Dance!" Kathleen called happily above the noise.

Sera stared dazedly at her before realizing she looked like a foolish, wooden statue among the swaying bodies. She began to move to the music, but her mind remained on the group in the corner. And the man. She was so focused on her thoughts and pondering over the strange sense of loss she'd experienced, that she didn't realize Kathleen was angling them toward the group until they were only feet away.

When she did realize it, she edged away, ignoring Kathleen's agitated glances. She moved to the center of the floor, mingling back in with the larger group. She'd be damned if she was going to turn into some groupie, and latch onto some guy she didn't even know. Kathleen stared up at her. "I'll be back!" she yelled above the music.

Sera nodded and mingled in with a group of girls from her dorm. They smiled warmly at her, and Danielle, another good friend of hers, playfully bumped her hip as she laughed happily. "Did you see the new guy?" she asked eagerly.

Sera rolled her eyes. Was every girl in this room infatuated with him? He was good-looking, yes, but they were all making fools of themselves. There were other guys at this party.

"Yeah," she mumbled.

Danielle grinned as she tossed back her long brunette hair. Her hazel eyes twinkled as she bumped Sera again. "Are you going to talk to him?"

Sera took a step back. "No."

Danielle shook her head before spinning in a circle. Her brown hair twirled around her as she stopped before Sera, beaming from ear to ear. She was a pretty girl with a small, pointy nose, high cheekbones, and a dimpled chin. Built like a dancer, Danielle was small, lithe, and graceful.

The fast-paced dance music cut off, and a slow song came on. Sera saw her opportunity to exit as couples started to fill the floor. She moved with Danielle toward the door but found herself unexpectedly blocked off. Frowning in aggravation, she tilted her head up to see who belonged to the body she'd walked into and who was now firmly blocking her way.

She froze as her gaze locked onto a set of brilliant green

eyes. They were so clear and mesmerizing she was certain no emerald could have compared. Her heart flip-flopped as she gazed at the man before her. The room seemed to disappear again as her entire body reacted to his presence.

It was him.

"Sorry," she managed to say around the sudden lump in her throat.

He smiled; his face and eyes lit up with it. "It was my fault. I was trying to stop you."

"Stop me?"

"Would you like to dance?"

Sera blinked in surprise. She didn't want to dance, she wanted to flee as quickly as possible, but her feet wouldn't move. Instead, without meaning to, she found herself nodding her agreement. He held his hand out to her as a small smile curved his full mouth.

Her gaze traveled to his elegant fingers as his hand clasped hers. An unexpected bolt of electricity ripped through her. She startled as her eyes shot back to his. He stared at her with a mixture of curiosity and amazement. She felt as if he stared straight into her soul. She felt completely vulnerable, bared to him, but no matter how much she disliked the feeling of vulnerability overtaking her, she couldn't tear her gaze from his.

Then he turned from her. Sera blinked dazedly as their contact broke. A shiver swept up her spine, but she managed to keep herself from revealing it to him. He led her to the center of the floor and turned to wrap his arms around her waist. Sera found herself staring at a broad chest as she rested her hands against it. She could feel the bunching of thick muscles, and radiating heat in her fingers.

Another shudder, this one of desire, rippled through her. Desire was not something she experienced; it was something she feared. She bit her lip to keep another shiver repressed as she tilted her head to look up at him.

She took in every inch of his perfectly sculptured face. His eyes were the brilliant color of new spring leaves. They seemed to glow with an inner light, and they radiated a magnetism that was utterly entrancing. His eyelashes were long, thick, and black as they shadowed the planes of his chiseled cheekbones. His nose was straight and narrow. His lips were blood red, and the lower lip slightly fuller than the upper.

Suddenly she longed, in a way she never had with anyone else, to kiss him. She had to know what his lips tasted and felt like.

Her hands trailed along his chest. She could feel every detail of his ridged muscles beneath his black shirt. His broad shoulders seemed to block out the rest of the room as he spun her around the floor. He was at least six feet tall, a good six inches taller than her. Cut short, his raven black hair waved around his gorgeous face.

He smiled as she hesitantly met his penetrating gaze again. She couldn't imagine why he was choosing to dance with her when he could have any girl here.

"What's your name?" he asked. He didn't seem to raise his voice, but she heard him clearly.

"Sera."

"Sera, that's unusual."

"You don't know my full name," she said with a playful grin, unable to believe she was flirting with him. She never flirted; she never even danced with guys. She went out of her way to avoid men altogether. It was easier that way, less upsetting. But now, she found herself unable to stop doing either.

He grinned at her and shifted his hold as he pulled her closer. "What would that be?" he asked; his voice was deep and husky. It sent chills of pleasure down her spine.

"Serendipity Hill."

He broke into a grin as he chuckled. "Well now, isn't that perfect. Sera, I think my meeting you was serendipitous."

She laughed and shrugged. "Who knows, maybe. What's your name?"

"Liam Byrne."

"Nice to meet you," she said as the music ended.

She felt a sense of loss as his arms fell away from her. "Would you like to go somewhere else?" he inquired.

Sera's gaze flitted around the crowded room. "Where?"

Liam was thrown off by her sudden hesitation and distress. His mind went from lust-filled thoughts of the bedroom, to making her feel safe and secure. "For a walk. It's hot and loud in here. Too loud to talk, and I would like to get to know you better."

She stared at him in disbelief, and then, to her astonishment, she found herself nodding in agreement as the music blared again. He took hold of her hand and led her off the crowded dance floor. She numbly followed behind, unable to believe she had agreed to leave with him. What was the matter with her? She knew better than to do this, knew better than to allow this to happen, but she couldn't stop herself.

She caught the envious glances tossed her way as they moved through the thick crowd. Suddenly, Michelle stepped in front of her.

"Where are you going?" she demanded, her eyes chillingly cold.

Sera pulled on Liam's hand, stopping him in the midst of the crowd. He turned back to her, a frown marring his forehead. His eyes traveled to Michelle, and his frown deepened. "I don't know yet," Sera answered.

"This is very unlike you Sera," she said coldly. "I've never known you to leave a party with someone. Has Kathleen finally succeeded in making you a slut?"

Sera's face flamed red with embarrassment. Michelle was supposed to be one of her best friends, why was she attacking her like this?

"That is uncalled for," Liam growled, taking a step closer to her.

Michelle's eyes blazed with vehemence as they landed upon him. Sera found herself trapped between them, her face on fire. She had no idea how to get away from either one of them, but she desperately wanted to bolt from this awkward situation.

"Well, Michelle, it is like you to be a bitch." Kathleen appeared at Sera's side; her jaw clenched as she leveled Michelle with a fierce stare. "Even I, who am well aware of how much of a bitch you can be, am astounded by this new level."

Michelle's eyes settled on Kathleen. They burned with an intense hatred, unlike anything Sera had seen before. A chill shuddered through Sera in the face of that hatred. Kathleen seemed not to notice it as she grabbed hold of Sera's arm and steered her away. She found herself pulling Liam behind her through the crowd as Kathleen plunged onward. They made their way outside where Kathleen released her arm, slid to the bottom step, and hugged her middle as she burst out laughing.

"Did... you... see... her... face?" she managed to wheeze out. "That was great!"

"Kathleen—" Sera started.

"Oh I know, she's a friend of yours," Kathleen waved a hand in dismissal as she sobered up. "But I love putting her in her place. Besides, I don't know how you can consider that stuck up bitch a friend."

"She's your friend?" Liam inquired.

"Yes."

"Good friends you have," he commented dryly.

"Hey!" Kathleen protested. "I'm a terrific friend. By the way, my name is Kathleen, and you are...?"

"Liam."

"Nice to meet you, Liam."

"You too, Kathleen."

Kathleen climbed to her feet and absently brushed at her wrinkled skirt. "I'm going to head back to the room; are you coming with me Sera?"

"I'll be there in a little bit."

Kathleen's gaze darted nervously to Liam. "Are you sure you're going to be all right?"

Sera smiled reassuringly at her. Regardless of Kathleen's carefree demeanor, Sera knew Kathleen worried about her. "I'll be okay. Why are you heading back so early?"

"I've had my share of entertainment, alcohol, leering guys, and bitches for the night," she said with a huge grin. "I'll see you later." She hopped off the stairs and skipped down the sidewalk. "Don't do anything I wouldn't do!" she called over her shoulder, "Which is nothing!"

Sera could hear her laughing all the way down the street. She turned back to Liam, who was watching Kathleen's disappearing figure. "She seems like fun," he commented dryly.

"She is. Lots of fun, and my best friend."

"I don't know you, or your friends very well, but I would suggest rethinking at least one of them."

Sera turned and headed down the sidewalk, kicking at a few loose stones. "Michelle is a little funny about some things," she admitted.

"I must have missed her sense of humor."

She laughed and turned to walk backward in front of him. "She doesn't have one, but she's a good person, once you get to know her. However, she's used to getting whatever she wants."

"And what did she want that she didn't get?"

Sera looked away; a blush stained her cheeks as a wave of shyness swept her. "She wanted you," she mumbled, unable to meet his eyes.

"And she always gets what she wants?"

Sera looked up at him, expecting him to be laughing at her. Instead, his face was expressionless, and his eyes were cold and remote. Sera stopped walking. He halted before her, his eyes focused on her, but remained distant.

"Yes," Sera said. "Michelle always gets what she sets her mind to. She's beautiful and smart, and not easily denied."

Liam's gaze searched her small, delicate face. He hadn't been wrong in his assumption earlier; her eyes were spectacular. They were a swirling combination of sapphire blue and vivid purple. The violet mingled with the blue in such a way it was almost impossible to discern one color from the other. He could become lost in those beguiling eyes if he wasn't careful.

Which he always was. He couldn't allow himself to get involved with someone, or to get attached. But, he found himself becoming intrigued with her. If he wasn't cautious, he might find himself liking her. That was something he couldn't do, wasn't capable of doing. He needed to stay aloof, and distant from her.

"I see," he finally replied.

She searched his face for why he was suddenly so detached, but he remained impassive. "Why does that make you angry?"

He smiled as he took hold of her hand and began to walk again. "It doesn't make me angry. I just don't like it when people assume things."

"Assume things?"

"She assumed she would always get what she wanted, and so did you."

"I'm not assuming anything," she retorted. "That's the way it's always been."

"Well, it isn't now."

"Besides, she won't give up. She never does."

"So?"

Sera looked down at the sidewalk. "You never know what the future holds."

"Wouldn't I have a say in it?" he asked, his voice tinged with ire.

"Yes," she said. "I didn't mean to upset you."

He squeezed her hand. "I know you didn't, but I don't want Michelle, and I think that's why she was so mad at you."

"Why?"

He smiled at her as he led her across the street. Sera realized they'd left campus and were heading into town. Cars packed the streets. People, mostly college students, were milling around outside the bars smoking cigarettes. Music filled the air as they passed the crammed bars and groups of people on the street. She couldn't help but smile as she noticed the envious glances of the women they passed.

They turned a corner and left the noise of the bars and restaurants behind for the closed shops. "She knew I had my eye on someone else."

"And who would that be?" she asked.

"Some blonde who wouldn't talk to me." Sera was pleased by the teasing glint in his eyes.

She laughed as she cast him a smile. "Who could with the swarm you had around you?"

He stopped walking, tugging on her hand to halt her. She stopped before him, tilting her chin up to gaze into his amazing green eyes. "I found a way to talk to you," he said huskily.

His voice sent shivers down her spine. His intense stare caused her to bite nervously on her bottom lip as his hand came up to caress her cheek. "There wasn't a swarm of people around me," she said as she relished in the feel of his touch against her skin.

"No," he whispered. "Just a bunch of leering guys who were too scared to talk to you."

Sera burst into laughter. "Oh, I don't think so."

His hand froze on her face as he stared at her doubtfully. "Didn't you notice them?"

Sera looked at him in confusion and took a step back. His hand fell from her face. A sense of loss enveloped her as the contact broke. "Notice who?" she asked.

He stared at her with the relentless intensity she was growing accustomed to. Her eyebrows rose inquiringly as she tried to discern what he was searching for, but she had no idea why he was looking at her like that. He gently placed his hand on her face and drew her closer. Her heart pounded as she rested her hands against his chest. The air seemed to crackle with electricity as his thumb brushed over her cheek.

She stared into his green eyes as they burned into hers. She was completely useless against the magnetic pull drawing her toward him. She closed her eyes as his lips brushed hers and sent a shower of sparks and heat throughout her body.

Her mouth opened, and his tongue delved into it. His hands thrust into her hair as he kissed her hungrily. Her whole body was on fire as she clutched at his back to pull him closer. He eased her against the cool cement of a store wall as his firm body pressed against hers. Her knees turned to Jell-O as his hands leisurely caressed the exposed skin of her stomach.

Suddenly, the loud burst of a horn ripped into her daze. She jumped as her mind cleared of its passion-induced haze. With frightening clarity, she realized she was alone, in an alley, with a man she didn't know. A man who was strong enough to do whatever he wanted to her.

Apprehension surged through her, and she pushed frantically at his solid chest. Needing him to get away from her so she could breathe. He pulled away from her, his eyes a darker, passion-clouded green. She took a shuddery breath as she tried to stop the shaking in her legs, and the pounding of her heart that no longer had anything to do with desire. Her eyes pleaded with him not to harm her as her hands slid away from his chest to clutch at the cool cement of the wall behind her.

"I'm not going to hurt you."

Shame flooded her face as she looked down at her feet. "I better get back," she finally managed to say.

"All right."

Sera blinked as he took her hand. Dread blazed through her, and she stiffened involuntarily. However, when he didn't make another move toward her, some of the dread dissipated. She knew many men would have been irritated by her refusal, by her sudden hot and cold. Liam seemed to take it all in stride as they walked toward the college.

It perplexed her, and she couldn't stop herself from casting wary glances his way. Not only did he make her melt just by touching her, but he also seemed to be a decent person. It was too good to be true, there had to be something wrong with him.

Liam tried to puzzle out the mystery that was Sera. He had finally seen what Mike was talking about. The trepidation and pleading in her eyes had constricted his heart. She reminded him of a frightened, trapped animal, and understood why Mike had said to leave her be.

It was obvious she'd been hurt in the past. But how bad it had been, he didn't know. His hand involuntarily tensed around hers as the thought of anyone mistreating her sent a flash of burning anger through him. What was the matter with him? He didn't know this girl from Eve; he shouldn't give a rat's ass about what happened to her in the past.

He chanced a glance at her as she walked along; her golden head bent as she studied the sidewalk. He frowned as he realized that, for some strange reason, he did give a rat's ass. He clenched his jaw as he turned to study the campus. She was the type of person he could truly come to like, and he couldn't take that chance.

They passed the party, which had begun to slow down. There was a scattering of people sleeping on the lawn, while others were spilling out the doors. The music was still going, but it wasn't as loud anymore. "Hey, Liam!" someone yelled drunkenly from the stonewall. "You get some, man?"

Liam was surprised by the deep blush staining her cheeks. He was certain he'd never seen anyone turn so red, that fast. He squeezed her hand for reassurance. "I see you've made some friends since you've been here," she said.

"I've never met him."

"It's Jason Riggs."

"He's an asshole."

"If you think so now, wait till you get to know him," she told him.

"Sounds like you like him," he commented dryly.

"Not at all, but you learn to deal with him."

"Has he ever done anything to you?"

Her face burned even hotter as she recalled some of the rude comments he'd made to her in the past. "No, just stupid comments, petty stuff."

He could tell by her tone it wasn't petty stuff to her. He glanced over his shoulder to see if he could still spot Jason, but the frat house was well behind them. He would talk with Jason later to make sure he didn't bother her again. His frown deepened as he realized he felt protective of this girl. Jesus, he needed to get away from her, now.

They turned a corner, and her dorm came into view. Disappointment filled her as she realized the night was ending already. Shaking her head to clear her conflicting emotions, she tugged on his hand.

"This is my dorm," she said, stopping in front of it.

"I'll walk you to your room."

She stared at him as she tried to figure him out. Was he being polite, or did he expect something to happen once they were in her room? But Kathleen had said she would be there so he couldn't be expecting anything. She was still busy trying to figure him out when they entered the building.

Liam was just as startled as she was. He'd planned to leave her at the door to the building, and go back to the party. There were probably some girls still lingering about who would be more than happy to spend the night with him. Instead, he found himself unwilling to leave her until he knew she was safely in her room.

"Do you live on campus?" she asked.

"At the Omega house."

"I don't picture you as a frat guy."

"It's better than living in a dorm. More freedom."

"I guess."

She stopped in front of her door and turned to face him. "Do you want to come in? Kathleen is probably still up." In fact, she knew Kathleen was still up, waiting to hear about everything that had happened.

"All right."

She opened the door and stepped aside to let him in. Kathleen was sitting on her bed, a beer in hand as she talked happily with Danielle. They both froze, their mouths gaping as they entered. "Hi," Kathleen finally managed to stammer out.

"Hey," Sera said. "What are you guys up to?"

"Nothing," Danielle answered, her eyes latched onto Liam.

"Beer?" Kathleen asked.

"Isn't it against the rules for you to have alcohol in the dorm rooms?" Liam asked teasingly.

"It's also against the rules for you to be here," she replied happily.

He smiled at her as she dug beneath her bed to pull out a cooler. Liam grabbed two beers from it, popped the top on one, and handed it to Sera. "How do you like this school so far?" Danielle asked unusually shy and hesitant.

"I'm, having a good time, so far."

"You have to watch out for some of the people," Kathleen said. "They can be funny." Her eyes settled on Sera. "It takes some people longer to realize that than others."

Liam looked over at her, his gaze just as intense as Kathleen's. "I figured that," he said.

A muffled knock on the door made them all jump. "Crap," Danielle said, ditching her beer under the bed. Sera grabbed Liam's can and shoved them into her desk drawer. It was bad enough there was a man in their room, but being caught with alcohol would surely get them expelled.

Heart hammering, she walked over to the door and cracked it a little. Michelle stood outside; her long auburn hair spilled around her beautiful face. "Can I come in?" she asked.

Sera stepped back, a knot of anxiety forming in her stomach. She wasn't in the mood for an intense encounter. Michelle swept into the room and froze when she spotted Liam sitting elegantly on Sera's bed, beers back in hand. He stared back at her with open disdain before standing and walking over to give Sera her beer. He managed a small smile for her as he casually leaned against the wall, his shoulder brushing against hers as he crossed his legs before him.

She didn't quite understand what was going on, but she knew he was trying to tell her, and everyone in the room, something. Michelle's dark eyes were filled with resentment as she stared at him. "Hello, everyone," Michelle greeted coldly.

"Hey," Danielle said nervously. "What's up?"

"I came to apologize for what I said earlier." The apology was meant for Sera, but Michelle's eyes remained locked on Liam.

Sera shifted uncomfortably as Liam stood straighter. She still didn't understand what was going on, but she could feel the anger radiating from him. He took a swig of beer and stepped away to place it on her desk before heading back to rest his hands upon her shoulders.

"I'd better get going," he said.

"All right."

Unbelievable disappointment welled inside her. She barely knew him, yet she felt as if something would be missing when he left. She took a deep breath to get her irrational emotions under control. She hadn't had that much to drink, but maybe the alcohol was affecting her.

"I'll see you tomorrow."

He leaned down and kissed her tenderly. Warmth instantly spread through her whole body. She had to clench her hand around her beer to keep herself from grabbing him and deepening the kiss. When he pulled away from her, there was a wealth of confusion in his eyes.

Liam studied her attentively. He hadn't meant to tell her he would see her tomorrow. He'd planned to walk out of this room, and never see her again. She was too dangerous. She made him feel things he'd never felt before. Things he wasn't supposed to feel, wasn't allowed to feel.

He found himself wanting to protect her, shelter her, and ease the distress he'd seen in her eyes earlier. He craved her with an intensity that was hardening him even now. She was the most delectable, entrancing woman he'd ever met.

Sera managed to nod a response before he turned away from her. He brushed by Michelle, not even looking at her as he opened the door. "Nice to meet you guys," he said to Kathleen and Danielle, pointedly ignoring Michelle.

"Bye," they said in unison.

He shut the door behind him, and they all remained silent for a few seconds. "Oh my God," Danielle gushed. "He is so hot."

"You had better spill!" Kathleen said, excitedly bouncing on her bed.

"Oh yes!" Danielle cried. "Where did you guys go? How was that kiss?"

Sera stared at them before she turned to Michelle. She was nonchalantly leaning against the door, but the set of her jaw belied her calm composure. "I'd better go too," she said as she stepped away from the wall. "I'll see you later, and I am sorry about earlier."

"It's all right," Sera replied dully.

Michelle swung the door open and closed it loudly behind her. "What is her problem?" Danielle asked.

"Bet you ten she tries to catch up with him." Kathleen scrambled off her bed and raced to the window.

"Kathleen—" Sera started.

"Never seen her walk that fast before," Kathleen commented.

Sera was unable to resist looking. Michelle was hurrying down the front walk, Liam just ahead of her. He suddenly turned around as Michelle walked over to him. Sera's heart began to speed up as they stood together beneath the street light.

"That bitch!" Kathleen cried, angrily slamming her hands on the sill. "That rotten bitch!"

"I can't believe it," Danielle whispered.

Sera felt as if someone had socked her in the stomach as the two continued to talk. "Well, if he wants her," she choked out.

"Screw that!" Kathleen snapped.

Michelle reached out to touch Liam's shoulder flirtatiously, but he took a step back from her. Sera watched in amazement as he turned and walked away from her. Michelle stood for a moment before turning and walking the other way. "Good for him," Kathleen muttered. "I knew I liked him for a reason!"

Sera turned away from the window and sat on her bed. "I can't believe her," Danielle declared. "She's got a set of balls."

"No, she's a backstabbing bitch! Now I hope you realize what she is." Sera stared at Kathleen in confusion. "She's not worth being upset over."

Sera blinked and shook her head. "I'm not upset about her."

"Then what's the matter?"

"I don't know; I guess I'm confused."

"About what?" Danielle asked, sitting next to her and handing Sera her beer.

Sera took a long swallow and began to twirl the beer in her hand. "I don't know what just happened."

"What do you mean?" Kathleen demanded, hands on her hips.

Sera stood and walked back to the window. The street was empty now. "I don't know. I just don't know."

"Sera," Danielle said. "You're not making any sense."

"I've never met anyone like him," she murmured. "No one has ever made me feel that way. He looks at me, and I melt. He touches me, and shivers run up and down my spine. He kisses me, and the whole world disappears, and I feel... well, I don't know how to explain what I feel. All I know is I feel more for him in the past hour than anyone I've ever met. How is that possible?"

"I don't know; maybe it's the alcohol," Kathleen joked.

Sera put her beer down. "Maybe you're right, but I don't think so."

"That's a good thing," Danielle said forcefully. "Why are you questioning it?"

"I don't know; have you ever felt like that?"

"No."

"Then there's Michelle—"

"Don't tell me you're concerned about that tramp!" Kathleen cried.

"No, it's not that. I just don't understand what in the world he could want with me when he could have her?"

Danielle and Kathleen's mouths dropped open. "Because he has good taste," Kathleen answered dryly. "It's obvious to the rest of us what Michelle is; you're the one who refuses to see it."

"I see it now," Sera whispered.

But too late. She always saw things too late. She'd considered Michelle her friend; she'd trusted her. But, after everything that happened tonight, she knew her trust was misplaced. Just like it always was.

And now there was Liam. She didn't know what to make of him, or the way he made her feel. She hated feeling this way; it only led to suffering. She found herself torn between wanting to see him again, and hoping she never would. She closed her eyes and wrapped her arms around herself as her body trembled with her torn emotions.

LIAM WALKED BACK into the frat house. The music had been turned down; the lights were dimmed to give the home a more romantic vibe. Although, how anyone could feel like screwing in the jumbled mess of garbage, and the stench of beer, he didn't know. However, some people obviously did. He could hear more than one couple having sex in the dance room, and knew the thumps over his head weren't drunks falling.

"Hey, how'd it go?"

Liam turned as Mike came strolling in from the back room with a cute brunette tucked under his arm. She grinned up at Liam drunkenly as she leaned heavily against Mike's side. Jack and Doug followed behind him; a redhead was under Jack's arm, and a brunette under Doug's. "Fine," he replied absently.

Mike flashed a drunken smirk as he leaned against the banister. "Told you so."

Liam scowled at him. "Told him what?" Jack asked happily.

"About Sera."

"Oh," Jack replied, his forehead furrowed. "You shouldn't have even bothered to try; she doesn't give it up."

"I didn't try!" Liam barked. "And don't talk about her like that."

He was even more astonished than they were by the hostility in his voice, and the tension filling him. Mike lifted a blond brow questioningly but didn't say anything. Jack and Doug both stared at him with expressions of shock.

"Well," Doug was the first to recover. "There are some girls back there who are more than willing."

The brunette giggled as she wrapped her arm around Doug's waist. Liam couldn't help the sneer of revulsion curling his upper lip. He looked away from her, his gaze traveled down the hall to the back living room. He could hear voices coming from there, most of them female. For a minute he was tempted. He was still partially erect from his time with Sera, and he wouldn't mind having someone relieve him.

Growing hard again at the thought of Sera, he took a step toward them and then stopped. He suddenly realized he wasn't in the mood for one of those girls. Frowning, and suddenly annoyed, he turned back around and headed for the stairs. His emotions were a rioting mess he couldn't begin to fathom right now.

"Where ya going?" Jack slurred.

"To bed," he muttered.

"Are you serious, man? There are plenty of girls back there!"

"Hey," Mike snatched hold of Liam's arm before he could escape. "You all right?"

Liam's jaw clenched as he gazed at his friend. Mike's eyes searched his face in bewilderment. "No," Liam responded as he pulled his arm free. "I'm not."

He turned away and stalked up the stairs.

CHAPTER THREE

Sera had slept in later than she'd planned, and now she was in a rush. She had to research her history report before meeting Kathleen and Danielle for lunch. Kathleen was still sound asleep when she'd left the room; Sera silently envied her lackadaisical lifestyle and carefree attitude. For once, she wished she could be more like Kathleen and still be buried beneath her blankets.

She shrugged off thoughts of Kathleen sleeping as she climbed the stairs to the library. She walked through the maze of hallways until she came to another set of stairs and climbed them. There were only a handful of people in the large room. Most students were still sleeping off Friday night, and it was only the truly uptight ones, like her, that were here.

She smiled at the librarian, who was used to seeing her, and headed for the back. The history books took up the last twelve rows, and she lost herself in them. Pulling down an armful of books on the bubonic plague, she headed for the beanbag chair in the corner. Slipping into the comfy chair, she opened one of the books and began to read.

"How's the book?"

She started and jerked back as someone slid onto the bag beside her. Her eyes widened in amazement as Liam smiled at her and leaned over her shoulder to look at the pages. Instantly, her heartbeat sped up as she gazed at his bent head. "Interesting topic to read first thing on a Saturday."

"I always like a reality check in the morning," she said, smiling happily and still a little dazed by his sudden presence. "What are you doing here?"

He sprawled out, crossing his long legs in front of him as he placed his hands behind his head. "I thought I'd prowl for good looking girls who come to the library at ten o'clock on a Saturday."

"You must be disappointed then."

He grinned as he touched a strand of her hair. "Nah, I think I've found one."

She smiled shyly as she leaned back in the bag. "Do you have a report to do?"

He laughed and dropped his arm around her shoulders. "Oh no, I don't make it a habit of coming to the library. I went to your room to see if you would like to go to breakfast. A very disgruntled, barely discernible, and extremely sleepy Kathleen informed me, and I quote, "Are you nuts? Mumble, mumble, mumble, nine thirty, mumble, mumble, mumble. She's probably in the library; she's crazy. Like you!" and slammed the door in my face."

Sera laughed. "You woke up Kathleen? That's never good!"

"So I noticed. I won't do it again."

His hand ran over her hair. She leaned her head against his shoulder. Closing her eyes, she allowed herself to drift into his caress. To her surprise, she didn't feel any revulsion. She hadn't felt it last night, at least not the revulsion, but she had attributed it to the alcohol in her system. She was more amazed to realize her lack of fear had nothing to do with the fact they were in the safe confines of the library, and everything to do with him. She could have stayed there forever.

"Don't let me interrupt you," he whispered, laying his chin against her head. "Continue reading."

"I can't; you're distracting me."

"Should I leave?"

That was the last thing she wanted to happen. "No."

He rubbed his hand along her hair and tilted the book so he could see it too. "Then we'll read it together. Nothing like a little death to start the day off right."

She chuckled and looked down at the book, but she couldn't seem to focus on the words. Her heart pounded rapidly in her chest, and her body tingled everywhere it touched against his. "You know what?" he whispered in her ear. "You're distracting me too."

She turned to look at him. His eyes were a brilliant green as they burned into hers. She shivered with excitement as he leaned down and kissed her. Instantly, she melted into his warm embrace and the pressure of his mouth against hers. His tongue brushed against her lips, and she instinctively opened her mouth to his soft caress. He entered her mouth unhurriedly; gently stroking her tongue, he sent sparks of passion throughout her whole body. He carefully pressed her back, gradually lowering himself over her, and enclosing her within the warmth of his embrace.

Something deep inside of her began to stir as she encircled her arms around his back. She felt as if she was losing control, as if there was no one in the world but them, and the profound emotions he arose in her. His kisses became deeper, more urgent. She met each of his thrusts eagerly, her fingers curling into his back as her whole body responded to his.

"Uh hum." Sera jumped, and Liam quickly moved aside.

She sat up to find Ms. Krinkle, the librarian, staring at them disapprovingly. "I think it would be better if you checked those books out, Sera."

"I'm sorry, Ms. Krinkle," she mumbled. She scooped up the books as her face burned with embarrassment. "I'll do that right now."

Unable to bear looking at Liam, she hurried down the long row of books. She walked up to the counter, handed over her college ID, and waited impatiently as a student worker checked her out. She turned to leave and realized Liam had disappeared. A sense of loss enveloped her, but she was in too much of a rush, and too humiliated, to think about it. She just wanted to get out of there as fast as she could.

She burst through the doors, grateful for the crisp air to ease the burning in her cheeks as she turned to head back to her dorm. Liam sat on a bench by the doors, a huge grin on his face. Dark sunglasses covered his eyes, adding an air of sensuality to him that was both thrilling, and disturbing.

"Glad you think it's funny."

"Sorry, I didn't mean to embarrass you." He stood and began to walk beside her.

"It's my fault."

"You were quite content until I showed up."

"It's all right."

Her head spun with the overwhelming confusion she felt. She had never lost control like that. Although she enjoyed it, she was also angry at herself for it. She knew better than to let herself get wrapped up with someone, knew better than to believe she could trust someone. But she couldn't seem to stop herself when it came to him. She needed to get away from him so she could try to sort out her confusing emotions.

"Have you talked to Michelle today?" he inquired.

"No, why?"

"We had a little chat last night after I left."

"Really?" she inquired innocently. "About what?"

"She apologized for the way she acted."

"That was nice of her," she said more casually than she felt. "I suppose."

Sera looked up at him. "You really don't like her, do you?"

He shoved his hands into the pockets of his leather bomber jacket. "No, I don't."

She wasn't paying any attention to where they were going until she realized they were at the frat house. Trash, empty beer cans, bottles, and plastic cups littered the lawn. The front door was open, and two kegs lay on the sidewalk.

"Looks amazing," she commented dryly.

"The cleanup crew will be by later."

"Cleanup crew?"

"We paid some guys to come by at twelve to clean up the yard and first floor."

"I hope you paid them a lot." She wouldn't like to be the one who had to clean up this mess.

He chuckled and took hold of her hand. Sera almost jerked away as a bolt of electricity sizzled through her. "Are you going to come in?"

She stared at the trashed house as she tried to calm her racing heart. Just moments ago she wanted to get away from him; now, she would like nothing more than to go in there with him. "I don't know if I should."

"You won't get into trouble. Girls are allowed in here," he teased.

"That's not it."

"Then what is it?" he inquired.

She chewed on her bottom lip as she turned to look at him. She couldn't see his eyes, but she knew he was staring intently at her. "I don't think I can control myself around you," she blurted before she could stop herself. As soon as the words were out of her mouth, she hated herself for saying them and wished she could kick herself in the ass.

He gently took hold of her arm. "Come on; I won't bite."

"Liam, that's not it, I mean... oh, I don't know what I'm saying," she finished lamely.

His hand on her chin soothed her as he lifted her face. The sunglasses rested on top of his head. His eyes were intense, but the tenderness in them touched her and melted some of her reserve.

"I know what you mean, Sera. It will be all right, I promise."

The last of her defenses crumbled at his words, and she followed him into the home. More beer bottles, cups, and piles of garbage littered the floors and stairs. The furniture was scattered around the house, holes dented some of the walls, and the entire place reeked of beer and something even less pleasant she didn't want to identify. She picked her way carefully around the trash, and the guy passed out at the top of the stairs.

At the second floor hallway, the trail of refuse continued to flow. A few people were lying on the floor, but all the doors were firmly closed. They moved around the clutter as he led her to another set of stairs. The stairway was gloomy, but unlike the others it was immaculate, making it obvious the party hadn't been allowed to spread past the second floor. Stepping out of the stairwell on the third floor, he led her to the third door on the right.

She hesitated before stepping inside. A full-size bed was pushed against the right wall with a black comforter spread over it. A small nightstand was next to it with a lamp and an alarm clock perched on top. There was a desk in the corner with a computer and phone. On the other side of the desk was a small green recliner. A small wooden entertainment center sat against the wall by the door with a TV and DVD player on it.

"Have a seat," he told her.

She set her books on his desk and stood next to it; she was a little too nervous to sit down. He smiled at her wryly and walked over to the closet. Opening the door, he knelt in front of a small refrigerator. "Want something to drink?"

"No, I'm fine."

He pulled out a bottle of water and shut the door. He turned to stare at her as he leaned against the door. She began to feel incredibly uncomfortable and foolish. She shouldn't be here. She didn't belong here. And she had no idea what he expected of her. Swallowing heavily, she fully realized the situation she'd put herself in.

She looked toward the door. It was only ten feet away, but it seemed like miles. Would she be able to make it there in time if something happened? Her gaze darted back to him. He was still staring at her, but he was frowning, and his eyes were questioning as they studied her.

He straightened away from the door and walked across the room to sit on the bed. "Do you want to go to a party tonight?" he inquired.

"Where?"

"The Phi Beta house."

Her gaze involuntarily shot back to the door. She swallowed as she forced herself to calm down. He was doing nothing wrong, nothing at all. She was acting like an idiot, and if she didn't stop he was going to notice. The thought mortified her brain into action. "How did you manage to get into the frat house so soon?" she asked in a desperate attempt to distract herself.

He smiled, and she had the distinct impression he knew what she was trying to do. "I was in the same frat at my old college. Before I transferred, I arranged it so I'd be able to move in here right away. Besides, I've known Mike, Jack, and Doug since we were kids."

"Mike's a good guy, not so good at math though."

"He never has been," he agreed. "Jack and Doug are good guys too."

She had seen them at parties over the years, even shared a couple of classes with them, but she'd never spoken to them. Although, they were among the few frat guys who had never bothered her, or stared at her like she was a piece of meat. They had always been polite, but distant. To her, that alone made them likable. "I don't really know them," she admitted. "Where did you go to school before?"

"Buffalo."

"What made you move to Massachusetts?"

He twirled the water in his elegant fingers. A shudder tore through her as she recalled those fingers on her body. She tore her gaze away from them and forced herself to look at him. Again, there was a knowing gleam in his eyes as he smiled at her. "I grew up near here, and I thought it was time to come home again. I know a couple of guys in this house, and Phi Beta, from high school."

"Then why did you go all the way to Buffalo?"

"Wanted a change of scenery, something new, but I'm not a big fan of the cold, and after last winter I decided to come back."

She raised an eyebrow. "This isn't exactly Florida."

He laughed and placed the water bottle on the floor. "No it's not, but it's also not as cold, or snowy as it is up there." He smiled as he slid back on the bed and leaned against the wall. "What about you, Sera?"

"What about me?" she asked warily.

"Why are you at this school?"

She sat on the corner of the desk. She tried not to show him how uncomfortable the question made her, so she forced herself not to bite her lip as she met his inquisitive stare. "It was far enough away so I could live at school, but close enough to my family so I could go home on vacations. Plus, this is a good school."

"Good reasons. Did you know anyone here?"

"No, but that was the point. I was looking for a new beginning, a chance to start my own life and make new friends. I like the way things have turned out."

It was only a little lie, and there was no reason to feel bad about it, she told herself. "That's good. Why don't you date?"

She blinked at the abrupt change of topic. Her hands automatically clenched upon the desk. "Excuse me?"

"Why don't you date? All the guys around here say you've never dated anyone on campus."

"You asked about me?" She couldn't keep the alarm out of her voice.

He watched her with an amused gleam in his eyes. For a second she was reminded of a panther studying its prey. Unfortunately, she seemed to be the prey. Apprehension prickled its way up her spine.

"Just a little," he admitted.

Sera had to fight against the violent shaking threatening to overtake her. "What did they say about me?"

He smiled at her and shook his head. "It was nothing bad. They just told me you didn't date anyone, that you never had, and not to waste my time. So, why haven't you gone out with someone else?"

Some of the tension eased from her, and she found herself able to breathe regularly again. Then his words caught her attention. Her brow furrowed as she stared at him questioningly. Why hadn't she gone out with someone else? Were they going out? Her heart did a hopeful flip-flop, but she buried it.

"Nobody ever asked me," she replied, "while they were sober anyway."

"That's because they didn't have the courage unless they were drunk."

"What about you then?"

He grinned cockily. "I don't need alcohol."

"Conceited," she commented dryly.

"Far from it. Not having the courage to do something just means you lose out on it. If you get rejected, so what, at least you tried. Besides, it isn't the end of the world."

She admired him for a courage she could never have. "So, how did you know it wasn't the alcohol in me last night?"

"I didn't. That's why I came by so early, I figured you might still be drunk." He grinned charmingly, and she felt the rest of her anxiety beginning to melt away.

"I didn't have that much to drink last night."

"No, but you never know how you're going to feel about someone the next morning."

"Oh, and how did you feel about me?"

"Very good," he said with a small smile. "Sit down." He patted the bed beside him.

She eyed him guardedly. She knew if she got close to that bed, and him, her thoughts and emotions would get all tangled up again. But she desperately wanted to get close to him, to touch him, and to have him touch her. Besides, she didn't think he would hurt her. He could have done that last night if it was what he'd intended. She released the desk and made her way to sit down beside him.

"Come on," he said and pulled her toward the head of the bed. "Lie down; you look tired."

She went rigid beneath his touch. Her eyes flew to his as memories suddenly assailed her. She found she couldn't breathe or even move. He slowly moved his hands away from her, and she was finally able to breathe again. His gaze was intense as he searched her face. Sera lowered her lashes before he could read too much in her eyes.

"It's okay," he said.

She fought back the tears threatening to fall. She had worked diligently to rid herself of her dread of men, and although she had gotten better, she still couldn't control some of her instinctive, involuntary reactions. She hated herself for it, hated herself for the weakness, and hated he'd witnessed it.

He slid his jacket off and lay down on the bed to give her some space. He didn't touch her, didn't force her to lie down. No matter how much he wanted to hold her, he restrained himself from grabbing her. Her back was rigid as she sat on the bed; small shivers racked her delicate spine. A raging anger suddenly tore through him. Something had happened to her; someone had hurt her. His hands clenched at the thought, and he had to take a deep breath to steady himself.

He never felt like this; never let his anger reach such a point. It was dangerous when it did; *he* was dangerous. But the idea of anyone harming her was pushing him toward a perilous edge. He didn't understand why he was unable to resist this girl, why she got to him in a way no one else ever had.

"You're safe with me, Sera," he said kindly.

She lifted her lashes to look at him. Tears shimmered in her eyes, and self-loathing filled them. Those tears touched something inside him, something savage and protective. He was tempted to pull her into his arms and shield her from the rest of the world, but he knew if he tried to touch her now, she would bolt like a frightened rabbit and never come back. That wasn't an option.

She bit her bottom lip, straightened her back in determination, and scooted back on the bed. She lay down beside him, forcing herself not to tremble as he wrapped his arms around her. She hated herself enough for letting him see her weakness without making it worse by shaking like a leaf in his embrace. He drew her closer, so her head rested on his chest.

She found herself relaxing. He'd given her no reason to fear him; it was unfair of her to do so. His warm body, steadily beating heart, and enticing aroma served to comfort and relax her even further. She stifled a yawn as she melted beneath his soothing touch.

"I can't stay long," she whispered, trying to keep her eyes open. "I'm supposed to meet Kathleen for lunch."

"Okay, just rest for a while."

He kissed the top of her head, and her eyes started to close. Liam remained staring at the ceiling long after she had drifted off to sleep. He couldn't quell the protective drive swelling through him as she lay trustingly in his embrace.

His body craved and responded to her in a way it never had to anyone else. But it was more than his body yearning for her. She was so warm, caring, and delicately fragile that he couldn't resist her. In the library, he had only planned to say hi and to see her, but he had lost himself in her dazzling warmth.

He couldn't seem to get enough of touching her. It was a treacherous game he played; one he was sure to lose. She'd been hurt before, and he could bring her nothing but more sorrow. It was against the rules, rules *he* had made for the safety of them all.

Sera stirred a little; her hand twitched on his chest. He clasped it and ran his fingers along her silky skin and delicate bones. Bones that could break so easily. He tensed at the thought. He was losing his mind, he knew that, but he didn't particularly care. He kissed the top of her head. Rules be damned, sanity be damned.

He didn't really know her, but for some reason, he knew he wasn't going to be able to let her go.

CHAPTER FOUR

Sera woke with a start. Her heart raced as she realized she didn't know where she was. The room was shadowed and unfamiliar. Loud, boisterous laughter echoed through the hall outside as people shouted to each other. Then she felt Liam's arm still wrapped around her waist, and she heard his deep breathing. She lifted her head to look at the clock on his nightstand. The bright red numbers announced it was five forty-three.

"Crap," she whispered. "Crap, crap, crap!"

She carefully lifted Liam's arm. His eyes instantly flew open. They were a brilliant green in the dim light of the room as they landed upon her. "What time is it?" he asked sleepily.

"Quarter to six."

"Oh." She stiffened as he pulled her back into his arms. "You missed lunch already."

She lay rigid for a minute before relaxing back against him. His arms were like steel around her, but she knew he would release her if she asked him to. He lifted her chin and kissed her. The brief touch sent a wave of warmth through her dissolving her remaining anxiety. Never had anyone been so kind to her. Her body yearned for his in a way it never had with anyone else.

He pulled away to stare at her. He seemed to be searching for something, but for what, she didn't know. His hands wrapped in her hair, drawing her against him as he kissed her. She melted against him, her body on fire as their tongues touched and teased. His kiss gradually grew deeper and more urgent.

An involuntary moan escaped her as she held onto his solid, well-muscled back. He groaned and nibbled at her lip as his hand caressed her neck, then her collarbone. She gasped when he cupped her breast. She moaned as he teased her nipple into a taut bud while his mouth kept firm possession of hers.

A loud bang in the hallway caused her to jump. With the contact broken, reality crashed down on her. She shouldn't be here, shouldn't be doing this. If anything, she had learned from past mistakes how quickly things could get out of control. How rapidly she could be betrayed. Her breath came in rapid pants as memories washed over her.

He brushed a loose strand of hair off her face. She flinched involuntarily, and his hand instantly fell away. She rolled away before she could see the disgust sure to follow her reaction in his eyes. Putting her head in her hands, she fought against sobbing out her self-loathing. She hated this weakness.

She wished she could be normal. She wished that night had never happened. She'd tried to forget about it, but she couldn't. It was always in the back of her mind, constantly haunting her, chasing her. Now she'd met someone she genuinely liked, who made her feel things she never imagined she could, and she was going to lose him. No guy, no matter how nice, would choose to be with someone who flinched every time he touched her.

"Sera," he whispered.

He sat up and laid his hands on her shoulders. She turned her head so he couldn't see her face. "I'm sorry," she whispered.

"For what?"

She shook her head, her long hair falling forward to obscure what little of her face he could see. A small tremor shook her, but she refused to look at him. He took hold of her chin with his thumb and index finger and turned her head, forcing her to look at him.

"There is nothing to be sorry for," he said firmly. "Okay?" She nodded, but self-loathing still filled her eyes. He was unsure of what to say, or do. "I won't do anything you don't want to do."

Her eyes flicked over his face as she thought over his words and tried to figure out if he was telling the truth or not. He seemed to be telling her the truth. He had to be. She was sitting with him, alone in a dark room, and he was making no move to do anything to harm her. Instead, he was only trying to reassure and comfort her.

"There's no rush," he assured her. "I'll wait until you're comfortable, until you're ready."

She had to fight back the wave of tears flooding her eyes. "Wait?" she managed to choke out through the lump in her throat.

He smiled. "Yes, wait. I like you, Sera. I want to be with you, with, or without sex. Understand?"

Her eyes widened as his words sank in. He could have almost any girl, at any time, why would he choose to wait for her? For someone who shrank away from him? For someone who was broken? She simply couldn't believe what she was hearing, but he seemed so honest, so sincere, and she wanted to believe him.

"Why?" she had to ask.

He stared at her as he tried to figure it out for himself. He liked her, he knew that, but he had liked girls before. Though none of them had ever made him feel the way she did or so protective before. And none of them had managed to arouse him as much as she did with just a look or a kiss. He was rigid right now, yet he was telling her he would wait for her.

It would be better for her if he left now, walked downstairs, and found the first girl he could take his lust out on. Instead, he found himself going limp at the thought. He was suddenly sure they wouldn't be able to satisfy him, and only she would be able to. Although they had just met, and he barely knew her, she helped to ease the loneliness of his bleak existence, and he was not going to let her go. He would have to someday, but not yet.

"Because I want to be with you. Okay?" he asked with a small smile.

She managed to smile back at him as her heart filled with happiness. He was surely too good to be true, but right now she didn't care. His thumb stilled on her chin as he leaned forward and kissed her. He pulled back and smiled as he held his arms out to her. She didn't hesitate as she fell into them. He hugged her against his chest, his chin resting on her head. To her amazement, she realized she'd never felt so safe before.

"Can I ask you something?" he inquired.

"Sure, what?"

"You may not like it, and you don't have to answer if you don't want to."

She nestled closer to his warmth. "Then ask."

"What happened to you before?"

Her breath froze in her lungs as her heart beat a staccato in her chest. "What do you mean?" she asked, trying to keep the tremor from her voice.

He stroked her hair. "I mean, what happened to make you so frightened?"

Agony tore through her as memories threatened to rush

forth. Resolutely, she turned her attention away from the past and made herself focus on the here and now.

"You don't have to answer me," he reminded her.

She didn't know why. Maybe it was because he hadn't pressed her, or maybe it was because she felt so incredibly, irrationally safe with him, but she suddenly felt the need to tell him... or at least tell him some of it. "Remember when I said I came to this school because it was close to home, but far enough away?"

"Yes."

"Well, that wasn't entirely true. To me, it wasn't far enough away from home, not nearly far enough, but I couldn't afford anything else. My parents only live three hours away, in New Hampshire, but I don't go home for the holidays. I stay with my grandmother on the Cape. Sometimes my mom comes to visit me, but she never stays long, and my father never comes."

She took a deep breath to steady herself as she reopened wounds which had never completely healed. "My graduating class was only thirty-two kids, and we all knew where everyone else was going. No one was coming here, so I did. No one from the following classes has attended here either."

He remained silent while she took another deep breath. Now that she was speaking, she suddenly found herself unable to stop. "In the middle of my senior year, I started dating this guy named Jacob."

Her voice broke off as she shuddered involuntarily. She hadn't said his name in years, just saying it brought cold terror to her gut. Liam stroked her hair and back, easing some of the tension from her muscles, and giving her the strength to go on.

"He was the quarterback on the football team of the town next to ours. Our town was too small for a team, so the kids in our school played on that team too. My friends and I went to all their games; it was the only thing to do on a Friday night. Jacob was outgoing and good looking. I thought I was the luckiest person on earth when he asked me to go out with him. My parents wouldn't allow me to date until I was a senior, so he was my first boyfriend.

"We had been dating for about a month when we went to my homecoming dance. I was crowned queen." Sera snorted as she recalled how happy she'd been that night, how childish, and naive. "It had been the greatest night of my life. After the dance, we went to a party at my friend Lisa's house. I never wanted the night to end, but I had a two o'clock curfew, so Jacob drove me home."

She closed her eyes as she tried desperately not to shed the tears pooling in them. She nestled closer to him, needing to know he was there, that Jacob was the past, and she would never have to see him again. That he couldn't hurt her anymore. Liam's hands massaged the back of her scalp as he hugged her closer to him.

"He was drunk, but I didn't care, nothing bad could happen to either of us," she continued in a strangled voice. "He pulled onto a side road and drove to a place we had gone to a few times before. It was private there; no one bothered us.

"He started to kiss me, and at first it was okay, you know. But then... I don't know; I don't know anything anymore." She blinked rapidly as she lost the battle against her tears and one slid free. "I can't believe I'm telling you this," she mumbled. "I haven't even told Kathleen. She'd be so mad at me if she found out I told you, and not her."

He clasped hold of her chin and lifted her head. She looked up at his handsome face as he tenderly stared down at her. "You don't have to tell me anything you don't want to," he assured her as he wiped the tear from her face. The tender gesture nearly undid her. She blinked rapidly against the flood of tears filling her eyes.

"I know, maybe that's why I can tell you. Or maybe it's because, for some reason, I don't know why, but I feel I can trust you." Although, she often put her trust in the wrong people. First Jacob, then her parents, and most recently Michelle.

"You can trust me, Sera," he vowed.

"I want to." His hand stilled on her cheek as something flashed through his eyes, something filled with longing and wistfulness. Sera's breath caught in her throat, and she knew she could tell him anything, trust him with anything.

She raised her hand and took hold of his. She couldn't tell him the rest if she kept looking at him. She would get lost in him and forget everything else. For a moment she wished for that, but she knew if he was ever going to understand her, then this was something he needed to know. She lowered her head and buried herself within the warm security of his powerful arms.

"Like I was saying, I don't know what happened, but everything seemed to go from blissful to frightening in an instant. I tried not to be scared, but I was. I had planned on losing my virginity to him that night, but suddenly I wasn't so sure I wanted to anymore. I told him to stop, if only just to give me a few minutes to calm down and relax."

Sera's voice became tenser as she continued. Memories washed over her, threatening to suffocate her with their intensity. She could suddenly feel Jacob's hands on her again, smell his stinking, alcohol-drenched breath; taste blood in her mouth.

"No matter what anyone says, I told him to stop. But, he wouldn't. He just kept saying this was supposed to happen, this was our night, and I had said I would. He ripped my dress, tore the front out of it. I started to cry, and he told me to shut up, to stop being a selfish bitch. I tried to make him stop, I screamed,

God did I scream, and I beat him until my hands were bruised and numb."

Sera's words tumbled out in a heedless rush revealing her intense grief. A fiery rage began to course through his veins as he thought of the man who attacked her, a man she had trusted. If Jacob had been standing in front of him, he would have killed him. He took a deep breath as he tried to fight against the animal thirst for revenge building inside him.

She took a hitching breath. "Then, he hit me," she continued, her voice small and extremely fragile. The sound of it tore at his heart, ripped into his soul. His arms squeezed around her in an attempt to block out the anguish of her past. It was impossible.

"That hurt so much," she whispered. "I nearly blacked out, but I knew if I did, he would do whatever he wanted to me. I somehow managed to claw his face as he continued to fumble and paw at me. He bellowed and smashed a fist into the side of my face. Blood spurted everywhere. It soaked him, and my dress, as it poured from my nose."

She forced herself to stay focused on the present and to get it all out. "I think it was all the blood that made him come to his senses. It coated everything. He started screaming at me to get out of the car, that I was getting blood everywhere and making a mess. He didn't have to tell me twice. I got out of there as fast as I could. I walked home through the woods, clutching my dress together, and leaving a trail of blood behind me.

"When I got there, I couldn't talk to tell my parents what had happened. My jaw was swollen shut, and I was in complete shock. They rushed me to the hospital, my mother in hysterics, and my father screaming about drunk drivers. It wasn't until a few hours later I was able to write down what had happened."

Sera stopped as tears spilled out of her eyes. She tried to

wipe them away, but now that they were flowing freely, they wouldn't stop. "Sera, you don't have to say anything more. I understand."

"There's more," she whispered, lowering her eyes.

He tried to raise her chin back up, but she kept her face firmly averted. She couldn't look at him when the shame was boiling up in waves, and the memories of Jacob's hands on her were so vivid and real. She didn't want him to see her humiliation.

"Sera—"

"I have to finish. I have to." She took a deep breath and forced herself to continue speaking. "To make a long story short, my father called me a liar. He said Jacob had told them I'd gotten drunk at the party, and taken off with a group of guys from his school. We must have gotten into a car accident, and I was trying to cover it up so I wouldn't get in trouble. The kids at school began to whisper about me behind my back, and my friends abandoned me. You don't remain popular by calling the star quarterback a rapist.

"It didn't matter people saw me leaving with Jacob that night, or that there had been no other guys around. No one would believe he could do such a thing. They all said I had asked for it. That I deserved whatever happened, and Jacob had done nothing wrong. Most of the guys already disliked me because I wouldn't date them, and I think the girls had always secretly hated me. They now had their excuse to turn their backs on me.

"By the time my father realized there had been no car accidents reported that night, and people had seen me leave with Jacob, it was too late. The damage had been done. I hated them for not believing in me, for not trusting me. The only person who always believed me was my grandmother. I moved to Cape Cod to spend the rest of my senior year with her. It took some finagling, but she managed to get me a resident tuition rate here."

He squeezed her chin gently, and she finally managed to lift her eyes to his. She was scared she would find disgust, or pity, in his gaze. Instead, she found a startling wealth of warmth and caring. The sight of it stole her breath away.

"I'm sorry for what happened to you, and I wish I could take it away. It never should have happened to someone like you. But the worst things always happen to the best people. I think you realize that," Liam said.

He bent his head and dropped a kiss on her trembling lower lip. He pulled away and wiped the tears from her face. "I don't know why I told you all of this," she whispered. "I barely know you. You must think I'm an idiot."

"You're not an idiot, Sera, and no matter what people said, or did, you did not deserve what happened, and you didn't ask for it."

It had taken her a long time to believe that, and there were times she still doubted it. She had always thought she'd done something wrong, that she'd encouraged it, but to have Liam say she hadn't made her feel better, stronger. For once, someone besides her grandmother believed in her and was on her side.

He lay back on the bed, pulling her down with him. She didn't fight against him as she lay down on top of him. His hands were relaxing as they rubbed her back and hair. She nestled closer, his warmth and security pushing the remains of her fear away.

Liam stared at the ceiling as she cuddled against him. He couldn't get over how small and delicate she was. Protective instincts he never knew he possessed raced through him. The anger still radiated just beneath the surface, but he refused to let her see it. He didn't want to frighten her with it.

"What do you say we order some pizza, rent some movies, and stay in tonight?" he inquired.

"What about the party?"

He knew the last thing she felt like doing was going to a party right now, and neither did he. "I'd rather stay here, with you."

She lifted her head to look at him. Her eyes were bloodshot from crying, but she was still exquisitely lovely. "I'd like that."

He smiled as he pushed back some of her glorious hair from her face. "Good."

She curled up against his chest and, within minutes, fell asleep again.

CHAPTER FIVE

Sera leaned against the doorjamb. The frat house was packed with people, more people than she had ever imagined it could hold. They bumped and jostled her as they made their way through the crowd. Kathleen stood by her side, swaying with the music as she surveyed the dance floor. It was so packed there was no room for them.

Danielle reappeared, slightly flushed and harried looking as she handed Kathleen another beer. "God, it's packed in here!" she cried.

Sera agreed as she studied the swarm of bodies. Kathleen ran a hand through her tousled, short bob. Even though they weren't dancing, the heat of the room was enough to make them sweat. She cast Sera a small smile as she stood on her tiptoes trying to look over the sea of heads.

Sera was still amazed Kathleen wasn't mad at her for not telling her about Jacob sooner, and for telling Liam first. At first, she'd been upset, more by the fact Sera had told Liam first, but she'd said she understood. Sera was even more astonished when Kathleen stated she'd known something had happened to Sera; she just wasn't exactly sure what.

She knew Kathleen, and patience was not one of her virtues. Kathleen loved gossip and hated being kept in the dark about anything, but although she had noticed it, she had never questioned Sera about her hesitancy around men or the fact she never dated. She simply tried to help Sera get over it, in her own way, by forcing her to go to parties and to interact with other people. Kathleen waited for Sera to tell her in her own time.

Sera loved her even more for her consideration and understanding. She'd been concerned Kathleen might have said she wasn't upset with her while in truth she was, but over the past three weeks, her best friend had shown no signs of resentment.

Sera returned her smile as she turned to scan the crowd again. She spotted Liam's dark head above the crowd as he wound his way toward them. Her heart immediately began to beat a little faster, and a small smile curved her mouth. She had spent every night of the past three weeks with him. They had spent a few nights hanging out in his room, watching movies, and talking. A few other nights were spent hanging out with Kathleen, Danielle, Mike, Jack, and Doug. Other times they had gone out to dinner, to the movies, and one ridiculous night of bowling where they both made fools of themselves and vowed never to do it again.

They went to parties, where every girl there hit on him, but he paid no attention to them as he stayed by her side, dancing with her, and never failing to make her feel as if she was the only woman in the room. He also never failed to make her feel safe and protected. When men leered at her and made rude comments, one look from him was enough to silence them, and send them on their way.

Sera had never been so happy in her life, never felt this

secure. He never pressured her, never forced her to do anything she didn't want to. When she stiffened involuntarily, he comforted her. When panic seized her for no reason, he understood and helped to set her at ease.

She knew she was falling in love with him, and it scared the hell out of her. She hadn't thought it was possible to fall in love with someone in three weeks, but she knew now she was wrong. With each day that passed, she found herself increasingly scared of losing him. There was only so much a man could take before he got tired of being patient. Although he showed no signs of that happening, she was certain it was only a matter of time. She just hoped she could get over her apprehension by then.

He stepped out of the crowd, flashing his dazzling grin as he handed her a beer. Sera took it and sipped as she studied him through lowered lashes. "Hey guys," Jack greeted as he appeared at his side. "This place is a madhouse tonight!"

"That's for sure!" Kathleen agreed.

Jack was bumped forward causing beer to slosh out of his cup. "Hey, watch it!" he yelled over his shoulder before turning back to Liam. "Can I talk to you for a minute?"

"Yeah," Liam replied. He turned back to Sera and kissed her. "I'll be right back."

He followed Jack into the crowd. "Well now, wasn't that sweet."

Sera turned at the voice in her ear. Michelle stood behind her, leaning casually against the wall as she surveyed her through narrowed eyes. Her long hair was loose and flowing around her elegant face. Despite the heat of the house, she somehow managed to look cool and refreshed.

Sera stared at her as she tried to sort through the jumbled rush of feelings rolling through her at the sight of Michelle. She hadn't seen her since the night she'd left her dorm room. She didn't know what to say to her now, or why Michelle suddenly seemed to hate her so much. She felt betrayed by her, and she was hurt, but she was also mad and getting madder.

"Hello, Michelle," she replied coldly.

"Haven't seen you around much." Nor had she attempted to either. Sera didn't say a word as Michelle casually brushed back a strand of hair. "You two make a cute couple," she purred.

"Don't they?" Kathleen inquired sweetly.

Michelle's eyes flashed to her as a cruel smile twisted her face. "You're a fool if you think he really likes you."

Sera's hand clenched on her cup. "I don't believe that's any of your business, Michelle."

"You're just pissed because he turned you down!" Kathleen retorted.

Michelle lifted her head haughtily as she tossed back her hair. "I wouldn't waste my time on someone like him."

"Oh, really, Michelle?" They all turned as Liam stepped beside Sera, his arm wrapped around her waist as he drew her against his side.

Michelle's eyes flashed angrily as she took in Liam. Kathleen snickered but hid her smile behind her hand. Danielle was frowning as she stood nearby. Liam's arm was like a steel trap around her waist. An odd sense of power radiated from him and frightened her. Sera's heart skipped a beat as his eyes landed on her. His face was pitiless, but there was a warmth in his gaze she knew was only for her.

"Hello, Liam," Michelle said calmly.

"Were you talking about me?" he inquired as he lifted his head to look at her.

Michelle raised her chin and stared back at him defiantly. "Yes."

He smiled at her, but there was no warmth in the gesture, or in his features. "Good, because I wouldn't waste my time on you either. So now that we're in agreement, don't you have somewhere else to be?"

The icy bitterness of his voice made the hair on Sera's arms stand up. "Yeah, I do," Michelle replied coldly.

"I would suggest going there."

Michelle glared at the two of them as she stormed past. Sera sighed as some of the tension eased from her body. Liam's arm around her waist loosened marginally, but he didn't release her.

"Want to dance?" he inquired.

She glanced back at the crowded floor. She hated the idea of pushing her way onto it, but the thought of being wrapped in Liam's arms was too tempting to refuse. "Yeah," she replied.

He led her out to the dance floor, easily cutting through the thick crowd. A small smile curved her mouth as she rested her head against his solid chest and wrapped her arms around his muscular body. His arms around her were warm, comforting, and completely sheltering. She felt perfectly safe, and completely at home, as she moved in time with him.

LIAM MOVED SWIFTLY through the thick crowd, searching for Mike, Jack, or Doug. "Hey."

He turned as Jack caught hold of his arm. "Hey."

"Come on."

Jack led the way to the back stairway and up the stairs. Liam followed behind; his thoughts jumbled as they made it to the second floor and continued to the third. Mike and Doug were standing outside Mike's room; their arms crossed over their chests as they talked quietly. This far up, the music was only a distant, thumping melody. Shouts and laughter wafted up from below, but the words were indiscernible.

Mike and Doug straightened away from the wall as he and Jack approached. An uneasy feeling began to fill him as he studied the intense looks on their faces. "We have to talk," Mike said briskly.

Liam knew what they planned to talk about; he just didn't care to hear it. "I don't have time right now," he replied.

Mike eyed him. "Then you're going to make time."

Liam folded his arms over his chest. "What is it, Mike?"

Mike looked at both Jack and Doug, but they appeared content to let Mike do the talking. "Come on."

Mike strode across the hall and thrust Liam's door open. He waited for all of them to enter before closing it again. Liam silently stood by the door as he eyed the three of them. "It's Sera," Mike said bluntly.

He had already known it was, but he still didn't want to deal with it. "What about her?" he asked coldly.

Mike perched on the edge of the desk. "Don't be difficult, Liam. You shouldn't be involved with her, and you know it."

"It's none of your concern."

"It *is* our concern! We're involved in this too!" Jack shouted.

"No, you're not."

Jack's hazel eyes narrowed as his solid jaw clenched. He was shorter and thinner than Liam, with a lithe, soccer player build. Right now, his light brown hair was a darker shade from sweat as it curled down to his collar and clung to the broad angles of his face. His nose was broken when they were twelve, and it was still a little bent to the side with a small bump in the middle.

"Really?" Jack inquired. "Go tell that to the girl across the hall. She's there for you, not us!"

Liam's arms dropped as he took an angry step forward. "Hey," Doug intervened. "Cut it out. Both of you."

Jack's eyes still simmered with resentment, but he took a

small step back. Liam glared at him, his jaw clenched, as his nostrils flared. "Look," Mike said, shooting Jack a warning glance. "All we're saying is you shouldn't be involved with her, Liam, and you know it."

Liam scowled at him, but he couldn't say anything to defend himself. Mike was right; he shouldn't be involved with her. "I know," he replied. "But I'm not going to let her go."

"Oh, for crying out loud!" Jack exclaimed.

"Jack!" Doug hissed warningly. Jack sneered at him. Doug didn't back down as his ocean blue eyes remained fixed on Jack. His dark blond hair was cut short, and right now stood in little spikes on top of his head from tugging at it, which had always been his habit when he was agitated. He was shorter and stockier than all of them, but he was wholesome and cute; a combination which always made people think he was younger than he was and had never failed to make women flock to him.

"Look, Liam, you can't keep seeing her," Mike said firmly. "First of all, we can't keep finding girls for you, second of all she's going to end up hearing about it, and then what are you going to do, tell her the truth? No, you're not. Third of all, you're just going to hurt her."

He was fuming as he glared at his best friends. "I know that!"

"Well then, don't you think you should end it soon... now?"

"No."

"Shit!" Jack exclaimed.

"Are you insane?" Mike demanded as his patience finally frayed. "Are you listening to yourself? You agree with everything, and yet you're still being an ass!"

Liam's patience and temper were close to exploding. It was the most selfish thing he had ever done, and he despised himself for it, but he couldn't bring himself to end it with her. The thought alone sent a cold bolt of dread through his heart.

"I'm not ending it with her."

Mike stood rigidly. "I cannot believe you're so fucking selfish. What about her? Don't you think she deserves better?"

"Yes, I do."

"Then end it with her!"

"No."

"Liam, you have to," Doug said calmly.

"No, I don't."

"You're a selfish bastard!" Mike exploded.

Liam rounded on him with his fists clenched. "Yes, I am," he snarled.

"You have no reason for hanging on to her!" Jack yelled. "None!"

"I love her!" Liam bellowed.

They gaped at him in amazement, but it was nothing compared to the astonishment jolting through his system at his words. He took a small step back as the realization slammed home. Jesus, what had he done? He never meant for things to go this far, never planned to care for her at all, never mind fall in love with her.

"Crap," Liam muttered.

"You can say that again," Jack mumbled.

"Liam, what can you offer her? Nothing. Your life, our lives, are nothing but death and blood. She deserves better than that. The only thing you're going to do is hurt her, you, and maybe even us."

"I know that, Mike, but I can't let her go. I don't know why; I just can't. Not now anyway."

"It will only get more difficult."

Liam ran a hand through his hair. He was still completely staggered by his sudden realization. He'd never expected to love anyone, especially not now. The only people he had cared about as a human were these three, David, and his family. How was it possible that now, when he was a monster, he could fall in love?

"You have to let her go," Doug said.

It would be the most challenging thing he'd ever have to do, but the most decent thing he'd ever done, human or not. "I know," he reluctantly admitted.

"Then—"

"All right!" he snapped. "I will. I'll end it tonight."

The thought tore through his heart and sent a fiery rage coursing through his veins. "It's for the best," Mike murmured.

"Shut up, Mike!" he spat.

They stared at him as if they had no idea who he was anymore; he wasn't entirely sure he knew who he was either. "The girl is across the hall," Doug informed him.

A muscle twitched in Liam's cheek. "Get rid of her."

"But—"

"I said get rid of her!"

"You need to feed, Liam," Jack said.

"I'll kill her if I do."

He spun away from them and flung the door open so forcefully the plaster cracked. He didn't care as he stormed down the hall and back toward the party. His breath was coming in rapid pants by the time he made it to the ground floor. He paused to gather his control before he walked back into the party. The last thing he wanted was for Sera to see him like this. He would scare the hell out of her.

Harnessing his willpower, he slowly regained control of his rapidly swaying emotions. Taking a deep breath, he forced himself to move out of the stairwell and back down the hall. There seemed to be even more people than before, and the smell of alcohol and sweat permeated the air. People bounced into him as he shoved his way forward, heedless of their cries of protest. He had left Sera by the dance floor, but she was no longer there.

He turned around and started shoving his way back through the crowd. He found Kathleen and Danielle at the doorway of the kitchen. "Where's Sera?" he yelled above the noise.

"She went to get another drink!" Danielle shouted.

Liam glanced at the keg by the front door, but she wasn't there. He turned and headed toward the back rooms. There were at least three kegs there. He stepped through the double doors and spotted her talking to a tall guy with brown hair. She was smiling, but she looked more than a little uncomfortable as she said something, and then turned to leave. The man's hand shot out, grasping her arm to stop her. He saw the tremor rocking her as she turned back to him.

For a moment, Liam saw nothing but red. Then, he was rapidly moving across the floor.

"I have to go," Sera told him.

"Can I get your number?" the man inquired.

"I have a boyfriend."

"So?"

Sera was unsure how to respond.

"So that means back off." Liam seemed to come out of nowhere to grasp the guy's arm.

The guy's mouth compressed as he turned toward Liam. "No one asked you, pal," he said coldly.

"Let her go!" Liam commanded.

Sera gaped in astonishment, unable to believe what was going on. The guy's hand fell from her arm, but resentment radiated from every inch of him. However, it was nothing compared to the wrath blazing from Liam. She was truly frightened as she gazed at his impassive face and fiery eyes. He looked like he was about ready to kill the guy.

"Hey, what's going on?"

Sera let out a breath of relief as Mike appeared at Liam's side with Doug and Jack behind him. "Nothing," Liam grated.

"I was just talking to the girl," the guy said coldly. "If you have a problem with that, then we can solve it."

"Yes, we can," Liam growled.

"I don't think so," Mike interjected, shooting a pointed look at Liam before stepping between them. "There will be no fighting, right, Liam?"

Liam's gaze remained locked on the guy in front of him. His whole body was stiff, and he knew he was close to breaking, close to a place he'd never been before. But seeing the guy touch Sera, and hearing what he'd said unleashed something inside him he hadn't known existed.

"Liam." Sera's voice and her small hand on his arm helped pull him from the fiery haze blurring his vision. He glanced at her. She stared at him with pleading, troubled eyes. Her lower lip trembled as she looked over at the guy, then back at Liam. "Please don't."

He stared at her, his jaw clenched as he released the guy's arm. "I think you'd better go," Mike told the man.

The guy looked at Mike and then at Liam. "Assholes," he muttered as he walked away.

Liam's jaw clenched, but he managed to refrain from going after him and beating him to a bloody pulp. His shoulders slumped, and he turned to look at Sera. "You okay?" he asked.

Her eyes rapidly scanned his face. His eyes were still filled with fury, but it was easing as the familiar warmth started to seep into them. She hadn't seen anyone look as wild, not since Jacob, and he had terrified her. It was a new side of him, a side she didn't like.

"I'm fine. He was just talking," she murmured.

He reached out to touch her cheek, but she flinched involuntarily away. "Sera..."

She shook her head as tears welled in her eyes.

"Will you come upstairs with me?" he asked.

She wrapped her arms around herself in a desperate attempt to stop the shaking rocking her body.

He stepped closer to her, and she tilted her head to look at him. "I'm not going to hurt you, Sera. I won't ever hurt you. I promise. Now, will you please come upstairs with me so we can talk?"

She stared warily at him before nodding. No matter what she just saw, Liam had never harmed her, and she believed he never would.

She didn't flinch from him, something he was extremely grateful for as he slid his arm around her waist. He turned back around to find Jack and Doug studying him with mixed expressions of concern. Mike frowned as he stared at Sera. Liam stopped at Mike's side. "It's not going to happen," he said quietly so Sera couldn't hear him.

Mike stared at him in disbelief before looking back at Sera. "Liam—"

"No, Mike, it's not going to happen."

"I hope you know what you're doing."

"I don't," he admitted before turning and leading her out of the room.

He knew he couldn't let her go right now; he wasn't sure if he'd ever be able to let her go. The thought of her with anyone else was enough to make him feel like killing someone. He loved her, and he intended to be with her for as long as he possibly could.

Tonight, he stood on a precipice he'd never thought to stand on before. His love for her had pushed him to it, but she somehow managed to pierce through his desire to kill and pull him back before he plummeted over. If he lost her, he would go over the edge. She was the only thing keeping him from the darkness and in the light. He couldn't let that light go, especially when his existence was so dreary.

He opened the door to his room and led her inside. Flicking the switch on, he turned to look at her. "You scared me," she whispered.

Liam winced. "I'm sorry, I didn't mean to."

He pulled her forward, enveloping her in his arms. He slipped his hand into her thick hair and held her against him. She resisted for a second before wrapping her arms around his waist and burying herself against him.

He held her for a long time, savoring her warmth, and the way she eased his bleak soul. He pulled away, bent down, and picked her up. Her hands instinctively clutched his shoulders as he flicked the switch off and carried her to the bed.

"Liam—"

"It's all right," he said. "I just want to hold you, Sera."

She didn't make another protest as he sat on the bed and pulled her down. She laid her head on his shoulder; her mouth pressed against his neck, her breath was warm on his throat. Her small fingers curled into his shirt as she nestled closer. She lifted her head; her delicate mouth parted as she gazed at him. Easing her head down, he kissed her, his tongue entwined with hers as she opened her mouth to his. Instantly, he began to harden and throb. He shifted so she wouldn't feel his obvious lust for her. Winding his hands in her hair, he leisurely imitated with his tongue what he longed to do to her body in long, smooth thrusts. She tasted so sweet he knew he would never get enough of her.

He stroked her breasts when she melted against him; her limp body trembled as her arms wound around his neck. She moaned as his hand slid up her shirt to cup her full, luscious breast. Her nipple became taut as he rubbed his fingers around it. He rolled her to the side, leveling himself beside her as his hands ran over her satiny skin, and his mouth continued to tease her. She was unbelievably soft and delicate, so enticing as her body moved against his and little erotic gasps escaped her.

It was sometime later before he forced himself to pull away from her. She stared up at him, her eyes clouded with passion, and her lips tantalizingly swollen from his kisses. He trailed his finger along her full bottom lip as she smiled. He wanted her so badly it nearly killed him to pull away from her.

He nestled her head securely in his shoulder. "Why did you stop?" she murmured.

She cuddled closer to him; her small fingers rested on his chest. "Because you're not ready yet, are you?"

"No, but you didn't have to stop."

She had no idea what she did to him. He couldn't take the chance of scaring her if they kept going, and he knew there was a risk he would. She was beginning to trust him, and he'd already scared her once tonight.

"Yes, I did."

She lifted her head to look questioningly down at him. "Why?"

He chuckled and pushed back her tousled hair. "Because you drive me crazy."

The frown and the questioning look in her eyes were enough to let him know she didn't understand. He took her hand; his eyes fixed on hers as he lowered it to his crotch. Her eyes widened as his shaft jumped through his jeans beneath her fingers.

Her fingers undid the button of his jeans and slid the zipper down. His breath froze as her warm hand slid inside; she pushed aside his underwear as she stroked him. His shaft jumped beneath her shy, hesitant touch as he sucked in a deep breath. "Sera you don't have to do this," he managed to choke out.

She smiled enticingly as her hand wrapped around him. He bit back a groan. "I want to," she whispered. "I just don't..." her words trailed off as a blush crept up her face, and her long lashes lowered to shadow her eyes.

A jolt of shock rocked through him as he understood what she was trying to say. To his surprise, and extreme joy, he realized she was even more innocent than he thought. He took her hand again. Her eyes flew back to his as he began to show her what to do, and how to please him.

He watched with intense rapture the myriad of emotions playing across her face. At first, there was a hint of fear, then wonder, and finally amazement. Passion clouded her eyes as she watched him. He eased his hand away and allowed her to touch and explore him on her own as he rolled her back to her side. She watched him as her hand continued to stroke and fondle him. He had to fight against the urge to spill himself as pleasure coursed through his body, but he wanted to wait to bring her over with him.

Placing his hand on her thigh, he ran it languidly up to the edge of her skirt and slid beneath. He watched her face for any sign she wanted him to stop, but there was only awe in her gaze. He pushed her panties down, his gaze focused on her as he slid his hand over her curls.

She bit her bottom lip as her legs clamped together. "It's all right," he whispered. "If you don't like it, tell me to stop."

Her eyes were tempestuous as her hand upon him stilled, and she studied him. Then, her thighs eased apart. Liam felt a moment of pure male satisfaction as he slid his hand lower and discovered her already wet with desire. It was good to know he drove her as crazy as she drove him, and she didn't even know what she was missing yet.

He was about to give her a hint.

He slid his finger inside her; an involuntary shudder ripped through him as he realized how wet and tight she was. She inhaled as he slid out of her, and then back in. Her face transformed from caution, to amazement, then to pleasure in a matter of seconds. Her mouth parted as her hand began to move on him again. He arched into her touch as he continued to make love to her with his hand.

He bent his head and reclaimed her mouth as his hand entwined in her hair. She arched into him, a cry escaping her as he began to move faster within her. He held her as she began to match his urgency, stroking faster and pushing him toward the brink. He parted her folds and used his thumb to caress her. She cried out, arching against him as her muscles clamped around his finger. He groaned as he finally found his release.

She collapsed on the bed, her muscles still contracting around him as she sighed contentedly. She had never felt anything so blissful or sweet in her life. "Hold on," Liam whispered.

He rolled out of bed and padded across the room. She heard him searching for something before he returned to her. He took hold of her hand and wiped it with a towel. It was only then she realized she had his seed on her fingers. A blush began to stain her cheeks as she shyly lifted her eyes to him. His pants hung loosely on his narrow hips, unbuttoned, and unzipped. He was so broad, and strong, and magnificent.

She looked back at his face to find him studying her with a bemused smile. He slid the jeans off revealing solid, muscled thighs. Sera's blush deepened as he pulled his shirt off to reveal his well-muscled abdomen and a V of black hair spreading across his chest and belly before tapering off at his underwear. She was still marveling at the amazing differences between his body and hers when he climbed back onto the bed.

"You can't sleep in your clothes," he said.

Moving ever so slowly, he took hold of the bottom of her shirt. He slid it up as she lifted her arms to allow him to slide it over her head. She remained silent as he pushed her skirt down. His hands skimmed over her legs and caused a shiver of delight to tear through her as he slipped it off. Her blush deepened as his gaze leisurely traveled over her body.

"You're beautiful," he whispered.

Her gaze flew to his. He smiled at her as he pulled her down and wrapped the blanket around them both. He rubbed her silky back as she nestled into his shoulder. A feeling of utter contentment stole through him as she snuggled closer to him. Her breasts were lush against his chest, and to his amazement, he found himself growing erect again. He closed his eyes as he gritted his teeth against the lust building within him. If he was this obsessed with her now, what would he be like when he finally made love to her?

He inhaled as he tried to get himself under control. Suddenly, he was assailed with the heady scent of her blood. It was sweet and enticing, utterly tempting. He had forgotten he didn't feed earlier. He was acutely reminded of that fact now.

He wouldn't hurt her. He'd burn in Hell before that happened. He closed his eyes as his baser instincts began to subside. He wanted to tell her he loved her, but the words lodged in his throat. Instead, he held her as she drifted off to sleep.

CHAPTER SIX

Sera slipped the black velvet cape around her shoulders and tied it at her throat. It swept along the floor as she moved to Kathleen's closet where her full-length mirror hung. Kathleen was cursing miserably in front of the small mirror on her dresser as she angrily shoved bobby pins into her hair. She was trying to get a long black wig to stay in place for the night, but Sera was certain she would rip her hair out in the process.

Sera was staggered by her reflection when she stepped in front of the mirror. Her long blonde hair was swept up and pinned neatly on her head. Spiraling tendrils framed her face. Her eyes shone a brilliant purple against the deep violet of her long, medieval dress, the sleeves were off the shoulder. An elegant gold choker, with fake blue stones hanging from it, was clasped around her neck. The painted flames on her face swirled out from her eyes and curled to her temples. They made her eyes seem larger and more mysterious.

She barely recognized herself as she stared in dumbfounded silence.

"There," Kathleen announced. "That should do it."

Sera turned to look at her. The long black wig hung down to Kathleen's waist and swished as she moved. Kathleen's Elvira dress was cut daringly low to enhance her large breasts. Her eyes were outlined in black, and she had painted a spider and a web on her right cheek. Her lips had been painted black, and she had placed long, black fingernails on. She looked utterly amazing and very sexy.

"You look fantastic," Sera said.

"Thank you," she replied, sweeping back her long black hair. "You look beautiful."

"Thanks, you ready to go?"

"Yeah, let's get Danielle."

Sera opened the door, and Kathleen swept past her, swishing her hair as she went. They moved down the hall, dodging the bats, spider webs, and witches hung from the ceiling. Kathleen knocked on Danielle's door and pushed it open. An eerie howl greeted them, and a skeleton laughed as its glowing green eyes lit.

"Hey guys," Danielle greeted as she shoved a pile of clothes on the floor.

Danielle had managed to get one of the few single rooms in the dorm. In her first three years, she hated her roommates. This year she'd decided she would rather be alone. She was much happier with the arrangement.

"You look so cute!" Kathleen gushed.

Danielle cast them a flashing grin as she tossed back her long brown hair. She'd dressed in a fitted gray leotard. Her hair was pulled into a ponytail, and gray ears were placed securely on her head. Whiskers decorated her face, and she had painted the tip of her slender nose black.

"You two look amazing."

"But of course," Kathleen cried as she spun in a circle.

"I'm ready." Danielle grabbed her small gray purse. "I hope this party is good."

"So do I." Kathleen bounced over to Sera as she opened the door. "The school party last year sucked! So, this one had better be good."

"It's a frat house," Sera said smiling. "Drinking, dancing, and passing out like always, only in disguise this time."

Kathleen laughed and skipped down the hall. "Like we won't know who it is through a mask!" she called, punching the button for the elevator. They stepped into it as Kathleen pushed the button for the first floor. "I can't wait to bob for apples in Budweiser, the Coors caramel apples, and beer bottle bats!"

They laughed as the doors opened and they stepped into the lobby. A handful of people were gathered, costumes on, waiting to go to parties. Streamers flowed from the ceiling to the floor, and decorations covered the walls in preparation for the trick-or-treaters tomorrow night. The three of them crossed the hall and exited through the thick wood doors. The crisp air and the smell of dead leaves instantly filled Sera's nostrils. Students strolled along the sidewalks, almost all of them wearing costumes, as they made their way toward whatever party they were invited to or bar they were spending the night at.

"Got your invite?" Danielle asked.

"I can't believe they sent out invitations," Kathleen said, pulling hers from between her breasts. "When did they get class, Sera?"

"Liam said they were doing something different this year, and they didn't have enough room for a lot of people. There will be no underclassmen unless they're in the frat or a girlfriend."

"There are still about a thousand people in the upper-class."

Kathleen pulled her dress down to expose more of her ample chest.

"They only sent out a hundred invitations."

"There are more people than that on the dance floor most nights," Danielle muttered.

"They're opening it up for the kid's tomorrow night," Sera said. "Everyone is invited afterwards."

At the frat house, they discovered a line winding all the way down to the sidewalk. "What is this?" Kathleen demanded.

"They're having a haunted house," a girl in an elf suit replied. "They're taking us in ten at a time."

"Yeah, but once you go in, you don't come out," a boy dressed as Robin Hood added with a sinister laugh.

"Oh cut it out, John," the girl replied, slapping him on the arm.

"Cool." Kathleen's eyes sparkled mischievously. "This should be fun!"

Sera stared up at the house. Jack-o-lanterns sat in all the windows on the lower floor, and candles flickered inside the pumpkins. In the attic, the lights were on, and a few people were moving across the windows. Sera realized they were the ones who had already gone through and had now begun the party. The line inched forward as they moved toward the doorway.

Halloween music poured out as the door opened to let in groups of people. No one appeared in the doorway, and no lights lit the foyer. Sera tried to peer inside, but it was impossible to see anything in the darkness. She glanced back through the line, her eyes landing on an Egyptian princess in a body-hugging gold dress. All her exposed skin was painted gold, except for her face, which was exquisitely layered with makeup. Her brilliant red hair flowed around her shoulders, and a gold tiara topped her head.

Sera felt a wave of annoyance as she stared at Michelle, who was flirting with a man dressed as a musketeer. He touched her shoulder, but Michelle slapped his hand away as she snapped at him not to mess up her makeup.

"How did that bitch get an invitation?" Kathleen demanded, hands on her hips.

"Kathleen," Sera warned.

"No way, Sera, that was the best thing about tonight!"

"She comes to all the parties here; I'm sure she's made more than a few friends. Just ignore her."

"You know I can't. She gives you dirty looks at all the parties, and she still won't lay off Liam. All she does is talk about what a jerk he is, but you know she's just waiting to make a move on him."

Sera felt extremely uncomfortable as she glanced back at Michelle. She was amazingly beautiful, and tonight it showed. She knew Liam couldn't stand her, but she had to be tough for a man to refuse, and Kathleen was right, Michelle did want Liam.

Finally making it to the front of the line, they found a man dressed as a troll who took their invitations. The door swung open, and Sera found herself faced with complete blackness. "Welcome to the House of Hell," a voice from behind the door said. "Enter at your own risk."

Sera walked into the foyer, followed by nine other people. The door closed behind them, and a small light came on to illuminate the floor around them. "Awesome," Kathleen whispered in her ear.

"This is ridiculous," a disdainful voice said from behind her. "How old are we?"

Sera bristled at Michelle's condescending tone and tried to push away her disappointment at having to go through with her. "Oh no," Danielle whispered.

A man stepped out of the shadows, startling them all, and causing Sera to take a step back. He wore a vampire costume and was covered with so much makeup Sera couldn't tell who he was. "I see you were brave enough to enter. I must warn you that not all of you will make it through alive. If you wish to leave now, please, be my guest." Sera bit back a smile as she recognized Jack's voice. She never expected to see him so dressed up for Halloween, and she found it charming.

"How corny," Michelle sneered.

"I see we have a disbeliever," Jack continued. "They are usually the ones who don't make it. Now, follow me to your death."

He walked away from them and toward the kitchen. They followed him down the dimly lit hall, past the swinging doors. "Welcome," he announced. "To the kitchen of death."

They stepped into an elaborately decorated death scene. On the kitchen table lay a torso with blood dripping from its neck and stumpy legs. A man stood by the sink holding a bloody knife; blood covered his white apron. "Have you brought me presents?" he asked, lowering the knife.

"Yes, master," Jack answered.

"You have done well. Come forward my children, and see what I have for you."

Sera cocked an eyebrow at Jack as he grinned down at her, his hazel eyes twinkling merrily. "Cute costume," she whispered.

"And you're looking lovely tonight," he said low. "Now move before I have to drink your blood."

Sera laughed as she moved forward, a little thrill of excitement flowed through her. She loved haunted houses. "Come." The man with the knife gestured them closer to the sink. They crowded around the sink to stare down at a bloody, decapitated head. "This was my brother. He stole my girlfriend; now I need a new one. What about you, sweetie?" he asked Kathleen.

"I love a man who knows how to protect himself," Kathleen replied laughingly.

"Oh, baby!"

They all jumped as the head in the sink uttered the words and opened its eyes to look at them. A few of the girls screamed and jumped back, and then everybody began to laugh nervously. "I need a girlfriend too," the head cried.

A shrill scream filled the air as a figure dressed in white came rushing at them. Sera yelped and stumbled into Danielle. "They're mine!" she shouted as she charged at them. "You can't have them!"

One of the men broke out laughing, and the terror fled Sera's body. "Come now!" Jack cried. "We must leave this room if we are to survive."

"This is awesome!" Kathleen enthused.

They moved through a pitch-black hall, bouncing against the walls as they felt their way along. Spider webs brushed annoyingly against her face, sending chills down her spine. The walls suddenly turned to mush, and Sera jerked her hand away as gunk enveloped her fingers.

"Ugh," Danielle cried. "What is this?"

"Brains," Jack replied. "Of those who didn't make it through."

"Well, it better not stain!" Michelle yelled from the back.

"Bitch," Jack muttered.

"You can say that again," Kathleen announced.

Jack laughed as Sera grinned. Suddenly, she bumped into something solid. "Sorry," she apologized when she realized it was a body.

Light suddenly flooded the room. Sera yelled and jumped

backward. The body was hanging from the ceiling staring down at her. "Help me," it cried as it grabbed at her.

"Shit!" she cried, her hand flying to her chest as Michelle laughed shrilly.

"Scared?" she taunted.

"Help me," it called again as she brushed past it and back into the shadows.

"We are about to enter the basement of torture," Jack announced.

A light flickered on. Sera eyed the rickety stairs before her, wondering if they would support her weight and the others. She swallowed as she followed Jack down the stairwell. An eerie feeling began to envelop her as the stairs rocked a little but held firm beneath them. The group followed behind her until they were all standing at the bottom. The only source of light was the bulb from above, and it was impossible to see anything beyond the ten-foot beam.

The light went out, and darkness descended. A chill went through Sera as Kathleen grabbed her arm. "I don't like this," Kathleen whispered.

Sera had to admit she didn't like it either. She wondered where Liam was in this blackness and wished he were with her. Something brushed against her arm, and she stifled the scream rising in her throat. Kathleen suddenly gripped her arm with enough force to leave a bruise.

"What the hell?" someone asked from the back.

"Something touched me!"

A large, hairy hand grabbed Sera's arm, and she screamed when a few other people did. A dim light suddenly came on. There was absolutely nothing around them. No hint of movement, and no place for anyone to hide. A shiver racked through her as she bit down on her bottom lip.

"Can we go to the party now?" a girl in the back asked nervously.

"Only the survivors will party," Jack taunted. "The dead will be dinner."

"Great," Kathleen mumbled, releasing Sera's arm.

They followed Jack into a dimly lit side room. In the middle of the room stood a man in surgical scrubs. A woman was lying on a medical table with blood pooling around her. The doctor looked up and pulled his mask down as he smiled at them. His teeth were gaping holes.

"Oh, more victims. I need practice!"

The young woman sat up. Blood flowed from her mouth, and her teeth hung grotesquely out. "Help," she begged. "Make him stop!"

The dentist came closer to them, a set of pliers in his hand. "I need more teeth for my collection!"

He held up a jar full of white teeth and waved it in front of them. "What about you?" he asked a girl dressed as red riding hood.

"How about you, goldie?" he asked Michelle. She laughed at him as he stopped in front of her. "Yes, you'll do," he grinned.

The lights went out and screams issued from everywhere. When the lights came back on, Michelle was pressed against the back wall, the dentist standing before her, laughing. "Let's go," Jack said, unable to keep the laughter from his voice.

The lights went back out, and Sera started to move forward cautiously. The wall suddenly gave out, and her hand fumbled into nothingness. Someone grabbed hold of it, pulling her to the side. She opened her mouth to scream when a hand wrapped around it, effectively cutting her off. Her heart hammered, and her chest heaved as she thrashed in the powerful grip.

"Shh, it's me," Liam whispered in her ear.

She slumped against him in relief as the panic fled. She

turned toward him, but she couldn't see anything in the dark. "You scared me!" she cried.

There was a clicking sound, and then a small light illuminated the alcove they were standing in. He lifted the tiny flashlight to look down at her. Sera smiled as she saw the Dracula costume he wore. The white shirt hugged his solid chest and broad shoulders. The black pants fit snugly against his solid thighs. The large bulge in his pants was obvious, and she had to tear her gaze away from it as heat washed over her face. Her gaze shot back to his twinkling green eyes as he smiled knowingly at her and propped his hand on the wall beside her head. His face was painted white, and blood dripped from the corners of his mouth, but all the makeup in the world couldn't cover his elegant good looks or his overpowering sensuality.

"You look beautiful," he whispered.

"I bet you say that to all your victims." She teased as she pressed her body against his.

"Only the ones I want to eat," he replied.

"Are you a tour guide?"

"I'm done with the tours; now, I'm hungry."

"I'm sweet," she whispered huskily.

"I know you are."

She fell into his warm embrace as his hands began to wander over her body and he kissed her leisurely. She tingled and burned wherever he touched as his hands ran up and down her back. She was just beginning to lose herself when the noise of the next group coming through woke her from her Liam induced haze.

She laughed and pulled away from him. Screams echoed through the air, and people began to laugh. He cradled the back of her head and kissed her again, his tongue delving into her mouth deeply as he gently pushed her against the wall. His hands skimmed down to cup her breast. A gasp of pleasure escaped her, and her hands dug into his back.

He lowered her dress to free one of her lace-covered breasts. He cupped it in his hand, his thumb rubbing tantalizingly against her nipple. His lips left hers as he bent to take the nipple into his mouth. His tongue caressed and teased it through the thin lace of her bra before nipping it softly. She wound her fingers into his hair as she arched against him; shivers of pleasure racked through her and caused her knees to go weak.

Screams filled the air again as the next group came through. Liam was slightly breathless as he pulled away. "We better go," he whispered. "Or we'll never leave."

She managed a small nod as disappointment coursed through her. She could have spent the entire night there, but she knew it was impossible. Taking a deep breath, she tried to calm her racing heart. He smiled as he wiped her cheek. "Makeup," he explained.

She adjusted her dress and stepped back to watch as he fixed his cape. She gazed at his powerful physique admiringly, unable to keep her gaze from the bulge in his pants that was even more noticeable than before. She finished straightening her dress to keep her mind distracted from the excitement coursing through her veins. Liam stepped forward and took hold of her arm.

She followed him through the passageways and back to the stairs she descended earlier. A group was coming down now. He turned off the flashlight as he pulled her beneath the stairs. A few guys stood there, smiling at the two of them as they waited to scare the unsuspecting people on the stairs.

"Tsk tsk tsk," Mike admonished and wagged a hairy finger in her face.

"Shut up, Mike," she whispered, laughing as she shoved his finger away.

He grinned at her and looked up as the group reached the bottom of the stairs. "Got you earlier," Mike whispered in her ear before he slipped his mask back on.

She shoved him playfully as the lights went out. Then they were pushing past. Liam took hold of her arm as the group began to yell and curse. "Don't touch me!" someone yelled. Someone else screamed, and the lights came back on as the group left.

Sera glanced around at the group surrounding her again. "See you guys upstairs," a Frankenstein monster said.

"No more detours!" Mike called after them as they made their way up the stairs.

She followed Liam through a few more passageways before she found herself at the back stairway. She had come to know the frat house well, but she was disoriented by the maze they'd erected. They hurried up the stairs and into the attic. People were spread out across the room. Music played, but not at the level it usually did. Drinks were passed around as people laughed and talked happily. They all sparkled in an amazing assortment of costumes, and glitter. Decorations hung across the room, and the faint sounds of Halloween music drifted up from the haunted house below.

Sera spotted Michelle as she floated past in a wave of gold. Kathleen came bounding up to her, a large smile on her face. "Did you have fun?" she asked, slyly glancing at Liam.

He flashed a dazzling grin. "Always tactful," he laughed.

"That's why you love me!" she cried. "That was a great haunted house. You would have loved it, Sera," she added mischievously. "Poor Michelle fell on the floor trying to get away from the headless horseman!"

Sera laughed and almost wished she'd seen it. "I'm going to get a drink," Liam said.

"All right."

He disappeared into the crowd, and she followed Kathleen over to where Danielle sat.

CHAPTER SEVEN

Liam stood by the keg and sipped his beer. The music was in full swing now that the haunted house was over. People were moving, dancing, laughing, and making out in the shadowed corners. Mike and Jack stood by his side, drinking, and commenting over the girls.

His gaze was focused on Sera as she sat with Danielle and Kathleen on an old couch. She was laughing happily as her eyes followed the people dancing. A man in a devil costume walked up to her and held out his hand. She shook her head, said something, and he shrugged and walked off.

"Looks like Lucifer wants your girl," Mike commented, his hairy werewolf hand was covered in spilled beer.

"Maybe Lucifer could get her to give it up," Jack said laughingly.

"What?" Liam inquired coldly.

Jack shifted uncomfortably as Liam turned to face him. "Well, did you get any yet?"

"Is that any of your business?"

Jack looked to Mike for help, but he was very engrossed on a dangling bat. "No."

"That's right."

"But if you do, could you let us know how it is?" Jack said with a laugh as he tried to break the chill in the air.

Liam forced a smile to his face as he turned his back on him. Anger was rapidly coursing through him, but getting into a fight with one of his best friends wouldn't do him any good. "There are some good-looking women here tonight. But then again, you can't see most of their faces!" Doug joked as he approached the keg.

They all laughed, and Liam felt some of the tension ease out of him. He glanced around the room, but his eyes quickly returned to Sera. She laughed as Kathleen gestured crazily. He couldn't help but smile as Sera's laughter rang through the room, and her violet-blue eyes sparkled brightly. She was unbelievably beautiful tonight. His heart and body ached from just looking at her.

A flash of gold cut across his line of vision as Michelle stepped up to the keg. "Hello, boys," she purred as she bent over to give them a clear view of her full breasts.

Liam looked away in disgust as everyone else bent lower with her. "You are looking exceptionally fine tonight," Mike said.

"I thought I looked exceptionally fine every day, Mikey."

"You do," Jack said eagerly.

"Thank you, Jack; you're a doll."

She stood back up, brushing her chest provocatively against Liam's arm as she studied him through lowered lashes. "Good party," she whispered in his ear. "I could make it even better."

She turned away from him, casually tossing her hair over her shoulder. "Well," Jack drawled. "You could definitely get some from her... again."

Liam glared at him as Jack moved swiftly past him and out to the dance floor. He didn't need to be reminded of his past mistakes. He ground his jaw as his hand clenched his cup.

"There is something wrong with that girl. Don't listen to Jack; he's an ass. I'm only going to say this because I'm drunk, and I'll deny it tomorrow, but if I had a girl like Sera, sex or not, I wouldn't give her up," Mike said.

"Weren't you the one telling me to break up with her two weeks ago?"

Mike downed the rest of his cup. "You know why I think that. It can't last forever, Liam, but for now, you might as well stay with her."

"I intend to," he replied icily.

"Good," Mike said, clapping him on the shoulder. "Now, I'm going to get laid. At least one of us should!"

Mike laughed as he hurried out to the dance floor. Liam shook his head in annoyed disbelief as he watched him mingle with a group of girls. He spotted Michelle again as she flirted with a bunch of guys. He resolutely turned away and walked over to Sera.

"Would you care to dance?" he asked, extending his hand to her.

She looked up at him and smiled. "Certainly."

He took hold of her hand and led her out onto the dance floor. Tugging at his hand, she stopped him at the edge of the floor. He turned to her, smiling as he wrapped her in his arms. She tilted her head back; her eyes appeared mysterious from the red flames curling to her temples. The creamy skin of her rounded shoulders was too tempting to resist. He ran his hands across them, pleased when he saw her eyes spark and her mouth part. He grinned as he pulled her closer against him.

Sera bit into her bottom lip, her hands clenched on his back as a familiar tightening started in her loins. Just a few weeks ago, the feel of his obvious arousal would have frightened her; now, it excited her. She stepped closer to rub against him. His abrupt inhalation, and the darkening of his eyes, caused her to smile with satisfaction.

Liam savored in the silky feel of her skin and luscious hair. He lifted his head; his gaze darted across the room to find Michelle watching them. Her eyes locked on his as she continued to talk to the group of guys around her. She stared hatefully at him and then glared at Sera. He kissed Sera's neck, his eyes never leaving Michelle's. He had begun to hate her for the way she treated Sera. But, he hated himself more. It was his fault Michelle despised Sera as much as she did.

He turned around and pulled Sera closer to him. He couldn't lose her, couldn't even bear the thought of losing her. He inhaled her precious, sweet smell. A scent he knew he would never forget.

Suddenly, a flash of gold was beside them. Liam stiffened as Sera pulled away. "I need to talk to you," Michelle said to Sera.

"I don't want to talk to you," Sera replied.

"Go away, Michelle," Liam informed her coldly.

"No, I think your girlfriend needs to know the truth." She spoke softly to not draw any attention to herself. She tossed back her thick red hair and smiled coldly at Sera. "Look, you need to know why I was so upset about the two of you."

"Michelle—" A tendril of unease squirmed through him.

"I have no idea what you're talking about." Sera frowned in confusion; her face reflected her innocence.

"Let's go," Liam said, grabbing her arm. He had to get her out of there before Michelle could say anything else.

"Wait!" Michelle cried. "I think you owe it to me to listen. For old time's sake Sera, please."

"I don't owe you anything," Sera replied coldly.

Michelle pitifully hung her head. "You're right; you don't owe me anything. I'm sorry to tell you this—"

"That's enough," Liam interrupted brusquely.

"But Liam and I slept together at the beginning of the school year. That's why I've been so upset. He just stopped speaking to me. He started completely ignoring me, for you."

Sera's eyes went back and forth between them. Her breath was frozen in her lungs as her heart began to hammer. Liam glared hatefully at Michelle.

"Is that true?" Sera demanded.

Liam knew he could lie, that she would believe him, but he couldn't bring himself to do it. She had bared her soul to him in complete trust; he couldn't betray her trust any more than he already had. "Yes," he grated through his teeth.

Sorrow burst through her eyes as her jaw clenched. She ripped her arm away from him and cast Michelle a scathing look before she turned and walked away. "I'm sorry!" Michelle called after her, a huge grin on her face.

"You bitch!" Liam hissed. "You goddamn bitch!"

Michelle turned to him, a sly smile on her face. "It's about time she knew. Were you ever planning on telling her? Because someone had to. I was just being a friend."

Liam stepped closer to her, forcing her to tilt her head back to look at him. "I will get you for this. Do you understand me?"

Alarm flickered through her eyes, but she covered it with a haughty expression. "No, Liam, I think I got you."

As much as he wanted to make her pay for what she had just done, he wanted to get to Sera more. He turned and hurried after Sera but was effectively cut off by Danielle and Kathleen. "What happened?" Kathleen demanded, her cute face scrunched and her hands planted firmly on her hips.

"Where did she go?" he demanded.

Kathleen tilted her chin defiantly. "I don't know. What did Michelle say to her?"

"Where did she go, Danielle?"

Danielle lifted her head and angrily met his eyes. "You should have told her," she whispered, cutting deeper into his heart.

"Told her what? What did you do?" Kathleen insisted. Then, her mouth dropped open, and her eyes flew back to Michelle. "You bastard! How could you? And with her? You cheated on her!"

It took all he had not to shake the girl. He didn't need this now. "I did not cheat on her," he growled. "Now, where is she?"

Kathleen glowered at him, her arms folded over her chest, and her mouth compressed in a severe line. "What's going on?" Mike asked as he appeared beside Kathleen.

"Your friend's a lying bastard!" Kathleen snapped.

Mike's mouth dropped as he looked at Liam. Liam was fighting every impulse he had to grab hold of Kathleen and shake the answer out of her. Instead, he fisted his hands and took a deep breath to control the growing fury inside of him.

"Where is she?" Liam ground out.

"Who?" Mike asked.

"Sera."

"She just went out the door."

"Thank you."

Kathleen moved to block him. "Leave her alone!"

Liam glared at her, but she refused to back down. "Kathleen, get out of my way."

"No, you've upset her enough, now leave her be."

"What is going on?" Mike demanded.

"He," Kathleen said, thrusting an outraged finger at Liam, "slept with Michelle."

Mike winced as he cast Liam an apologetic glance. "How'd she find out?" he asked.

"You knew?" Kathleen cried, whirling on him.

Liam moved swiftly past her while she was distracted. He hurried through the mess of labyrinths built for the haunted house, becoming increasingly agitated with every step he took. He would like nothing more than to rip Michelle's throat out. But he was angrier at himself than he was with her. He should have told Sera. He never should have let her find out like this, but his concern over losing her kept him from telling her.

He made his way to the first floor and stopped. Sera hadn't gone outside. The eerie music that played when the door opened hadn't gone off. He froze to listen, but he heard no footsteps or sounds of movement. He headed back up the stairs, knowing if she had made her way down, she would have left. He went a different way through the maze, and back up to the second floor. He rounded a corner, stepping into one of the scenes set up between two bedrooms.

All that was left was a large table and two dining room chairs. Sera was sitting in one of the chairs, her head resting in her hands. "Sera—"

"Go away, please."

"Sera—"

She dropped her hands to look at him, her eyes were wet with tears, but her jaw was set. "Go away, Liam, now."

"I have to talk to you."

"No. You could have talked to me before, and you didn't. Now, I don't want to speak to you."

"Sera just let me explain."

"You've had your chance to explain," she replied icily. "You chose not to. You opted to have me think one of my best friends suddenly hated me for no reason. You could have told me. You made your choice, now I've made mine. Go away."

Liam made his way cautiously into the room. He knew if he moved too fast, she would bolt. "Would you have had anything to do with me if I had told you?"

A tear streaked down her cheek "Yes," she whispered.

"You would have kept talking to me if I told you I got drunk, slept with your best friend, and left without even saying goodbye? You would have thought I was a piece of shit, and you wouldn't have said one word to me."

A few more tears slipped free as she realized just how easy walking away from Michelle had been for him. He hadn't cared about her at all; he had just used her and left her. Sera's heart broke when she realized she didn't know him as well as she'd thought. She had known there were other girls in his past, but she hadn't thought he could discard them as if they were nothing.

"Lying was much better though," she whispered.

"I didn't lie."

She laughed coldly and shook her head. "You acted like you didn't know why she was behaving the way she was. You lied to me."

She choked back a sob as she buried her head in her hands again. "Sera, please don't do this."

"I didn't do this," she whispered. "I told you things I'd never told anyone, you son of a bitch." She wiped angrily at her face. She hated herself for crying like this in front of him, but she couldn't help it. Her heart was breaking into a million pieces.

Liam felt a fresh rush of anger at the reminder of what that bastard did to her. He clenched his jaw against the sudden bloodlust ripping through him. He swore if he ever found Jacob, he would kill him. But now was not the time to let his temper get the best of him. Now he had to make her understand as her tears tore at his heart.

"Please don't cry, Sera. I'm sorry; I never meant to hurt you."

She shoved back her chair and jumped to her feet. "Go away, Liam; I don't want to see you."

"Listen to me, I made a mistake, but I didn't lie to you."

"Liam—"

He walked across the room to her.

"Stay away from me!" There was a wealth of vehemence in her voice, but he ignored it as he took hold of her hands. She jerked them away. "Don't touch me!"

"Sera, I love you."

Her head shot up so forcefully he thought she might have given herself whiplash.

"Don't," she whispered. "Don't."

"I'm sorry about what I did, I made a mistake, but I do love you."

She took a hitching breath as she shook her head in denial. "How could you say something like that? How could you?"

He didn't know what else to say. He stepped forward and took her into his arms. She sobbed as she angrily pushed at him in a desperate attempt to free herself. "Stop," he whispered. "Stop."

"Get away from me!" she yelled, but he refused to release her. He needed to get through to her. He couldn't lose her; he just couldn't. "How many times have you used that line?"

He cupped her face in his hands and forced it up. Tears slid down her face as she glared at him. "I have never said it to anyone before," he said. "Never! You are the only person I have ever loved."

She stared at him as her eyes searched his face. "How can I believe you?" she whispered tremulously.

He closed his eyes against the agony ripping through him. "You just have to," he answered. "I'm telling you the truth."

Tears caused the makeup of her flames to trail down her cheeks in red and orange streaks. He tenderly wiped them away with his thumb as she fell limply into his embrace. He held her against his chest as he smoothed her hair and kissed the top of her head. He was suddenly unable to stop himself from kissing and touching her. He wanted her so badly he burned with it.

"I love you," he said again, kissing her neck and tasting her sweetness. She buried her face in his shoulder as sobs continued to rack through her. "Come on," he urged as he took hold of her hand.

He led her through the maze and up the stairs to his room. He settled her in before walking down the hall to the bathroom. Music blared from upstairs as he washed the makeup off his face and tried to get his thoughts together. The water did nothing to ease the tense anxiety in him. He hung his head as self-disgust rolled through him.

With a deep sigh, he shoved away from the sink, grabbed some paper towels, and wet them before making his way back down the hall to his room. He opened his door, closed, and locked it behind him. Sera was standing by the window. She had taken her cape off; her exposed skin glistened like pearls in the moonlight as it streamed over her.

He wanted to talk to her, to try to explain, but he didn't know what to say. Instead, he moved across the room to stand behind her. Resting his hands on her shoulders, he relished in the feel of her satiny smooth skin. She went rigid beneath his touch but didn't move away from him.

"Why didn't you tell me?" she whispered.

Liam closed his eyes and inhaled deeply as he tried to gather his thoughts. "I didn't want to lose you," he answered honestly.

She turned to face him. His breath froze in his chest at the sorrow in her startling eyes. Gently, he tilted her chin up and used the paper towels to wipe the makeup from her tear-stained face. She kept her lashes lowered as he worked. When he finished, he tossed the towels aside, and her gaze finally met his.

"You wouldn't have lost me."

There was so much warmth in her gaze he knew he didn't deserve her. She was too good, too innocent and pure for the likes of him. "In the beginning, I would have."

"I told you what happened to me on the second day I knew you. I trusted you then, and you said I could, but I couldn't. If you had told me about Michelle then, you wouldn't have lost me, but now..."

Her voice trailed off as she rapidly blinked back tears. Liam bowed his head to press his forehead against hers. "I meant what I said. You can trust me. But at the time, I didn't think you needed me to tell you about it. The conversation we had that night had no place in it for what happened between Michelle and I. After that night, I should have told you, but I didn't."

"Why didn't you?" she asked tremulously.

His hands clenched on her shoulders. "Because I didn't want you to think less of me for it. I preferred to pretend it didn't happen. Can you understand that?"

Tears slid down her cheeks as she nodded. She could understand that. There were things she would prefer to forget, but she still felt betrayed. Maybe he couldn't tell her that night, and she could see why, but she wished he'd told her later. She wouldn't have been upset with him, and maybe she could have tried to talk to Michelle, but she didn't think Michelle would have spoken to her anyway.

"I can understand that," Sera whispered, lifting her head so she could look at him. "But I wish I hadn't found out this way."

"So do I," he said hoarsely. "So do I."

"How could you use her so easily?"

Liam's jaw clenched, a muscle twitched in his cheek. "Sera,

I didn't use her, she was there, and I was there, and sometimes things just happen."

"She apparently thought it was more."

"I don't believe she did. She's just aggravated I didn't chase her around, and follow after her like everyone else," he said honestly. "We met, and we slept together, that is all it ever was."

She was tempted to ask how many others there had been that he'd experienced the same thing with, but she couldn't bring herself to do it. She didn't think she could handle the knowledge.

His hands clasped the sides of her face as he lifted it to him. She stared at him, her eyes misty in the moonlit room. He couldn't seem to get enough of looking at her, of touching her, of holding her. Her breath shuddered through her. "Liam."

The sound of her whispery voice heated his loins and caused him to grow instantly erect. He bent and kissed her, his mouth sliding over hers. She shivered and her mouth parted. She was sweet and warm as her tongue met his with the same urgency.

He stroked the exposed skin above her dress, relishing in the silkiness of it. She shivered again as her breath rushed out of her. He should stop, he should pull away, but he couldn't bring himself to release her. He was almost wild with his need for her. He would hurt her, or he would push her too fast, but tonight he must have all of her.

His hands slipped across her shoulders and around to the back of her dress. His hands hesitated upon the zipper as he waited for her to tell him to stop. She moaned and pressed closer to him as he broke the kiss. Her passion-clouded eyes met his in the moonlight.

"Liam?" she asked questioningly.

He closed his eyes as he inhaled a steadying breath. "I want you, Sera, I want all of you," he added, so she got the point.

She was unaware of how seductive and enchanting she was when she smiled at him like that. "And I want you," she whispered.

His hands clenched upon her as a muscle twitched in his cheek. "You don't have to do this." The words nearly killed him to say, but he had to give her a chance to get away from him now before he could no longer control himself.

"I want to."

The words sent a firestorm of yearning to his elongated shaft. He inhaled a deep breath to steady himself before he ripped the dress from her. Instead, he slid the zipper down; the rasp of metal was loud in the hushed room. His hands caressed the swell of her back and trailed down to her waist. She was so unbelievably small in his arms. He could feel the rapid pounding of her heart through her delicate ribcage.

She took a step back. Her smile was enticing as she allowed the dress to slide off her shoulders and pool at her feet on the ground. In the moonlight, she was ethereal. Her skin shimmered; her eyes were smoky as her hair spilled around her in silvery gold waves. Her body was amazingly perfect. He sucked in his breath as his gaze traveled over her. Her full breasts were pushed tantalizingly high in her bra. The material was thin and lacy, revealing her dark nipples. Her stomach was flat, her waist tiny, her hips small and round. Lacy white panties shielded the juncture between her thighs. He could never get enough of looking at her.

Liam's heart leapt in his chest as his prick jumped with enthusiasm. She was exquisite, perfect. He forced his gaze back to hers. She stared at him uncertainly as a blush crept into her cheeks. He opened his arms to her. She hesitated before stepping into his embrace.

He enfolded her, his head lowering so he could whisper in her ear. "You're exquisite."

She shivered as her arms wrapped around his broad back. Lifting her face to his, she kissed him. His hand wound into her hair as he pulled her head back for better access. Pleasure filled her as her body arched against his.

Liam tried to slow down before he lost complete control and ravished her, but he couldn't stop touching her. A firestorm raged through his body, searing his veins, and causing all the blood to rush into his groin. He pushed his pelvis against hers. She moaned as he rubbed provocatively against her, and a shudder ripped through her body as her movements matched his.

Her hands slid down his shoulders, and she began to unbutton his shirt. Liam released her mouth; his arms held her loosely as he watched her long, delicate fingers work the buttons. Her head was bent as she focused on her task. Slipping the last button free, she lifted her head to his. Passion clouded her eyes, her lips were swollen from his kisses. Her gaze never leaving his, she slid the shirt off his shoulders and down his arms.

Her eyes were round as she gazed at his broad, well-muscled chest. Her fingers ran over his smooth skin as she relished in the feel of his muscles and the small tufts of black, wiry hair. He was a perfect carving of masculine strength and beauty. She should have been frightened by the hunger in his gaze; instead, she found herself even more aroused by it.

His hands slid along her back. She couldn't suppress the shiver that raced through her, heated her blood, and caused her whole body to melt. He easily unclasped her bra and let it float to the floor. His eyes darkened even more as he gazed at her heaving breasts. He clasped one gently, and her mouth parted with faint inhalations as she arched against him. He ran his thumb teasingly along her nipple, watching as her passion rose. She was more desirable and responsive than any woman he had ever known, and he had known many. None of them responded to him with such open abandon. None of them ever made him this hard and aching.

He bent his head to take her nipple into his mouth. Her fingers wound into his hair as he stroked her with his tongue. He nipped her, and she spasmed in his embrace. "Liam!" she gasped.

He pulled away from her, grabbed hold of her hips, and lifted her onto him. She blinked in surprise and then wrapped her legs around his waist. A cry of ecstasy escaped her as she settled against his erect shaft. He groaned as he lifted her up and slid her back down. Her eyes slid closed as she tilted back in his embrace, her back arching to give him easier access to her breasts.

Laying her down, he stepped back to admire her exquisite body as he unbuttoned his pants and kicked them aside. Sera's eyes were dazed with passion as her eyes settled on his cock. Apprehension briefly flashed through her gaze. Then, she met his eyes again and opened her arms to receive him.

He climbed onto the bed and wrapped her in his arms. He touched her everywhere, unable to stop his hands from roaming over her, from feeling every perfect curve. Her breasts pressed firmly against his chest as she arched eagerly against him.

He slid her panties down her long thighs, savoring in the touch of her as he slid them off easily. Moans escaped her as he caressed every inch of her body while his mouth made love to hers. One hand touched her breast while another slid down to stroke her stomach, her hips. She arched beneath him as his hand slid through her golden curls. He unhurriedly slid lower, his hand cupping her mound. He was pleased to find her already wet as he slid a finger into her warm body. Delight ripped through her as he began to move in and out. Her hands dug into his back as she lifted her hips against him, matching the leisurely pace he set as he slid smoothly back and forth.

Liam watched her as erotic moans escaped her throat. His dick ached, but he was determined to give her as much pleasure as possible before the pain. He fondled the nub above her wet sheath. Tremors rocked through her body as she dug deeper into his back.

"Liam!"

The sound of his name on her lips nearly caused him to explode. He couldn't wait any longer. He slipped his hand from her. She moaned her disappointment as she arched her hips demandingly against his. He nearly tore his underwear off as he shoved it down his waist and legs. Finally free, he grabbed her hips as he leveled himself between her enticing thighs. She watched him intently.

He rubbed against her, watching for any sign this was not what she wanted. It would kill him to stop, but he would. She lifted her hips against him as she opened herself to him.

He lowered himself over her and took her mouth with his again as he began to slide into her. His body was tense as he parted her inviting folds. She was so tight, so warm and inviting. It took every ounce of willpower he had not to thrust brutally forward and end his torture. Instead, he inched forward, his arms trembling from his weight. Then, he reached it. The barrier. He didn't want to cause her discomfort, but he was unable to stop.

With a moan, he shoved forward, burying himself to the hilt. She cried out as pain shot through her eyes, her teeth bit her lip and her hands spasmed on his back. He didn't move as he stared at her. "Are you all right?"

"Yes," she breathed as her muscles eased around him. He stroked her face as he leisurely reclaimed her mouth. She trembled beneath him, but her thighs released their firm hold on his waist. His tongue entwined with hers as he tried to ease the rest of the tension from her body.

Gradually he withdrew from her before easing back in. The familiar pleasure he gave her began to return. He moved at a leisurely pace in and out of her, allowing her to get used to his invasion as he deliberately stoked the fires in her again with his mouth and hands. His whole body was taut as a bowstring, but he forced himself to calm down. It was the most difficult thing he'd ever done. He'd never felt anything as exquisitely tight and wet as she was.

His willpower was rapidly unraveling. She began to move with him, her hips and body arching against his as she met each of his thrusts. Her long legs wrapped around his waist, pulling him deeper into her. Her soft moans and enthusiastic reception were driving him beyond the brink of control. He wanted to tell her to slow down, that he couldn't restrain himself, but he was past the point of speech. Waves of pleasure washed over him as he drove in and out of her.

Sera's hands dug into his back. She'd never known anything could feel like this, never even imagined how wonderful it would feel to have Liam inside her, filling her, becoming one with her. Her whole body quivered as she neared a point she didn't understand, came close to something almost frightening.

He thrust vigorously into her and pushed her to the brink. A cry tore from her as her body exploded with unimaginable pleasure that swept through her in fierce waves. Her muscles clenched around him as the force of her climax ripped his from him. With a savage yell, he drove himself to the hilt and spilled everything he had into her.

He almost collapsed on top of her but managed to catch himself in time. Instead, he wrapped his arms around her and rolled, so she lay beside him. Her body trembled against his; her breath came in pants as she wrapped her arms around him and nuzzled his neck. He was unable to believe the force of the orgasm she managed to rend from him. Never in his life had he expected to find someone like her.

He kissed her cheek as his hands ran over her body. "I love you too." Her breath was a mild breeze against his neck.

Anguish and pleasure crashed through him in tangled waves. Until then he hadn't realized exactly how much he needed her love and warmth. He pulled her flush against his chest. He didn't deserve her. He shouldn't have her, but he was never going to let her go.

CHAPTER EIGHT

Liam blinked dazedly against the sunlight filtering past the thick curtains. He groaned and rolled away from the light. Sera slept beside him, the blanket tossed aside to bare her shoulder, back, and butt. She was an amazingly tempting sight to wake up to first thing. Unable to resist, he kissed her shoulder as his hands wrapped around to fondle a full breast. She instinctively arched into his touch. They had made love over and over again last night, but he still couldn't get enough of her.

She stirred as her eyes flitted open, she blinked uncertainly, and then she turned to him. She smiled sleepily as she trailed her fingers over his chest. "Good morning," she whispered huskily.

"Good morning."

He lowered his head to take her mouth in his. She opened to him as their tongues lazily entwined together. "Liam!"

The loud banging on the door made them both jump. Liam muttered a curse as he lifted his mouth from hers. "What?" he demanded.

"Get up man; we have to go!" Mike yelled.

Liam glanced at the clock and swore again. "I'll meet you guys there."

"You've got the car. Get your lazy ass out of bed!"

"Give me ten minutes!"

"Whatever," Mike mumbled as he walked away.

Liam dropped his head against her tempting shoulder. "Sorry about that."

She kissed the top of his head. "I should go anyway. Kathleen's probably waiting to attack me with questions." It wasn't a pleasant thought, she didn't feel like having to explain everything that happened last night, but she wouldn't be able to refuse her. Kathleen would be as persistent as a bee on a flower until she got the whole story.

He propped his head on his elbow as his hand leisurely caressed her tender breasts. He looked so young and sweet that it melted her heart. There was a shadow along his strong jaw, his hair was a tousled mess, and the lazy gleam of satisfaction in his brilliant eyes warmed her. "I have to go; we have a basketball game at the park. Are you going to come over tonight?"

She smiled slyly at him as her eyes twinkled mischievously. "I don't know; I'll have to think about it."

He grinned. "Really?"

"You'll have to help me make up my mind."

He trailed a finger from her collarbone to her stomach. He circled her belly button, dipping temptingly low, before circling her belly button again.

"And how do I do that?" he whispered as he nibbled on her ear.

Sera became a quivering mass beneath him as his hand slid down to cup her. "I think you're making a good start," she panted. His smile was pure satisfaction as he slid a finger into her warm body. "What about the game?"

"They'll wait; I have the car, remember?"

She smiled at him as he seized hold of her mouth.

Sera turned over on her bed and placed her finger in the book so she could look at Kathleen. "You look beautiful," she assured her.

"You sure?" Kathleen asked as she nervously fiddled with her hair.

"I'm sure."

"Why don't you come now?"

She lifted her book. "I have to get some studying done. Besides, the haunted house won't close until ten."

Kathleen patted her hair. "I would stay with you, but you know how I hate to be cooped up."

"If you stayed with me I'd never get any studying done. Go ahead; I'll meet you there in about an hour."

"Okay." Kathleen grabbed her coat from the hook by the door where Sera had hung it for her. "I'll see you soon."

"Yep," she agreed.

Kathleen cast her a grin as she opened the door, locked, and shut it. It had taken Sera a long time to get Kathleen into the habit of locking the door when she left. Now she did it all the time, even if Sera was still in the room. She rolled onto her back and buried herself in the book. She was just beginning to lose herself when a knock at the door pulled her out of Sociology. She glanced at the clock; it was already quarter after nine. She hadn't realized it was so late already. Sighing impatiently, she closed the book and climbed to her feet.

"What did you forget this time, Kathleen? Besides your key?"

Sera unlocked the door and flung it open. She froze, unable to move as she stared at the man before her. The world seemed to tilt briefly before coming back into focus. With a startled cry, she tried to slam the door closed, but he put out his hand and blocked it. "Now, is that any way to treat an old friend?"

Her scream lodged in her constricted throat as Jacob pushed the door open. She was forced back as he pushed his way inside. Stumbling awkwardly, she quickly righted herself as she launched at him. "Get out of here!" she cried.

He shoved her backward and knocked her to the floor. Sera scrambled away and jumped back to her feet as he closed and locked the door. "Just calm down, Sera."

"Get out of here, now!"

"I just came to talk to you," he said calmly as he turned to face her again.

"I have nothing to say to you. Leave."

He walked toward her as she steadily backed away from him. She found it extremely difficult to breathe as she inhaled rapid, short breaths. Jacob was taller than Liam was, and broader through the shoulders and chest. He could, and would, squash her like a bug.

Suddenly, there was nowhere left for her to go as she backed herself into the wall. Panic leapt through her as he continued to hone in on her. She was such an idiot. What was she thinking when she'd left herself with nowhere to go? She stared breathlessly up at him, terror ripping through her as he stopped just inches away. Her legs trembled as his face loomed over hers. His breath against her cheek caused nausea to twist through her stomach as the familiar stench of it filled her nostrils.

He placed his hands against the wall by her head. "I just want to talk to you."

Sera took a trembling breath as she tried to steady herself. She almost closed her eyes and cringed away as he lowered himself to look directly into her eyes, but she wouldn't give him the satisfaction. Instead, she forced herself to tilt her chin and defiantly meet his gaze. His brown eyes focused on her. Unwillingly, she looked away as memories, and nausea, shook her. Tears threatened to fall as she swallowed the lump in her throat.

"How you been, Sera?" he inquired.

"Fine," she managed to choke out.

"You look good, but then you always did. Would you like to know how I've been?"

"No."

"Well, I haven't been too good. Some people believed that nasty little lie you told about me. I was kicked off the football team and lost my scholarship to college, thanks to you."

She met his gaze. "It wasn't a lie."

He laughed and took a step closer, his solid chest brushed against hers. A shudder of revulsion ripped through her as he leered down at her, disgustingly close, and amazingly real. Looking at him now, she couldn't recall why she'd thought he was so perfect. He was handsome, in the classic, all American sense, but there was a wealth of depravity in his brown eyes. She didn't understand how she'd never seen it before. It had to have been there, but she'd been so enamored with him she'd refused to acknowledge it.

Now the evil inside him blazed at her. It seeped into her soul, caused her mind to go numb, and her legs to tremble so much she was afraid she would collapse.

"We both know you wanted it."

She wrapped her arms around herself to ward off the chill racking her. He turned away and walked around the room. She frantically searched for the nearest thing to hit him with. "Nice place you got here. Your roommate's kind of a pig though," he remarked.

"I think it's time for you to leave, Jacob."

He stalked back to her. She lurched desperately for the lamp on her desk. Her trembling hands knocked it over as she clumsily grasped at it. "Oh God," she cried in frustration as it tumbled to the floor and broke in half.

He grabbed hold of her arm and spun her around. She screamed as he lifted her up and flung her onto the bed. The force of it knocked the breath out of her, but she somehow managed to find the strength to scramble back. He grabbed her leg and jerked her toward him.

"No!" she screamed as she kicked crazily at him. "Get away from me!"

He pulled her across the bed and climbed on top of her. Sitting on her legs, he grabbed hold of her hands and pinned them above her head. She screamed again, bucking wildly as she tried to rip her hands free. He squeezed her wrists as he shifted both of her wrists into one hand and placed his other hand over her mouth. Tears of frustration rolled down her face as she fought to get free.

Liam stood by Mike as the next group passed them. "There are only two groups left. Then we can go party. Or, at least I can." The wolfman mask covered Mike's face, but Liam knew he was grinning beneath it. "Then again, I'd rather be at your party."

Liam shook his head. "I'm sure you'll find your own."

Mike laughed as he pulled the mask off. "God, this thing is hot. I need a beer."

Liam winced as screams from children echoed through the halls. He was beginning to get a headache from all the high-pitched shrieks. Glancing at his watch, he discovered it was only quarter after nine. He rubbed at his pounding temples. He couldn't wait to end these tours. His throat was sore; he was hungry and tired. He had led ten groups of screaming children and their parents through already. He wanted to get out of here and see Sera. It was the only thing keeping him going.

Mike began talking again, but Liam had stopped listening to him. A knot worked its way into his belly. He frowned as he tried to figure out where it was coming from. Becoming completely still, he used his mind to probe the area around him as he scented the air for the source of the unexplained fear. He turned into himself, searching for anything that would explain it.

Then he realized the fear was coming from Sera.

"I have to go," he blurted, cutting Mike off in mid-sentence.

"What?" Mike asked dully.

"I have to go. Find someone else to do the last tour."

"You can't just leave Liam."

"I have to. Get my car and meet me at Sera's dorm."

"Liam, wait!" Mike grabbed hold of his arm and swung him around. "What is it? What's wrong?"

"Let go!" he ripped his arm free. "It's Sera; she's in trouble, just meet me there."

Mike gawked at him, but Liam didn't wait for a response as he turned to run. Liam burst through the front door as the next group was getting ready to come through. They stared at him in astonishment, but he barely noticed as he started to run toward her dorm.

"I HEAR YOU HAVE A NEW BOYFRIEND," Jacob's mouth hovered near her ear. Sera squirmed beneath him as she tried to turn her head away. "Are you giving it up to him?"

Sera choked against his hand. He smiled chillingly as he

licked her ear. Bile rose in her throat, and it took everything she had to shove it back down. She would probably choke to death if she threw up now.

"I'm going to take my hand away so you can answer me. If you scream again, I'm going to gag you, understand?" he asked.

She nodded as a tear slipped down her cheek. She hated herself for the sign of weakness, but she couldn't stop it. He eased his hand away, and she felt something cold press against her throat. She tried to retreat further from him, but it was impossible as he smiled down at her.

"Yes, it's a knife," he said. "Now, answer me."

Her heart hammered in her chest, and she couldn't stop shaking. "Are you sleeping with him?" he demanded, his face twisting into a sneer.

A wave of defiance washed over her as she tilted her chin. "Yes, I am."

He smiled coldly as he leaned down to kiss her. She turned her head away in a desperate attempt to get away from his repugnant touch. His hand twisted cruelly in her hair as the knife pressed more firmly against her throat. "That's what your friend said."

Revulsion swamped her, and it took everything she had not to vomit as he ran his hands over her body. "Stop it." She tried to squirm away from him, but he pressed the knife more firmly against her throat. "What friend?" she asked as his words registered.

"Your girlfriend called me. She told me where you were. I decided to visit you to finish what we started."

With a violent jerk, he ripped open her shirt. Sera cried out in distress and horror as his hand ran down to the edge of her jeans. Tears spilled from her eyes as she bucked crazily in an attempt to dislodge him. "I'll slit your throat, you bitch!" he spat. "Stop moving!"

Sera whimpered as his hand cruelly squeezed her breast.

"You feel good," he purred as he licked her ear.

A knock on the door froze his movements. "Are you expecting anyone?" he asked in a low voice.

"No," she answered honestly.

"Get rid of them." The knife cut into her flesh. She could feel blood running down her throat. She froze, unable to move, unable to breathe as she fully realized he would kill her. "Now!"

She inhaled sharply. "Who is it?" she called.

"It's me, open the door," Liam replied.

Her heart gave a little skip of hope that quickly faded. Liam was big, but Jacob was bigger and obviously crazy. She didn't want Liam to get hurt, and Jacob would kill him... or her. Hopelessness filled her as she resigned herself to what she had to do. Jacob would hurt her, but she wasn't going to let him hurt Liam too.

"I'm not feeling well," she called out.

"Sera, open the door!" he yelled.

The annoyance in his voice puzzled her, but she didn't have time to figure it out, and right now she didn't care. "Just go away, Liam." Her voice cracked as tears spilled down her face. "I can't see you tonight."

Jacob gripped her hair painfully and dug the knife in a little deeper.

"I don't want to talk to you! I... uh... I just need to be alone. I have to study!"

Silence came from the other side of the door, and she held her breath as she prayed he would stay there all night. "Fine," he finally said. "I'll talk to you tomorrow."

She almost screamed for him to help her, but she kept her mouth closed as tears flowed freely and her hope vanished. Jacob's eyes sparkled with malice. She closed her eyes, unable to look at him anymore, unable to think anymore.

The loud crash startled her eyes open. Jacob gasped as he was ripped off her. The knife sliced her as she was thrown to the floor. She cried out as she fumbled at her injured neck. Blood spilled between her fingers, ran down her arm, and dripped onto the ground. She sat numbly, barely hearing the crashes around her, and the grunts of a fight.

She stared dazedly at her bloody fingers as her mind spun in directions she didn't understand. She couldn't grasp a single thought. Liam was suddenly before her, his face pinched, and blood streaked his mouth and cheek.

"Are you all right?" he demanded. "Sera, are you all right?"

She was unable to answer.

He gingerly explored her wound. "Don't move."

He swiftly strode over, shut the battered door, and slid the chain lock into place. She watched his legs as he walked to the other side of the room in search of something. He came back with a towel he put against her neck. She winced in response.

"You'll be okay," he whispered. "It's not deep. Just hold this on your neck."

He took her trembling hand and placed it on the towel, forcing her to hold it. He brushed back her hair and kissed her forehead. "I'll be right back, okay?"

She watched as he walked away. She wondered where Jacob was, but she couldn't seem to ask the question out loud. She heard him shuffling around on the other side of the bed. Loud music gradually began to register, and she dimly recalled the Halloween party going on downstairs. That was why no one had heard her, why no one came sooner.

"Sera, do you know who this is?" Her hand fluttered up to clutch her torn shirt together as shivers racked her body. The blood was drying on her fingers, but she could feel more seeping into the towel. "Sera," he said more firmly. "Do you know who this is?"

"Is he still here?" she croaked, the words sounding alien to her ears.

"Yes. Do you know who he is?" She nodded as her hand fell into her lap. "Who is he, Sera?"

"Jacob."

A sneer curved his mouth as he looked down at his feet. "Jacob?"

Sera started to cry as blood spilled onto her lap and seeped into her jeans. "He said I ruined his life!" she sobbed, her body shaking. He climbed over the bed and grabbed the towel. He pressed it against her neck as he wrapped his arms around her. "He said it was my fault. That I asked for it. I didn't though. I didn't."

He rocked her back and forth as sobs tore from her throat. "I know you didn't," he whispered. "You didn't. How did he know you were here?"

She tried to stifle her sobs, but tears continued to roll down her face. "I don't know. He said a girlfriend of mine called him, but Kathleen wouldn't do that. I know she wouldn't!"

Liam's muscles became locked. "What about Michelle?" he grated.

Sera shook her head as her trembling hands clutched at his shirt. Her tears soaked his shirt and wet his skin. He hated her tears, hated seeing her so tormented, but he didn't know how to take it away from her. "I never told Michelle, and Kathleen wouldn't tell her." she choked out.

"Would she tell anyone else?"

"No."

Kathleen wouldn't have told anyone else; he knew that. He'd bet money Michelle was somehow involved in this. He kissed Sera's bent head as her sobs eased.

"I need you to listen to me," he said in a mellow tone. "You need to keep this towel against your throat. I'm going to take you down to the bathroom. You're going to take a shower, you're going to change, and you're going to come right back here. You can't let anyone see you though, okay?"

"Okay," she muttered.

He disentangled himself from her and stood uncertainly. Her knees were drawn up against her chest. Blood had soaked into the towel and seeped down her neck to stain her torn shirt and jeans. Rage and helplessness battled through him in alternating waves. He should have been here to stop this from happening, but he'd been too late, and she had suffered even more because of it.

He forced himself to turn away from her before he couldn't. Before he scooped her up, carried her from this building, and took her where no one could harm her again. He moved around the room, gathering the stuff he would need. When he finished, he went back and helped her stand. He led her to the doorway and pulled the chain off. Her legs suddenly buckled as she slumped against him. He wrapped his arm around her waist to keep her up as he shoved the battered door aside.

Mike stood on the other side with his hand raised to knock. His hand fell limply to his side as he took in Sera. "What happened?" he demanded.

"Go inside, I'll be right back," Liam ordered briskly.

Mike nodded as he slipped past Liam. He led her down the hall to the bathroom, flicked the light on, and walked her in. Opening one of the glass doors of the shower, he turned the water on and adjusted the temperature. He stripped her clothes and held her at arm's length. She tilted her head back to look at him through glazed eyes.

"Sera, you need to do this for me, do you understand?"

"Yes," she whispered.

"I'm going to leave clean clothes on the sink. There's a

bandage with them. You need to put it on your throat when you get out, all right?"

"Yes," she whispered.

He kissed her forehead. "Meet me in the room when you're done."

She bowed her head as he led her into the shower. The fog in her mind began to lift as she ducked her head under the stinging needles of water. He watched her raptly from the doorway. "I'll be all right," she assured him.

"Are you sure?"

"Yes."

He squeezed her arm and closed the door. She stood under the water, letting it pound against her as it eased some of the tension in her sore muscles. Blood pooled around her feet and flowed down the drain. She picked up the bar of soap and began to scrub herself vigorously. She slumped weakly against the wall as she started to cry again.

CHAPTER NINE

"What happened?" Mike demanded the minute Liam entered the room.

"Don't," he said coldly.

"Don't! Are you kidding me? Liam, he's dead!"

"I know that!"

Mike took a deep breath to calm himself. "What happened?"

Liam stared dispassionately at Jacob's corpse. If he weren't already dead, Liam would kill him all over again. He had finally met Jacob and done what he'd wanted to do, but it suddenly didn't seem like enough. He wished he could bring the bastard back to life so he could destroy him all over again.

"He was attacking her," he grated.

Mike ran a hand through his hair. "Who is he?"

"Jacob."

"Who is Jacob?"

"I don't have time to explain now. We have to get him out of here before Sera comes back."

"She doesn't know he's dead?"

"In case you didn't notice, she's in shock. Now help me get rid of him."

"Fine, but I better get a full explanation later," Mike said.

"You will."

Mike helped him strip the sheets from Sera's bed and wrap Jacob in them. "Your car's out back, in the alley."

"Can you take him down by yourself?"

Mike lifted him and flung him over his shoulder. "Yeah. I'll meet you down there."

"Is Michelle at the house?" he asked, stopping Mike in the doorway.

"I don't know."

Liam nodded as Mike strode out the door. He instantly busied himself with cleaning up the mess in the room. He sopped up Sera's blood, and the little bit of Jacob's, with towels he tossed into a plastic bag. She'd been in the bathroom for a while, but he could still hear the shower. He had one more thing to do before he could make sure she was all right. He crossed the room, picked up the phone, and dialed the house number. His eyes searched the room for anything he might have missed, but the room appeared to be spotless.

"Is Kathleen there?" he yelled into the phone the minute someone answered.

"Who?" someone drunkenly shouted above the music, and the distinct chant of, "Strip, strip, strip!"

"Kathleen! Little blonde, big chest!"

"Oh, yeah, hold on."

The harsh clatter of the phone dropping made him flinch. "Hello!" Kathleen called into the phone.

"Kathleen, it's Liam."

"Hey! Whassup?" she asked drunkenly. "You comin ta join the party?"

"Kathleen, sober up!" he snapped.

The sounds of the party began to fade. "What's wrong?" she asked, no longer having to scream into the phone.

"I just need to ask you a question."

"Is Sera okay? What's wrong?" Her voice raised an octave with every word.

"She's fine; everything is fine. I was just wondering if you had told someone about Jacob?"

"Jacob who? Wait a minute... oh, the ass?"

"Yes."

"No, of course not! Why? Don't tell me he tried to contact her. Bastard! No, I never told anyone. I wouldn't do that. She doesn't think I did, does she?" she asked in a shrill rush.

"No, no," he assured her. "Nobody thinks you did; I just had to make sure."

"What did he say to her?"

"Nothing, don't worry about it right now."

"Of course I'm going to worry about it. I'll be right there."

"No. Stay there; we're coming over."

"Are you sure? Does she need me? Are you sure she's okay?" Kathleen demanded.

"I'm positive. Just stay there. Is Michelle there?"

"Yeah, she's here. Where else would she be?"

"I'll be right there."

"Okay."

Liam hung up the phone and walked over to the door. He fiddled with the latch and put the screws back in as he fixed it to the best of his ability. There was nothing he could do about the splintered jam, but he didn't care. He looked into the hall as Sera emerged from the bathroom with a towel draped over her arm. Her hair hung wetly around her shoulders; her clothes were wrinkled and damp. The bandage was placed securely against the wound in her neck, a fact he was incredibly grateful for.

He stepped away from the door as she walked into the room. Her eyes still looked a little dazed, but she seemed calmer. Her skin was a livid red. His teeth ground together as he realized she'd scrubbed herself raw. "Feeling better?" he asked.

She looked around the room before focusing on him. "Yeah."

"I need to go to the frat house. I need to talk to Michelle."

She looked at him questioningly as she dropped the towel on the floor. "Why?"

He clasped hold of her arms. "I just do, and you're coming with me."

"Okay," she mumbled.

He was desperate to ease the lost look in her eyes, but he didn't know what to do to help her. He pulled her against him as he attempted to comfort her. "It'll be all right," he whispered. "He's never going to bother you again."

"Where is he?"

"He's gone."

She didn't seem to know how to take this as her forehead furrowed. Taking hold of her arm, he led her out the door to the elevator. They descended, and he walked her out the back, avoiding the main lobby, and the party. His car was parked by the door. Mike was leaning against it; his arms crossed over his chest as he stared at them. Liam opened the door for Sera and helped settle her into the car. She sat numbly as he hurried to the other side and Mike slid into the back.

He drove back to the frat house and pulled into the driveway. Throwing the car into park, he turned to look at her. "I need you to stay here."

"Why don't I take her in?" Mike suggested.

Liam shook his head as he squeezed her hand. "Will you be okay here?"

"Yes."

He kissed her as his hand lingered on her cheek. He hated to leave her, but he had to go inside and take care of this. "Stay with her," he ordered Mike.

He forced himself to release her as he flung the door open and climbed out. Mike hopped out of the back seat and slammed the door shut. "Liam, let me take her in," he said quietly.

"No, she stays here."

"Liam—"

"I have something I have to do. She's staying with me. Just watch her, I'll be right back."

Liam turned away and hurried into the house. Climbing the stairs, the music became louder as he ascended. Making it to the attic, he flung the door open to a packed room that shook with music and reeked of alcohol.

He hurried through the crowd as he searched for Michelle. Kathleen found him first. "Where is Sera?" she demanded her hands on her round hips.

"Outside," he answered as he peered over her head through the crowd.

"Is she all right?"

"She's fine. Where's Michelle?"

"She was on the dance floor. I'm going to see her."

He grabbed Kathleen's arm and halted her in place. "Not right now, okay?"

Kathleen glared up at him. "She's my best friend!" she protested.

"I need to do something first. Let me do this, Kathleen. I promise it will be worth it."

Kathleen relaxed in his grasp. "All right, but you tell her I love her, and I'll talk to her soon."

"I will, I promise."

"I'll help you find Michelle."

He found her first though. A group of men surrounded her by the back wall. He moved through the group and leaned against the wall beside her. He took her drink out of her hand and sipped from it.

"Did I say you could have that?" she asked coldly.

"I'm used to taking what I want." He smiled at her as he handed her cup back.

"Where's the wife?"

"Who?"

"The little wifey. Where is she tonight?"

"I don't know and don't care."

"Did you two have a lover's quarrel last night?" Her voice was husky and seductive.

Anger blazed through him at the reminder, but he managed to keep it under control. "Can't quarrel with a lover unless they are your lover."

Michelle glanced through the crowd, and he followed her eyes. Kathleen was standing off to the side watching them. Doug stood beside her, his mouth hanging open. Kathleen grabbed his arm and pulled him away as she shot Liam a look over her shoulder. Liam didn't know if Kathleen had done it on purpose, or if she was really pissed, but the look she gave him could have frozen Hell.

"Is that why you're here?" Michelle inquired through lowered lashes. "Need a little relief?"

Revulsion washed through him at the thought, but he managed to keep his face impassive as he turned back to her. "Thought we could both use a little relief."

Her eyes flew to his as she smiled slyly. "That may be true, but I don't plan on going there again, not after the way you treated me last time."

"We both know we only wanted one thing that night."

"Maybe so," she whispered huskily. "But you didn't have to be so mean to me after."

"Ah, but I had to."

"And why is that?"

"Because I can't resist a challenge."

She lifted a delicate brow as her mouth curved. "A challenge?"

He laughed coldly and turned to face her as he propped his hand on the wall beside her head. He leaned in so close that his chest brushed against hers. Her body arched into him as her mouth parted. He pushed down a shiver of revulsion as he forced himself to smile. "Everyone said I couldn't get near Sera. I proved I could. I never refuse a challenge, and now it's gone."

"So she finally gave it up," Michelle purred. "I thought you cared for her."

"Now, Michelle, you should know better than that."

"What's that supposed to mean?"

He rested his lips against her ear. "I'm just like you. All we want to do is please ourselves."

She laughed and tossed back her hair as she stared up at him. "I'm not like that."

"Oh really?" He brushed back her hair. "Well, I know you pleased me, and I know I pleased you."

"Oh really?" she inquired as she sipped her drink. "What makes you think that?"

He glanced pointedly down at the hardened nipples pressed against his chest. "You do. I think we need to do it again."

She touched his chest lightly. "So you can make me look like a fool again. No thanks."

He grinned and leaned closer to her. "Whatever you say, sweetie. It's your loss."

She stared at him as he took a step back. "I can't leave this party with you," she said.

He had her. "I understand, beautiful. We'll meet somewhere else."

"Where?"

"Meet me in the park, by the gazebo. We'll have a little picnic and enjoy each other."

"All right."

"Ten minutes." He rubbed his finger along her lip. "Don't be late."

"Oh, I won't. You be ready for some real pleasure."

"I already am."

He turned and walked rapidly through the crowd. Kathleen was standing by the keg with Doug, Jack, and Danielle. They were all staring at him with mixed expressions of surprise and distrust.

"You better know what you're doing," Kathleen grated.

Liam poured himself a drink and took a long swallow. "I do."

"If you hurt her again, I'll kill you," she said flatly.

Liam shot her a look as he tossed the rest of his beer in the trash and walked away.

"Where are we?" Sera murmured.

"The park."

"What are we doing here?"

Liam sat back in his seat and turned to face her. Her eyes were a vivid purple in her pale face. Her bottom lip trembled, but her eyes were dry. "I need to take care of something."

"What?"

"Michelle."

"How?" she whispered.

"She's going to meet me here."

"What are you going to do?"

"Try not to think about it right now. Come here."

He pulled her into his arms. She laid her head in his lap; her small hand curled around his thigh as her eyes drifted closed. He stroked her hair as he took in her pale face and the thick bandage on the side of her neck. His hand clenched as he ground his teeth.

He lifted his head to meet Mike's gaze in the rearview mirror. Liam looked away from him before Mike could see how close the demon in him was to breaking free. He looked out at the night. It was eerily hushed. There were no moon or stars, but he could see the trees. A steeliness stole its way through his body. He wanted to kill Michelle and anyone else who had ever caused Sera harm. He continued to stroke her hair as he tried to keep himself grounded with her.

He glanced at the clock. "I have to go," he said. "I'll be back soon; will you be all right?"

"Yes."

He took off his jacket and lifted her head to slide it underneath her. "I love you," he whispered. She curled into a ball as he opened the door and stepped out. "Come on," he said to Mike.

Mike looked dumbfounded before he thrust his door open and stepped out. "You don't want me to stay with her?"

Liam glanced back at Sera. She looked incredibly small and so wounded it tore at his heart. He hated to leave her alone here, but he needed Mike. He shut his door and waited for Mike to do the same.

"No," Liam said. "I need you with me." Mike looked warily back in the car. It was obvious he didn't like the idea of leaving her alone either. "I'll kill her, Mike. I need you there to stop me."

Mike closed his mouth and nodded.

∼

A PAIR of headlights swept over the interior of the car. Sera listened as another vehicle pulled up and turned off. A door opened and shut. She rose to watch Michelle hurry down the path toward the gazebo with a case of beer in hand.

For the first time, Sera felt some emotion penetrate her numbness. She had to fight the urge to get out of the car and confront her. She didn't know how, but she knew Michelle had something to do with Jacob showing up tonight. She looked at the keys in the ignition and was half-tempted to start the car and run her over with it.

Instead, she sat back in the seat and watched her disappear.

∼

LIAM WATCHED as Michelle walked toward him with her hips swaying seductively. "Hello, sexy," she purred as she placed the beer on the gazebo step.

"Hello, Michelle."

She smiled as she hurried up the steps. She froze just inches before him as terror spread over her features and she gaped at him.

∼

SERA GRABBED the keys from the ignition and climbed out of the car. She was freezing, and she needed something to do to take her mind off what was going on in the park. She walked around to the back of the car and slid the keys into the lock.

Pulling Liam's jacket closer, she inhaled his pleasant, reassuring scent as she flung the trunk open.

She reached in to look for a blanket or clothes and froze. Jacob stared back at her. Wrapped in her clean, white sheets, his head was turned toward the side and his eyes open in unseeing horror. Sera stumbled back in revulsion as a scream caught in her throat. She tripped and fell to the ground. A guttural cry ripped from her as she scrambled backward like a crab.

Her breath came in heavy, lurching wheezes, and she couldn't stop the rolling revulsion racing through her. She turned onto her knees and vomited, her whole body heaved as she knelt upon the chilly ground. When her stomach was empty, she wiped the back of her hand over her mouth. She couldn't find the strength to stand.

Liam was a murderer. He killed Jacob. Jacob was dead. Her mind spun, one thought would not stay for more than a second or two. Nothing made sense. Everything was wrong.

Finally, when she could breathe normally again and move without feeling nauseous, she shoved herself to her feet. Stumbling to the car, she slammed the trunk closed without looking in it. She couldn't handle that awfulness again. The keys fell to the ground, but she didn't notice as she took a trembling step back.

Her gaze drifted to the path Liam, Mike, and Michelle had traversed. She didn't want to go, but she knew she had to. She had to see Liam and learn what was going on. Stumbling forward, she headed toward the path. Her heart lurched with every step, and her breath came in heavy pants as she broke into a run.

Tree branches slapped her face and hands as she stumbled blindly through the night. She tripped over a log and fell to the ground. Her hands and knees stung from the impact, but she didn't notice through the panic constricting her heart. She climbed back to her feet and started running again. The gazebo loomed before her as she finally made it to the park.

She froze as something inside told her not to go any further. She could see Liam and Michelle in the gazebo. Michelle gestured excitedly; her voice drifted through the night, but the words were indiscernible. Liam's voice was angry and insensible.

Sera started to creep forward. A part of her told her to run, to leave, and never look back. Another part of her, the bigger part, told her to keep going. This was Liam; he loved her; he would never hurt her.

Liam looked up and spotted Sera standing at the edge of the woods. He froze as his eyes latched onto her. Michelle turned toward Sera, her body stiffened and then relaxed. Liam's arms remained locked on the banister behind her as Sera approached.

Sera looked like a ghost, pale and ethereal as she moved toward the steps of the gazebo. Her long hair billowed like a banner behind her as it whipped in the wind. Michelle turned back to Liam; apprehension still filled her eyes, but there was a glimmer of hope in them now. Sera climbed the steps; her eyes were turbulent as they met Liam's before going toward Michelle. Sweat beaded her brow and matted her hair to her face. Her breath came fast, and he knew she'd run all the way here. He just didn't know why. He turned his attention away from her and back to Michelle.

"I think you have something to tell her," he said.

"I called Jacob," Michelle admitted.

Sera's jaw clenched. "How did you know?" she grated.

Michelle looked at the ground as she wrapped her arms around herself. "I knew something must've happened to you," she whispered hesitantly. "You never spoke of your home. You never go back there; you were always so skittish around men..."

Her voice trailed off. Sera's breath froze in her lungs. Liam's face was utterly inhuman as he stared at Michelle. She willed him to look at her, to show some sign he was still the man she loved. But his gaze never traveled to her as he kept Michelle pinned in.

"Tell her everything!" he barked.

Michelle jumped and tensed. Sera shivered and buried herself deeper into Liam's jacket. Her gaze flew to the back of the gazebo as Mike took a step forward. She hadn't seen him standing there. Relief washed over her when she realized there was someone else here to help. Nothing bad would happen.

"I... I did some investigating," Michelle stammered, drawing Sera's attention again. "I called your old high school and got in touch with your parents. At first, no one would tell me anything. But, a couple of weeks ago I got ahold of one of your yearbooks, and I managed to get in touch with someone from your class..."

Michelle's voice broke off.

"Who?" Sera asked.

"Lisa Evans."

Sera closed her eyes against the wave of sorrow crashing through her. Lisa had been her best friend, and it was Lisa's party they were at that night. Lisa saw her leave with Jacob. She never said a word, and she had been one of the first to accuse Sera of lying. Betrayal, fresh and new, tore through her, wrung tears from her eyes, and shook her body.

Liam turned his head to gaze at Sera. Tears slid down her pale cheeks. She looked so small, vulnerable, lost, and hurt. The impotence he felt caused his hands to clench on the rail. It took everything he had not to rip Michelle's throat out. A gasp escaped Michelle as she gazed at him in wide-eyed alarm. Her body began to tremble.

"Please don't kill me," she whispered pleadingly. "Please."

Liam closed his eyes and took a deep breath. There was enough blood on his hands tonight, and no matter how much he wanted to, he couldn't kill her. Not with Sera there. She would not see that side of him. As far as he was concerned, she would never know it existed.

"What did Lisa say?" Sera asked.

Michelle nervously licked her lips as she stared at Liam. Her heart raced so fast he could see it leaping in her throat.

"Answer her," he grated.

Michelle jumped and blurted a response. "She told me you accused Jacob of trying to rape you, and that it was a lie. She said once everyone learned about the lie, you took off to live with your grandmother, and no one heard from you again. She put me in touch with one of Jacob's friends, who gave me his number."

"So you called him?"

"Yes."

"You told him where I was. You told him about Liam and I. Why would you do that?"

The betrayal in Sera's voice ripped through Liam. His hands clenched so firmly on the wood he was sure he would tear it free. Michelle's eyes flitted back to him. She swallowed convulsively as she tried to find the words to speak.

"She said it was a lie. He said it was a lie. I thought he should confront you on it. Make you face up to your lies."

"I didn't lie!" Sera yelled.

Michelle jumped again; she glanced hopefully at Mike. Liam's temper was coming to a dangerous boiling point. Michelle was suffused in a reddish haze. If he didn't get away from her soon, he would kill her.

"I know that now," she whispered. Her head bent as sobs racked her body. "Please don't kill me, I'm sorry. I *am* sorry."

"No one's going to kill you," Sera assured her.

She wasn't so sure no one was going to kill her though. Jacob was dead. Liam had killed him. The deadly look on his face, and the wrath emanating from him, sent a shiver of alarm down her spine. She didn't know this man before her; she reminded herself. She had no idea what this man was capable of doing. And right now, he seemed fully capable of anything.

"Please," Michelle whimpered.

"Why?" Liam demanded. His voice was a whiplash of malice that sent waves of alarm crashing through Sera.

"I just thought... I just thought if you saw what a liar she was you wouldn't want her anymore. I didn't know it was true! I swear I didn't!"

"That makes it all right?" he hissed.

"Liam," Sera whispered.

For a moment, her words didn't penetrate the killing frenzy enshrouding him. Then, Sera touched his arm. He turned to her, his eyes spitting fury, as a snarl curved his mouth. Her hand fell away as she took a trembling step back. Mike stepped in between her and Liam. The utter terror suffusing Sera's face finally penetrated through to him.

Sera's heart hammered. For a second, Liam's eyes had been a blood red that sent instinctive terror ripping through her. She was tempted to turn and flee from what she glimpsed in him. What was he? Tremors racked her body, adrenaline raced through her, but her legs refused to move.

She knew what she'd seen, what she'd glimpsed, and yet her heart and soul, would not allow her to run from him. She loved him, no matter what, but right now she was utterly petrified of him. She glanced at Mike, but he must not have seen it. Otherwise, he would have fled by now. Wouldn't he?

She glanced back at Liam. His eyes seemed to clear, and the coldness left them as he gazed at her. His body sagged as he shoved himself away from the banister. "Get out of here!" he spat at Michelle.

Michelle glanced at Sera but didn't stop as she lurched down the steps and ran into the woods. Sera's legs threatened to give out as she was left alone with Liam and Mike. Liam could do anything he wanted to her; he could kill her like he had Jacob. And yet, something inside her said he wouldn't. That no matter what, he wouldn't allow any harm to come to her. Plus, Mike was there, he would help her if she needed it.

Liam took a step toward her, but she held up a hand to stop him as she shook her head. "Are you all right?" he inquired.

"No."

"Let's get you out of here."

"No."

He stared at her in confusion and took another step toward her. Mike took a small step away; his eyes were watchful as he glanced between her and Liam. "What's wrong?"

Sera took a deep breath, her shoulders shook, but she was determined to know everything. "Where is Jacob?"

He froze as he stared at her. "Sera—"

"Where is he?" Her voice was a little shrill.

Liam stared at her in dismay. Shit, this was all going wrong. The rapid beating of her heart told him she'd seen something in his eyes when he'd turned to look at her. How much she glimpsed, he didn't know. "He had a knife."

"So you killed him?"

"It was an accident."

"Why didn't you call the police?"

"Sera, please calm down."

"Don't tell me to calm down!" she screamed.

"I panicked all right," he said. "I just panicked."

"You seemed pretty calm to me."

"I didn't know what to do." He took another step toward her. "It was an accident."

That was a lie, he'd meant to kill Jacob, and he'd enjoyed every second of it. But he couldn't tell her that. She was already looking at him like he was a monster. If she knew the truth, she would run screaming into the woods and never look back.

"Then we'll go to the police now," she whispered.

"Sera, I can't do that."

"Why not? If it was an accident—"

"They'll say I tried to cover it up, they won't believe me," he said.

"They'll understand it was an accident. They'll know you stabbed him in self-defense; he had a knife, he was attacking me, and you stabbed him."

He moved a step closer to her. "Sera, I can't do that."

She lifted her eyes to meet his. They were full of despair as she gazed at him in confusion. He wanted to ease the sorrow in her gaze and make her forget everything that happened tonight, everything she'd seen. "My life would be over. I'd go to jail. Everything I've worked for would be gone."

He stopped before her and gripped her arm. A sudden spark rolled through her eyes, an acknowledgment that made his stomach heave, and his heart hammer. She stared at him in dawning horror. "Sera," he whispered.

"If you stabbed him," she whispered. "Then where's the blood? My sheets are clean."

He tried to grab her, but she took a step away from him as her hand flew to her mouth. Liam closed his eyes against the revulsion and trepidation in her gaze. "Sera—"

"My God," she whispered. "What are you?" His eyes flew to hers. His arms fell limply to his sides. Her eyes searched his face pleadingly, but he made no move toward her. "Liam—"

"Let's go."

Her gaze flew to Mike. He stood with his arms folded over his chest as he stared at her in resignation. It felt as if a sledgehammer slammed into her stomach as the breath rushed out of her. Mike knew what was going on, what Liam had done. He had helped him afterward; that was why he was here. He would be no help to her.

Her legs turned to Jell-O. She panted as she hung her head and fought desperately against passing out. Hands clasped hold of her and lifted her up. She couldn't offer a protest as Liam swung her into his arms and carried her down the steps of the gazebo. She was confident she was being taken to her death, but she couldn't find the strength to fight against him.

CHAPTER TEN

Mike opened the door to Liam's room and stepped back to let him enter. Liam carried Sera swiftly inside. Her body was unyielding against his; her hands curled into fists in her lap. He shifted his hold on her to pull the blankets on the bed back. Sliding her in, he pulled the covers up around her as she lay unmoving. "Just get some sleep," he whispered. "We'll talk in the morning, all right?"

Her eyes were dull and glazed as she looked at him before turning away to look out the window. She hadn't spoken a word to him since the gazebo. He didn't know what to say or do. He naively thought he could avoid all this.

It wasn't the kind of a secret you could keep from someone who was as close to him as Sera was. Deep inside, he knew that. He just never wanted to acknowledge it. Now it was slapping him in the face.

He turned away from her. Mike stood in the doorway, his gaze intense as he studied Liam. "We need to talk."

"Tomorrow."

"Liam—"

"Tomorrow, Mike!" he barked.

Mike's gaze was intense and irate as he studied him. His eyes closed as he nodded briskly and left the room. Liam stood in the quiet room, unsure what to do. Finally, he strode across the room and slid tiredly into the easy chair. He watched as she continued to stare out the window, hoping she wasn't afraid of him, certain she was. How could she not be?

"You're safe here," he told her.

"Am I?" she muttered.

He winced at the words. "Yes, you are."

He turned to look out the window, unable to stand the revulsion in her gaze any longer. The moon had finally risen; its pale light spilled in to illuminate the room. He looked back at her as she lay motionless. He watched her for a long time as her breathing steadied. He knew she was still awake.

LIAM WOKE with a start and nearly toppled out of the chair. His neck and back ached, he felt as stiff as a board. He groaned as he straightened his aching joints, and opened his eyes. The sun was just touching the horizon. His bones cracked as he walked over to shut the blinds before it woke Sera. She was sleeping on the bed, her head buried beneath the blankets. His heart and body longed to hold her as he watched her for a minute.

He forced himself to turn away and head for the door. He opened it cautiously, stepped into the hall, and made his way to Mike's room where he pounded on the door. "What?" Mike yelled.

"Open up," Liam grated.

He listened as Mike stormed over to the door and swung it open. Mike glared at him from bloodshot eyes. "When I want to talk you tell me to go away, but it's all right to wake me up at six thirty in the morning!" he snapped.

Liam glowered at him as he swept into the room. A young brunette sat up in bed; she blinked sleepily at them as the blankets fell to expose her nude body. Liam scooped her clothes off the floor and threw them at her. "Get out," he ordered.

"What?" she cried as she scrambled to gather her clothes. "Michael?"

"Go on." Mike collapsed onto the couch.

The girl cast him a scowl as she tugged her shirt over her head. "You're an asshole!" she spat.

Mike laughed and draped his arm over his eyes. "Bye, sweetie," he drawled as Liam opened the door, and closed it behind her.

"You know, one of these days I'm going to come barging in on you and Sera," Mike mumbled. "Kick her out of the room naked."

"Don't even think about it," Liam warned.

Mike removed his arm from his eyes and looked up at him. "Then again, I doubt she'll be sticking around for much longer. You've messed up, Liam, bad. What are you going to do about it?"

"I was hoping you'd have some suggestions."

"You could make her forget, take the whole night away from her."

Liam closed his eyes as he slumped onto the bed. He absently rubbed his temples to ease some of the pressure in his skull. The idea was completely and utterly tempting, and the easiest thing to do. He could make her forget about Jacob's body and everything that followed afterward. He wished he could take everything about Jacob away from her, but that would take more power and capabilities than all of them had. Plus, he would have to change Kathleen, Danielle, and Michelle's memories. It would be too much, but he could make her forget enough to make her no longer frightened of him.

"I don't know if I can."

"Why not? You have the power and ability to do it."

"It's not that."

"Then what is it?"

The truth was, he wanted her to know, he wanted her to know it all, and he wanted her to decide what she was going to do. If she left him, then he would deal with it, but if she stayed there would be no barriers between them. He wouldn't have to worry about her finding out, wouldn't have to worry about losing her.

Liam lifted his head to look at him. "I don't know if I want to," he admitted.

Mike's brow furrowed as he swung his legs off the side of the chair and planted them on the floor. "What do you mean?" he asked.

"I want to tell her the truth."

Mike's mouth dropped as he stared at him in stunned amazement. What he suggested went against all the rules, rules *he* made to keep them all safe. Right now though, he didn't care about the rules.

"Why?"

Liam had expected Mike to explode. Instead, he was still staring at him in astonishment. "Because I can't do that to her, I can't change her memories; I can't invade her mind like that. I won't do it."

"You don't have a choice, Liam," Mike grated through clenched teeth. "You've screwed up bad. I don't know what you want me to say, but you've got to do something. Other people need to be protected. You know that. If you can't do it, then one of us will."

"No one," he said firmly. "Is going to harm her, in any way, do you understand me?"

Mike looked away from him to stare angrily at the poster on his wall. He sighed as he ran a hand through his disheveled blond hair. "There may be no other option. You have to understand that. I know how you feel about her, but—"

Liam launched to his feet, his hands clenched into fists as he glowered at him. "No! You don't know how I feel about her," he spat. "If you did, you would realize what you're suggesting is not, and never will be, an option."

Mike's eyes shot back to his. "You need to talk to her. See how things go, but you have to realize what all of this could mean."

"I do realize what it could mean."

"No, I don't think you do," Mike's eyes were suddenly weary and resigned.

"Yes," Liam grated. "I do. What you don't understand is I will kill anyone who tries to hurt her; that includes you."

Mike looked as if he'd punched him in the jaw, Liam had never threatened any of them, but he would kill them to protect her. "Go talk to her, Liam, see what she says. Maybe there's nothing to worry about, but if there is—"

"No!" he interrupted. "I'm not kidding, Mike, you stay away from her; do you hear me?"

"Yeah, I hear you," he muttered. "I couldn't do anything to her anyway; you know that."

"Don't tell anyone else about this."

"Whatever, you're the boss." Liam strode to the door. "What are you going to say to her?" Mike asked as he opened the door.

He turned to look at him and shrugged helplessly. "I don't know yet. The truth."

Mike snorted as he shook his head. "We don't have to be

concerned about what to do with her after that; she'll be locked in the loony bin."

Liam shot him a scathing glare as he slammed the door. He hurried back to his room and opened the door. Sera had rolled over. The blanket fell away to reveal her exquisite face. She looked angelic and peaceful in her sleep. He dreaded the hurt he was going to inflict on her.

He sat on the edge of the bed and touched her shoulder. Her eyes opened, and she stared up at him, a smile spreading across her beautiful face. Then, suddenly, it was gone. Remembrance crashed over her features and shuttered through her eyes. She bolted upright; her hair tumbled around her face and shoulders. Her eyes were huge, and a vivid, startling purple.

"Sera, we need to talk."

"Are you going to be honest with me?"

"I never wanted to lie to you."

"Really? Because it's all you've ever done. I feel like I don't even know you. You've been this one person, this person you've let me see, or wanted me to see. This person who I fell in love with, but you're not that person. And now this. This! Who are you, Liam? *What* are you?"

Tears spilled down her cheeks, and she angrily wiped them away. She was mad at herself for crying, and she was furious at him. "I'm going to be honest with you, about everything."

She laughed and shook her head despairingly. "How am I supposed to know that?"

Her words cut into his heart, and he winced involuntarily. "I deserve that, but it will be the truth, Sera, I promise."

She snorted and looked away; she rubbed her hands along her arms to ward off the chill racking her. "I hope so, Liam, I really hope so."

He stretched his hand out to rub her cheek. She jerked away from his touch, her eyes burned with a resentment bordering on hatred. He dropped his hand away. He was going to lose her; no matter how much she loved him she wouldn't be able to deal with this. She was going to walk out of this room and never look back. But, she was going to hear the truth first. She deserved it, and no matter how much he never wanted her to be, she was involved now.

He stood and walked across the room; he paced as he ran his fingers through his hair. "I told you why I didn't tell you about Michelle, but I didn't tell you about all the circumstances surrounding her—"

"Don't you think you should tell me about last night first?" she cut him off abruptly.

"No. Last night happened because of her. It will be best to explain her first."

"Fine."

"I met Michelle two days before school started. We were throwing an end of summer party here, and she came to it. I didn't pay much attention to her at first, which I don't think made her very happy. But it was a game I was playing. I knew by not paying attention to her, she would want me more. She was a challenge to me. She wasn't as tough to get as she pretended to be. By the end of the night, I'd had too much to drink, and I had her. It was quick, it was over with, and it didn't mean anything, not to me anyway.

"Apparently, she thought it meant more, which I *am* sorry for. She came by here a couple of times after, but I didn't talk to her. When she confronted me about it, I told her the truth. It was a one-night stand, nothing more, and it was never going to be more. She didn't take it well, and I can't say I blame her. I was a jerk, I know it, but I can't take it back. But I wasn't by myself; she was there too.

"Then, a couple weeks later, you showed up. I saw you before you saw me. Everyone was talking about you, and guys were fluttering around you like moths, but you didn't notice. I didn't know what to make of you. Some said you were stuck up, mainly the girls, but then I saw you with Kathleen and Danielle, and how open and happy you were with them. The guys said pretty much what guys say. They wanted to sleep with you, they wanted this, or they wanted that. Except for Mike. He told me to stay away from you. To leave you alone. For Mike to say something like that... well, it just amazed me and piqued my curiosity. I had to meet you."

"Did I become a challenge too?" she asked as her chin lifted defiantly.

He didn't want to tell her this, but she wanted the truth, and he was going to give it to her. "Yes," he admitted. "You weren't a challenge in the same way Michelle was, but you were a challenge."

"Good to know," she mumbled bitterly.

"You wanted the truth." A jolt of anger made his voice harsh. "I'm giving it all to you, Sera. You were a challenge simply because I had to know more about you, not because I just wanted you in my bed like Michelle—"

"This is just getting better," she muttered.

"Don't do that!" he retorted. Her hands fisted as her chin jutted out but she didn't say anything more. "All I wanted from Michelle was a one night stand. I wanted more from you. Otherwise, I would have gone to any of the many willing girls around here after the first night we met, but I didn't. You were not, and are not, just a stupid conquest; you never have been. That first night, I saw what Mike had been talking about. I saw the vulnerability in you, the fear, and I knew I shouldn't become involved with you, that I should stay away. You'd been hurt, and I could do nothing but bring you more hurt."

"Then why didn't you leave me alone?" she asked.

"I don't know!"

His frustration had come to a boiling point. She jumped in surprise and then winced. Liam took a deep breath and forced himself to calm down. She was scared of him already; he didn't want to frighten her anymore, especially when he hadn't even told her the worst part yet.

"I don't know," he repeated. "You are unlike anyone I ever met, and I wanted to know all about you. The more I learned about you, the more I loved you. I think I've loved you since the first night. No matter what happens, I will always love you, and I will protect you from anyone who tries to injure you. Even if you never speak to me again, I will still protect you."

She stared at him, crying silently as her hands shook in her lap. He walked over to the window and stared out the blinds as he gathered his strength before turning to face her again. "If you decide to leave, I won't blame you, but no matter what you cannot reveal to anyone what I am going to tell you. If you do, I don't know if I can protect you. I don't think I could stop them from coming after you. They would kill me to get to you. Do you understand me?"

"I don't want anything to happen to you," she whispered tremulously.

"Are you worried about me?" he asked incredulously.

"Yes."

He closed his eyes and turned back to the window. Anguish filled him, and a love greater than he ever thought he could experience engulfed him. "You know," he said. "I never thought I could love anyone like I love you. I never thought I would meet a person like you. I didn't believe they existed."

"Liam—"

"No one is going to harm me, Sera. You just need to promise me you won't tell anyone, please."

"I won't tell anyone anything you don't want me to."

He felt as if his skin was flayed away and his soul bared as he turned back to her. "I'm a vampire."

The words hung heavy in the air as she stared at him. Then, she began to laugh. Hitching in a deep breath, she managed to stifle her laughter as she stood. Her eyes blazed with fury, and her jaw clenched as she turned to him. "You know, there is something wrong with you. I've had it. If you don't want to tell me the truth, then don't. But don't pull this bull with me. I'm going to the police!"

"Sera—"

"No!" she shouted. "You have done nothing but lie to me. I've had it. I've had it with you! You've won whatever game you were playing. You've won! You can run around and tell everyone you made a fool of me; I don't care!" She turned and stormed toward the door. "You rotten bastard!"

He moved swiftly across the room. He was ahead of her before her hand stretched for the knob. She froze, unable to believe he'd moved so fast. Suddenly, her mind flashed back to the red in his eyes, and the killing rage radiating from him last night. The lack of blood on Jacob and on her sheets. For a moment, she wanted to believe him. For a moment, she did.

Then her mind snapped back into place, back into reality. There was no such thing as vampires. They did not exist. He had done nothing but lie to her from the beginning. She couldn't believe this insanity. It was impossible. Lifting her chin, she glared at him, her eyes full of a ferocity that rocked him.

"You can't go to the police. I'm not lying," he said coldly.

"Get out of my way!" she spat as her hands clenched at her sides.

He stared at her as he took a step closer. "Sera..."

She took a couple of steps back. Her annoyance vanished as despair washed over her. She'd had too much. She simply couldn't take anymore. "Stop, please," she begged. "Just stop it. I can't take this anymore. Do you have any idea how much you've hurt me? All I wanted was the truth. Even though you killed him, I didn't care! I would have helped you. I would have done anything for you! Just leave me alone, let me go."

She stood with her head in her hands as her shoulders shook with her sobs. He grabbed hold of her hands and forced them away from her face. "I'm not lying to you," he growled.

She lifted her eyes and froze. His eyes were a scarlet shade of red. His beautiful face twisted into something unrecognizable, something unreal and horrifying. His long, inhuman teeth hung over his bottom lip. They looked deadlier and sharper than any lion's teeth.

Her eyes widened, her jaw dropped, and then she screamed. He slammed his hand over her mouth, silencing her before she could make much of a sound. Liam wrapped his arm around her waist and pulled her flush against his chest. She clawed at his hand and kicked backward with such frenzy he almost lost his hold.

Tightening his grip, he lifted her off the floor. Her body shook and heaved as she dug into his skin. "Sera, stop it," he grated in her ear. "Stop."

She continued to scream against his hand as her chest heaved with her inhalations. He hissed as her teeth sank into his palm. "Damn it!"

He dropped her onto the bed. She bounced back up and scrambled to get away. He grabbed hold of her ankle and pulled her back as she cried out. "No!"

He clamped his hand over her mouth again. Her small fists beat impotently against his chest as he straddled her. Seizing hold of her wrists, he clamped them firmly together against her stomach. Her muffled cries became softer as tears spilled down her face.

She stopped fighting and went still beneath him. Her nostrils flared as she watched him through terrified eyes. He kept his hand over her mouth while he tried to steady his breathing and the pounding of his heart. This was not the way he wanted this to go.

"I'm going to take my hand away. Don't scream, Sera. I mean it."

She nodded, and he eased his hand from her mouth. She inhaled deeply; a tremor raced through her as she shivered beneath him. Blood stained the corners of her lips, his blood. He wiped it away gently. She winced and turned her head from his touch.

His head bent in defeat. Of course, she would be repulsed by him. He was a monster. But he hoped maybe, just maybe, she would accept him. He knew now she wouldn't. The knowledge ripped his soul to shreds.

"You're the one who wanted the truth!" he spat.

She flinched as his words tore at her. Yes, she wanted the truth, but who in their right mind could ever imagine this was it? That he was a monster and a killer. No one could. No one who was sane anyway, and right now she wasn't entirely sure she still was.

She couldn't stop the mind-numbing horror filling her. "You're hurting me," she croaked out.

His grip on her wrists eased, but he didn't release her. "Look at me, Sera."

She bit her bottom lip as she took another shuddery breath. She forced herself to turn her head, open her eyes, and look at him. The monster was gone. It was Liam hovering over her, his green eyes haunted with turmoil. His jaw clenched so firmly a muscle in his cheek jumped wildly. Even though the creature was gone, he was still deadly.

Another tremor raced through her. She had seen the

ferocity in his vivid red eyes, the snarl twisting his features into something inhuman, something she didn't recognize. He could kill her in the space of a heartbeat. Rip her throat out and drain the blood from her before she even had a chance to scream, let alone struggle.

He made no move to attack her.

The realization gradually sank in and eased the tension in her muscles. Warmth, and love, suddenly flashed through his eyes, melting the coldness in them, making him more human. A sob broke from her. She bit her lip to try and stifle it. The coldness settled back over his gaze and instantly shut out any warmth.

"Now, are you going to listen to me?" He waited for her to nod her acknowledgment. "Good, because not only does my life revolve around this, but so does yours, and so do four others I care about. Do you understand?" She could only manage another weak nod. "You can walk out of my life, Sera; I will understand if you do, but you cannot breathe a word of this to anyone. Do you hear me?"

She took a deep breath and nodded. She would have told him anything he wanted to hear. If there was any chance of her being able to escape, then she would do whatever it took.

"Good. Because if you do, I don't know if I can protect you."

"You'd kill me?" she breathed.

The wrath emanating from his eyes caused her to recoil. Instinctive terror surged through her, and she began to thrash in his grasp. His hands tightened on her wrists as he held her in place. Pain shot down her arms; she cried out as tears sprang to her eyes. His grasp instantly loosened.

"Sera, stop it. I don't want to hurt you." His words sank slowly in, and her resistance ceased. She lay, panting beneath him, as she met his sincere gaze. "I told you I would protect you no matter what, and I meant it. But there are others. I can't stop them all. I can't let you go if you're going to tell anyone."

Sera laughed as she shook her head. "Who would believe me anyway, Liam? They would lock me in a nuthouse if I started talking about a vampire boyfriend in a frat house."

"Believe it or not, some people would believe you. We can't afford to have that happen, okay?"

"Yes."

"Do I have your promise you're not going to say anything?"

"If I say no, what will you do to me?"

His eyes reflected his torment. "Take you away from here, keep you away from people. I would hate to do it, Sera, but I can't risk our lives. You may grow to hate me for it, you probably hate me now, but it's something I'm willing to live with. As long as you stay alive and safe, then nothing else matters."

There were no lies within his eyes. There was only a desperate need for her to understand and concede to his will. She couldn't believe he would let her leave this room if she gave him her word not to say anything. What kind of monster would do that?

Eventually, she realized he wasn't a monster. He was still *her* Liam. He could have killed her many times already, but he hadn't. He didn't have to let her go. He could make her do whatever he wanted. He was ten times stronger than she was, and she was certain she hadn't even seen a hint of what he was truly capable of doing. She didn't hate him; she didn't think she could ever hate him. She was terrified of him right now, as she had every right to be, but she didn't hate him.

"Do you promise Sera?"

"Yes," she whispered.

His head bent as he took a deep, shuddery breath. He released his hold on her and sat back. She levered her arms beneath her and scooted back on the bed as he stood and walked away. Rubbing her tender, bruised wrists, she watched him in disbelief. He was going to let her go.

"You can leave."

His back was rigid as he stood by the desk. He didn't turn as she climbed unsteadily to her trembling legs. She looked at the door and then back over to him. "You're letting me go?" she asked in disbelief.

Liam closed his eyes as pain seared through his entire body. "Yes," he grated. "I don't expect you to stay with me, Sera. I know what I am, what I can never give you."

"And what is that?" she whispered.

He couldn't look at her; she was the only bright thing in his entire joyless life. When she left, she would take all the light with her, and leave him to drown in the dark. But he couldn't expect her to stay. He was a demon. He survived on blood. He could destroy her with a single flick of his wrist. He had nothing but blood and death to offer her.

"A life, Sera, I can never offer you a life. I won't age; I won't die. I can offer you nothing. Now go, before I change my mind and decide I don't care about anything, but keeping you with me no matter what it means, no matter how you feel about it."

Sera's gaze traveled back to the door. Her heart was ripping to shreds in her chest. She had never known such physically emotional suffering in her life. She couldn't breathe through the constriction in her chest; she could barely see through the tears burning her eyes. If she walked out of this room and left him, then a part of her would cease to be. But, if she stayed, then she gave up her hopes of a family, of children. She would grow old and die. He would stay young and alive.

She could always join him. Horror shuddered through her at the thought of drinking blood, and her mind instantly shut out the possibility. She couldn't do that, no matter what, she couldn't do that. She had to give him up. She had to. Tears streaked her face as she took a stumbling step forward and halted.

"Go, Sera," he muttered. "Leave."

She sobbed as she fell against the door. "Liam," she whispered.

He didn't turn to her. He kept his eyes firmly shut as he waited for her to leave. It took every ounce of strength he possessed not to grab her and keep her from leaving him. It took all he had not to grab her and force the memories from her mind. But he could not, would not, do that to her, to himself. It was better to end it now, to let her leave, instead of having to give her up in five years, ten years, when he loved her even more.

The touch on his arm caused his eyes to fly open. Immersed in his grief, he hadn't heard her approach. "Sera," he managed to choke out.

"I don't want to leave," she whispered.

He fought back the hope threatening to choke him. "I can offer you nothing."

"You can offer me you. I just want you."

He was frozen as his conscience waged war with his heart. His heart won out. With a groan, he pulled her snugly against him. "I hope you understand what this means," he said hoarsely.

"Yes."

"I'm never going to let you go now. Do you understand that?"

"I don't want you to."

His heart contracted as his hands convulsed around her. He buried his head in her fragrant hair. He had never done anything to deserve her. He didn't understand how she could love him so willingly, so freely, and so openly. She clung to him, her head buried in his chest, completely vulnerable, and giving.

He held her for a long time, unwilling to release her. She

yawned, and he took a small step back. He lifted her and crossed the room in three long strides to lay her down on the bed. "Lay with me," she whispered.

He climbed in beside her. She nuzzled closer to him as she savored in his strength and warmth. He held her in his arms, clinging to her as if he was a drowning man and she was his life raft. Which, she was.

CHAPTER ELEVEN

Liam's back was pressed firmly against the wall; he had one leg drawn up, and his arm draped over it. Mike sat across from him in the easy chair, which he'd turned sideways in, so his long legs dangled casually over the side. He was smoking a cigarette; the ashes drifted to the floor as he ignored the ashtray in his hand.

"Well," Mike said. "I'll take care of Jacob's body."

"Thanks."

"No problem. What about her?"

"She'll be all right."

"You said she was pretty shaken up. Great way to tell her too. I mean, you drop a bombshell on her and then transform yourself into a monster. That's not easy to take."

"She wouldn't believe me."

"Did you honestly expect her to?"

Mike took a long drag of his cigarette. The smoke curled out of his nose as he finally remembered the ashtray and snubbed it out. "I don't know what I expected."

Mike snorted, pulled out another cigarette, and lit it. "Well, I guess you had to tell her."

"Yes."

"I don't know what to say to you, Liam."

"Then don't say anything."

"You know this goes against all of our rules."

"Of course I know it. I made the rules!" he barked.

Mike took another drag and flicked an ash to the floor. "Yeah, I guess you did."

Liam rubbed at his throbbing temples. "You'll understand one day."

Mike chuckled. "I don't think I will. As long as you think it'll be all right, then I won't argue with you. But, I don't like it. I don't want to see either one of you get hurt."

"She won't be hurt."

"I hope you won't be either."

"I won't."

"Yeah well, I'll stand by you no matter what."

"Thanks."

Sera stirred slightly, and he looked down at her. His hand ran through her hair as she rolled over and buried her head in his lap. She opened her eyes and looked dazedly up at him. She sat up and rubbed the sleep from her eyes.

"Hi, Sera," Mike greeted.

She started, and her hands fell to her sides as she turned to look at him. He appeared casual in the chair, but there was an air of tension around him that belied his demeanor. Her heartbeat kicked up a notch as she suddenly understood why he had been there last night. "Hello, Mike," she greeted.

He smiled as he flicked an ash to the floor and swung his legs leisurely back and forth. "How are you doing today?"

Her eyes jumped to Liam, and then back to Mike. "Sera," Liam said as he clasped her hand.

Mike's eyes were an intense blue as they burned into her.

He snuffed his cigarette out and dropped the ashtray to the floor. "I suppose you've figured out I am too."

Sera's gaze flew back to Liam's. He squeezed her hand, willing her to be okay. For a minute, she stared at him. Then her eyes sparkled, and a smile curved the corners of her full mouth. She turned back to Mike. "I have."

Liam pulled her into his arms, nestling her against his chest as he met Mike's gaze above her head. Mike stared back at him as he lit another cigarette and took a long drag. He looked down at Sera, his brow furrowed in puzzlement as he studied her carefully.

"I didn't know you smoked," Sera mumbled.

He blew a small smoke ring. "Only once in a while."

Liam was glad Mike refrained from telling her he only smoked when he was agitated and troubled. "Good thing you don't have to be concerned about lung cancer."

Mike's eyebrows shot up; he grinned as he took another long drag. "Yep."

"So who are the other three?"

"What?" Mike asked.

Sera lifted her eyes to Liam. "You said four others needed to be protected. Obviously, Mike is one, but who are the other three?"

Liam's hands tightened on her. They had never exposed themselves before. Mike's eyes focused on him and narrowed pointedly. Liam silently dared Mike to make any objection, but he didn't. Instead, he took another long drag of his cigarette and stubbed it out.

"You haven't met David. He's going to college in Pennsylvania," Liam said.

"And the other two?"

"Doug and Jack," Mike answered. Sera felt as if someone

punched her, but she didn't say anything. "Look, you're obviously taking this rather well, but..."

"You don't trust me."

"No, I don't."

Sera bit her bottom lip as she lowered her eyes from his intense stare. Liam's arms were warm and secure around her. Liam trusted her, he would keep her safe, but she wasn't sure it would be enough. He said he couldn't protect her from all of them. If they decided she was a threat, they would kill her, and Liam, to get to her.

She lifted her head to gaze at him. His eyes were turbulent, but the love in them was unmistakable. "Do you trust Liam?" she inquired.

Mike's eyes flickered toward Liam. "Well, yeah," he said hesitantly.

"Then you should trust the fact *he* trusts me."

Mike frowned thoughtfully. "I guess I should."

Sera dropped her head against Liam's chest and snuggled closer to him. He smiled as he met Mike's startled gaze. "Amazing," Mike mumbled.

Liam didn't have to ask what was amazing. He was holding it securely in his arms. The piercing ring of her phone caused them all to jump in surprise. Mike grabbed it off the desk and tossed it over to Liam. "Hello."

"Where is Sera?" Kathleen demanded loudly.

"She's right here; hold on," he said, handing the phone to her.

"Hello," she said.

"What is going on?"

"Nothing."

"Don't give me that! Something is going on. Liam came in last night and took Michelle out of the party, did you know that?"

"Yes, Kathleen," Sera replied tiredly. "I was in the car."

"Why?"

"We had a few things to straighten out, that's all."

"Oh, that's all! Really? There's more going on, and I want to know what it is."

"There is nothing else going on, Kathleen," she said firmly. "I wouldn't lie to you." Sera closed her eyes and took a deep breath as guilt washed through her. She was lying now, but there was no way she could tell Kathleen that. "I'd had it with all of Michelle's crap and decided to confront her on it. I knew she wouldn't leave the party with me, so Liam came to get her."

"Why did Liam want to know if I had said anything about Jacob?"

Sera closed her eyes as memories flowed over her. A fierce shiver racked her and almost caused her to drop the phone. Liam grabbed her shoulders and tried to take the phone from her. She shook her head, holding up a hand to ward him off. She had to deal with this sooner or later, and Kathleen would only become more adamant if Liam took the phone now.

"He called me," she managed to say.

"Oh, Sera, that must have been awful!" Kathleen cried. "Did Michelle tell him where you were?"

"Yes."

"Oh God, I swear I didn't say anything to her Sera. I swear it!"

"I know you didn't."

"How did she find out?"

"It's a long story, Kathleen. Can we talk about it later?"

"Oh, oh yeah." Sera could hear the unhappiness in her voice, but there was nothing she could do to ease it. "Um, Sera, the door to the room is broken. What if it was him? What if he came here? I should call campus security and—"

"No!" Sera nearly shouted.

"But what if he came here?"

"He didn't."

"Sera—"

"Kathleen please, there is nothing to worry about. Liam broke the door last night. I was so upset after Jacob called I accidentally locked myself out." She was normally a horrible liar, but suddenly they were pouring off her tongue as if she was accomplished at it. She'd never felt so awful before.

"Oh, okay. Well, that's good then. I'll just have maintenance come and fix it. Your sheets are gone too, but I guess I don't have to ask what happened to those if Liam was here," she added with a laugh.

Sera winced as she vividly recalled Jacob's body wrapped in those sheets. "No," she mumbled. "No, you don't."

"Are you sure you're all right?"

"I'm fine," she answered tiredly. "I'll be back later today, okay?"

"Okay. If you need anything, call me."

"I will," she promised.

She hung the phone up and tossed it back to Mike. He placed it on the desk and turned to face her, a look of admiration on his face. "Well," Mike said. "It's good to know you think fast in a pinch."

Sera rubbed at her pounding temples. "I hate lying," she mumbled.

"You're going to have to get used to it." Liam and Sera glared at Mike. He held up his hands in surrender. "Well, you are!" he protested. "And trust me, it doesn't get any easier. Wait till people start to ask questions about what happened to Jacob. I just hope no one knew he was coming here or saw him."

Sera hadn't even begun to think about that. Her mind had been too overwrought with everything else going on to start wondering what would happen when Jacob was reported missing.

"I doubt he let anyone see him," Liam said. "He came here for a reason, and he wouldn't want anyone to be able to testify against him."

"But he might have told someone. He might have told Michelle," she whispered.

"No, he wouldn't."

Sera spun toward him. "You can't know that!"

He clasped hold of her hands. "No, I can't," he said. "But we also can't know if he told anyone else. Worrying about it now won't do any good. If something happens, we'll worry then. Okay?"

She searched his face before nodding her consent. "What about the body?"

"I'm going to take care of that," Mike answered. "Speaking of which, it's getting pretty late. I'd better go."

"Thanks, Mike," Liam said.

"No problem. I'll let you know how everything goes."

He climbed to his feet and left. Sera turned to look at Liam; her hopelessness radiated from her body. He pulled her down onto the bed with him. "Things will be all right," he assured her. "I promise."

She lifted her head to look at him. Her eyes burned into his as she leaned down and kissed him. "I don't want to think about it anymore," she whispered. "I don't want to think about anything right now."

She kissed him again, her mouth warm and lush against his as she opened to him. His passion built as she melted against him. He rolled her over, resting himself on top of her as his mouth ravaged hers. He needed her with a nearly consuming hunger. His hands roamed over her body, relishing in the feel of her warm skin as he shoved her shirt up.

Sera pulled eagerly at his shirt in her craving to feel his skin, to feel his solid body flush against hers. He sat up and ripped his shirt and jeans off. Sitting beside him, she pulled off her clothing to expose her splendid body. He studied her before pulling her against him.

He was wild with need, desperate to feel her, to be inside of her. Frantic to have her ease the torment of the past day and wash away the horrible memory of blood on his hands. He pushed her back on the bed, kissing her savagely, as his hands explored every inch of her satin skin. She moaned and lifted herself against him, her body begging him for more.

He drove himself into her with such force he was afraid he'd hurt her. But she showed no signs of discomfort as she arched beneath him and her hands dug into his back. Her moans and furious movements urged him to a faster pace as he drove in and out of her. He forgot everything as he was swept up in her body, in her movements, in the pleasure she gave him. Her hands grasped his buttocks, begging him for more, bringing him closer against her.

She cried out as the orgasm ripped through her. Her muscles tightened around him as her body shook. He drove forcefully into her, emptying himself with a loud groan of pleasure.

She collapsed on the bed, her body still trembling from the waves of pleasure racking her. She smiled sleepily at him as she caressed his face. Sweat beaded along his brow, matted his black hair, and made him look even sexier. She shivered as he nibbled on her lower lip.

His heart swelled with love as he rolled her onto her side. How he had ever gotten so lucky to find her, to have her, he didn't know. She should have run screaming from him, from everything he was, from everything he had done, and could do.

Instead, she gave him her heart, her body, and her soul.

Even before he became a monster, he hadn't been a good man. There was nothing in his life to explain the kind of wholehearted love she gave him.

"I'll always love you," she whispered. Liam's heart skipped a beat as his arms convulsed around her. "But you have to promise me, no more lies, no more secrets."

"I promise I will never lie to you or keep another secret from you."

"Good."

"I love you too," he whispered.

Sera glanced up from her history book as Mike slid into the seat across from her. "Hey," she greeted.

He smiled as he leaned back in his seat and draped an arm casually over the back of it. "Cafeteria food will kill you."

Sera grinned as she pushed the remains of her salad aside. "Not all of us are lucky enough not to have to eat it."

He snorted a chuckle. "True."

"So to what do I owe the pleasure of your company?"

He glanced around the crowded cafeteria. Sera had been there for so long she had tuned out the noise level; it now penetrated her ears again. "Not much. Just saw you sitting here and thought you might like some company."

"Keeping tabs on me?"

He frowned as his arm dropped from the back of the booth. "No. I don't understand why you're taking this so well, but I do trust, Liam, which means I trust you."

"I didn't take it well at first," she admitted.

"I know, Liam told me." She bit her bottom lip as her gaze fell to the table. "Do you love him?"

Sera's eyes flew up to his. "With all my heart and soul," she said fervently.

Mike's eyes clouded as he leaned across the table. "You do realize he won't age; he won't—"

"I know, Mike," she interrupted briskly. "I know everything."

"Then what do you plan to do?"

She scanned the cafeteria. "I don't think this is the best place to be talking about this."

"They're not listening to us," he replied flippantly. "Besides, I doubt they could figure out what we were talking about anyway. So, what do you intend to do?"

"I don't know."

Her eyes flew to his as he took hold of her hand. "I trust you, Sera, I do. But you need to think about this. This way only leads to unhappiness."

"I know that," she whispered. "I do. I tried to leave, Mike. I was at the door. He would have let me go, but I couldn't. I just couldn't. I know what I did when I went back to him. I can't let him go."

"And he can't let you go."

"He would have let me go yesterday."

Mike opened his eyes to stare at her. "I don't think he would have, Sera."

"You didn't see him," she whispered. "He would have let me go."

"I honestly don't think he would have. I have never seen him like this. I've known Liam our entire lives. I was there the day he broke his arm, the night he lost his virginity."

Mike's face reddened as he looked at her with chagrin. Sera met his gaze with a slightly amused smile. For all his bluff and bluster, Mike was more like a giant teddy bear.

"I don't think I want to know the circumstances surrounding that."

He snorted as he smiled. "No, you don't, but my point is he's my best friend, and he threatened to kill me if I hurt you."

Sera gasped loudly.

Mike laughed harshly, released her hand, and leaned back. "That was my reaction too. He won't let you go, Sera, but his life is going to be a lot longer than yours."

"So, what are you saying?"

"I don't know exactly. Look, most of this is none of my business, but some of it is. I like you, Sera, and I trust you to do the right thing. I think you will."

"And what would the right thing be?"

"You'll figure it out in time. Just don't take too long."

"I won't."

"Good."

She felt extremely uncomfortable in the following silence. "How did everything go last night?" she asked.

He frowned as he ran a hand through his hair. "Good. It's all taken care of; there's nothing to worry about."

"Where—"

"It's taken care of."

Sera knew he wouldn't tell her more. "Trying to make the moves on my girl?"

She smiled as Liam slid into the booth beside her and draped his arm around the back. Doug and Jack slid in beside Mike, shoving him against the wall. He scowled ferociously at them. Sera's heartbeat picked up as she realized she was surrounded by four men who could easily kill her.

She instinctively moved closer to Liam. He cast a curious glance at her before draping his arm around her shoulders and pulling her closer. "Hey, guys!" Kathleen cried as she bounded eagerly up to the table. Danielle looked a little breathless as she came up behind her. "I'm glad I found you!"

"So am I," Danielle muttered.

Sera stifled a laugh as Danielle slumped into the booth beside Liam. She knew how difficult it could be to keep up with Kathleen when she was in a mood. Kathleen chose to ignore Danielle as she grabbed an empty chair and pulled it over to sit down. "What do you guys have planned for tonight and tomorrow?"

"Classes," Sera answered instantly, not liking the way this conversation started.

"Nothing much, why?" Mike asked.

Kathleen grinned cheerfully as she practically hopped up and down in her chair. "I have an idea."

"That doesn't sound good," Mike said with a grin.

"Oh, it's an excellent plan. If you're willing to miss a couple of classes." Kathleen gave Sera a pointed glance. "You want to have fun, relax, and get away."

"So far it does sound like a good plan."

Sera groaned.

CHAPTER TWELVE

"Turn right up here," Kathleen directed from the backseat.

Liam turned the car onto a small dirt road beginning to get slick from the wet snow accumulating on it. "Are we going to get snowed in?" Doug asked.

"Nah," Kathleen answered. "My dad leaves a plow truck here. There are a few snowmobiles too, so we'll be able to get around no matter what."

They bounced along the road over potholes and rocks. Sera's head pounded with every rut they hit. She closed her eyes and forced herself to picture the cabin at the end of the road. She had come here with Kathleen once during their freshman year and loved it. When Kathleen suggested coming up now, she instantly jumped at the chance to go, despite her reservations about missing classes.

She had fallen behind already; she didn't need to fall behind any further. But the idea of spending a couple of days at the cabin, with Liam, was too tempting to refuse. She could do some studying and crack down when they got back. So what if she didn't get straight A's this semester, in the grand scheme of things it didn't seem that important anymore.

The cabin was at the top of a steep hill and set back in a grove of trees surrounding it on three sides. Snow was beginning to cover it, and old snow had been plowed into a big pile at the end of the road. Behind the large cabin, mountains loomed high against the night sky. Kathleen's family stayed here through the summer and visited it often in the winter.

Liam pulled the car up and turned the engine off. "Thank God," Jack said, throwing his door open. "My legs are killing me."

They piled out of the car, and Sera took a deep breath of the crisp air. Snow filtered down the back of her parka and caused a chill to run down her spine. When they left Massachusetts the weather forecast had predicted a chance of snow showers in Vermont. When they reached Vermont, they'd begun to predict at least six inches.

The wind howled around them, and Sera pulled her parka closer around her. "We'll get the stuff," Mike said. "You guys go inside and get the heat turned on."

"No problem," Kathleen said as she eagerly rubbed her bare hands together.

She bounded through the snow toward the cabin with Sera and Danielle following more cautiously behind. They huddled together on the huge, wraparound porch as Kathleen dug the keys from her pocket and threw the door open.

Kathleen flicked a switch, and the lights came on. The living room on their right had a large, cathedral ceiling with old wooden beams running across the top. The beams were the same dark mahogany as the floor, while the walls were a light, oak color. A large stone chimney took up the farthest wall, tapering as it went to the ceiling. Two large, creamy white couches furnished the room along with a forest green recliner, and a glass coffee table in the middle of the room. A long bar took up the far back wall. A green bumper ran around the edge of it. The wall behind it was a mirror, and alcohol bottles lined the glass shelves.

Kathleen turned down the hall on the left-hand side and flicked on another light switch as they passed a doorway on the right. The pale blue of the small half bath was warm and comforting. Kathleen moved on to the kitchen and to the thermostat on the wall. The floor of the kitchen was light blue linoleum. In the center was a small island crafted from light oak wood. The kitchen counters were pale yellow tile, and the cabinets were stained the color of dark wood. The long and shimmery curtains were a yellow that brightened the whole room.

Sera paused in the doorway and smiled as she leaned against the frame. She loved the cabin, with its elegant beauty and comfy furnishings. The smell of wood permeated the air to mingle with the hint of spices, crisp apple, cinnamon, and vanilla from the candles and potpourri scattered throughout the house.

"This place is beautiful," Danielle whispered.

"Thank you," Kathleen said as she turned up the thermostat on the wall. "I love it up here, but I never have a chance to come. Lack of transportation and all."

"We have to come here a lot more," Danielle said.

Sera looked around as a sense of peacefulness settled over her. This house was like a real home, a home she wanted to have one day, with a family of her own. A family nothing like hers. Her children would know they were loved and cherished.

Sorrow flickered through her as she realized the family she pictured would never be. Not as long as she was with Liam. Sera closed her eyes and took a deep breath to ease the pressure building in her chest. She forced herself not to think about it, not now. For now, she was going to enjoy her time here, and she wasn't going to let any depressing thoughts interfere with that.

Kathleen flicked another switch to illuminate the back porch. "Would you give me a hand?" she called over her shoulder.

Sera walked out to the screened in porch. Snow was billowing down outside as the wind howled through the trees. "It's getting nasty out there," Sera said as Kathleen began to grab piles of wood.

"We'll light a fire and cozy up," Kathleen said with a sly grin. "Just grab some wood for me."

Sera piled wood into her arms before following Kathleen back to the living room. "Danielle, why don't you put on some hot chocolate," Kathleen called over her shoulder.

The door opened with a blast of cold air as Mike, Doug, Liam, and Jack piled through. "Shit, it's cold!" Mike called, dropping his arm full of bags on the floor.

Kathleen grinned at him and playfully bumped his hip as she walked past him. "It *is* winter," she said.

"Actually, Miss Wise Ass, it technically still is fall," he retorted.

"Where do we put this stuff?" Jack asked as Doug slammed the door.

"Just leave it there for now. I'll get the fire started. The heat takes a while to warm up this place."

"Awesome place," Doug said. He took in the large staircase before him and the chandelier over his head before turning to follow Kathleen into the living room. "Sweet," he said, plopping onto one of the couches.

Sera grinned at him as she placed the logs next to the fireplace. Kathleen began to stack wood carefully inside of it. Liam sat on the other couch, while Jack slid in next to Doug. Mike plopped into the recliner and popped out the footstool. "I could stay here forever," he said as he closed his eyes and leaned back.

"I'm sure my parents would love that," Kathleen quipped as she lit a piece of paper and placed it under the logs.

"Do they know we're here?"

"They know Sera, Danielle, and I are here. They wouldn't appreciate you guys, but what they don't know won't kill them, right?"

"True, true."

Kathleen stood as the logs began to smoke and a flame sputtered to life. She shut the grate and stepped back with a look of pride on her face. "Hot chocolate's done!" Danielle called from the kitchen.

"Great," Kathleen said as she held her hands over the fire. "Who wants some?"

"I do," everyone said at the same time.

"Jack or Bailey's?"

"I'm in heaven!" Jack cried. "What could be better?"

"You actually getting laid," Mike retorted.

"Screw you."

Mike laughed and leaned further back in the chair. Sera shook her head as she headed back to the kitchen to help Danielle carry out the pot of hot chocolate and cups. When they came back to the living room, Kathleen had pulled out bottles of Jack, Tequila, and Bailey's from the bar and set them on the table.

"There are three bedrooms upstairs," she was saying. "One down here. The little bathroom's down the hall, and the full bath is upstairs."

"So what are the sleeping arrangements?" Mike inquired, his eyes focused on Kathleen.

She grinned at him flirtatiously. "Well now, we'll just have to figure that out later, won't we?"

Sera put the hot chocolate on the table, poured herself a glass, and added a generous shot of Bailey's to it. She sipped it as she slipped onto the couch next to Liam and kicked off her shoes. The fire crackled and sputtered as it filled the room with warmth. Liam slid his arm around her shoulders, and she snuggled closer to him.

"I figured Sera and Liam could have the room down here." Kathleen sipped her hot chocolate as she settled onto the floor. "Danielle and I will take my room, and the three of you can figure out the other two."

"Sounds good to me," Danielle said as she sat next to Sera.

She glanced over at Liam as he sat watching the flames. The light danced across his face and reflected in his eyes. A wave of possessiveness swept through her. He was hers, and she was never going to let him go. No matter what happened, no matter what she had to give up for him.

She looked back over at the flames, feeling completely at peace in Liam's warm embrace. No one spoke as the fire crackled and the room steadily heated. The grandfather clock in the corner chimed ten o'clock. "This is wonderful," Danielle finally said.

"Yeah," Jack agreed. "I can't wait to go skiing tomorrow."

"The ski hills are about two miles down the road; we'll take the snowmobiles out there. There's a hill right behind the house, I've come down it a few times, but it's not very big, and it's a bitch to climb."

They fell back into a lulled silence, watching the flames as they started to sputter down. Kathleen got up to toss more logs onto the fire then settled back down. An hour drifted by with little conversation.

When the clock chimed eleven, Sera stood and stretched her legs. "I'm pretty beat," she said.

Kathleen stood up and stretched. "I'll show you the room."

Sera followed her back to the main foyer. She stopped to pick up her bags as Kathleen walked to the side of the staircase. "We don't use this room often," Kathleen was saying. "But it's private," she added with a sly grin and a wink.

Kathleen stopped in front of the door behind the staircase and swung it open. Sera hadn't seen this room the last time she'd been here. Stepping inside, Kathleen flicked on the light switch. Sera looked in the small room and smiled. An oak bed, dresser, and an antique nightstand furnished the small room. A brass lamp with a rose-colored shade sat on the nightstand, and the entire room was done in a pale, rose color.

Liam appeared in the doorway behind her. "Very nice," he said as he rested his hands on Sera's shoulders.

Kathleen grinned. "I knew you'd like it. I'll leave you guys alone. See you in the morning."

Sera had to fight the urge to grab her and tell her to stay away from Mike as she left the room. She kept her arms by her sides though as Kathleen left.

"What's wrong?" Liam inquired as he placed his bags by the dresser.

"I think Kathleen is planning something with Mike."

He looked up at her as he opened a bag and pulled out a sweater. "That bothers you?"

"Yes. I don't want him to hurt her."

"They're both adults."

"That's not what I meant." Sera put her bags down and walked over to the small window. "How do you survive?" she asked. She hadn't asked yesterday because her mind hadn't thought of the question, but it did now, and she needed to know.

"Sera..."

She folded her arms over her chest as she turned back to him. "You said no more secrets, no more lies."

He ran a hand through his hair as he studied her. "I know what I said, and I meant it, but there are some things better left unexplained."

"I want to know," she whispered.

He leaned a hip casually against the dresser. "You won't like it."

"I don't care. I need to know."

"Fine," he relented. "It's easy enough to survive in a frat house; there's parties almost every night of the week. At first, it feels like an annoying hickey, and then it goes away."

Sera blinked as she contemplated his words. The thought of it disturbed her. How many girls had he done that to? She hated to think about it. Then, another more hurtful thought occurred to her. He had never taken her blood. Suddenly she felt as if there was something wrong with her, something about her he didn't want.

She turned her mind from those thoughts and focused her attention back on him. "Did you sleep with them all?" she whispered.

"Sera, come on," he groaned.

"Did you?" she asked.

His eyes flashed as he clenched his jaw. "Most, but not all."

Sera closed her eyes as pain clenched around her heart. Why had she even brought any of this up? All it did was upset her, and yet she couldn't stop herself from asking, from knowing. "How often," she had to stop and swallow heavily before finishing her question. "How often do you have to... to ah do this?"

"At least four times a week, preferably every day. Are you happy now?"

No, she wasn't happy. The thought of it turned her stomach in ways she hadn't thought possible. That was a lot of girls. A lot more than she ever wanted to consider. "How did all of you become like this?"

He blinked at her, obviously thrown off by her change in topic, and from the look on his face, more than a little relieved. He pulled out another sweater, opened a drawer, and dropped it in. "I've known Mike, Doug, Jack, and David since we were kids. We went to school together, lived near each other, and joined all the same teams in high school. We were never apart. During our senior year, I met this girl at a party. She was beautiful and vibrant, and she could have had anyone she wanted. For some reason, she wanted me.

"I saw her at a few more parties after that, and then she vanished. Last year, I ran into her again. She was at a frat party at my house in Buffalo. At first, I was amazed she even remembered me. It wasn't until later I realized she'd been looking for me."

He broke off as he bent and grabbed another sweater. "Why?" Sera prompted.

Liam shook his head. "Honestly, I don't know. For some reason, she fancied herself in love with me. She kept tabs on me over the years and always knew where I was. She came back for me last year because she thought I was finally mature enough to be changed. Of course, I didn't know that at the time.

"I left with her that night. However, unlike the last time, she didn't just feed off me and leave. She changed me. She was lonely, and she wanted someone to spend the rest of her life with."

"And you didn't want to be that person?"

Liam ran a hand through his hair. "No, I didn't. I didn't know her, or what she was. When I found out what she did to me, I freaked out. I took it about as well as you did. The last thing I wanted was to see her again, let alone spend eternity with her."

Liam grew silent as he seemed to drift off to another place. It appeared he forgot she was there as he relived his own, tortured memories. "What about the others?" she prompted.

Liam's gaze remained briefly unfocused before settling on her again. "The others are my fault," he mumbled bitterly.

"You changed them?" she blurted.

"No. She did."

"Then how is that your fault?"

"She changed them to get to me. When I refused her, she went after them. She thought if the others joined her, I would come to her too."

"But they didn't?"

"No, they didn't. Their reactions were just as strong, and volatile, as mine. When I found out what she had done, I swore I'd kill her if I ever saw her again."

"Have you seen her since?"

"No. She changed David last, probably because she found him last, and then she disappeared. None of us have seen her since."

"Is that why you came back here to college?"

He picked up another sweater and dropped it in the drawer. "Yes. David's coming back at the end of this semester. It's easier when we're all together, and the frat house is a perfect place for us."

"Why?"

Liam winced as he realized the mistake he'd made. They had just gotten off this topic, and he knew he was going to have to tell her the truth. "Because there are lots of girls who we can control, and attract to us, even if they're sober. But when they're drunk it's easier to make them forget we fed off them."

"They remember?" she asked in astonishment.

Shrugging, he grabbed another sweater. "Sometimes they know what's going on, but we can make it so they don't."

Her hand fluttered to her throat. "Have you ever done that to me?"

The sweater dropped from his hand. "No, I haven't. I wouldn't do that to you."

"Well, why not?" she demanded.

"Because those girls are more like cattle. I care way too much about you to do that to you."

She was suddenly very confused. She didn't want him drinking her blood, yet she didn't want him going elsewhere for something she could give him. Mostly, she just didn't want him not to want her that way.

"Is there something wrong with me?" she inquired.

"Are you serious?"

She nodded, unable to speak.

"There is nothing wrong with you, Sera. Would you have preferred it if I took it from you, without your knowledge?"

"No."

"All right then."

"But—"

He sighed angrily and slammed the bureau drawer shut. "There are no buts, Sera. I wouldn't drink from you without your permission."

Sera couldn't meet his gaze. She felt like a fool. She was acting like an idiot.

"I can tell you I've been very tempted," he said.

Her eyes flew back to his as she gaped at him. He gave her a sly smile as he leaned against the bureau and folded his arms over his chest.

"Seriously tempted," he said. "Your neck is very delicate, appetizing, and I can smell your blood, even from here. It's amazingly sweet."

The feral gleam in his eyes was utterly thrilling, and terrifying. A shudder worked its way through her as she instinctively responded to him.

She forced herself to take a deep breath. There was still so much she wanted to know, and she couldn't allow herself to be distracted now. "Did you attract me to you?" she asked.

"No. I talked to you; it's different."

Sera's forehead furrowed as she recalled how the world seemed to disappear the first time she'd seen him. Had he used whatever powers he possessed to make her feel like that? Had he been using his powers on her all along? "I have never used anything on you."

"That first time I saw you..." her voice trailed off as her throat constricted.

"Never, Sera. I felt something the first time I saw you too, but I have never used my powers on you. I could have made you forget what you saw the other night, changed your memory, but I didn't do it."

"Why not?"

"Because for better or worse I wanted you to know, I needed you to know who and what I am."

Sera's heart melted, and she found herself suddenly able to breathe easier again. "Then what is this ability to attract people?"

"There's a power inside me that draws people in, but they don't do anything they wouldn't want to otherwise."

"Even letting you feed off them?"

"We have to survive, Sera, what would you suggest we do? Kill them?"

"No!" she cried in horror. "But it seems wrong."

"Because it's not the nicest thing to do to a person, but most of them don't know what we're doing, and the ones who realize it, well, we just bend their will to ours and force them to forget it. No one leaves unhappy."

"Bend their will?" she croaked. "How?"

"It's easier when someone has been drinking. You just make them forget. It doesn't hurt them, and they don't even know we're doing it."

Sera wished again she hadn't started this conversation. Her mind was beginning to spin. She didn't want to know what else he could do. What all of them could do, but there was one more thing she had to know. "How have you been feeding since we got together? Are you still sleeping with all these girls?"

"No!" he cried indignantly. "Of course not. Sleeping with them was a bonus. It was a bigger rush, more power, more thrilling."

Nausea twisted in her stomach as she shook her head, attempting to clear her befuddled mind. "More thrilling?"

Liam was silently kicking himself in the ass. He should have kept his big mouth shut, but she was being so obstinate and aggravating right now. His brain wasn't having enough time to tell his mouth to stay closed.

"Sera, come on; you don't want to hear this."

She bit her bottom lip. No, she probably didn't want to hear this, but she had come this far, and she couldn't turn back now. "Yes, I do. I need to understand."

He groaned as he straightened away from the bureau. "Because we're pleasing ourselves in more than one way. The blood is a giant rush, and sex on top of it makes you feel like you could rule the world. Are you happy now? Is that what you wanted to know?" he demanded savagely.

She blinked back tears as her stomach threatened to empty itself. "No," she choked out.

The distressed look on her face was enough to help calm him down. "It's my past, Sera. I haven't slept with anyone since I met you, I don't ever want to, but I cannot change my past. No matter how much I wish I could now that I know you."

Sera took a steadying breath. "How are you feeding now?"

"I don't have to have sex with someone to feed from them. I can make the marks go away almost instantly. I can feed on them, and ten minutes later send them back into a party as if nothing happened. Their neck may be a little redder, or they may appear to have a tiny hickey, but no one is ever the wiser. They don't even know I was there."

Sera felt even sicker. She closed her eyes as she tried to block out the nausea in her stomach. She felt as if he was cheating on her, even though he wasn't. But she couldn't help feeling he was going to someone else for something she could give him. Something he had never asked her for *or* seemed to want from her.

What had she gotten herself into? What was she doing here? With him? With all of them? And now Kathleen was vulnerable to Mike. She wanted to run from the room, grab her friends, drag them out of the cabin, and flee back to safety. She opened her eyes to find Liam staring at her with a mixture of resentment and indignation.

"Changing your mind?" he sneered.

She'd wanted to know, and as promised, he'd told her the truth. She had brought this on herself. She knew what he was when she stayed in his room yesterday. She had made her choice and wasn't going to leave now. He needed to survive. She couldn't turn her back on him because she didn't like the way he did it.

"Kathleen," she whispered.

"Mike won't hurt her. I know he likes her and cares about her as a friend. If things progress, I'm not sure if he'll feed on her."

Sera felt like she was abandoning her friend, but there was nothing she could do. She couldn't go barging up there and tell

Kathleen to stay away from Mike. It wouldn't happen. In fact, it would only make Kathleen more determined to go after him.

Liam turned away from her. His shoulders slumped as if the weight of the world rested on them. She walked over to him, wrapped her arms around his waist, and rested her chin on his back. He remained rigid before his hands enclosed hers. He turned around, and she tilted her head to look up at him. He was so unbelievably gorgeous it made her tremble with longing. She ran her hands down his shirt and slipped them underneath to feel the warm skin pulled taut over his ridged abdomen. She pushed the shirt up. He lifted his arms so she could tug it over his head and toss it to the floor. Stepping back, she took the time to admire his solid chest.

She smiled as she stepped closer. His muscles rippled beneath her touch as he stopped breathing. Her smile deepened as she realized the full extent of the power she had over him. The power only a woman could hold over a man. She dropped a kiss on his chest and tasted him. His hands wrapped into her hair as he pulled her head away and lifted her mouth to his. She kissed him passionately, her tongue entwining with his as her body tingled with anticipation.

His hands leisurely roamed over her. Breaking the kiss, he pulled the sweater over her head and unhooked her bra. His eyes were clouded with passion as he gazed at her. His hands skimmed to the waist of her jeans as he unbuttoned them and bent to slide them down her legs.

She stepped out of them and kicked them across the floor. Stepping back to him, she pressed her full breasts against his chest as she slid her hands down to his jeans button and easily undid it. He watched her as she undressed him, making no move to stop her or touch her. She pulled his jeans and underwear down. Her eyes flicked to his erect cock as a wicked thought crossed her mind. Before she could have second thoughts, she knelt before him.

Liam inhaled sharply as he realized her intent. He caressed her cheek as she bent forward and ran her tongue along his hard shaft making it throb beneath her touch as she drew him into her mouth. His hands dug into her hair as his hips arched into her. Moving slowly, her tongue flickered along his head as she tentatively began to explore him. At first, she was hesitant, and more than a little afraid, but she became more confident as she felt his excitement rise and his hands guided her. Her hands wound around to grab his firm ass and draw him deeper into her mouth.

He groaned as his head tipped back and his body trembled with pleasure. He had never seen anything as erotic as Sera kneeling before him, making love to him with her delicate mouth. He stroked one of her breasts, relishing in the feel of the taut nipple as he rolled it in his hand.

Her mouth and tongue moved faster, and he knew he couldn't take much more of the exquisite torture. He pulled away suddenly and bent to pick her up. He lifted her as if she weighed no more than a feather. She smiled as she wrapped her arms around his neck.

He turned the light off and laid her on the bed. Even without the light, he could see her in perfect, beautiful detail. Her body trembled in anticipation as he spread her legs and kissed her delicate inner thigh. His eyes locked with hers as he levered himself between her thighs. She stared at him with a mixture of trepidation, and anticipation, as he parted her folds with his fingers and bent to her.

Pleasure soared through her as he pushed his tongue inside. She wound her fingers into his hair as he lifted her and pulled her against him. His hand rubbed against her outer nub as his tongue dove ever deeper. She was like molten lava and sweet honey rolled into one. Her body began to tremble uncontrollably, and she cried out as sparks of pleasure shot through her. He drove relentlessly into her, and her body arched against him as he savored every drop of her sweet juices.

He pulled away, leveling himself over her as he captured her mouth again. She lay trembling beneath him, sated, yet still aching for more. For all of him. Her hands wrapped around his back as she lifted herself against him. He teasingly rubbed the head of his shaft against her. She moaned and arched more frantically as she begged him with her body to take her. He couldn't resist her anymore as he drove into her with a loud groan. She cried out loudly as he stretched and filled her with exquisite heat.

She met his urgent pace with her own as she rocked against him. Her hands held onto his sweat slickened back as she wrapped her legs around his waist and drew him deeper into her. She relished in the feel of his body against hers. He left a trail of kisses across her face, her ears, and her breasts causing her blood to heat everywhere his mouth touched.

When he moved away from her neck to kiss her ear, she captured his head with her hands and guided it back to her neck. "Sera," he breathed in her ear. "No."

"Yes," she whispered. "Yes."

His body was trembling as he waged an inner battle with himself. A battle she was determined to win. She dug her hands into his hair, refusing to let him move his head away from her neck. She wanted this, she needed this, and she was going to get it. She had to know what it felt like. She eased him closer to her; his breath was warm and ragged against her throat. She felt trepidation trying to steal through her, but she refused to give into it.

"Please, Liam," she begged. "I need to know. I need to feel."

He began to slide in and out of her. She lifted herself to

take more of him into her as she held his head firmly in place. She moaned; her hands clenched in his hair as she turned her head to allow him better access.

She could feel the need driving his body savagely into hers. He still resisted. "Sera," he groaned.

"Please, Liam!"

Even if he wanted to fight her, he couldn't anymore. He could smell the sweetness of her blood; hear it pounding through her veins. It was too tempting, and she was so willing. He wanted her in every way. He needed to taste her, to have her. Suddenly, he felt like a feral animal, needing to mark its mate as his and only his. With a cry of possession, he sank his teeth deep into her neck.

She let out a startled cry as pain blazed through her. She fought against it for a second, but then it began to fade, and an overwhelming mix of emotions filled her. She could suddenly feel his overwhelming pleasure as he drank from her and moved within her. She could feel his thoughts and his love. Delight spread through her body as she realized she was helping him, joining with him, and they were one. She was satisfying the deep hunger pulsing through him.

She moved more quickly against him as his ecstasy spread throughout her entire body and his need became fevered. His urgency drove her to primitive levels she never knew existed, and never dreamed her body and mind could attain. Her nails clawed his back as shivers of delight ripped through her, causing her to arch high and tighten around him as her body shook with unending waves of ecstasy. She felt his orgasm rip through him, felt his pleasure as it poured from him into her mind and body.

He pulled away from her neck and looked down at her. His mouth was tinged with her blood, and the hungry, frenzied look in his eyes revealed the thing inside of him. But his eyes were also filled with a love so intense it melted her heart and made it impossible for her to look away from him.

She suddenly realized why he had never fed from her. He didn't want to hurt her. He was afraid whatever was inside of him would take control, and he wouldn't be able to stop himself. She also realized just how hungry he was, how badly he needed blood.

She let out a breath as anguish for him bloomed in her chest. He touched her face as the turbulent look gradually left his eyes. "Do I scare you?" he whispered.

She wanted to tell him, no, but she couldn't. "Yes," she admitted. "And no." She stroked his cheek as she sensed the distress her words caused him. "I know you would never hurt me," she whispered. "But—"

"But, you can't help but be afraid," he finished for her. "I understand."

She ran her finger over his lips and wiped away her blood. She held it before him, and he took it into his mouth, gently sucking on it. "You're not feeding well," she said.

He released her finger. "It's all right."

"No, it's not. Why aren't you feeding as often as you should?"

He dropped his hand away and eased himself out of her. He propped his head on his elbow so he could stare down at her. "Sera—"

"If it's because of me—"

"It's not because of you," he assured her. "It's just..."

"You feel guilty," she said as realization dawned on her. She felt an acute sense of guilt, along with relief. She'd thought he also enjoyed being with other women, even if he wasn't sleeping with them. Now she realized he didn't enjoy it, he felt as if he were betraying her, and he was depriving himself because of it.

"Don't worry about it."

"Of course I worry about it. I worry about you. I admit it bothered me, but I realize now it's something you have to do to survive. I don't want you depriving yourself because of me."

"I'm not."

"Yes, you are. I can feel it in you; your mind was in mine. I could feel your desperation, your need. Don't lie to me about this."

He caught her hand and dropped a kiss on it. "I'm not lying. Granted, I'm not feeding as well I used to, but I can handle it. Okay?"

She studied the planes of his face and the firm set of his jaw. "Yes," she said grudgingly. "Does your mind mingle with everyone?"

He smiled as he began to stroke her shoulder and down toward her breast. "No," he said as her body began to respond to his touch. "Only if I let it. I always keep my mind shut out of theirs, and theirs shut out of mine. It keeps them from knowing what's going on, and I don't care how they feel."

His finger caressed her nipple and teased it back to erection. "You knew what I was feeling too?" she asked, her voice husky with pleasure.

"Uh huh, every thought, every sensation." His hand skimmed along her body, and down between her thighs. "Did you enjoy it?"

"Yes," she whispered. She hadn't thought it was possible after everything she had just experienced, but her body was beginning to ache again.

His lips traveled down her neck, and then up to her ear. "Good," he murmured as he nibbled at her earlobe.

"Did you?" she breathed, as he pushed her down and lowered his body over hers.

"Immensely." His hands traveled over her body as his eyes

burned into hers. "Do you want to try something else?" he asked as his fingers slid into her.

She stared into his eyes as her body came alive with electricity. She ran her hands along his back, feeling the tautness of his skin, the sweat still coating them both, and the texture of his muscles.

"What?" she asked, her voice choked with passion.

"You can taste me," he said as the demanding movement of his hand caused her to moan. "Not enough to change you, but enough to let you inside of me again."

He kissed her neck; his tongue flickered out to brush against her flesh. "Do you want to?" he groaned.

He lifted his head to look into her eyes, kissing her, as his hand slipped away from her. It was the hopeful look in his eyes that made her want to do anything for him.

"Yes," she whispered. "I want as much of you as possible."

He lifted himself from her and stood up. She admired his naked body as he opened the closet door and searched through his bag. He grabbed something and came back to her. His body glistened with sweat and his erect prick pulsed in the dim light of the room. He moved with the elegance and grace of a powerful jungle cat.

A shiver of pure possession ripped through her. This big, powerful man was all hers, and she was never going to let him go.

He slid in beside her; his eyes fixed on hers as he slid on top of her, teasing her with his cock. His eyes locked onto hers as he put whatever he had grabbed on the pillow. His hands skimmed down her body, and back up to her face as he slid into her. He touched her adoringly as his eyes burned passionately into hers.

Her immense love for him was consuming her as she kissed him, touched him, loved him with her heart and body. He made love to her slowly, caressing her, enjoying her, and making her ache all over with need.

He had never tasted anything so sweet, so wonderful. Her blood flowed through his body, burned in his veins, and made him stronger. He wanted all of her, everything, and he knew he would never be able to get enough of her. Her hands roamed all over him as she learned every aspect of his amazing, perfect body.

"I love you," she whispered.

"I love you."

She could feel her desire mounting as he moved languidly within her. He stretched his hand over the pillow and brought out a knife. She watched nervously as he made a small slit at the base of his throat. Blood welled against his beautiful skin and began to flow forth. He guided her mouth to his neck and pressed her against him.

The blood was warm against her lips, metallic in her nostrils. She hesitated for a moment, suddenly frightened and unsure. His hands tensed upon her hair as he waited breathlessly. She could sense how bad he wanted this, how bad he needed it. She wanted to cry for the loneliness she felt in him. She couldn't deny him this. She could deny him nothing.

"Liam," she murmured before opening her mouth to him. The blood trickling into her mouth was warm and surprisingly sweet. She closed her mouth around him and began to drink deeply, sucking on his skin as she reveled in the taste of him. He moaned as he held her closer, urging her to drink deeper and to take more.

His body began to move faster with his urgency. She drank deeper, her body alive with pleasure as the need building within her reached a fevered level. She moaned as she clung to him, wanting more of him, needing more as his blood, his body, and his mind filled her. She experienced the possession he felt for her, and she knew he would never let her go, that she was his. At one point in time, that fact would have frightened her. Instead, it only served to arouse her further. He may think she belonged to him, but he also belonged to her, and she was never going to let him go.

His mind begged her to take more, to have it all. She responded by biting remorselessly on his neck and causing a fresh surge of blood to fill her. He moaned and pounded into her, grasping at her body frenziedly as an animalistic need overtook him.

Her body arched against his with the same wild need as his blood, and mind, overtook her. She was suddenly like a crazed animal that couldn't get enough. She wanted all of him in her. Their actions became uncontrollable as their bodies ground together, and their minds whirled.

Her body exploded in a blur of pleasure as lights filtered through her eyes. He cried out and thrust deeply into her as his body found its sweet release. She held him as she continued to taste him, and love him, and wanting desperately for him to feel her love like she felt his.

"You have to stop," he said.

It took her a minute to realize his words hadn't been spoken but were floating into her mind.

She didn't want to stop though; she didn't want him to leave her. She wanted to stay like this forever, feeling his love, and the peace it brought her. He rubbed her head as his own aching need spread into her body. Along with his fear.

His fear finally made her pull away. She expected to feel an enormous sense of loss, but she didn't. As she stared at him, she knew she would never feel alone again. She had found her home.

She kissed him as he licked the blood off her lips. He stared at her with a tenderness that melted her heart. "Nothing will ever separate us," he whispered. "You are inside of me, and I am inside of you."

"Yes," she whispered.

Her eyes drifted closed as exhaustion slipped over her body. She could barely keep her eyes open as he settled in beside her and pulled her into his arms. He kissed her, and she smiled as she snuggled into his chest. She drifted off to sleep with the security of knowing nothing could tear them apart.

CHAPTER THIRTEEN

Sera briefly forgot where she was as she stared at the unfamiliar rose-colored room. Finally remembering she was at Kathleen's cabin, she sat up and looked around the empty room. She was disappointed to find Liam gone already; she had planned a wonderful way to wake him up. She got up and slid on a pair of jeans, a turtleneck, and a sweater.

Standing in front of the mirror, she pulled down the collar of her turtleneck. She was startled to see the two dark marks visible on her neck. Liam had said they disappeared almost instantly, but they were vivid against her pale skin. She touched them and winced as they were a little tender. She would have to remember to ask him why they were still there.

Her gaze traveled to the window. Snow was still heavily falling outside. The wind was blowing forcefully, and large snowdrifts had begun to form. There was well over a foot on the ground already, and in some places, it looked to be two or three feet deep. The few inches of snow predicted seemed to have turned into a blizzard overnight. Swallowing nervously, she stared in amazement before turning away.

Digging out her hairbrush and toothbrush, she headed down the hall. The smell of eggs, bacon, and toast assaulted her nose, and her stomach rumbled in enthusiastic response. People were in the kitchen, moving around and talking as pots and pans banged together.

She slipped into the bathroom and pulled her hair into a ponytail. She brushed her teeth, placed her toothbrush on the sink, and left. Following the voices to the kitchen, she found Kathleen standing by the stove, happily scrambling eggs. Mike and Jack sat at the kitchen table, sipping coffee, and talking quietly. Danielle sat at the island, a cup of coffee and a plate of food in front of her.

"Good afternoon," Kathleen called out cheerfully. "It's about time you woke up."

Sera walked over to the coffee pot and poured a cup. She sipped it as she watched the snow falling rapidly outside. "Good morning," she replied. "I thought it was supposed to stop snowing last night."

"No such luck," Jack said. "While we were sleeping the storm turned into a nor'easter. It's not supposed to stop until tomorrow. They're calling for over three feet of snow. We might be here for a while."

"The ski resort is closed," Kathleen informed her as she slid a plate of eggs in front of Sera. "So are all the roads. They've declared a state of emergency."

"Thanks." They smelled delicious, and her stomach rumbled again. "These are good," she told Kathleen around a mouthful.

"Just call me Betty Crocker," she replied as she tossed the frying pan into the sink. "Doug and Liam went to get more firewood. By the time we need it, it should be dry. I dug out the flashlights and candles already. We'll probably lose the electricity sometime today, and the phones are already down."

Sera shook her head as she watched the snow fall with a heavy heart. The sky was gray and filled with thick white flakes. "Looks like a mess."

"It's going to be a real mess when the electricity goes," Kathleen said. "Hope you guys like cold food. I'm going to cook up some chicken and steak now, so we have something to eat later. I don't know what you're going to eat, Sera. I hope you like a lot of cold beans and salad."

"I'll make myself some rice," she said. "I'll be fine."

"Freaking vegetarians," Kathleen mumbled as she turned away.

"Maybe we'll just eat each other," Jack said flippantly.

Mike kicked him under the table, and a look passed between them. With horrifying clarity, she realized normal food wouldn't keep them satisfied. They had been counting on going to the ski resort, meeting people, and intermingling. "Crap," she said.

Mike gave a barely discernible shake of his head. Jack's eyes narrowed as he studied her. Danielle paused with her coffee cup halfway to her mouth as she cast Sera a questioning look. "What?" she asked.

"Oh, uh, nothing, I just hate it when the power goes out." She grabbed her plate off the counter and made her way over to where Kathleen was washing dishes. "The eggs were delicious, thanks."

"No problem," she replied as she took the plate from her hand.

Sera pulled a pot out of the cabinet and grabbed some packages of rice. She began to cook as Kathleen scrubbed enthusiastically and hummed under her breath. The screen door on the porch opened, she listened as Liam and Doug stacked the wood they had found.

"What a mess!" Doug cried as he shook the snow off his

jacket and head.

"There's well over a foot out there now, and some of the drifts are over four feet high." Liam rubbed his hands together as he blew into them. His eyes twinkled when they landed on her. She smiled back at him, suddenly feeling a little shy as she recalled everything that passed between them during the night. Her skin was starting to burn as he walked over and kissed her. "Good morning, sleepy head."

"Good morning," she murmured.

He chuckled as he tugged on her ponytail. "You think you're a little shy now, wait till you see what I do to you tonight," he whispered in her ear.

Sera's face flamed redder, even as her body began to tingle with anticipation. "I'd suggest everyone take a shower now," Kathleen said. She closed the freezer and turned to them with a chicken in her hand. "While there's still hot water."

"I'm first." Danielle stood and hurried out of the room.

Liam leaned casually against the counter and folded his arms over his chest as he turned to face Mike and Jack. The heat radiating off his body was enough to get her flustered. Sera frowned as she eagerly attacked the rice and stared at the white world surrounding them to distract her mind from the yearnings of her body.

"What is that?" Sera's attention was pulled away from the window, but she was too late. Kathleen had already grabbed her turtleneck and pulled it down. She jerked away from her and pulled it up to protect her neck. "Nice hickey," Kathleen teased.

Sera turned and looked at Liam, but he was staring at Mike and Jack. Jack's eyes were as large as saucers as they darted back and forth between him and Sera. Mike's eyes narrowed as he stood suddenly. "Can I talk to you?" he said to Liam.

A sinking feeling began to form in her stomach as she frantically stirred her rice. Liam glanced at her, but she hastily averted her eyes. She was scared to meet his gaze, afraid she would only see accusation there. "Yeah. I suppose you want to talk too," he said to Jack.

"I think we should all talk," Mike replied. He looked over at Doug who remained by the door, looking extremely uncomfortable as he shifted from foot to foot.

Sera listened to their footsteps as they headed upstairs. "What was that all about?" Kathleen asked as she slid the chicken into the oven.

"Boy talk," Sera replied with a shrug that belied the anxiety filling her body.

"So, you obviously had a good night," Kathleen taunted.

Sera couldn't help the grin spreading over her face or the blush. "Kathleen—"

"Oh, come on, it's written all over your neck and now your face," Kathleen replied laughingly. "I'm just glad you're happy. You love him, don't you?"

"Yes, I really do."

Kathleen put a pot of water on to boil. "I can see he loves you too."

Sera grinned at her, unable to keep the stupid smile off her face. "What about you? Did you have a good night?" she asked, trying to keep her voice as casual as possible.

"Slept like a baby."

"Alone?" Sera asked teasingly, even though her heart hammered with apprehension.

Kathleen grinned at her and pulled out a potato peeler. "Are you insinuating something?"

"Maybe."

Kathleen laughed happily and pulled out a potato. "I slept alone. All night. Well, unless you count Danielle in the next bed."

Sera felt a huge sense of relief as she turned back to her rice. "Do you like Mike?"

"Yeah, I do. However, I also like him as a friend, and I don't want to ruin that."

"What are you going to do?"

"Just see how things turn out. Go with the flow."

"Sounds good." Even though it didn't.

Liam stood by the window in the room Mike had slept in last night. Mike's clothes were laying across the small chair in the corner, and scattered on the floor. Doug stood by the other window, Jack sat on the bed, and Mike was pacing restlessly back and forth. "I don't even know what to say," he finally said.

"Then don't say anything," Liam replied coldly. "I don't see how it's any of your business anyway."

Jack snorted and leaned forward. "You know why it is. What is going on, Liam? Because the last time I checked, no one was supposed to know anything about us. Anyone who found out was supposed to be killed."

"First of all," he growled as he turned to face them. "She didn't find out, I told her. Second of all, if you even think about laying a hand on her, I'll kill you myself. Understand?"

Jack stared at Liam. "Are you serious?" he demanded in disbelief.

Mike snorted and stopped pacing to look at him. "He's serious."

Jack sat back. "We weren't supposed to tell anyone, unless we changed them," Jack finally said. "Which we agreed not to do without consulting each other first. Since none of us were asked, and Doug and I didn't even know she knew, I'm going to say that rule is shot. I don't know what you're doing, but you better let us in, and now."

Liam sighed angrily and began to pace. "Look, she knows, but she isn't going to say anything. As for changing her, that isn't going to happen."

"So she's going to grow old and die, and you're just going to pine away, forever young. You're right, you have thought this all out," Jack spat sarcastically.

Liam wanted desperately to punch him in the face. "If that's the way it is," he hissed. "Then yes!"

"I hope she wants that too. To be attached to a young guy, while she grows old. To never be married, to never have children. To constantly have to move, so people won't notice you're not aging. Great life you're giving her, Liam, truly."

His fists clenched as he took a step forward. Mike stepped in front of him and put a restraining hand on Liam's arm. "That's enough!" Mike said firmly. "We're not going to sit here and fight with each other! It's done and over with. Besides, Jack has a point."

Liam whirled on him.

"Hey, calm down!" Doug yelled. "Just calm down, all of you."

Liam forced himself to take a deep breath as he tried to steady his nerves. He wasn't angry at them; he was angry they were right. He turned away from them and walked back to the window. Leaning his head against the pane, he let the cool glass calm the fire in his body. The truth hurt, it always did, but he hated having it slapped in his face.

"Look, Liam," Jack said. "I don't want to fight with you, but you kept us in the dark on this. You purposely left us out. You must have had some concern she would say something about us."

"Maybe at first, but I would have stopped her."

"You would have killed her?"

Liam lifted his head from the glass and turned to face him. "No, I would have locked her away from the world, and from you, but I never would have killed her."

Jack shook his head in disbelief. "Shit, Liam. Shit."

"She's not going to say anything," Mike said as he ran a hand through his tousled hair. "There's more," he glanced at Liam, who shrugged. They might as well know it all now. Liam turned away as Mike filled them in on everything that happened with Jacob.

Jack sat with his eyes closed as he rubbed at his temples. "Are we safe?" Doug asked.

"For now."

"What do you mean, for now?" Jack demanded.

"So far nothing has been mentioned, and I got rid of the body."

"Where?"

Mike sighed and glanced back out the window. "An old stone quarry in Quincy. By the time someone finds him, if anyone ever does, we'll be long gone."

"And if people start questioning his absence?"

"They haven't yet."

"It hasn't even been a week!"

"We'll worry about it then!" Mike exploded. "For now, leave it be!"

"Wait till David finds out about this mess. Or do you not plan on telling him too?"

"I'll tell him," Liam stated. "When he moves out here."

"Fine."

Mike swore and resumed his pacing. "Why didn't you get rid of the marks, Liam?"

He could have gotten rid of the marks, he should have gotten rid of them, but pride and possession kept him from doing so. He liked knowing that, beneath her turtleneck, she was marked as his and no one else would have her.

He wasn't about to explain that to them though. "I just didn't."

Mike closed his eyes and turned away from him. "She knowingly let you feed off her?" Doug asked in disbelief.

"Yes."

"Crap," Jack muttered.

"From the cut on your neck, I'd say you returned the favor," Mike stated.

Mike stopped pacing again as the three of them turned to him in disbelief. "Will you change her?" Jack demanded.

Liam closed his eyes. Before, the answer would have been a simple no. But now, now, he couldn't bear to lose her, and he would if she remained human. But he couldn't force it on her; he couldn't make her do anything she didn't want to. He knew he would lose her if he did. "If she asks for it."

"Crap," Jack mumbled again as Mike resumed his pacing.

"Do you think she will?" Doug inquired.

"I don't know."

"I think she will," Mike said.

Liam's eyes went to him as he stopped pacing. "Why do you say that?"

Mike seemed to be gazing at something beyond this room. "She loves you, Liam. She allowed you to feed on her; she fed from you. You two are growing closer by the minute. It's only simple logic she won't want to lose you either."

A spark of hope began to bloom inside him, but he shoved it aside. There was no way to know what Sera would decide to do, and he wasn't going to pressure her. Dwelling on it now wasn't going to help.

"Jesus," Doug muttered.

"Well now, this is getting interesting." Jack climbed to his feet and walked over to join Doug. "Will you at least tell us if it happens?"

"Yes."

"No more secrets Liam, we're all in this together. You should have told us about Jacob sooner. We're at risk too."

Liam turned away from them. They were right, but he had been so worried about Sera, and what they might do to her, he hadn't spared them more than a thought.

"I think it's obvious we can trust her," Doug said.

"Yes, we can," Liam insisted.

"We can," Mike said. "Trust me, I was worried at first, but she won't do anything to hurt Liam. She'll die before that happens."

"Don't say that!" Liam snapped.

Mike stopped pacing. "It's true, Liam. She isn't immortal. If things start to go wrong with Jacob, if the hunters realize we're here, and they come for us, she is the one most closely linked to Jacob. It's her they'll go after."

Liam had been too concerned about everything else to even think about that. Even if they did find Jacob's body, he didn't think the police would put two and two together, but the hunters would. They would read about how he'd been killed, and they would know. And Sera would be their logical choice.

"Fuck!"

They didn't speak as Liam began to pace the room and mutter curses under his breath. "You two said not to worry about it, for now," Doug reminded them. "So don't."

"That was before I realized she is in more danger than we are!" Liam snarled.

"For now, there's nothing we can do. We can't even leave here. Which brings us to a more pressing problem right now," Mike said. "Food."

"Well some of us don't have that problem," Jack mumbled. Liam was about to start yelling at him until he realized Jack wasn't being his usual ass self. His face was drawn and pale as he looked at Liam with blank eyes. "Having them trapped in this house with us is not helping."

"I'm not going to touch her again. It's too soon."

"At least you've gotten something recently. The rest of us are hungry and tired, and their presence is killing us."

"It is," Mike said. "We didn't feed yesterday, and it's starting to get to us now. There's no way we're going to last another day, maybe two, if we can't get out tomorrow. It will start to get to you too."

"It's going to be difficult to control soon," Doug muttered. "We have to figure something out."

Liam looked out the window at the brilliant, white world. "Shit," he muttered as he ran his fingers through his hair. He knew they were right. Even though he had fed sooner than they had, it would start to get to him too. He didn't know what he would do when it did. He did know he wouldn't be able to go near Sera.

"Animals," he said, dropping his hand to his side. "We're going to have to get our hands on some animals."

"How?" Doug asked. "Go tramping through the woods in search of a rabbit?"

"What's up, Doc?" Jack quipped with a stupid grin on his face.

Liam laughed as some of the tension drained out of his body. Doug smiled and turned to look out the window again.

"Well," Doug said. "We do have supernatural powers; I guess it's time to put them to use."

"A rabbit won't even be an appetizer right now," Jack said.

Mike walked over to the window and looked out at the endless snow. "There aren't any other options."

"Well, men," Jack said. "It's time to get in touch with our hunting instincts."

CHAPTER FOURTEEN

Liam stepped off the porch and into the blinding snow. He clapped his gloved hands together as he huddled deeper into his coat in an attempt to ward off the chill of the whipping wind. He watched in disbelief as Danielle, Sera, and Kathleen rolled a giant ball of snow. They were laughing as they shoved and pushed at the huge ball, seemingly oblivious to the blizzard around them.

His gaze settled upon Sera. Her hair had fallen loose from its ponytail to hang in damp curls around her beautiful, reddened face. Her laughter filled the air, and he felt a smile tugging at the corners of his mouth in response.

"What are you doing?" Mike called to them.

"Building a snowman," Kathleen yelled back. She laughed loudly as she fell on her ass.

Sera helped her to her feet as the four of them walked over to join them. "Awfully big snowball. How do you plan on getting that one on top of the other one?" Jack asked as he pointed to the larger ball five feet away.

"That's what we have you big strong men for." Sera punched him playfully on the arm.

"Good plan," Doug commented dryly. "Glad we were informed."

"Well, now you know," Danielle said as she clapped her snow-covered mittens together. "So you can help us."

Unable to keep his hands off her, Liam pulled Sera into his arms. Her eyes sparkled as she tilted her reddened face up. "Don't you think you should go inside?" he asked.

"Nope," she said with a grin. "We're going to get Frosty together, and you're going to help."

"Actually," Liam said. "We were going to go for a walk."

Sera's brow furrowed. "In a blizzard?"

"You won't get far, the snow is too deep, and it's tough to walk through," Kathleen told them.

"That's okay, it'll be good exercise," Doug said. "Plus, I need to stretch my legs before we can't go anywhere."

"Not a bad idea; we'll come with you, right girls?" Kathleen said enthusiastically. "I'll show you the lookout. You'll love it. It's an old tree house where you can see everything for miles around. The mountains will be beautiful with all of this snow."

"You know, we weren't planning on going that far," Mike said.

"The look out's about half a mile away. It won't take us long to get there."

Liam's arms constricted around Sera as Mike shot him a look. Sera looked up at him, and then over at the others. Her brow puckered in confusion before her eyes widened in dawning realization. Her hands tightened on his jacket as she turned toward Kathleen. "I would rather stay here and finish the snowman."

"We can't finish it without their help," Kathleen retorted.

"We can roll the last ball and wait for them to come back,"

Sera insisted. "Besides, I'm getting pretty cold. If we walk through those woods, just think about how much colder we'll be."

Kathleen stomped her booted feet. "Yeah, I guess you're right," she relented.

Liam blew out a breath of relief as Doug and Jack swung shocked and impressed eyes toward Sera. Pride bloomed in his chest as he hugged her closer. "We'll let them get cold, and when they get back, they can put the snowman together for us."

"Ouch," Jack said as he grinned happily. "That's just wrong."

Sera grinned as she stood on her toes to kiss Liam. "Right?" she asked as she batted her eyelashes playfully.

"Blackmail is illegal," he whispered in her ear.

"Yes," she murmured. "But so is what I am going to do to you later."

He laughed loudly and kissed her; he was secretly pleased her shyness seemed to be slipping further away. His dick hardened as he thought about exactly what he was going to do to her tonight. "I'm going to hold you to that." He let her go before he decided to forgo the walk and carry her back into the cabin for the rest of the day.

"You'd better. Be careful."

She tossed an enticing grin over her shoulder before bouncing back over to Danielle and Kathleen. She sat on Frosty's stomach, a smug look on her beautiful face as snow fell to coat her hair, and clothes.

"Don't be too long!" Kathleen called after them. "It's going to get dark fast tonight!"

"We won't!" Mike yelled back.

They trudged through the knee-high snow into the woods. "I guess it's all right you told her," Jack said after a while. "She is kind of cool."

"She's more than cool," Mike joked. "She's hot."

"Oh yeah," Jack said eagerly. "She is definitely hot."

"Don't make me have to threaten to kill you again," Liam replied as some of the tension left his body.

"You might have too," Doug said as he slapped Jack on the arm. "I think he's in love."

They all laughed as they trudged their way up the mountain.

SERA CLAPPED the excess snow off her gloves and stepped back to look at their three massive snowballs. The snow was coming down faster, and the wind had risen to a thunderous crescendo. Branches cracked loudly as the trees bent and swayed from the force of the gale.

Her hands and feet had long ago gone numb, and her hair was a tangled, wet mass. Kathleen and Danielle had already gone inside to warm up. Sera knew she should go before her feet froze in the snow, but she couldn't stop staring into the woods.

She turned and headed back to the cabin. She wasn't going to make them magically reappear by standing there and staring. She wiped the snow out of her eyes as she pushed back an annoying piece of hair whipping across her face. "Hello!"

Sera almost fell over as she spun awkwardly around. A young girl waved to her from the edge of the forest. Sera waved back as the girl made her way forward, the snowshoes strapped to her feet made her journey easier. Sera stared in amazement and curiosity. She didn't know what could bring someone out in these conditions. The girl stopped before her; her black hair billowing in the wind contrasted sharply with the white surrounding them.

"Hi," Sera greeted in disbelief.

The tiny girl was amazingly beautiful. She had striking features that were delicate and sweet. Her nose was small and sloping, her full lips a deep blood red color. Her eyes were shimmering, blindingly brilliant, emerald orbs. Sera stared at her in amazement, and the girl stared back with a smile on her pouting lips. She was small and petite, at most she was five three, and only weighed a hundred pounds with all her snow gear.

"What are you doing out here?" Sera asked worriedly. "Is everything all right?"

The girl laughed easily, a sweet, tinkling sound that carried through the air. "Oh, yes," she said happily. "I live in the cabin about a mile down the road. I was going stir crazy, so I decided to go for a walk."

"Well, why don't you come inside and have some hot chocolate with my friends and me?"

"Oh, who are your friends? Maybe I know them."

"Kathleen's parents own the cabin, and she's inside with Danielle now. A few of our other friends went for a walk."

The girl studied her before she turned to look at the woods. "A walk, huh?" Something flickered over her delicate features that caused a chill to run up Sera's spine. The girl smiled as she shook back her midnight hair. "No, that's all right. I was heading to my friend's cabin. They'll be worried if I don't show up. Maybe I'll stop on my way back."

Sera felt as if there was something wrong with this girl, but she didn't know what, and she couldn't just let her walk through a blizzard without trying to help her. "Are you sure you don't want to come in and warm up for a couple of minutes first?"

"No, I really should be going. My name's Elizabeth by the way, but everyone calls me Beth," she said as she extended a small, gloved hand.

"Serendipity, but everyone calls me Sera. It's nice to meet you."

"That's unusual, pretty though. It's nice to meet you too."

"Thanks. Have a safe walk."

"I will. Have a good day."

Sera hurried back to the cabin and climbed the steps. She swung the back door open and stomped the snow from her boots as she pulled her gloves off. She stripped her jacket off and hurried into the warm kitchen. Danielle and Kathleen were sipping hot chocolate and bickering over a crossword puzzle as they sat at the island.

"They back yet?" Kathleen asked.

"No, not yet."

"For not wanting to go very far, they've been gone a while," Danielle said.

"Well over an hour," Kathleen muttered.

Sera poured a mug of hot chocolate and held it in her numbed hands to help warm them up. "They'll be back soon," she said as she took a sip.

"I hope so; it will be night soon."

Sera moved over to the island and stared unseeingly at the crossword. The heat was rapidly sinking into her as shooting pains lanced through her numbed fingers. "I just met a neighbor of yours," she said to Kathleen.

Kathleen frowned as she lifted her head from the puzzle. "A neighbor?" she asked. "Where?"

"Out back, after you guys came inside. She was walking through the woods."

Kathleen plopped her pen on the counter. "We don't have any neighbors, Sera."

Sera frowned as she took a sip of her hot chocolate. "She said she was from a cabin about a mile down the road."

Kathleen chewed on her bottom lip as she glanced back at Sera. "That's funny."

"Why?"

"Well, that would be the old McDonald place. His wife died last year, and Mr. McDonald died last month. As far as I know, no one bought the place."

"Maybe she was a grandkid or something?"

Kathleen picked her pen up. "Yeah, maybe."

"She said she was going to a friend's cabin."

Kathleen glanced inquisitively at her as she lowered her pen again. "Sera, were you hallucinating or something?"

"No, I swear! Her name was Beth."

"The closest cabin is five miles away. Unless she was planning on spending all night walking, I doubt that's where she was going."

"I'm just telling you what she said."

"Maybe you misunderstood her."

"No, I understood her just fine."

"Then she must have been lying."

Sera glanced back out the window. She couldn't see anything through the snow blasting against the pane. Apprehension gnawed at her stomach as she noticed the sky darkening. She took another sip of hot chocolate and placed the cup on the counter. "Maybe," she replied. "But why would she?"

Kathleen wrote down an answer.

"Are you sure that's right?" Danielle demanded.

"It fits, doesn't it? She may have been too shy to come inside."

She didn't seem at all shy to Sera, but she couldn't think of any other reason. "Maybe," she agreed absently. "Do you think they're okay?"

"I'm sure they're fine, stop worrying about it. Why don't you take a shower before the electricity goes out? I'm sure they'll be back by the time you're done."

The idea of a shower was very tempting. She was exceptionally numb, and she needed a distraction from her anxiety. "That sounds like a good idea. I'll be back in a bit."

"The towels are in the hall closet!" Kathleen called after her.

Sera gathered dry clothes and practically leapt up the stairs as the warm shower beckoned to her. Stripping out of her wet clothes, she adjusted the shower to the hottest temperature she could stand and stepped inside. The driving needles and fiery warmth helped to melt some of the tension from her body. Once the sting of her frozen extremities began to fade, she savored the warmth of the water, and the steam rising around her while she leisurely washed her hair.

The shower curtain suddenly ripped open. She cried out as she instinctively covered her naked body. Liam grinned at her as he stepped into the large tub. "Jesus!" she gasped, her hand flying to her heart. "Don't do that! Didn't you ever see Psycho?"

He laughed as he wound his hands into her wet hair and pulled her closer to him. She scowled at him, not ready to forgive him for scaring her.

"Sorry," he mumbled as he dropped a light kiss on her mouth. "But the idea of sharing a shower with you was too tempting to resist."

Her irritation began to melt as he nibbled on her lower lip. Her hands fluttered to his chest. "You're freezing!" she cried as she dropped her hands.

He grinned at her as he stepped under the warm water. "Come here and warm me up."

She raised a haughty eyebrow at him. "You come in here, scare me to death, take over my hot water, and expect me to be accommodating?"

The sensual grin he shot her warmed her more than all the hot water in the world. "Yes."

She couldn't stop the small smile playing at the corner of her mouth. He tipped his head back to let the water run down his face and plaster his hair back. Sera's mouth went dry as her heart began to pound rapidly in her chest. He was magnificent. Water slid over his bronzed skin, ran over his broad shoulders and chest in tantalizing rivulets that made her wish her hands were the water. He was already rigid, and the throbbing tip of his shaft glistened with beads of water.

She swallowed heavily as her body grew taut with anticipation. She looked up to find him watching her with a small smile and a feral gleam in his emerald eyes. He opened his arms to her, and she went into them eagerly. His mouth was savage as it seized upon hers. Sera was instantly swept away by his ardent need and her own.

His hands grabbed hold of her waist as he lifted her up and thrust deeply into her. "Hold onto me," he grated hoarsely in her ear.

She wrapped her arms and legs around him as he turned her into the wall. He braced her firmly and used his hands to guide her movements as she slid leisurely up and down, him. The water ran over her, flowing down her breasts and dripping off her nipples. His mouth took hold of one of them; he sucked upon the sweet bud as he licked the water from her skin.

She cried out, arching against him as her fingers curled into his neck. His eyes landed upon the marks on her neck. *His* marks. His body tensed as a powerful hunger ripped through him. His teeth instantly lengthened, and the animal inside of him sprang forth. An inhuman urge to mark her once more gripped him. He wanted her sweet blood, needed the resurgence of strength it gave him. He wanted to brand her as his own again so everyone would know she belonged only to him.

His hands tensed upon her hips, his need became savage as he relentlessly drove into her.

Her hands dug into his back as she sensed his urgency and met it. His mouth began to water as her head fell back and he could see the blood throbbing through her veins. He almost drove his teeth into her neck. Almost took her against her will. He managed to take a ragged breath and rip his gaze away from her tempting throat. He had to stop; he had to get away from her before he lost all control and devoured her completely.

"Sera," he grated. "Stop. We must stop!"

His words barely pierced her erotic haze. When they did, she dropped her head to gaze at him. His face twisted with beastly need, his teeth long and pointed. She could see the struggle for control in his clenched jaw and flaring nostrils. Although he drank from her last night, he had never looked like this. This Liam was feral, primitive, and utterly deadly.

"I can't," he somehow managed to say.

He gritted his teeth as he tried to regain control of himself. He had never lost it before, and he wasn't about to lose it now. Not with her. He took a step away from the wall and released his hold upon her.

"Get out of here, Sera. Stay away from me for a while."

"No."

"Sera!" he growled as he took hold of the hands wrapped around his neck.

"I said no."

Anger blazed through him as he met her determined gaze. "Damn it, Sera; I'm going to hurt you!"

"No, you won't. I know you won't." Her simple words managed to dampen some of the beast within him.

He groaned as his hands convulsed upon hers. "It's too soon."

"Will it change me?"

"Not if you don't drink from me, and I can control myself."

"Then control yourself."

"It's not that easy," he groaned. "Not with you."

Her smile was seductive as she lifted herself up and slid back down his cock. She rubbed her erect nipples against his chest and nipped at his bottom lip. She rose again and slid leisurely back down, her muscles clenched as she drew him all the way into her. He made no move to meet her actions as he stood stiffly. She felt so exquisitely good, but she was playing with fire, and she was going to get burned. He couldn't let that happen.

Sera rode him slowly, determined to melt his resolve; determined he would give her what she wanted. And she wanted all of him; consequences be damned. She bit lightly into his neck. "Sera!" he grated.

She couldn't stop herself from smiling. No matter how much he tried to fight her, and himself, she knew she would win. She nibbled at his neck as his hands grasped her hips. His grip was bruising, but she didn't care. She bit into his earlobe, tugging on it as he trembled and groaned.

Suddenly his grip eased as he pushed her against the wall. His body was hot as he throbbed and pulsed within her. His head fell to her shoulder, and she could feel his teeth pressed against her skin. His breath was warm as his inhalations became ragged and harsh. His body trembled as he fought for control.

"Take me, Liam," she whispered. "Make me yours."

He shuddered violently as her words drifted over him. All his control frayed. He drove fiercely into her as the creature within him took over. She tilted her head back as she rode him with abandon. He didn't know why she wasn't afraid of him, why she didn't want him to stop, and right now he didn't care.

All he wanted was to own her, to have her, and to have her know she was his, and only his.

With a savage growl, he bit deeply into her. She cried out in ecstasy as her hands tore at his skin and the overwhelming urgency for more threatened to destroy them both.

It was a while later before Sera was able to rouse herself from her languid state. She felt thoroughly sedated, deliciously satisfied, and very well used. Somehow, they had managed to make their way to the plush rug upon the floor. She curled one hand into it and smiled with contentment as she nestled closer to Liam.

His hand clenched upon her hip. She lifted her head to gaze down at his exquisite face and vivid green eyes. There was a haunted look in them as he searched her face. "Are you all right?" She smiled and nodded. "You should have let me stop."

It was the self-contempt in his voice that caused her hand to still, and her smile to fade. "No."

His hand took hold of hers as he levered himself onto his elbow. "I could have hurt you."

The sweet smile flitting over her face tugged at his heart. "No, you couldn't have."

Her blind trust and absolute belief in him caused an overwhelming wave of love to fill him. He had done nothing to deserve it, nothing to deserve her, and yet, he had her. Her eyes were dreamy as she gazed at him. Never had she looked more beautiful. A subtle glow radiated from her dreamy eyes. Her golden hair cascaded around her to spill onto the floor in a damp, wet mass he found impossible not to touch.

"Come on, let's get you dressed."

"Do we have to?"

"Unless you want to spend the rest of the night in this bathroom," he said briskly.

She grinned saucily. "This rug is rather comfortable."

To his amazement, Liam felt himself growing hard again. Her body was supple beneath his and utterly tempting. He didn't know what was wrong with him. His need for her wasn't diminishing at all; it was growing stronger each time he took her. He had fed on her last night, caught a few rabbits today, and fed upon her again, but suddenly he found himself hungry for more of her.

He would kill them both if this kept up. He shoved himself off the floor and to his feet. "Come on," he said more briskly than he had intended.

He took hold of her arms and pulled her to her feet. "Is everything okay?"

"Yes." He tossed her clothes to her and turned away. He couldn't look at her anymore. He needed to get out of this room. It was growing smaller by the second.

Sera tugged her jeans on as she watched him. His back was tense, and his jaw clenched as he stalked over to turn the shower off. The water had long since grown cold, and the steam in the room had evaporated. She slid her turtleneck on and then tugged on her sweater. He stood by the sink, pulling on a pair of jeans as he kept his back to her. It was then she noticed the claw marks marring his smooth, taut skin. She couldn't believe *she'd* done that to him. A blush burned her face as she lowered her gaze. What had he turned her into?

She bit her bottom lip as she searched for something to turn her mind away from her thoughts. "Was your walk successful?"

"Yes. You ready?"

His clipped tones drew her attention back to him. She frowned as she pulled her turtleneck higher. "Liam, what's wrong?"

He kept his back firmly to her as he gathered the clothes off the floor. "Nothing."

"Are you mad at me?" she asked in confusion.

"No."

"Then why are you acting like it?"

He scooped the last article of clothing from the floor and shoved them onto the counter. He ran a weary hand through his hair as he turned to face her. "I'm not mad at you, Sera."

No matter what he said, his voice was still cold and strained. She stared at him in confusion. "Then what is the problem?"

He frowned as he studied her. She was a little paler than normal, and there were shadows under her large, luminous eyes. "How do you feel?"

"I feel fine."

"I've taken a lot of blood from you, Sera, are you sure you're all right?"

"I'm fine." Though her words did nothing to ease the harshness in his face and the coldness in his eyes. "Liam, what is wrong?"

He opened his arms to her. "Come here." She hesitated before stepping into his embrace. "I'm not mad at you. I'm mad at myself, and I'm confused."

Alarm constricted her heart. Was he confused about her? About the way, he felt about her? "About what?" she asked in a strangled voice.

He pulled slightly away and tipped her chin up with his finger. "About the loss of control I have when I'm around you."

She frowned at him. "What do you mean?"

"Sera, what happened earlier shouldn't have. I should have been able to stop myself from changing, from feeding off you. But I had no control; it just took over. And now I would like nothing more than to do it again."

He expected to see dread or revulsion in her eyes. Instead, they clouded with passion as she bit into her enticing bottom lip. "Oh," she whispered.

Sera shivered with want as his words stirred something deep inside her. She had no idea what she was becoming, what he brought out in her, but words that should have warned her to stay clear of him, at least for a little while, only served to make her tremble with want and need. Was it because his blood coursed through her veins? Was there now part of a vampire inside her?

The thought should have terrified her, it didn't.

He tugged at the edge of her turtleneck and pulled it down. He gazed at the two marks marring the creamy perfection of her skin. *His* marks. His eyes dilated as his teeth instantly lengthened. He wanted to brand her again, to taste her again, and to fill her veins with his blood.

He ground his teeth as he willed the demon inside him to subside. Gradually, he was able to regain some control of himself and meet her eyes again. "I thought you said the marks faded," she whispered as she watched him.

"They do when we use our saliva to make them close faster."

Her brow furrowed. "Why didn't you do that with me?"

His eyes flashed red for a second. "Because I wanted you to bear my mark. I want everyone to know you're mine. And you are mine, Sera. No one else is ever going to touch you."

Normally, she would have been irritated by his high-handed, possessive tone. She would have been enraged at the thought of anyone thinking they owned her. Instead, she found herself thrilled by it.

"I mean it," his eyes flashed again as the creature within neared the surface. "If anyone touches you..."

She placed her finger over his mouth to silence him. A muscle in his jaw twitched as his eyes gleamed violently.

"I am yours, Liam," she whispered. "Only yours."

He closed his eyes as he fought against the vampire seeking to break free and finish what it had started. Finally, her words sank in and helped ease his need. "Good."

"And you're only mine, right?"

He opened his eyes. He smiled at the ferociousness in her gaze as he traced her swollen lower lip. "Yes."

She grinned as she stood on her toes to kiss him. "We better go before they send a search party for us."

She pulled her turtleneck back up. Liam's hands clenched as he fought the urge to rip it back down so everyone could see what was beneath it. He knew he couldn't risk Kathleen and Danielle realizing it wasn't a hickey she bore though.

CHAPTER FIFTEEN

BY THE TIME they made it downstairs, the electricity had gone out. Kathleen had already placed candles around the house, and they followed the light of them into the kitchen.

"So, what do you guys want to do?" Mike asked when they entered.

Sera glanced around. Mike, Doug, and Kathleen were sitting around the middle island and smiling knowingly at them. Jack and Danielle were sitting at the table arguing over the same crossword puzzle from earlier. "How about strip poker?" Doug suggested with a mischievous grin.

"Sounds like a plan to me," Jack said eagerly.

"Count me in," Mike said. "Girls?"

"I'll get the cards," Kathleen volunteered.

Liam's stance was rigid as he took a step closer to her. "I don't want to play," she said.

"Of course you will!" Kathleen retorted as she held a candle above the kitchen drawer she pawed through. "It will be fun! Right, Danielle?"

"Sounds good to me," she answered.

"You're playing, right Liam?" Jack asked.

"No," he replied.

"Oh, come on man, lord knows when you'll get a chance to see another girl naked."

Kathleen laughed as she continued to fumble through the drawer. "Who said I wanted to?" Liam retorted.

"Ugh, you guys are sickening," Kathleen closed the drawer and held up a pack of cards. "For crying out loud Sera, you need to see more than one naked man in your lifetime."

Sera shook her head. She could feel the anger radiating off Liam, and she knew this was not a good idea. "I don't want to strip," she said.

"Don't worry," Kathleen said as she grabbed hold of her hand. "We're going to win this game."

"No," Liam said.

"Come on; it will be fun!" Kathleen urged.

"Yeah," Mike enthused.

"I know I wouldn't mind seeing some fine female flesh!" Jack cried eagerly.

Liam was so fast she never saw him move until his arms were locked securely around her waist. "I said no," he said.

Even Sera was astounded by his behavior as she turned to look at him. Kathleen gaped at him as Danielle froze in the middle of standing up. Doug, Jack, and Mike all turned to look at him.

"Liam," she said soothingly.

The set of his chin and the twitching muscle in his cheek let her know he wouldn't tolerate this. She recalled his words in the bathroom, and she knew, without a doubt, he would attempt to kill everyone here before she ever removed an article of clothing. She would not allow that to happen. Besides, she didn't want to play. The idea of seeing Liam stripping was more upsetting to her than having to remove her clothes. A spark of anger shot through her as she thought about Kathleen and Danielle looking on what was hers.

"I don't want to play," she told them. "Why don't we play rummy, or something else?"

Kathleen stared at her, and then back up at Liam. "Fine, can I talk to you for a minute, Sera?"

She knew Kathleen almost as well as she knew herself, and she knew what Kathleen had to say was important. Her mind instantly shot to Mike. If there was any way she might be able to help her friend from being hurt, then she was going to do it.

"Yeah, sure."

"Good. Come on, Danielle."

She squeezed Liam's hands reassuringly. They eased on her waist and finally released her. She cast him a small smile before following Kathleen out of the kitchen. She didn't head to the living room but veered sharply to the left. Sera lifted an eyebrow but followed her down the hall. Kathleen swung the door to Sera's room open and stepped inside. She waited for both of them to enter before closing it.

"What's going on?" Kathleen demanded instantly.

"What are you talking about?" Sera inquired.

Kathleen planted her hands firmly on her hips. "I mean, what is going on?"

"Kathleen—"

"No!" she cut off abruptly. "Okay, you don't want to play strip poker, I understand that. I've known you for three years now, and I know it's not your kind of game, but what just happened in there?"

Sera's mouth dropped further with every higher pitched word Kathleen shouted. "What are you talking about?" she asked.

Kathleen's nostrils flared as she inhaled harshly. "What am

I talking about?" she sputtered in disbelief. "What am I talking about?"

"Kathleen, calm down."

Kathleen took a deep breath and closed her eyes before opening them again. "Sera, he's so possessive of you! He's so... oh, I don't know. You didn't see the look in his eyes. For a second I thought they were red!"

Sera's heart leapt into her throat, but she managed to keep her face completely impassive. "That's crazy, and I have no idea what you're talking about."

Sera worried Kathleen was going to start screeching again. Danielle headed her off. "I thought I saw the same thing, but it was only the candlelight. However, I think I know what Kathleen is talking about."

Sera cast her a glance. "And what would that be?" she asked.

"Has he hit you?" Kathleen demanded.

"What?" Sera was so aghast the word barely squeaked past her throat.

"Has he hit you?" she almost screamed.

"Kathleen, calm down, please," Sera said.

"Don't tell me to calm down!"

Danielle turned to her. "You need to calm down."

For a moment Sera was afraid Kathleen's head was actually going to explode off her shoulders. Then, she took a deep breath, closed her eyes, and seemed to gain some control of herself. "I'm calm," she said. Her clear blue eyes landing upon Sera again. "Has he hit you?"

"Of course not."

"Sera, I am not kidding here. You're my best friend, and I love you. I don't want to see you hurt."

"Kathleen—"

"No!" she snapped. "He acted like he owned you! He acted

like you didn't have a mind of your own. You two love each other, fine. But what happened in there was not normal, and you know it!"

What happened wasn't normal, she knew that, but she also knew Liam would never hurt her. He would die before he ever harmed her. She knew that, as surely as she knew she needed air to live. She also knew she had felt the same way as Liam about the idea of anyone seeing him naked. Maybe it wasn't normal, maybe it wasn't right, but it was the way it was. He was different, their relationship was different, but there was no way Kathleen, or Danielle, could understand.

"Kathleen, I think you're misunderstanding—"

"No I'm not!" she yelled. "Has he abused you?"

"Never!" Sera cried.

"Because if he has, I'll kill him!" Kathleen continued as if Sera hadn't spoken.

"Kathleen—"

"Has he? Has he hit you?" Kathleen was close to screaming like a banshee again. Sera winced at the shrill tone.

"No!" she yelled. "He would never hurt me. Now calm down!"

Kathleen began to pace as she mumbled under her breath. "Sera," Danielle said serenely. "We're just worried about you."

"There's no need to be."

Kathleen took a deep breath and spun to face her again. "He was acting like the men you hear about," she said. "The ones who think they own their wives or girlfriends. The ones who beat them. If he's doing anything wrong, please tell us."

Tears bloomed in Kathleen's eyes as her lower lip began to tremble. Sera crossed to her and hugged her. "He's not," she vowed.

Kathleen hugged her back as sobs rocked her body. "Would you tell me if he was?"

"Yes Kathleen, I promise I would tell you if he was."

"You didn't tell me before," she whispered so quietly Sera barely heard her.

"This is different Kathleen."

She took a step back. "He really hasn't?"

"No. I wouldn't stay with someone like that. But Liam would never hurt me. He would chop off his own hands before he ever raised one against me. He really would, Kathleen."

Kathleen's stare burrowed into her. "If you say so. But if I ever see one unexplained bruise on you, or if I ever see him mistreat you, I will beat the shit out of him, agreed?"

The idea of Kathleen trying to beat Liam was even funnier than the idea of Liam hitting her. "Agreed," she vowed.

"What is the matter with you?" Mike demanded.

Liam turned to him as Sera, Kathleen, and Danielle disappeared down the hall. "What do you mean?"

"You didn't see yourself. Are you trying to get us all killed? Do you want to give us all away?"

"I don't know what you're talking about."

"Your eyes were red," Doug said. "For a second Liam, your eyes were red."

Liam frowned as he folded his arms over his chest. "What is going on?" Mike asked.

"I don't know," he admitted reluctantly.

"What do you mean, you don't know?" Jack demanded.

"I mean, I don't know."

"But something is going on?" Mike prompted.

Liam ran a hand through his hair. "She's mine."

"We all know she's your girlfriend, now what is your point?"

"My point," he grated. "Is that no one else is going to see her."

"It's only a game," Doug muttered.

"Not to me!" he shouted.

"Liam, I think you need to tell us what is going on because it's pretty clear to me you're close to losing it," Mike said.

Liam's jaw clenched as he stared at them. "I don't know what's going on. All I know is I can't control myself when I'm around her."

"What do you mean?" Jack asked.

"Exactly what I just said."

They exchanged bewildered looks before turning back to him. "I think you're going to have to be more specific," Mike insisted.

"I don't know how to be. I've never felt like this. I've never acted like this. I've never lost control like this. You're trying to get me to explain something I can't. All I can tell you is I will kill anyone who tries to harm her. I will kill anyone who tries to take her from me. I will never let her go."

"Yes, we understand that, but there's more going on here, Liam," Mike said. "That doesn't explain your lack of control."

"Didn't you hear me?" he spat. "I can't control myself when I'm around her! At all!"

"Are you afraid you'll hurt her?" Doug asked.

Before his answer would have been a resounding no. Now, he wasn't so sure. "I might," he reluctantly admitted. "I don't want to, and she's sure I won't, but I can't stop myself."

"Stop yourself from what?"

"From tasting her! From having her!" he cried.

"Maybe you should get away from her for a while, at least until we can figure out all of this," Doug suggested.

"That is not an option."

"Liam—"

"No!" he cut Mike off forcefully. "That is not an option!" His teeth began to lengthen as his hands clenched at his sides.

"Jesus," Jack muttered. "Okay, it's not an option, just calm down."

Liam ground his teeth and took a deep breath. What was the matter with him? He closed his eyes and leaned against the wall as he rubbed at his temples. Maybe he should get away from her before he hurt her, or someone else. But even the idea of leaving her brought the beast forth again. Bloodlust and a wave of possessiveness burst through him, seizing his muscles and shaking his control.

"Okay, we'll figure this out," Mike said. "But you need to control yourself, Liam. You're going to lose it, and you can't afford to do that in front of Kathleen and Danielle."

"I know."

"You will lose Sera if something happens to her friends."

His eyes flew open, and they all took an involuntary step back. "Nothing is going to happen to them, and I will not lose her!"

"Hey, guys! Come on!" Kathleen called. "Let's play cards!"

Liam glared at them before turning and leaving the room. "What is going on?" Jack demanded.

"I don't know," Mike said.

"What are we going to do? He's snapping."

"I don't know."

"You're not helpful!"

"I don't see you putting forth any ideas!" he retorted.

"We're not going to figure it out now," Doug intervened. "And he will shred us to pieces if we even try to interfere."

"Yes, he will," Mike agreed.

"Maybe it just needs to work itself out," Jack muttered.

"Well, it's going to have to, or he's going to lose it, and the consequences will be devastating. Come on, let's go."

They followed Mike out of the kitchen and into the living room. Candles were set around the room. Their tiny flames cast shadows over the walls and added a cozy aura of warmth. Kathleen and Sera were pulling the cushions off the couches and plopping them around the coffee table.

They settled in as Danielle began to shuffle and deal out the cards. "Five card draw," she announced. "Nothing wild."

Sera poured herself a glass of Peachtree Schnapps and orange juice. Everyone gathered drinks and sat back to stare at their cards. Liam slipped his hand onto her leg and squeezed her thigh.

Liam stared at his cards as everyone laughed and joked around him. His thoughts were tumultuous; he couldn't get a handle on himself. Sitting this close to Sera, he could smell her temptingly sweet blood; hear it pounding in her veins. He'd always been able to smell blood, and hear it, but not like this. Before, he could shut it out. Before, it never pulsed inside of him in an answering rhythm that enhanced his hunger. It had never called to him like this.

It took every ounce of control he possessed not to take her and brand her again.

Time seemed to drag at an excruciating pace. Every second was pure torture. His hands clenched upon his cards. Sera placed her hand on his thigh. He shifted as he instantly became erect. Seizing hold of her hand, he forced it to remain still. The smile she sent him was completely knowing, and utterly enticing.

"Witch," he murmured.

"Yep," she agreed happily.

"Okay," Kathleen announced. "Let's see what we've got."

He laid his cards on the table as a knock on the door resounded through the living room. "I'll get it," Sera volunteered as she hopped to her feet. She had already lost most of her change, and she stood no chance of regaining it.

"Who could that possibly be?" Kathleen pondered as she scooped her winnings up, again.

Liam turned to watch as Sera disappeared into the foyer. The minute she stepped out of his sight, he wanted to go and make sure she was safe. "Hi," she greeted. "Sure, come on in, you must be freezing. Have you been out there all day?"

"Yeah," a girl replied. "I got lost. I just found this place again."

"That's awful," Sera said. "We were just playing a game. I'll introduce you to everyone."

Liam frowned as he stood. There was something familiar about the girl's voice. Mike, Jack, and Doug rose as Sera entered the room, followed by a small girl. Liam's heart began to jackhammer rapidly; the breath froze in his lungs as he gaped in disbelief at the beautiful woman behind Sera. "Guys this is—"

"Beth," Mike breathed, silencing Sera in mid-sentence.

"Hello, everyone," Beth said, a sly smile on her face. "Am I interrupting something? Dinner perhaps?"

Liam's breath gradually returned to him. Jack and Doug remained frozen, staring in awe. Kathleen's eyes were wide as she looked everyone over. Danielle stood beside her; her eyes narrowed as she watched Beth. Beth scanned the room as she idly trailed her hand across the back of the couch.

"Lovely place," she commented as she moved closer to Liam. "How are you doing, Liam?"

Liam glanced over at Sera. She was only ten feet away, but it suddenly seemed like a mile. She stared at him in confusion, her eyes startlingly violet in the candlelight. "You know each other?" Kathleen asked in disbelief.

"Yeah," Mike said. "We do."

"You could say that," Beth responded as she glanced around the room. "I see you four are back together, but where's David?"

Sera's hand flew to her mouth. Liam's head turned toward her as panic burst through him. He took an instinctive step toward her as Beth focused on her with gleaming eyes. "Who's David?" Danielle asked.

"Just an old lover," Beth replied nonchalantly. "Like all the guys in this room."

"Who are you?" Kathleen demanded.

"Oh, I'm just an old friend, long forgotten." Her eyes remained locked on Sera; her head tilted to the side as she studied her. "Oh my," she finally said as a grin spread across her face. "You've been tasted, and marked."

Sera took a step back, Liam turned to face Beth.

"I can smell it on you. I can smell *him* on you." Beth's eyes filled with unbridled wrath as she focused on Liam. "I never thought I would see it happen, did you, boys?" She circled the room as her gaze moved over Mike, Doug, and Jack. "I never thought Liam would settle down with someone, never mark his territory. But she does smell like you, Liam, and her blood is very sweet. You reek of it."

Liam's hands clenched into fists. He could feel the beast fighting to rip free. Beth was a threat to all of them, but she was especially a threat to Sera. "What do you want, Beth?" His voice revealed his barely contained temper.

Beth released a tinkling laugh that would have been beautiful if it wasn't filled with ice. "I love it."

Liam glared at her as she smiled sweetly. She looked away from him and back to Mike, Doug, and Jack. "Hello boys, how have you been?"

Doug looked extremely uncomfortable, but Jack and Mike glared at her. "Fine, Beth," Mike grated out. "You?"

"Oh, I've been better."

"I don't know what's going on," Kathleen said. "And I have a feeling I don't want to, but I think it's time for you to leave."

"So soon!" Beth cried in mock indignation. "No, I don't think so. These guys owe me, and they're going to pay up, especially since I'm so hungry."

"Well," Sera said as her eyes locked on Beth's. "There's chicken and rice in the kitchen. I'll get you some if you want."

"You think you're cute, don't you?" Beth's eyes narrowed angrily. "Well, I don't. Don't push me, sweetie; I won't be as gentle as Liam here."

Sera's chin tilted in indignation as her eyes flared.

Beth let out a false, hateful laugh, and turned back to Liam. "You picked a live one, literally." She spun back around to Sera and forced a smile to her face. "You remind me of me, and I don't like that."

"Neither do I," Sera replied.

Beth started to move around the room again. "I like this place. I could live here."

"That's good to know," Kathleen said. "But, I don't care. I would appreciate it if you left."

"But I'm just getting to know everyone." Beth walked closer to Mike, Jack, and Doug. "Then again, I already know you three. Created you, made you what you are, and how do you repay me? How do you thank me? You leave me, that's how." She ran her finger along Mike's chest as she walked past him and moved on to Doug. "I don't know what's wrong with me. I'm not mean, and I'm not ugly." She trailed a finger across Doug's chest as she continued to ponder aloud. "Maybe it's just because of what I am. What do you guys think?" She asked Jack as her finger trailed over his chin.

"I'll agree with that," Kathleen said.

Beth turned to her and smiled. "Sweetie, you don't know

what you're involved with here, but I would suggest keeping silent before I rip your throat out," she hissed coldly.

Kathleen took a frightened step back. "I think it's time for you to leave," Liam growled.

Beth laughed and walked back to him. "Oh, Liam, trying to get rid of me again? Why? Is it because of her?" she asked as she nodded to Sera.

"It's time to go."

Beth's eyes flashed red; it was obvious she was close to losing it. "I'm not ready!" she spat. "I think I might even stay a while, now that I've been invited. Know what I mean?"

Fury boiled inside of him as he clenched his fists. "I know what you mean. I think you better figure out what I mean when I say it's time for you to leave."

"Do you boys want me to leave?" she called over her shoulder.

"We didn't leave you because we wanted to be around you," Jack replied.

Liam let out a snort of laughter. "It doesn't look like you're wanted, Beth."

"I could have told you that," Kathleen said coldly.

Beth's eyes flashed again, and then she smiled. "Yes, but it was your lover who invited me in."

Her head tilted back to gaze at him as she stopped before him and rested her hand on his chest. Hungry and ferocious, her gaze traveled to Sera. The sight brought the beast within him rushing to the front.

"Ah, so it has begun," Beth whispered.

Her words managed to suppress the monster within him. She knew what was going on, knew what was happening to him. "What has begun?" he asked.

She grinned as her hand stroked his chest. He grabbed hold

of it and squeezed. Her eyes filled with pain as she fought to pull free.

"What has begun?" he demanded harshly.

She finally managed to rip her hand free. Her jaw clenched as her eyes burned a brilliant, blood red. Then, she smiled as she took a step closer to place her hands on his chest again. "I'll never tell," she taunted.

Liam shoved her back. Beth stumbled, regained her balance, and came up spitting. He braced himself for her attack, but it didn't come. Instead, she took a deep breath and smiled chillingly. "Get out of here!" he spat.

"Yes, I think I will go," she said. "But I *will* be back." She turned to walk away. Liam launched forward to block Sera before Beth could get near her. Beth's eyes blazed as he grasped hold of Sera's arms and pushed her firmly behind him. Mike and Doug moved forward to stand beside him, while Jack stood behind Sera.

"She's dead, Liam. I will get her," Beth vowed. "I'll get the other two as well."

Her words ripped the beast out of him. His eyes blazed as his teeth instantly sprang forward. "I'll kill you if you ever come near her again Beth. Do you hear me?"

"I'm older and stronger than you."

"Not all of us though," Mike said.

Beth's eyes flickered toward him before settling on Liam again. "I will get to her, and I will drain her dry."

The room suddenly became a shade of red as the bloodlust tore from him. Sera's hand grabbed hold of his arm as he surged forward.

"Liam, no!" she cried as she pulled him back. "Not here! Please!"

Mike and Doug moved forward swiftly. They were certain there would be a bloodbath, certain his rage would cause him to go after Sera, as well as Beth. Mike had never seen him so incensed, so far out of control. Jack seized hold of Sera's shoulders, ready to rip her out of the way if Liam spun on her. They were all stunned when he froze in mid-launch and took a shuddery breath to try and control himself. Beth's gaze flicked to Sera.

"Don't even look at her!" he shouted.

Beth's eyes flew back to his. "I'll see you soon," she vowed.

Liam's jaw clenched, but he made no move to go after her. Sera's hand kept him grounded as it pacified the raging demon straining to break free. Beth turned away from them and headed to the door.

Liam waited for it to open and close before turning to Sera. Fresh anger blazed through him as he spotted Jack's hands upon her shoulders. "Get your hands off her!" he spat.

Jack's hands fell limply to his sides. Sera tilted her head to look at him. There was a wealth of confusion and love blazing out of her. "Are you okay?" he demanded.

"Yes." She stepped forward to wrap her arms around his waist and bury herself in the security of his chest.

He enfolded her, drawing her close. Gradually the beast within him began to ease as he held her. After a few minutes, he lifted his head to gaze at his friends. They gawked at him.

He knew exactly how they felt because he felt the same way. His control was slipping further and further away. Sera could reach him now, but he wasn't sure she would be able to reach him for much longer, and he didn't want to think about what would happen if he lost complete control.

What if next time he turned on her in his fury? He couldn't bear the thought of that happening, but even thinking about letting her go made him want to destroy everything around him. If the idea was enough to make him almost crazed, what would the reality do to him? He didn't know what was happening to him, but he knew he had to figure it out before it was too late. And Beth knew the answer.

"I want to know who that was and what is going on!" Kathleen demanded from the other side of the room. "And I want to know now!"

Sera rested her head on his chest. She wanted to bury herself in him and shut out the rest of the world. "You have to tell them something," she whispered.

"Doug, do you have your cell?" Liam asked.

"Yeah."

"Call David."

"I don't know if it's going to work up here."

"Screw the phone! Give me some answers, or get the hell out of here!" Kathleen commanded. "I'm sick of this crap!"

"Get it to work!" His hands clenched on Sera as his patience began to fray. "Now!"

He turned toward Kathleen. She stood with her hands on her hips; her jaw clenched as she glared at him.

"Until we talk to him, we can't talk to you," he said more calmly. "So, you're going to have to wait."

Kathleen opened her mouth and then closed it. He turned back to Doug. "Get him on the phone and tell him what's going on."

"Now you want to let everyone in," Doug muttered as he walked away.

"Mike would you go get some blankets, mattresses too. It might be better if everyone slept in here tonight."

"Yeah, I think you're right."

"Jack, would you help me bring in some extra logs?"

"Sure."

"You two," he said to Kathleen and Danielle. "Stay in this room and stay together."

"Whatever," Kathleen angrily threw herself into the recliner.

"Come with me."

He took hold of Sera's hand and led her from the living room. He almost went down to the bedroom but quickly changed his mind. No matter what was going on, he knew if he got her in there, he wouldn't be able to keep his hands off her. He led her into the kitchen and sat her at the island while he helped Jack gather wood.

"What are you going to tell them?" she asked.

"I don't know," he admitted. "We'll decide that when David gets here."

"There's a blizzard outside, Liam. I don't think David is going to get here."

"He will," Jack said. He stepped back into the kitchen with a bundle of wood balanced carefully in his arms. "Can I ask you a question?"

Liam straightened to look at them. "Sure," she said.

"Why are you doing this? You don't have to stay, you don't have to be a part of this, and you would probably be safer if you left."

"Safer from who?"

"From Beth, from..." his voice trailed off, but his eyes flicked toward Liam. Liam's hands clenched upon the logs as he stepped back into the kitchen. "From us. We don't exactly live a normal, safe life."

"I want to be here, and I am safe."

There was a scrutinizing look on Jack's face as he studied her and then Liam. "Yeah, I guess you are."

"I know I am."

"Liam," Doug said as he appeared in the doorway. "David's on the phone. I left it on the stairs, that's the only place I can get any reception."

"Okay. Here, take these." He handed the logs over to him. "And take her into the living room. Make sure she's safe."

He followed them to the foyer and watched as Sera followed Doug into the living room. He almost went after her to bring her back, he hated having her out of sight, but he needed to talk to David, alone. He grabbed the phone off the stairs and sat down. "Hello."

"Hey." David's voice was distorted by static. "Sounds like you got a mess up there."

"You could say that. How much did Doug tell you?"

"Enough. I can't believe you told your girlfriend."

"Don't start, David."

"I'm not. How did Beth find you guys?" David inquired.

"Same way she always finds us I guess, but this time she left a mess for us to clean up."

Another wave of static swept through. "Yeah, what do you want to do?"

"I don't know yet. Tell them the truth?"

"Have you lost your mind?"

"I don't know, maybe," he admitted.

There was silence as static crinkled over the line. "There's more, isn't there?"

"Yes, we need you here."

"In a fucking blizzard?"

"Yes, if you can. Things are... I don't know what they are, not with me, not anymore."

David took a deep breath. "This doesn't sound like you, Liam."

"It's not." He hated to admit it, but it was true.

"All right, I'll see what I can do. Guess I'm leaving school sooner than I planned. How do I get there?"

"I don't know, hold on. Kathleen!" he yelled.

"What?" she snapped.

"I need you for a second."

He listened to her rustling around in the living room before she stomped up to him. "What?"

"I need you to give a friend of mine directions to get here."

"No way, I've had enough of your friends."

"Kathleen, this is important. If you want any explanations, then you're going to have to wait until he gets here."

Resentment was written all over her face as she snatched the phone out of his hand. "This is what you do," she spat. She rattled off directions from the main highway and threw the phone back at Liam.

She turned and stormed away. Liam picked up the phone again. "Got that?"

"Yeah, I managed to copy the rapid fire. Sweet personality. You want to tell that girl?"

"Maybe, I don't know. How long do you think it will take you to get here?"

"I can probably get a flight out tonight, but I don't know what airports are open in that area. Or how I'm going to get there from the airport. I don't know, hopefully tomorrow, maybe the next day."

"Just see what you can do. We won't do anything until you're here."

"All right. One more thing."

"Yeah?"

"Do you love her?"

"More than anything."

David sighed. "All right, I'll see you soon. Bye."

"Bye."

Liam hung up the phone and sat for a few minutes as he tried to sort out his mangled emotions.

CHAPTER SIXTEEN

Sera woke slowly the next morning. The blanket was pulled firmly over her head, and she snuggled in deeper seeking warmth. It was then she realized Liam was no longer with her, and that's why she was cold. She sat up quickly.

Recently rebuilt, the fire's bright flames leapt high as it crackled, and the smell of wood permeated the air. Kathleen was passed out on one of the couches, and Danielle was curled up in the recliner. Mike had abandoned his spot on the other couch, and Jack was gone from his mattress on the floor. Doug remained on his mattress next to the couch, his mouth open as he snored.

Muffled voices from the kitchen drifted to her. She wrapped the blanket around her as she stood and made her way toward them. Their voices drifted to her, but she couldn't make out any of the words. When she entered the doorway, they stopped talking and turned to look at her. She glanced curiously at them as she made her way to the coffee pot and began to gather the ingredients.

"What's going on?" she asked as she turned to face them.

Liam stood and made his way around the island to her. She stared at him, suddenly very disconcerted by his behavior. He seemed distant again. "Is everything all right?"

He brushed back a strand of tangled hair. "Yes," he assured her.

His face was still remote, but the familiar warmth was back in his brilliant eyes. "Sera, when you opened the door last night you invited Beth in like you knew her, did you?" Mike asked.

Her eyes flicked to him. "I had met her before."

Liam stiffened. "Where?"

"She came by when you guys were on your walk, and Kathleen and Danielle had come back inside. She said she lived in the cabin down the road and was walking to her friend's house. We talked for a few minutes, and she left. Kathleen said the people who used to own that cabin are dead."

"That's probably where she's staying," Jack said.

Sera drew her cold hands into the blanket. "I don't know."

Liam stared at her for a minute, and then looked over at Jack and Mike. "You want to come with me, Jack?"

Jack slid off the stool. "Absolutely."

"How far away is it?" Liam asked her.

"Kathleen said it was about a mile down the hill."

He reached under the blanket and clasped hold of her cold hands. She smiled as warmth swiftly spread through her body. "I have to go." She opened her mouth to protest but closed it when she saw the haunted look in his eyes. "I have to find her."

The snow was still falling, although it seemed to have eased, and the wind had died down. But how much was out there? Her gaze returned to Liam as she bit nervously into her lip. "Mike and Doug are going to stay here to make sure you're safe. I want you to stay inside. Okay?"

"Yes."

He squeezed her hands and released her. She grabbed his

shirt before he could turn away and stood on tiptoe to kiss him. For a second he was unresponsive, then his mouth seared into hers before he pulled away. Sera's breath caught in her throat at the savage gleam in his eyes.

"Be careful," she whispered.

"I will. Come on, Jack."

Sera watched as they bundled up and walked out the door. A wave of loneliness and loss swallowed her. She closed her eyes as she fought against it.

THE GRANDFATHER CLOCK chimed out five o'clock as Sera sat, sipping hot chocolate, and watching the flames. Kathleen sat in the recliner, her eyes frozen on the flames as she twirled the mug in her hands. Danielle sat before the fire, her knees drawn up, and her arms wrapped around them. Mike and Doug had wandered off, bored, and tired of the silent treatment Kathleen had been giving them all.

"You know, don't you, Sera," Kathleen finally said.

Sera felt her heart clench. She had been wondering when Kathleen would confront her. "Know what?" she asked as she tried to bide her time.

"What's going on, you know."

"Kathleen—"

"Sera, you're my best friend, but if you lie to me one more time I'll never talk to you again."

Sera winced. "I can't say anything," she finally said.

Kathleen looked back at the fire. "Yes, you can. I don't care what they say, or what you may say, but there was something wrong with that girl. Something's not right. She's dangerous. I could sense that, and she puts us in danger somehow. And so does Liam. There's something wrong with both of them." Her gaze darted nervously toward the door. When she spoke again, her voice was so low Sera had to strain to hear her. "Maybe there's something wrong with all of them. I think we deserve to know what."

Sera stared down at her mug as steam rose in waves. She desperately wished Liam were here to help, that any of them would show back up and help. Her glance fell on the clock. Where was he? He'd been gone for so long. Way too long.

Uneasiness had officially turned into full-fledged panic three hours ago. There was so much snow out there, it was cold, and Beth said she was stronger than he was. Was he laying out there somewhere injured, maybe dying? He wasn't completely immortal. Vampires could still be killed somehow, couldn't they?

"Sera," Kathleen said. "Answer me."

She took a deep breath as she tried to ease the growing knot of anxiety in her chest. "I can't say anything, Kathleen," she said again.

"If your life were in danger, I would tell you why."

"It isn't my secret to reveal, Kathleen." She wasn't going to tell her that her life wasn't in danger, it was, and Kathleen knew it. To lie to her now would only cost Sera her best friend.

"It *is* your secret if you know what it is, Sera."

She looked over at Kathleen, who stared at her with tear-filled eyes. "I promise you will have answers soon enough."

"We'd better. I'm serious, Sera, no more lies."

"No more lies, Kathleen," she promised. The fact she may have just lied to her was something she didn't want to contemplate.

"Good."

"But some things are better off not knowing."

"What's that supposed to mean?"

Sera took a sip of her hot chocolate and pulled her blanket

more firmly around her. "Just what I said. Sometimes it's better not to know. The truth isn't always the answer, but just the beginning."

Kathleen didn't speak as she turned to stare at the flames again. A loud knock on the door startled them all. Sera's hot chocolate spilled onto her blanket as she jumped up. Liam and Jack wouldn't knock, but maybe, just maybe, it was them.

"I got it!" Mike yelled as he ran into the foyer. He pointed sharply at Sera. "You three stay in there."

Doug came into the hall as Mike flung open the door. Cold air and snow blasted into the house. "Jesus! You made it! Come in," Mike said.

Sera watched as a tall figure set a pair of skis down on the porch outside before stepping into the flickering candlelight. "How you doing, man?" Mike asked as he embraced the man.

"Been better. Sure as hell been warmer. Help me get these freaking boots off. They're killing my feet!"

Sera moved toward the foyer as Mike shut out the blasting wind. Doug turned to look at her but didn't stop her. "Come on in."

Mike frowned at her. "I told you to stay in the living room."

"Don't start, Mike," she muttered.

He shook his head as he grabbed her shoulders, turned her around, and gave her a nudge forward. "Come on, let's get David warm."

She scowled at Mike's highhanded manner and shot him a look. She would have argued with him, but the pleading look in his eyes froze her words. He was just trying to make sure she stayed safe. She glanced over her shoulder as Doug clasped hands with David and slapped him on the shoulder.

"Where are Liam and Jack?" David inquired.

"They went to look for Beth. They've been gone all day."

Sera settled back onto the couch as Doug came into the

room, followed by a very wet, very unhappy looking David. His boots clumped loudly over the hardwood floor as he settled into the recliner.

Tall and athletically built, David's light blond hair was wet and windblown. It added a boyish charm to his angled face. His eyes were a brilliant electric blue. His lips were thick, and a deep ruby red that were now chapped and sore looking. His nose was elegantly carved, but it was the only thing about him that wasn't perfect. It had been broken at one point, and was a little crooked, but it only seemed to add to his appeal.

He was almost as good looking as Liam, and Sera found herself staring at him in astonishment. She looked over at Kathleen and Danielle, who were both gaping at him. "This is Kathleen, Danielle, and Sera," Mike introduced as he gestured at them. "This is David."

"Well now," David said as he glanced at them. "Don't we all look cozy."

"Oh yeah," Danielle replied sarcastically. "We're a happy bunch!"

"How far did you have to ski?" Doug asked as he helped David struggle out of his boot.

"About ten miles. Freaking roads are a mess. Shit Doug, leave my feet attached to my body!"

"Sorry," he muttered.

Sera watched in amusement as Doug and David tugged and pulled at the boots. Finally, they managed to get them off. David pulled his leg up and began to massage his feet. "Do you have any dry clothes?" Mike asked.

"My bag by the door. I'll get them when I can feel my hands and feet again." David looked them all over again. "Which one of you is Liam's girlfriend?" Sera raised an eyebrow as his eyes settled on her. "You?"

"Yes."

David studied her a minute longer before turning away. Sera scowled at him. She had the distinct feeling he wanted to say or do something but hadn't.

"Hey!" Kathleen shouted. "I do recall a promise that revolved around this man!"

Sera closed her eyes and shoved the blanket off her. "We'll wait until Liam gets back," Mike said.

"We've been waiting all day! I'm tired of waiting!"

"He'll be back soon," Doug said.

"I don't care!"

Sera stood up, suddenly exceptionally pissed off. She was tired of Kathleen's demands and tired of all the lies. She was tired of being worried about Liam, tired of staring at the clock and not having him return. She needed him here. She felt as if a part of her was missing without him. She paced over to the window. It had grown dark out, but she could still see snowflakes as they continued to fall.

"How much snow is out there?" she inquired.

"About three feet," David replied absently.

Sera closed her eyes. Where was he?

"Would someone please tell us something," Danielle pleaded.

Sera turned and walked out of the room. "Where are you going?" Mike demanded.

"Bathroom!" she called over her shoulder.

She walked right past the bathroom and into the kitchen. Hastily lacing up her boots, she grabbed her jacket and slid it on. She suddenly couldn't stand being in the cabin one minute longer. She didn't care what Liam had said, he left her here, and she needed to get out before she went insane. Flinging the back door open, she plunged into the thigh-high snow. The wind howled around her, and the frigid air seared her lungs as she trudged toward the woods.

"Sera!" Mike yelled as she made it to the edge of the woods. "Sera! Get back here!"

She deftly ignored him as she plunged into the forest. Her breath came in ragged pants, and her legs ached from trying to get through the thick snow, but she forced herself to keep going. Suddenly, her foot got caught on a tree branch. With a cry, she fell into the snow. Her fingers were cold and raw as they buried into it. She clawed at it as tears of frustration blurred her eyes. With a muffled cry, she collapsed, not caring about the cold as it seeped into her bones. She was just glad to be free.

"Goddamn it!" Mike roared as he shoved his way through the tree branches toward her. "What are you doing?"

"I needed to get out of that cabin. I couldn't take anymore of the anger," she answered. He loomed over her, a sinister scowl on his face as he planted his hands on his hips. She couldn't help but laugh at him.

His scowl deepened as he stared at her in disbelief. "I'm glad you think this is funny. Are you trying to kill me?"

"Of course not."

"Liam will kill me once he finds out you did this! Sera, get up!"

"He's not going to care."

"Not going to care! He's going to rip my head off! I found her!" he called out as footsteps sounded to their left.

"Is he coming back?" she asked.

"Of course he is."

Sera found herself unable to meet his gaze. "He's been gone a long time, Mike, I'm worried."

"There's nothing to worry about; now come on, get up."

She had to gather her courage for her next question. It was something that had been nagging at her all day. Finally deciding the best way to ask was just to say it, she turned back to him. "Do you think he might stay with her?" she whispered.

Her distress finally seemed to penetrate through to Mike as he sat in the snow next to her. "Are you serious?"

"Yeah."

"No, Sera, he will not stay with her. He's more than likely going to kill her if he finds her."

"But she said she was stronger than him."

He ran a hand through his tangled hair. "She knows more about her powers, and she's more adept at using them than we are, but he will kill her."

"He seemed so unhappy when he left this morning," she whispered forlornly.

Mike tilted her chin up with his finger. "Trust me; he will be back. I've known Liam my entire life, and I've never seen him as happy as he is with you, or as possessive. He would walk through Hell to get back here for you, okay?"

She gnawed on her lower lip as she nodded. David burst out of the woods beside them. He was panting as he glowered at them. "Are you two trying to freeze to death? Get out of the freaking snow!"

Mike laughed and laid back. "I don't know; I think Sera's got the right idea. That cabin was driving me crazy too. The infuriated estrogen level was getting a little too high."

"Hey!" She punched him in the arm as he grinned up at her.

"You two have lost it," David muttered. "This shit sucks! I should know, I've been stuck in it for hours!"

"It's worse in there," Mike said. "Trust me."

"Yeah," Sera agreed. "I don't want to go back."

"You two are going to freeze to death out here, and then Liam is going to kill Doug and me."

"Oh, stop bitching," she said. "I'll freeze to death, not you; you don't die."

David gaped at her as Mike burst out laughing. "She's got you there!" Mike cried.

Sera laughed and picked up a handful of snow to throw at him. She caught him square in the face, stopping his laughter in mid-tirade. He blinked in surprise and then grabbed a handful of snow. She tried to scramble away, but it was too late, he grabbed the back of her shirt, and shoved snow down her sweater. She squealed as a freezing tremor racked through her. She jumped on him and began tossing and throwing snow.

"Children!" David yelled.

Sera stopped attacking Mike and lay panting on the ground. "I say we get him," she whispered.

Mike grinned at her, and they both hopped up and sprinted toward him. David didn't have enough time to get out of the way before Mike knocked him into the snow. Sera grabbed handfuls of snow as she charged forward to help Mike. They rolled around, shoving snow at each other as they squealed and laughed away some of their tension.

"What are you doing?" Liam roared.

They all froze, snow falling from their hands, as they stared guiltily at one another then at him. Liam and Jack stood a few feet from them. Sera's delight at seeing him vanished in the face of his obvious wrath. Jack looked extremely uncomfortable as he glanced at the three of them, and then at Liam. He took a small step away from Liam. Liam's eyes burned with fire as they landed on Mike's hand on her arm. Mike instantly released her.

"I told you to watch her!" he barked at Mike.

Mike ran a hand through his wet hair. "I am watching her."

"Hey, I do have a mind of my own! I'm not a child!" Sera yelled indignantly.

"You're acting like one!" Liam retorted.

Sera's mouth dropped open. She knew he was angry, and she supposed he had a right to be, but he was the one who left her alone all day. And now that she was finally having fun, she was not about to stop just because he was mad.

"Really?" She climbed to her feet and brushed the snow off her. David and Mike nervously shuffled along behind her.

"Yes, really."

"That's good to know."

She gathered the snow from her clothes and threw it at him. "What are you doing?" he demanded.

"Being a child."

She ran at him and flung herself forward. The force of her small impact was enough to knock him into the snow. He cried out in surprise as she shoved snow in his face. Then, he started to laugh as he rolled her over and pinned her down. She grinned up at him. His hair was now white, and wet, as it hung around his magnificent face. His eyes lit with desire, and her body immediately arched into his. For a moment, she forgot about everyone else as she gazed at him.

"Get him!" Mike yelled.

They were suddenly on top of them, throwing and tossing snow, screaming and yelling happily. Liam rolled off her as he tried to fend them off. She was instantly on her feet and joining in the fray.

Ten minutes later they lay spent and panting. Sera stared up at the stars, happy, tired, and freezing. Snow adhered to her clothes and skin. Her feet and hands were numb, but she didn't want to move. She didn't want to go back into that cabin to face Danielle and Kathleen.

"Come on," Liam said as he extended a hand to her.

"Do we have to?" she asked.

"You'll freeze to death."

"I think I might prefer it."

He smiled down at her as he took hold of her outstretched hand. "I'll give you a piggyback ride," he offered.

She wrapped her numb, wet legs around him as she tightened her arms around his neck. He carried her through the woods, moving with a swiftness that startled, and enthralled her. She nuzzled her face into his neck as she sought his warmth and strength. She kissed his cheek and rested her head on his shoulder.

"I love you," she whispered.

"I love you too." Her smile was so angelic it melted his heart. He forced himself to look away from her before he was completely lost. "How have you been?" he asked David.

"Cold, and she seems to enjoy keeping me that way."

Sera laughed as she nestled closer to Liam. "Did you find Beth?" Mike asked.

Liam's hands tensed on her calves. "No, she wasn't there. She was at one point in time, though; she left enough signs of that. We looked for her, but she seems to be gone, for now anyway."

"Wonderful."

They moved out of the forest, and Sera lifted her head to look at the cabin. It looked so peaceful, but she knew how much looks could be deceiving. "Well, guys," Jack said. "Here goes all hell."

"Yeah," Liam muttered.

"It'll be okay," she said.

He squeezed her hand, and David opened the door. "Have you decided what we're going to do?"

"No," Mike answered. "We'll decide that now."

"Why don't you go join them," Liam suggested as he set Sera down. "We'll be right there." She stared at him for a minute before leaving the porch. "Sera!" She turned to him, a puzzled look on her face. "Stay here."

"Liam," David said quietly.

"She stays."

She had been out of his sight all day, and it had eaten him up. He had done nothing but think of her. She probably shouldn't be here now, but the minute she turned to leave he realized he didn't want her where he couldn't see her anymore. He didn't know what was going on inside of him, but he did know it was getting stronger, and it was getting worse. When he came across all of them in the snow, he'd almost attacked David and Mike. It was only the fact she was present and might be injured that halted him. He had never even gotten into a fist-fight with any of them, but he'd felt the insane urge to kill them both when he'd seen them with her.

"She is part of what we need to talk about." David took a step back as Liam glared at him. "It's not what you're thinking," he added quickly.

"If it concerns her, then she stays," Liam insisted.

"She may not want to hear what I have to say. You may not want to hear it. I'm telling you, Liam, let her go."

He glanced at Sera standing just outside the doorway. He turned back to David and shook his head. "I can't."

David ran his hand through his hair. "Fine, but just remember I warned you. Can we talk in here?"

"I don't want to be too far away from Kathleen and Danielle, just in case. But they shouldn't be able to hear us."

"I can go if you want me too," Sera said.

"No," Liam said brusquely.

She didn't say anything as he walked over and pulled her into his arms. Leaning against the counter, he braced her between his legs and relished in the refreshing, sweet scent of her hair. His body quickened as he heard the blood rushing through her veins. He could smell himself inside her. The realization caused his mouth to water and the beast to stream forth again. His hands clenched on her as he closed his eyes in an attempt to keep the demon at bay.

"So, what do we tell them?" Mike asked. "Do you think they could handle the truth?"

"I don't know," Sera answered. "I didn't handle it too well, and I love Liam."

"We can't tell them the truth," Jack said.

"Do you have another idea? Because I know I've been racking my brain for hours, and I can't think of one," Mike said.

"Can we force them to accept another truth?"

"You can't do that!" Sera cried.

"It may be the only way," Doug said. "It will be trickier since so much time has elapsed, and they're not drunk, but with all of us we should be able to do it."

"There has to be another way."

"Sera, there may not be."

Liam's breath warmed her neck. It sent shivers down her spine at the same time tears sprang to her eyes. She turned to him. "Liam, please," she pleaded. "I don't want to see them hurt."

He clasped her face in his hands and held her. "They won't even know what happened."

"And if Beth comes back and tries to harm them?"

The tears in her eyes, and the quiver in her voice, tore at his heart. He didn't want to see her hurt, but telling Danielle and Kathleen the truth only placed all of them in more peril. This was for the best, and she had to realize that.

"We will keep them safe, Sera," he vowed.

Tears slid down her cheeks as she stared at him with melancholy eyes. He wiped the tears away with his thumbs. "Promise?" she breathed.

"Yes, I promise. We all promise, right?"

"Yes," they answered.

"It really won't hurt them? Are you sure?"

"I am absolutely positive."

Sera's lip trembled as her head fell forward and tears spilled down her cheeks to wet his hands. He pulled her against him as she cried silently into his shirt. He closed his eyes against the anguish filling him.

"Go do it," he ordered in a hoarse voice.

It took all he had to keep Sera standing.

"We need to talk about something else first," David said.

Liam ground his teeth. "I think it can wait!"

David looked at Sera and then back at him. "No, Liam, it can't."

"David," Mike warned.

"Mike, this cannot wait. You're losing it, aren't you? Losing control of your ability to keep the demon at bay?" His gaze focused on Liam.

Liam stared back at him relentlessly. "Yes."

David ran his hand through his wet hair. "I thought so."

Sera pulled away and tilted her head back to stare at him. His jaw clenched, and his eyes gleamed dangerously as his nostrils flared. "Liam?" she asked questioningly.

He glanced down at her before looking away, but she'd already seen the torment in his eyes. Her hands clenched on his shirt. She'd known he was struggling to be around her, but she hadn't realized how bad it was until right now. She had pushed him yesterday; she had completely ignored his need to get away from her, in her own need to be close to him. She was doing this to him. She felt like the most horrible person in the world.

She took a step away from him, but he grabbed hold of her waist and pulled her back.

"No," he said so quietly she knew no one else had heard him.

"But—"

"I said no!" his eyes flamed with fire as his jaw clenched.

"But it's because of me!" she protested as she squirmed to

get out his embrace. His hands clenched on her. She winced in response, and he immediately eased his grip. "It is, isn't it?"

"Yes." It was David who answered her. Sera stopped struggling as she turned to look at him. David's eyes were pitying before he looked at Liam. "You've tasted her?" Liam nodded sharply. "And she tasted you?"

Sera's face flamed hotly.

"Yes," Liam grated.

"But she's not one of us," Doug stated.

Sera felt herself turning redder as she realized they knew everything. "No, she's not," David said. "That's the problem."

"What is that supposed to mean?" Liam spat. His body trembled; his arms locked around her were as taut as a bowstring.

"I met some of our kind in Pennsylvania—" David started.

"How did you know they were our kind?" Jack interrupted.

David shot him an aggravated look. "Like knows like," he explained hastily. "You'll see when you meet others. Trust me." His gaze returned to Liam and Sera. "After I talked to you, I went and asked them about our relationships with humans. We aren't meant to be with them, not seriously anyway."

"They told you this?" Liam demanded.

"Yes. You have marked her as yours, Liam. When you let her feed on you, she became a part of you, and vice versa."

"Beth did the same thing!" Liam seethed.

"It's not the same, Liam, and you know it! You never loved Beth, but you love Sera, and the thing inside of you needs her to be with you, forever. When we fall in love something happens, something changes. Inside, we are savage, and we need to mark our mates. You will kill anyone who hurts her; you will kill us."

"So he says," Mike muttered.

"So he will," David said firmly. "You'll also destroy her."

"No, he won't!" Sera cried.

David's eyes were sympathetic as they met hers. "Yes, he will. He will turn you. He's fighting it now, but he will. He can't let you go Sera, not in any way. The demon inside him senses the mortality in you, the frailty of your life, and it will not have it."

"Then I'll let her go," Liam said even as his arms tightened upon her waist.

"No!" Sera was horrified and broken at the mere thought.

"Sera—"

"You can't," David said flatly.

"Of course I can," Liam insisted.

"No, you can't!" Sera denied.

"No, he can't," David reasserted vehemently. "Don't give me that look; you can't, Liam. Even now, while you're saying the words, you're changing."

Sera twisted to look up at him. He diverted his head, but not before she caught a glimpse of red eyes and elongated teeth. "Liam," she whispered as she touched his cheek.

He took her hand and pulled it away from his face. "Don't!"

Tears welled in her eyes, but she withdrew her hand from him. She could feel him trying to put a wall between them, and she didn't know how to stop it. He was determined to keep her away from him.

"Look," David said. "I'm going to tell you what they told me about this. First of all, you can't let her go. We don't often find our mates, in fact, the two vampires I met are over two hundred years old, and they've never found theirs. From what they've been told, once we find our mates, if they are human, then all control for the vampire is lost. What you're going through now, Liam, is nothing. It will only get worse until you make her yours in every way. If you send her away, you will go insane; you will become a threat to everyone around you. She is the only thing keeping you from losing your sanity now.

"Simply put, you can't let her go, and she can't stay human."

"What about Beth?" Liam demanded. "We exchanged blood."

"You didn't give two shits about Beth, and no matter how much she fancies herself in love with you, she's not. She's obsessed with you because you didn't want her. You never had a problem with walking away from Beth, but I bet going for that walk today almost drove you crazy, didn't it?"

Liam refused to answer the question. "I thought so," David continued. "Our mates are ours. We know them when we find them, if we find them. It's instantaneous. You might not have recognized it at first, but if you look back over everything, I'm sure you realize it now, right?"

Liam's resentment at David's words was growing by the second. However, he was right. Every minute he spent away from her today was horrendous, and he desperately needed to get back to her. The beast within him was clawing to emerge every second they were apart. It was only the knowledge Mike and Doug would keep her safe, and he needed to find Beth to ensure Sera stayed that way, that kept him going.

David was also right about Liam not being able to leave her. His need to get her away from him, before he injured her, was nowhere near as strong as his urge to drag her from the room and take possession of her in every way possible. One thing was for sure, his need for her was growing, while his control was weakening.

He took a deep breath and met David's intense gaze. David was also right about another thing. From the beginning, he needed to speak to Sera, gone out of his way to meet her. He told himself to stay away from her, yet he hadn't been able to do so. So far, David was right about everything, and Liam was certain this conversation wasn't going to end well.

"He was going to let me leave his room," Sera said. "After he told me what he was, and I was terrified. He was going to let me go."

David contemplated that for a minute. "He may have said that; he may have even let you walk out, but I can guarantee you wouldn't have gotten far, and he wouldn't have let you go for long. You went back to him?"

"I didn't make it out the door."

"Listen to me, Liam, she's not even one of us, and she's already possessive of you. Your blood has started making changes in her also."

"He hadn't bitten me then!" Sera cried.

"That doesn't matter. A part of you recognized him. You have instincts, Sera; they knew you were meant to be together. That you are soul mates. If you left that room, he would have come for you, and I don't think you would have put up much of a fight."

Sera lowered her head. "No," she admitted in a whisper. "I wouldn't have."

"His biting you did not precipitate this, it only sped things up a little. He's tasted you, he wants you, and he will change you. His blood in your veins marks you as his. If he had changed you, then we would be able to smell him on you, always." David's eyes shot back to Liam. "You want us, and our kind, to know she is yours. It's our kind who you think are the most dangerous to her."

"I can control this," Liam grated. "I can fight this."

"No Liam, you can't fight this forever. You will not allow her to die a mortal death; you won't even be able to tolerate the risk of losing her for much longer. It will not happen. Look, if we never find a mate, then it doesn't matter. They said there is a vampire who is almost a thousand years old and has never found his. You have already killed for her, Liam. You have never lost control like that before, and you will lose it again. If she dies, then you die. You will either go insane, be destroyed, or you will kill yourself."

Sera didn't speak as she absorbed everything David was saying. If she died, then Liam died. If she stayed with him, then he wouldn't allow her to be human. It was all too much to grasp right now. Suddenly, she didn't feel so good. Liam's arms tensed around her as he supported most of her weight. "So what are you saying?" Liam demanded.

"She can't stay mortal. Instinctively, you will not allow it, and as long as you keep fighting it, the people around you are in danger. Including her."

"I am completely capable of controlling myself. I only killed Jacob because of what he was doing to her!" he hissed.

Sera shivered as she huddled deeper into Liam's embrace. "And when you lose control again, what then?"

"It won't happen."

But it would, Sera knew it would. She could feel it in him. She had seen it come over his face many times in the past few days. Saw it today, when he'd come upon them in the snow. Saw it yesterday when Jack had been holding her shoulders. Saw it when they were in the shower. He would go after them, and it would be her fault. But what could she do? She couldn't become one of them; she just couldn't. She couldn't drink blood, and she couldn't be a monster. She didn't even eat meat! She would have to give up her hopes of a home, and a family.

Sera closed her eyes as anguish tore through her. What good would a home, or a family, be if she wasn't with Liam?

"It will happen Liam, and it will probably happen with her."

Sera's eyes flew back open as her heart lurched into her throat. "He won't hurt me!" she choked out.

"He will change you. There is no chance he won't. It's only

a matter of *when* he will, and from the looks of him, I would say it is going to be very soon."

Sera shuddered as revulsion ripped through her.

"That is not true," Liam grated.

"Yes, it is. Now the only question is, will she be willing, or will you force it on her?"

Four sets of utterly inhuman and savage eyes turned toward her in the candlelight. Liam's arms tightened around her. She was terrified to look at him, completely terrified of everything happening.

"Well, Sera, what will it be?" David asked.

A choked cry escaped her as her legs buckled. Liam swung her easily up. His jaw clenched, and his eyes were burning orbs of hopelessness as they flashed from red to green and back again.

"Take care of those two," he ordered, as he strode across the kitchen.

"Liam, what I said is true," David said.

He paused in the doorway to look back at him. "I know."

Sera dropped her head against his chest and began to sob softly.

CHAPTER SEVENTEEN

LIAM SAT on the bed and cradled her in his lap. He held her tenderly, allowing her to sob out her sorrow as he kept his head buried in her hair. He could smell her blood, hear her heartbeat, but it didn't arouse the beast in him now. The monster within seemed to be effectively buried by the sorrow racking her.

He stroked her long golden hair that was still damp from the snow. Reaching behind him, he pulled one of the blankets forward and wrapped it around her as he rubbed her arms to warm her even more.

Minutes ticked by endlessly. Eventually, her tears dried as she lay trembling against him. He noticed how small and frail she was as he shifted his hold on her. At the thought, he felt the demon surge forth. Closing his eyes, he willed it to go away. Now was not the time or the place. She needed him now.

"Feeling better?" he asked.

She shook her head and buried herself within the blanket. He pulled it away from her face and caressed her tear-stained cheek as she lifted her chin to look at him. Her eyes were a vibrant violet, even though they were bloodshot and swollen from her tears. Her lower lip still trembled a little.

A wave of protectiveness washed through him. He hated to see her cry, and it was his fault she was crying now. Everything was his fault. "Damn!" he shouted. "I'm sorry, Sera. I am so very sorry."

Her lids dropped down; her long, gold-tipped lashes were wet as they shadowed her pale cheeks. "It's all true, isn't it?" she whispered.

His hands convulsed on her. He wanted to tell her David was wrong, that no matter what he could control himself around her. But he promised her he would never lie to her again, and he knew David was right. He was controlling himself now, but only because of her tears. He was aware that one of these days he would snap, and it would be soon.

"Yes, I think it is. If I had known, I would have left you alone," he grated hoarsely. "I would have stopped myself from seeing you. I would have left the country, the continent if necessary. I would have done whatever it took not to inflict this on you, Sera. But I can't now. I just can't."

The torment in his voice tore at her heart, ripped through her soul, but she was so scared and confused. She knew he would have left her before things had gotten this far, but she also knew if he had left, if she had never seen him again, she would have always been empty without him. He would have haunted her dreams, and she knew somehow she would have found him again.

"I would have found you," she whispered.

He released a small groan. "Sera—"

"No, Liam, I would. If you hadn't come back for me, I would have found you. I love you."

"I would have left before it ever came to that."

"I've loved you from the beginning. I loved you before I met you," she told him as a dawning realization came over her. "I was ready with Jacob."

His hands convulsed on her. She turned to him knowing already the demon was there. His face was strained as he fought to bring it under control.

"But, I began to panic," she said. "It suddenly felt wrong; it felt awful. I was waiting for you. Somehow, even then, I knew you were out there."

He fought to control his temper. The thought of what Jacob did to her made him wish the bastard was still alive so he could kill him again. A shudder ripped through him, and he almost bellowed from the rage encompassing him.

A butterfly touch on his cheek drew his eyes open. She stared at him with a mixture of trepidation and love so powerful it shook him.

"I was waiting for you," she whispered again.

Something inside him broke. He hauled her against him, holding her as close to him as he could. It wasn't close enough. Her arms wrapped around his neck as she pressed herself against him. "What have I done?" he groaned.

Her hands clenched upon him as tears spilled free again. She could feel the distress and self-loathing radiating from him. "I love you, Liam. I love you so much it hurts." Her voice was choked with sobs as she clung to him.

His hands were bruising as they dug into her. She winced but didn't make a sound. She could feel his desperation, he needed her, and she wasn't going to let him down. "I don't deserve you."

She laughed as she buried her face in his neck. Her tears wet his skin, but they were no longer tears of grief for herself, but for him. "Yes, you do. I can't live without you. I can't even breathe when I think about the possibility. If this is what was meant to be, then that's fine. I would let you change me anyway; it might have taken me a little longer to come to it. But this is all right, Liam. It is."

"Sera," he moaned.

"It's all right."

She pulled away from him and tilted her head so she could gaze into his tortured face. She pulled her hair away from the wounds in her neck. His eyes gleamed as they fastened upon her wounds and his teeth instantly elongated. He closed his eyes, his face twisted with anguish as he fought to bring the demon under control.

"I can't, Sera."

"Liam, it's all right. I want this," she assured him.

"Not tonight. You'll need blood right after. Unless you want to feed off Danielle and Kathleen, I can't."

Sera froze as that thought hit her. Blood, she would have to drink blood. An involuntary shudder of revulsion ripped through her. He pulled her hair back over the marks before they tempted him even further.

"Blood." She was unable to hide the disgust from her voice.

"I can feed you, Sera. You need never feed off anyone but me if that is what you want." That was what *he* wanted. The thought of her even going near someone else twisted his stomach and brought forth a rush of violence.

"Not my friends," she whispered. "Not them."

"No, never them. I promise. But until I can find someone else, this cannot happen."

She dropped her head to his chest and yawned. He lifted her easily as he stood. Pulling the remaining blankets back, he laid her on the bed. He thought about undressing her but firmly decided against it. The thought of her naked body hardened him. The sight of her naked body would push him over the edge, and all common sense would go out the window.

He could not be with her again until he was ready to

change her. She smiled sleepily at him and raised her arms. He climbed in beside her and gathered her into his arms. He closed his eyes as a wave of contentment stole through him. The beast was at bay. She was going to be his, and nothing would ever change that.

Sera woke with a start. The night closed in around her as she strained to see anything. She stretched out a hand and felt Liam's solid figure. It reassured her, but she couldn't get rid of the dread creeping through her belly. She sat up and tossed the blanket aside as she walked over to the window.

The moon lit the backyard, revealing bare trees and an endless sea of white. The howling wind blew snow across the yard. She stared for a moment longer but couldn't see anything worth worrying about. She turned and crept to the door.

Creeping down the shadowed hallway, she felt her way to where the stairs began. Her hand found the banister, and she used it to guide her toward the kitchen. Two candles still burned within the room, but their flames were sputtering in the small nubs of wax left. She crossed the linoleum to where Kathleen left some candles on the counter and used the flames to light four more.

Taking one of the candles with her, she moved to the back door and opened it. There was nothing in the dark yard, but the hair on the back of her neck began to stand up. She froze for a second and then spun quickly. Nothing was behind her, but she was sure something or someone was watching her. She turned back to the night and stepped back. The wind howled across her, blowing snow into the room, and knocking out her flame.

Terror suddenly ripped through her as she took another

step back. The force of the sudden impact sent her flying to the floor. The scream in her throat was cut off as the air was knocked out of her lungs. Something was on her, clawing at her, and ripping into her shirt and chest. She couldn't breathe, she could hardly even move. Then, the eyes were there, brilliant red eyes staring hatefully at her.

The air rushed back into her lungs as she opened her mouth to scream. A hand shot over her mouth, stifling her. She gasped as Beth's face appeared above her. It was twisted and evil as she leered down at her. "I told you I would get you!" she hissed.

Sera bucked wildly in a desperate attempt to get away, but although Beth was smaller than her, she was amazingly strong—almost as strong as Liam, who could kill her with a flick of his wrist. The sudden knowledge Beth could do the same sent her heart beating so powerfully she feared it would rip out of her ribcage.

Beth's eyes gleamed maliciously as an evil smile curled her mouth. Her lips pulled back to reveal her deadly teeth. Sera screamed against her hand, but only muffled cries of fright escaped. Beth surged forward, her mouth ajar, and her fangs gleaming as she lunged at Sera's throat with deadly intent.

Air rushed back into her lungs as Beth was ripped off her. Sera's lungs were finally able to expand again as she drew in a ragged breath. Rolling to the side, she watched in astonishment as Liam appeared within the candlelight and flung Beth across the kitchen. Beth slammed into the back wall with so much force the cabinet doors popped open. Pots, pans, and cans fell to the floor with loud rattling crashes and dull thumps. Beth instantly sprang back to her feet as a hiss escaped her.

The hair on Sera's neck rose as she scrambled backward. The answering hiss from Liam was nearly as frightening as Beth's. She could almost smell the bloodlust emanating from the two of them. Sera's mind and body screamed at her to run, but she couldn't get her shaking muscles to obey the command.

Liam spun around and caught Beth as she launched herself at him. She spat and fought in his grasp as she dug her long nails into his forearms. Liam bellowed with wrath and flung her away. She skidded across the floor and crashed into the fridge.

"What the hell?"

Sera turned as David, Jack, Doug, and Mike came skidding into the kitchen. Their eyes widened as they took in the spectacle before them. "What's going on?" Kathleen cried. Mike spun back around to block the doorway. "Get out of my way!"

Mike refused to budge from the doorway as he turned his head to see what was going on. Beth stood; her eyes were vivid and hateful as she lifted her chin. She spun and bolted out the door, seeming to blur and disappear as she moved. Liam took a step after her, and froze; his body was tense and shaking.

His ruby gaze darted back to Sera. Sera's mouth gaped open, and her heart leapt into her throat as he came at her. A scream tore from her as he seized hold of her arms and ripped her off the floor. "What were you doing?" he roared.

Fresh terror spurted through her in the face of his rage. A rage now focused solely on her. All his control was gone.

"What were you doing?"

He punctuated each word with a small shake. "Liam!" David shouted. "Liam, stop!"

David's words did nothing to dim the fury blazing through him. The hands on his arms ripped a shout from him as they tried to pull him away from Sera. He released Sera and spun toward them as he instinctively shielded her from whoever was behind him. David and Doug took a hasty step back, their hands raised in surrender.

He turned instantly back to her. Tremors racked her body as she stared at him with a petrified look in her eyes. Her shirt was ripped from her collar to mid-chest. Blood marred her porcelain skin. The sight of the blood further unraveled him.

He took a step forward. She whimpered as she scuttled back a few feet. At any other time, the sign of her distress would stop him. It didn't now. The fact she was almost killed shattered all his control. He would not lose her. He would not take the chance of losing her.

Sera had seen what was inside of him before, but not like this, never like this. Before, she had always glimpsed something of Liam inside. There was nothing there now. There was no flicker of green in his bloodshot eyes, no hint of softening in his contorted features. He had lost complete control, and he showed no signs of regaining it.

She wanted him to change her. She wanted to be with him. But not like this. He looked as if he was going to kill her.

She scrambled back, but he was on her in an instant. Sera screamed as her hands flailed wildly. He grabbed them and pinned them down. Pain blazed through her wrists, but it was nothing compared to the terror constricting her chest and throat. "Sera!" Kathleen screamed.

Hands grasped his shoulders and tried to rip him away. "Liam, don't!" Doug yelled. "Don't do this!"

He spun and lashed out with his fist. Doug was flung into the kitchen cabinets as if he weighed no more than a twig. His own eyes flashed red before he took a deep breath and steadied himself. Liam looked at the others, but they made no move to come near him.

His eyes focused on her again. The smell of her blood was thick in the air; the riotous fluttering of her heart was hammering in his head. He pushed her hair back and pulled her forward. She cried out as she fought against him. Her thrashing only made him more determined. He was going to make her his for good. He was going to make sure no one ever hurt her again.

"Liam, please," she whimpered as his teeth skimmed her neck. She choked out a strangled cry. "Please not like this. Not like Jacob."

He was pulled back, ready to strike, when her words slammed into him with the force of a sledgehammer. They rocked his body and soul as they knocked the demon out of him. He released her wrists as he pulled away from her. Her eyes were tumultuous and terrified, her hair a tangled mess about her beautiful face. Blood marred her delicate cheek and chest, the smell of it was heady and enticing, but he did not go after her again.

"Get away from me, Sera!" he grated. "Get away now!"

She needed no further encouragement as she scrambled to her feet and stumbled around the island. Jack reached out to steady her, thought better of it, and dropped his hands back to his sides. She had taken a risk with mentioning Jacob's name. She knew it would either drive him into a further rage or help him come to his senses. She was incredibly grateful it went her way.

"Get her out of here!" Liam spat. "Get her out now!"

"Sera!" Kathleen yelled. "Sera, are you okay?"

"She's fine," Mike answered when it became obvious Sera couldn't do so.

"Get out of my way! I want to see her! Now!" Danielle and Kathleen were both screaming and shoving at Mike.

"Get her out of here!" Liam bellowed. "And take care of them!"

Mike pushed Kathleen and Danielle back as they fought to get away from him. "Everything is fine," he said slowly. "Jack, help me."

"Let us go!" Kathleen screeched. "He's hurt her! I know he has!"

Mike took hold of Kathleen's chin and forced her to look at him. She was fairly spitting as she beat ineffectively at his chest. "Everything is all right," he said. "Sera just had a nightmare, but she's fine now." Her eyes began to glaze as his power wrapped into her mind. Beside him, he could hear Jack whispering the same words to Danielle. "You saw for yourself she was all right. Now, go back to sleep."

Kathleen looked dazed as she turned to leave. Danielle followed behind her. Mike sagged against the wall.

"We can't keep doing this," Jack muttered.

Mike nodded his agreement as he turned back to the kitchen. David and Doug were before Sera, blocking her from Liam. Liam was standing by the sink; his hands clasped on the counter so forcefully he was shaking. With his head bowed, hunger radiated from him like a heat wave.

"They're gone," Jack said.

David and Doug glanced back at them. "Would you please get her out of here!" Liam grated.

David and Doug backed up, pushing Sera with them without touching her. Sera's gaze was focused on Liam's trembling back as she shuffled away. She wanted to go to him, to soothe him, but she knew he would lose it again, and this time he wouldn't come back.

A sob rose in her throat, but she suppressed it as she tore her gaze from him. She was lucky to get away before; she couldn't risk not being able to get away again. Her breath froze in her lungs as her legs instantly planted themselves. David and Doug bumped into her and immediately jumped away when Liam lifted his head.

"What is that?" Sera cried.

Four sets of red eyes hovered just outside the window. "Shit!" Jack exclaimed.

"Get her out of here!" Liam yelled.

He turned and raced out the door in a blur of motion.

"Liam!" Sera screamed and lurched forward. "No!"

Doug grasped her shoulders and pushed her back. "Stay with her!"

Jack grasped her shoulders and released her as if she'd burned him. The minute she was free, she bolted forward. David blocked her off as Mike and Jack ran out the door.

"If you go out there, you'll only distract him and get him killed," David said. "If you go out there, he will bring you back in here, and he will finish what he started. There will be no stopping it this time."

Sera glanced at David before looking longingly at the door. She knew what those eyes were, knew what they represented, and Liam was out there with them now. She needed to help him.

"There's nothing you can do to help him. Come on, let's get you cleaned up," David said.

She didn't move for a second, and then her shoulders slumped in defeat. She turned and woodenly walked out of the room.

CHAPTER EIGHTEEN

SERA NUMBLY ACCEPTED THE PEROXIDE, cotton balls, and bandages David handed her before he walked over to sit on the other couch. She fumbled with the peroxide, spilling some on her dirty jeans before finally managing to get it on a cotton ball. She winced as she gingerly cleaned the jagged tears in her chest. Her hands trembled as she ripped the plastic wrapping around the large bandage, and taped it to her chest.

She closed her eyes as she took a deep, steadying breath, and tugged anxiously at her torn shirt. "He's all right," David said kindly.

Sera nodded. "I know."

"Can you sense him?"

She frowned. "Sense him?"

"Yes, can you sense him, feel him?"

"No. I just know he's all right, for now."

"He'll be okay. He's strong."

"Who were they?" she whispered.

"Probably some of Beth's friends. I'm sure she's created a

few others along the way, and some of them stayed with her. Or, she's gathered some here to help. We're not all the same, Sera. Some of us are brutal killers. They relish in their power, thrill in it. The more you drink, and the more you kill, the stronger you are. They may be here just because Beth promised them a bloodbath."

Sera's hands trembled as she anxiously pulled at her shirt. "Liam, Jack, Mike, and Doug aren't killers. They won't be as strong as them."

"No they're not, but they will be all right. Liam's fury alone will be enough to overpower them. They just want the pleasure of the blood. He's trying to keep you safe, that is a far stronger motivator."

"Oh God," she moaned. "He needs to come back."

"He will. They'll drive them away, but he won't follow them. He won't go far from you, not now."

She felt numb as tears slid down her face. She had to believe David was right. If Liam didn't come back, if he got hurt, if he was killed....

Her heart shattered at the thought as she began to tremble. *Please God*, she prayed silently. *Please let him come back to me.* "I can't live without him," she whispered.

David clasped his hands together and leaned forward. "No, you probably can't."

Sera choked on a sob as she bowed her head and fiddled with her shirt. "Can they come in here?"

"No, they weren't invited. Only Beth can come in here. Sera—"

"You okay?" Sera jerked around as Mike appeared in the doorway.

She leapt instantly to her feet. "Where is he?" she demanded.

"In the kitchen, but..." Mike blocked her before she could go through the doorway. She glared at him as she tilted her chin defiantly. "You need to stay here."

"I—"

"No, Sera, not now." His stance was so rigid she knew arguing with him was useless.

"Is he all right?"

"He's fine; he's just a little, ah... he's a little crazed right now. Jack and Doug are with him."

"Are you sure?" she asked anxiously.

"Yes, why don't you sit down and relax."

"What about you guys, are you all right?"

She scanned him, but he seemed fine. "Yeah, we're all fine. They took off when we went outside. I think they wanted to let us know they're here. That they're watching us."

Sera's gaze flickered toward the kitchen. She wanted to go to him; she needed to go to him. "I can calm him down," she whispered.

"Not now you can't," David said. "Now, you will only push him over the edge."

"But he needs me!" she cried as she whirled to face him.

"Yes, he does, but not like you are. Not with what is going on. He will finish what he started earlier, Sera; don't doubt that for an instant."

For a second, she didn't care, but it was only for a second as she recalled the way he'd been earlier. He would never listen to reason now. He would only attack her again. He wouldn't even give her the chance to offer herself to him. As much as she wanted to be with him, she knew she couldn't let it happen like that. He would harm her, no matter how unintentional, he would. And he would hate himself for it.

She bowed her head as she turned and walked back to the

couch. Her heart was breaking as tears rolled down her face. She slid limply onto the couch and hung her head in her hands.

"Do you understand now that what I told you all yesterday was true?" David asked.

She lifted her head to look at him through blurry eyes. "I understood earlier."

David frowned as he glanced over at Mike. "You want to be changed?"

"I won't lose him. I can't. It... it hurts to even think about it, to say it. You can't imagine how much it hurts."

"No, we can't."

"Why hasn't he done it already?" Mike asked his voice filled with confusion.

She turned her eyes to him. "He said I would need blood, and Kathleen and Danielle... I can't. I just can't."

"Crap," Mike muttered. "I never realized... I forgot."

David dropped his head into his hands. "We need to get out of here."

"Maybe the roads will be open tomorrow," Mike said hopefully.

"I doubt it. We're miles from the highway, on a bunch of back roads. I wouldn't be surprised if they didn't get here for another week."

"He doesn't have a week, and neither does she."

"I know that!" David retorted.

"What happens if I don't have blood?" she inquired.

They both turned wary, troubled eyes on her. "If you don't get it within the first day, the transformation won't be complete. You'll die."

"Or turn into a creature stuck between the worlds. Something completely twisted—an utter monstrosity. You would have to be destroyed."

"You could have left it at I'd die," she said dryly.

"We'll figure out something," David said.

"What?" she muttered.

"I don't know, but we're going to have to do it soon. Very soon."

THE FEATHERY TOUCH on her cheek woke her the next morning. She smiled as she nuzzled into Liam's hand. Then, the events of the night crashed back over her, and her eyes flew open. He was kneeling before her, his eyes clouded and his face impassive.

She sat up slowly. Her neck and back were stiff from sleeping on the couch, what little sleep she had managed to get. She waited for him to come to her all night, but he hadn't, and eventually, exhaustion won out. She glanced around the living room, but they were alone.

She returned her attention to him. She had changed her shirt last night, but his gaze settled on where the bandage was. "Are you okay?" he asked hoarsely.

"Yes."

"I hurt you."

"No—"

"Yes, I did!"

Sera winced at the anger radiating from his voice. "Liam—"

He gripped her arms and pulled them forward. Sera tried to jerk them back, but he was already shoving the sleeves up. Bruises marred her upper arms and the delicate bones of her wrist. His breath rushed out of him as he gazed upon the ugly, dark marks. Marks he inflicted. He dropped his head as self-loathing gripped him.

"You didn't mean to," she whispered as she brushed back his raven hair. "It wasn't you."

"It was me!" he spat. "It *is* me!"

Her lower lip began to tremble as tears filled her eyes. He thought he had himself under control enough to see her, to come near her. He'd been wrong. His composure was rapidly unraveling as he thought about what could have happened to her, what Beth could have done to her, what he could have done to her.

He dropped her arms and stood swiftly. "Liam, please don't shut me out."

He couldn't shut her out if he tried. He couldn't get her out of his mind, out of his body, out of his soul. She was a part of him, and he needed her more than the blood keeping him alive.

"I have to go somewhere," he said.

"Where?"

"David and I are going to take the snowmobiles out."

"You can't!" she cried. "You can't go out there! Those things are out there! She's out there!"

He knew what was out there better than she did. He was aware of what they wanted, and that was her. "Liam," he heard her stand, but he didn't turn to face her.

"Sera stay away, just stay away." She sat back on the couch. "I have to go. This is something I have to do."

"Why?"

He ground his teeth as he moved further away from her. He could smell her blood. The memory of what it tasted like caused his teeth to lengthen, and his mouth to water. "I have to find food," he grated.

"You can just go into the woods!" she cried.

"For you. I have to find food for you."

She inhaled harshly as her hand fluttered to her throat. "Oh," she said dully as realization sank in. "I see."

"When I come back..." he grated.

Sera bit into her bottom lip. "I know."

"Good." He turned and walked from the room. He had to get away from her, now.

"Liam." He froze in the doorway as her voice drifted over him. "Please be careful."

"I will be."

"I love you."

He closed his eyes, clenched his jaw, and forced himself to leave before he couldn't.

SERA GAZED out the window as dusk descended. She had long ago retired to her room, unable to face Kathleen's enthusiasm, Danielle's cheerful laughter, and Mike, Doug, and Jack's pitying glances. Her thoughts were in such turmoil she could barely understand what they were saying to her, let alone try to function.

She turned away from the window and woodenly moved toward the bed. These were her last hours as a human. Despair filled her as she slumped to the mattress. She wondered if it would hurt. It was a little uncomfortable when Liam bit her, but he hadn't taken it all before. He would now. When he changed her, when she died, would it hurt? It had to; dying couldn't be easy.

She shuddered as she wrapped her arms around herself. She was sitting here, waiting for death to come, for her death. She should run, she should flee into the night and never look back. But she couldn't move. She had nowhere to run, and even if she did, she knew she would return to him.

The waiting was killing her. The creeping by of minutes was making her edgy. She wondered where he was. She knew he was safe, she could feel that, but she still wondered where he was and when he would return to her.

She bit her bottom lip as she clasped her hands together. She could leave. If she left now, then she would be able to put some distance between herself and the cabin. There was another snowmobile; she could take that and go. No one would know until it was too late.

A muffled knock at the door caused her to jump. "Sera, are you okay?" Mike asked.

"Yes," she called back.

"Let me know if you need anything."

"I will."

He had come down at least twenty times since she had locked herself in over two hours ago. She knew he was worried, but he was driving her insane. Her nerves were frayed enough without being startled every ten minutes by his incessant need to check on her. She should have gotten used to expecting him, but her thoughts were too discombobulated to even try to remember Mike would be coming by every few minutes.

She stood back up and began to pace the room. Suddenly she stopped, her head tilted to the side, as she looked at the night beyond the window. Liam was back. She knew it, felt it. She walked over and closed the blinds. Her hand trembled as she stepped back. A steel cord of resolve strengthened her spine. She knew what she had to do.

LIAM AND DAVID stomped the snow off their shoes as they entered the back porch and quickly shed their wet winter clothes. It had taken hours, and miles of snow, but they eventually found an open rest area. It took almost as long to wait for enough people to stop there but eventually, they had. He'd fed until he couldn't feed anymore, and then fed again.

He needed to make sure he had enough for Sera; that she would get enough blood for everything to go smoothly. He had seen the things that got stuck in between human and vampire, and they were horrendous monstrosities. He would die before he allowed that to happen to her.

"You going to be okay?" David asked worriedly.

"Yeah."

Now that he'd fed, and the moment was nearly upon him, he was much calmer and more relaxed. He almost went insane on the ride to the rest area and drove like a bat out of hell all the way back with the monster clawing at his insides. But now, here, he felt somewhat in control of himself again. For the first time since yesterday afternoon, he had a firm grip on himself.

His heart contracted when he saw Sera wasn't in the living room. "You're back!" Kathleen greeted happily.

"Where's Sera?" he demanded.

"In her room," Kathleen replied. "Taking a nap."

His gaze swung to Mike. "You left her alone?" The idea of it rattled his newly found composure.

"She's perfectly capable of taking care of herself!" Kathleen retorted.

Liam's jaw clenched, but he refused to look at her. "She's fine," Mike said. "I've been checking on her, and don't forget I can sense Beth's presence too."

"Who's Beth?" Danielle asked.

"Oh crap," Jack moaned in disgust. "Good going, Mike. I'm not doing it this time!"

"Doing what?" Kathleen demanded haughtily.

David chuckled under his breath as he stepped into the room. "Be gentle," he mumbled to Liam. "I'll do it," he volunteered.

"Do what?" Kathleen and Danielle asked in unison.

Liam couldn't help but laugh as he turned on his heel and headed down the hall. He paused at the door, suddenly hesitant. He didn't know what would happen when he saw her, didn't know what he would do. He only hoped he could keep himself under control for as long as this took. He didn't want to hurt her any more than was necessary, any more than he already had.

He took a deep breath and pushed the door open. Shadows enshrouded the room; the blinds were closed against the night. His eyes instantly adjusted to it. "Sera," he said.

She was sitting on the bed, the blanket wrapped around her as she gazed at him. "I knew you were back," she whispered. "I felt it."

He frowned as he stepped into the room and closed the door. "Are you okay?"

"Yes. Did you succeed?"

"Yes."

"Good." The word caused his entire body to tighten. "Does it hurt?"

He wanted to tell her it didn't, but he couldn't. "Yes."

"A lot?" she asked tremulously.

"Sera," he breathed.

"I'm not changing my mind. I'm just scared."

"I understand that."

"I wanted to leave. I wanted to run. I don't want to die. But I couldn't leave you. I couldn't make my legs go. I just couldn't."

Her words brought the beast surging forth. He inhaled deeply to calm it. "I'll try to make it as easy as possible for you."

She stood and moved toward him. The shadows shifted and moved around her as she stepped from their embrace. "I know you will."

His hands shook as he grabbed her shoulders. She smiled as she released the blanket. It slipped smoothly down her body to puddle on the floor at her feet. The shadows hugged every inch of naked flesh as her hair cascaded freely down her back in thick, golden waves. Her full breasts heaved with her rapid inhalations. The white bandage covered her delicate skin from her collarbone to mid breastplate, and the sight of it was enough to drive him mad. His hands clenched on her. She was trembling, but she didn't move away from him.

"Make love to me," she whispered. "Do it then."

He groaned as her words shoved the creature aside and brought forth the man. He easily scooped her into his arms and carried her across the room. Depositing her on the bed, he fell on top of her in a heedless rush as his mouth seized hers. She whimpered as her hands dug into his hair. She pulled him closer against her as her tongue intertwined with his.

His hands caressed her breasts until her nipples hardened. Now that he was here, with her, he suddenly wanted to savor every second, and to relish in the feel of her. He wanted to memorize every inch of her glorious, silken body.

He kissed her lovingly as he tasted the sweetness of her mouth. Somewhere along the way she managed to slip his sweater over his head. She ran her hands along the rigid muscles of his back. They shifted and bunched beneath her touch as she tasted him. The hair on his chest was wiry against her cheek; the bristles on his chin rubbed her delicate skin. She teased his nipples, bringing them to life as he had done to hers.

He kissed and explored her as he made love to her with his fingers and mouth. There was no urgency, no rush as he moved over her. Although she was trembling with anticipation, wet with need, he didn't take her, and she didn't rush him to do so.

His jeans were somehow removed. He rubbed the head of

his cock against her temptingly wet sheath but still didn't bury himself within her. He wanted to spend the whole night feeling her, tasting her, teasing her, but her body became too tempting to refuse.

Sera trembled as he rubbed against her, and slid a little way in before pulling back out. She arched against him, moaning her dismay and making her urgency known with her writhing movements. She needed him now. She wanted him to fill her, to stretch her, to be a part of her. He slid leisurely in again, going a little further this time before pulling back out. She nipped at his shoulder to show her displeasure.

He chuckled as he slipped back into her. "I intend to drive you mad with want," he whispered in her ear.

"You already are!" she gasped.

He slid back into her and buried himself to the hilt with a groan of possession. Her legs tightened around him as she arched into him. He moved slowly within her, his mouth on hers as he made love to her with deliberate tenderness. His lips slid over her neck, her shoulders, her delicate collarbone and trembling breasts.

He moved his hand between their bodies and rubbed the quivering nub between her thighs. He watched as her eyes clouded with passion, her lip trembled, and her body bucked beneath him. She cried out as her fingers dug into his back, and her muscles contracted deliciously around him.

His smile was pure satisfaction as her legs loosened, and she fell, limp and trembling, to the bed. She gazed dazedly at him as a content smile curved her full lips. "We're not done, love," he murmured. "Not by a long shot."

He took possession of her mouth as he began to move within her again, sparking the fire of passion back to life. Sera was amazed to find her body responding to his again. She hadn't known it was possible to feel so completely sated and still want more. As his hands stroked her, and his body moved within hers, she found herself swept up with him again.

He waited until he knew she was close and he could push her over the edge anytime he wanted. He wished he could go on like this all night, but his restraint was slipping further away with every moan of pleasure. She felt so good it took all he had not to end his torment and spill into her. But he was going to wait for her. This time, he would go with her.

He smoothed the hair back from her neck, and his eyes latched onto the marks. The animal did not burst free, but came leisurely, and at his command. "It's time Sera," he whispered.

Her glazed eyes met his. "Yes."

He bent his head to her neck as she turned her head to allow him better access. He bit into her. Sera cried out as her hands dug into his back. He drove into her as her blood filled his mouth and flowed down his throat. She moaned as her body ground against his. As her blood flowed, he brought her to the brink of the abyss and with a final, deep thrust, he drove them both over.

She cried out as she fell back against the bed, her body trembling, weak, and very sated. Liam held her shaking body as he felt her begin to weaken. He also felt her utter trust, blissful contentment, and the unconditional love she possessed for him. Her hands on his back began to slacken, her grip on his waist eased.

Finally, he pulled away. She lay on the bed, pale, and unmoving. Her lashes curled against her slender, delicate cheek. A sense of urgency enveloped him as he grabbed the dagger he had left by the bed. He cut the base of his throat and scooped her up. He clutched her head and pulled her forward. Her head lolled back; a whimper escaped her as he lifted her to the blood on his neck.

"Drink, Sera," he ordered briskly.

She didn't respond at first, and panic flashed through him. Had he taken too much? He had never done this before, but the demon inside instinctively withdrew from her when he made it to a certain point. He knew he'd taken enough to kill her as he could hear the weak flutter of her heart within her delicate ribcage.

"Sera, drink!"

The butterfly brush of her lips against his neck tightened his body. And then her mouth enclosed on him. His hands dug into her thick hair as he cradled her skull. At first, she simply lay there and allowed the blood to trickle down her throat. He could feel it slipping inside, drifting into her veins, and burning through her body.

Then, her hands clenched upon his back, and she clamped down. Liam groaned with ecstasy as her mouth sucked on him. He was filling her in every way, making her his in every way. He grew erect inside of her but didn't move. Suddenly her mind filled his. Pleasure swamped him, followed by an urgent longing for more. There was no fear anymore as she bit down more forcefully. Liam's hands clenched on her head as he ground his teeth against the urge to begin moving within her, to take her in every way again.

He pulled out of her, and she bit harder as her displeasure radiated through him. He didn't have to tell her this was the easy part, he was certain she already knew; that she could feel it in him. She was growing sated from his blood as she neared the end. Her heart fluttered and skipped a beat. A stab of agony ripped through her and tore into his mind. He groaned as she whimpered and trembled.

She was panting as she fell back. "Sera, it's going to be painful, but it doesn't last long."

Her eyes were clouded and hazy as they met his. Her lips

were swollen from his kisses, and covered with his blood. His finger lingered upon her luscious mouth as he wiped the blood away. Her body arched off the bed as a cry of agony tore from her. He buried his face in her hair as she bucked and kicked beneath him. He wished he could take all her anguish away, absorb it into himself, but he couldn't.

They all had to go through the agony of dying and being reborn.

A scream tore from her throat as she twisted away from him and drew her legs up against her chest. He allowed her to turn to the side but kept his arms wrapped around her. She buried her head in his chest as shivers racked her body. Sweat poured from her as she moaned and whimpered in agony.

He tried to comfort her, but there was nothing he could do. She screamed again as her body jackknifed off the bed. He grasped her shoulders and pinned her back down. A wail erupted from her; her fingernails ripped into his forearms as she attempted to jerk free. Her head whipped back and forth as she arched and bucked.

A cry escaped from her as she curled back into a ball. Tears streaked her face as she lay sweating and shivering. Liam grabbed the blanket and wrapped her securely within it before drawing her against his chest. He knew from experience the worst of it was over, but it would be a long time before the spasms and shooting pains subsided.

He brushed her damp hair from her face and lay beside her as he encircled her protectively. "It will be all right," he promised. "The worst is over."

She whimpered in response as another shudder racked through her, and she trembled within his grasp. "Hold on, Sera. It will be all right."

He continued to calm her with his words and gentle touch. It was after two in the morning before she finally drifted to sleep. He lay awake long after, fighting against waves of self-hatred and exultation. He had hurt her deeply. Even now, in her sleep, she whimpered and moaned every once in a while. But no matter how much he hated himself for it, she was his; she was finally all his. No one would ever take her from him. Ever.

CHAPTER NINETEEN

Sera's lids fluttered open and then closed again. She felt so weak, so drained and exhausted. She inhaled deeply as she tried to gather the energy to move. A million different scents assailed her at once. Apple, vanilla, cinnamon, wood, sex, and blood permeated the room. Beyond the door, she could smell eggs, bacon, waffles, syrup, and butter. The smell of snow and something feral drifted in from outside.

She could hear the pots and pans in the kitchen, catch bits and pieces of the conversation out there. Outside, a squirrel yelled as it fled from its tree and crashed into another branch. Her eyes opened. She could make out every grain of wood on the door, and see the scratches on the brass handle.

She closed her eyes again; she was too tired to assimilate everything now. Liam lay beside her; his strong arms encircled her as his firm body spooned hers. She could smell herself on him, in him. She could hear the thumping of his heart and the blood pulsing through his veins.

"The world is different."

She didn't have to look at him to know he was awake. "Yes,

it is. It will take a little while to get used to, but eventually, you'll adapt."

"It's so loud."

"That's the worst part. I'll teach you how to tune it out."

"Soon?" she asked hopefully.

"Yes. How do you feel?"

He pushed back strands of her hair. She turned slightly to look at him. His face was as magnificent as she recalled, but suddenly she could see every bristly hair on his cheek and jaw. She had thought his eyes a pure green, but there were flecks of gold within their depths. She frowned and closed her eyes again.

"I'm tired," she whispered as she stifled a yawn.

He dropped his head to her shoulder. "You need to feed."

A tremor of revulsion and delight racked through her. Suddenly, she was starving, but she knew food wouldn't satisfy her. "Come here."

She opened her eyes as he pulled her into his arms and rolled her over. She looked down at him as her hair fell across his chest. He smiled as he pushed her hair over her shoulder. The marks on her neck were vivid against her creamy skin. He eased the bandage from her chest off. His eyes focused on the scratches marring her delicate skin, but they appeared to be healing well. Her gaze followed his, and she gasped.

"You'll heal faster now."

"I can see that!"

He stroked her cheek with his thumb. She turned into it, nuzzling him as her eyes drifted closed. "Are you hungry?"

Her eyes sprang open. Surprise, revulsion, and hunger radiated from their depths. "It's all right," he said. "You only need to feed from me, remember?"

Her gaze traveled down to his neck. A spark of something

shot through her, something she didn't understand, but it rocked her body. She looked away, ashamed and frightened.

"It will be just like last night," he soothed.

He could feel the tension in her, the yearning to fight against him and what she was feeling. He remembered that feeling. He fought so relentlessly in the beginning, but in the end, the demon had given in to Beth's demands and its own urgent needs. He had been repulsed and frightened, but the feeling faded.

"I know how you feel; it will fade, Sera, I promise. But you must. The change isn't complete yet, not until you feed. You need the blood." That spark shot through her again. "I fed for the both of us yesterday."

Her body trembled from the turbulent battle she waged, and her eyes flashed from blue to violet, to a vivid red. Her elongated teeth caused blood to flow forward as she bit her bottom lip. She whimpered as she instantly released her lip.

Liam's eyes locked on that trickle of blood. He pulled her down to him, lightly licking her lip as he used his saliva to close the wound. Her teeth pressed against his lip as he stroked her mouth with his tongue. He pulled her away from him and guided her head down to his neck.

"Sera, you must," he urged.

Her mouth was warm and wet as her teeth pressed against his neck. He shuddered in anticipation as his hand dug into her skull. He wanted this so bad his entire body tensed with anticipation, and his breath froze in his lungs.

"Sera," he breathed.

Her teeth sank deep. Liam's hands convulsed on her as a wave of pure ecstasy shot through him. Her mind opened to his. In the beginning, her hunger was the only thing he could sense, but it started to ease as she filled herself on him. Then, other emotions began to come through. He could sense her revulsion, but beneath that was pure pleasure. Possessiveness radiated from her, and he smiled as he recognized the feeling.

A sense of completeness began to steal through him as he caressed her hair and back. She whimpered as she squirmed against him. Her desire slammed into him so fiercely it hardened him instantly. Her thighs parted as her hands dug into his neck and she bit deeper to convey her urgency to him.

He rubbed his cock against her, pleased to find her wet with longing. He slipped into her, stretching her tight muscles as he filled her completely. She sighed in contentment as her bite eased and he filled her in every way.

SERA WOKE AGAIN SOMETIME LATER. She felt sated, still a little tired, but utterly complete and blissful. Her head nestled onto Liam's steel shoulder. She snuggled closer as she dropped a light kiss on him. He murmured in his sleep and turned to envelop her in his embrace.

"Go back to sleep," he mumbled.

"I think we've slept enough. It's already afternoon."

"I know."

Of course he knew, she had known without having to look too. "I can't believe Kathleen hasn't come in to drag us out of bed."

"Neither can I," he admitted ruefully.

"Liam."

"Hmm," he replied sleepily.

"What can kill us?"

She knew he was instantly wide-awake. "Why?"

"Well, I am one of you. I know what I've heard about vampires, but you can go out in the sunlight, so what else isn't true?"

"Sunlight can kill us."

"Huh?"

He chuckled at the confusion in her voice. "Some of us," he amended. "We can all still go into the sunlight because we haven't become cold-blooded killers of humans. Whether the human is good or bad, their death has an effect on a vampire. The more you kill, the stronger you become, but the more limitations are placed on you. Vampires that kill lose the ability to be in direct sunlight, they will die from it. Beth can't be in it."

Anger rippled through her at the mention of Beth's name. Her hands dug into his back as a wave of possessiveness shook her. He was hers, and that was final. Liam's chuckle only served to infuriate her more. "I met Beth during the daytime." The name was bitter on her tongue.

"You met her during a snowstorm. There was no direct sunlight."

"Oh," she mumbled. "You've killed."

"Yes, I have," he grated, and he would do it again if anyone attempted to harm her. "And the sun has become more grueling for me. It stings my eyes more, burns my skin more. It also tires me out faster."

"I'm sorry."

He pulled back to look down at her. "For what?"

She shrugged as she caressed his well-muscled chest. "It's my fault the sun bothers you now. If it hadn't been for me, you wouldn't have killed Jacob."

An involuntary growl escaped him at the name. She smiled as she lifted her lashes to gaze at him. It was good to know she wasn't the only one who became angry and possessive. "It's not your fault," he grated. "And I will kill anyone else who tries to harm you. No one will take you from me."

"No, they won't," she promised as she rubbed his chest. "No one will take you from me either, right?"

"Right."

She feared he would meet someone else, someone better though. He would grow tired of her and move on. He could have any woman he wanted, and he already had. Eternity was a long time; there were a lot of women out there. Prettier women, smarter, sexier, better.

"Would you ever leave me?" he inquired.

"No!" she cried in horror. The mere thought of it ripped her heart to shreds and brought instant tears to her eyes. To lose him would destroy her.

"That's the way I feel, Sera. I can sense your thoughts, and you're wrong. There is no one better, no one else for me. You are it."

"But—"

He placed a finger over her trembling lower lip. "No buts. Don't you remember what David said? Together forever. The passion only grows."

"What if he was wrong?"

"He was right about everything else."

"What if you don't want me in a hundred years? What if you grow tired of me? Or you meet someone else?"

"Sera, stop it. I will never leave you, never find anyone better. There is no one better. Look in me and feel it for yourself if you don't believe me." She searched his intent gaze. "Open yourself to me."

She allowed herself to open to his thoughts. She couldn't exactly read them, not like she could when she was feeding from him, or he from her, but she could sense them. She knew he loved her and cherished her, but she suddenly sensed the full depth of his emotions toward her. It shook her to the core as she recognized in him the same feelings living within her.

She pulled out of him as she searched his intense gaze with awe. He would never leave her, never grow tired of her, she felt it; she knew it. She brushed a strand of black hair off his forehead. "Eternity is a long time."

He pulled her closer. "Not long enough."

"No, it's not," she agreed. "So what else can harm us?"

"Crucifixes and holy water are like the sunlight. The more you kill, the less you can tolerate them. Otherwise, a standard stake through the heart, beheading, and fire are the other ways."

"Oh. I've seen you eat regular food, does it do anything for us?"

"No. We can eat it, but it doesn't fill us. Eventually, you even lose a taste for it. Alcohol still affects us, but it takes a lot more for it to do so."

Sera frowned, there were so many foods she enjoyed, she especially didn't want to lose a taste for cheesecake. She winced as Kathleen's shriek suddenly pierced through her ears and into her skull. "Ow!" she cried as her hands flew to her ears.

He grabbed her hands and pulled them away from her head. Her face scrunched with pain as Danielle and Kathleen both screamed. "Look at me, Sera; listen to me, not them."

She focused herself on him as he explained how to control all her new senses and her new world.

CHAPTER TWENTY

It was late afternoon before they finally emerged from the bedroom. "It's about time you guys got up!" Kathleen cried. "I was beginning to think we would never see you again!"

Sera blinked against the sunlight as she stepped into the snow. The giant snowman had been assembled. He was sporting a carrot, black button eyes, a gray ski hat, and a cigarette dangling from where his mouth was supposed to be. "Yours?" she asked Mike.

"But of course, and if we don't get out of here soon, Frosty's going to be parting with his mouth."

Sera was suddenly hesitant to meet his gaze, to meet any of their gazes. "The electricity's back on," Danielle said. "And the phone lines are working. We called the town, and they stated that they should have the roads plowed tomorrow."

"Thank God," Jack groaned.

"Being snowed in wasn't such a bad thing!" Kathleen protested. "I thought since it's almost the weekend, we might as well stay and check out the ski resort."

Jack and Doug groaned. "I agree," David commented as he clapped snow from his hands.

"What?" Mike demanded.

Liam wrapped his arm around Sera's waist. She glanced up at him, but his face was impassive. "I think we should abandon ship before it starts snowing again," Doug said.

"I'm with him," Jack agreed.

"I trekked ten miles through the snow to get here. I think I deserve a little relaxation and fun," David argued.

"Why did you do that?" Danielle asked.

Jack rolled his eyes and walked away. "Damn idiots can't keep their mouths shut, we can't keep changing their memories," he muttered as he walked to stand beside Liam.

David shrugged as Mike and Doug scowled at him. "Felt like some skiing," he muttered.

"See!" Kathleen cried. "We should stay. It's not fair to expect David to come out here for nothing!"

"Why don't we talk about this later," Mike suggested.

"I think that's a good idea," Liam said.

Sera glanced back up at him. His face was still remote, but the flicker behind his eyes told her something troubled him. She frowned at him questioningly, but he shook his head and kissed her forehead.

Sera cast a sidelong glance at Jack. His hazel eyes were knowing as he grinned at her. Sera felt a blush creep up her cheeks as she lowered her gaze again. She chanced a glance at Mike, Doug, and David to find them all eyeing her with that same knowing gleam in their eyes and identical goofy grins. She focused her gaze on her boots.

Liam scowled at the four of them. Their grins grew bigger, and Liam gave up trying to intimidate them. "Well, come on!" Kathleen cried. "I'm starting to freeze. Not all of us have been in bed all day!"

She nudged Sera as she bounced through the snow to the house. Sera shook her head as she turned to follow her back to the cabin. "So, how are you feeling?" Mike asked as he appeared at her side.

"Fine," she muttered.

"Mike," Liam growled warningly.

Mike laughed as he slapped Liam on the back. "I can see your good humor has been restored."

Liam couldn't help but smile as Mike grinned. He could feel her chagrin, but he couldn't stop the pleasure sweeping over him. She was his now, and he was hers. He pushed the back door open and stepped aside to let her enter. Everyone filed into the tiny space, bumping and jostling as they tried to remove their snow gear.

Doug knocked into Sera and instantly jumped back as he shot Liam a worried glance. She looked up, her brow furrowed with apprehension as she turned to Liam too. He felt a spark of annoyance when Doug touched her, but it faded almost instantly. He smiled reassuringly at her as he pulled off his jacket. Her frown vanished as she returned his smile with a carefree air he hadn't seen in a while.

"Thank God," Doug muttered.

Sera silently agreed as she pulled off her scarf and hung it on the hook. It was so much more enjoyable to have this Liam back with her. Until then, she hadn't realized just how much she missed his smiles, laughter, and easygoing demeanor. He had changed so fast she couldn't recall what he'd been like before. She was frightened by the new alterations in herself, and the world around her, but she wouldn't change a thing, and she would do it all over again just to have him with her once more.

Love burst so intensely through her that she couldn't keep herself from running over and throwing her arms around him.

He grunted and wrapped his arms around her. "I missed you," she whispered.

He closed his eyes as he held her. He hadn't realized how bad he'd been until now, how close he'd come to being something he'd never wanted to be. But everything was all right now; *he* was all right now. She made him complete. He glanced over her head at Mike, Doug, David, and Jack. They were no longer grinning stupidly but staring at them in amazement.

"Oh, for crying out loud, you guys have been in bed all day, could you please stop pawing each other!" Kathleen cried.

Sera pulled her head out of Liam's shoulder; she smiled and kissed him. He grinned as he released her. Kathleen grabbed her arm and pulled her out of the mudroom. "Now that we've got you for a few minutes, I'm not letting go!" she declared as she shot a pointed glance over her shoulder.

Liam finished pulling his jacket off and hung it on the hook. "It's good to have you back," Jack said.

"Yeah," he mumbled.

"So, are we going to stay or not?" David asked.

Sera, Danielle, and Kathleen were gone as he entered the kitchen, but he could hear their voices drifting in from the living room. "If we get the chance to get out of here, I say we take it," Doug said.

"I agree," Jack muttered.

"Beth is still out there, she will come back," Mike said as he cast a worried glance at Liam.

"What are we going to do when we go back? She found us here, and she's already found us at the college," David said. "It will be harder to protect them at the school. They'll be more open."

Liam shifted as he crossed his legs before him and folded his arms over his chest. He could feel his anger steadily growing. Instantly, his mind sought Sera. He could feel her happiness, her joy as she laughed and talked with Kathleen and Danielle. He took a deep breath as her presence helped to pacify him.

"So what are you suggesting we do?" Mike demanded.

David glanced warily at Liam. "Honestly, I think the two of you should leave."

Liam stood away from the counter. "And go where?"

"Somewhere, anywhere."

"She'll find them," Mike said. "She'll track him through her blood, and she'll find them. Leaving isn't going to do them any good."

"And what about Kathleen and Danielle?" Jack asked.

"I think Beth will leave them be if Liam and Sera are no longer around," David answered.

"But you can't be sure," Liam said coldly. "And I can't leave them unprotected."

"We would still be here."

"Leaving isn't going to solve anything," Liam replied. "Until Beth is dead, there will be no peace," he said. "When we get back to the college, Sera will stay with me."

"Kathleen and Danielle?" Mike asked.

Liam closed his eyes and shook his head. "I don't know. I'd like to say Beth would leave them alone, but I know she won't. She'd kill them, or turn them, just to hurt Sera."

"Maybe it would be better if we did stay. At least we're all together, and if the ski resort opens tomorrow, we won't have to be concerned about food."

"Beth can come in here anytime she wants," Jack remarked.

"But with all of us here, she can't get to them. Not if we stay aware and awake," David said.

"So, for now, we stay," Liam confirmed.

CHAPTER TWENTY-ONE

Sera beamed from ear to ear as she stopped with a whoosh of snow. Pulling her goggles up she watched as Liam slid to a graceful stop beside her. He grinned as he pulled his goggles off.

"I'm glad we stayed," she gushed.

"Way to leave the rest of us in the dust!" Danielle panted as she skidded to a stop.

Jack and Doug halted behind her, breathing heavily as they scowled at her. "You're the ones who said you wanted to race!" Sera reminded them.

"That was before we realized you were hell on skis," Jack muttered. "I think Mike's still stuck in a tree somewhere."

Sera glanced up the hill as Mike cautiously picked his way through the snow toward them. She had to bite back a smile as she spotted the twigs stuck to his boots, clinging to his parka, hat, and scarf. "I hate this stupid sport," he muttered as he stopped before them.

"What did you hit?" Danielle demanded.

His scowl deepened as he angrily ripped a twig from his jacket. "A briar patch." Unable to stop herself, Sera burst out laughing. Mike's scowl deepened as he pulled another twig from his hat. "Glad you think this is funny."

"You would too if it was one of us," Liam replied with a grin.

Kathleen bounded up to them; she'd given up on skiing a couple of hours ago. "They're having a dance tonight! What happened to you?"

Mike muttered something as he pulled his glasses off. "Mike has trouble following the signs," Liam answered.

Sera laughed even more. "Oh, shut up!" Mike snapped.

Kathleen snorted and then laughed. "Anyway, they're having a big dance," she continued between bouts of snickering. "A kind of reopening celebration. We have to go!"

Sera immediately stopped laughing as she glanced at Liam. The smile slipped from his face as his jaw clenched. "I don't think so," Jack said as he popped his skis off. "Riding back to the cabin in the dark isn't such a good idea."

"I know the trails like the back of my hand," Kathleen replied airily.

"After you have a few drinks in you, I doubt it," Mike told her.

Kathleen glowered at him as she planted her hands on her hips. "At least I don't lose the trails in broad daylight! Besides, if you guys want to go back, that's fine, but I'm staying."

"Kathleen—" Sera started to protest.

"Come on, Sera. We've been cooped up in the cabin for three days now. I want to have some fun! Besides, have you seen some of the cute guys here? I'm going to that dance, with or without you!"

Sera closed her eyes and threw her hands up in defeat. There was no arguing with Kathleen once she made up her mind. "Fine," Mike said as he tossed his skis aside. "Whatever you want, Kathleen."

Sera was startled by the amount of resentment in his voice. Kathleen scowled at him as she spun on her heel and stormed back to the ski resort. Danielle glanced at them before hurrying to follow her. Sera bent over to pop her skis off; her earlier elation was gone. "There was no need to get so snippy with her," she told Mike.

"You do realize what will happen when the sun sets," Mike said.

"Yes, I do, but Kathleen doesn't, and you made sure of that. Getting mad at her isn't going to do any good. Arguing with Kathleen is like waving a red flag in front of a bull. I would have convinced her to go back eventually, but you can forget it now."

"Sorry," he mumbled.

"I'm taking you back," Liam stated bluntly.

Her mouth gaped as she spun on him. "No, you're not!" she declared.

"Sera, you are not staying here."

"I'm not going back to the cabin and leaving them here!" she cried. "That is not going to happen."

"You are not going back there in the dark!" he grated.

Sera's hands fisted at her sides. "I am not going to leave them. Besides, Beth can get into the cabin too."

"I'll be there, and someone else can come back with us."

"So there are even fewer people here to protect them. No way."

"Sera—"

"I am not going back!" Liam's eyes flashed violently, but she didn't care. She wasn't going to back down from this. Her friends wouldn't be harmed because of her. "They are at risk because of us, and I will not abandon them."

"You are not staying here."

She snatched up her skis. "If you force me to leave, so help me, Liam, I will go after Beth myself."

His nostrils flared. "What?"

"I will go out of my way to find her, to bait her. I will do whatever I can to draw her out, as long as it means they're safe. Do you understand me?" she demanded.

He tried to grab her, but she took a hasty step back. His eyes flashed dangerously again.

"I may belong with you, but that doesn't mean you own me!" Sera declared. "I still have a mind of my own, and whether you like it or not, I am staying. And right now, you're pissing me off!"

She slammed her skis into his chest, spun on her heel, and stormed after Kathleen and Danielle. Liam fumbled awkwardly with her skis, too shocked to do much more.

"Well now, it seems like Kathleen isn't the only one you shouldn't wave a red flag in front of," Jack chuckled.

Liam glowered as he thrust the skis at him. "Shut up."

Jack laughed as he caught the skis. "You really pissed her off; bet you're glad you'll be spending eternity with her now!"

Liam cast him a furious look as he spun and headed toward the lodge. His friends echoing laughter only served to infuriate him further with each step he took. He made his way through the small crowd gathered in the main room of the lodge. Sera's anger was like a homing beacon as he left the main room and strode down a hallway.

He found her sitting on one of the leather couches in a small sunroom at the far end of the lodge. There was no one inside as she stared out the multitude of glass panes making up the entire back wall of the room. Potted plants and trees filled every available nook and cranny. Deer heads hung on the wall by the small fireplace.

He crossed the small blue throw rug to stand beside her. She didn't turn away from the window as she watched the skiers coming down the hill. The setting sun washed over her in soft rays that lit her porcelain skin and highlighted the vivid violet blue of her eyes. He took a minute to admire her delicate beauty.

"You don't own me, Liam."

He turned to watch another group of people coming down the hill. "Sera, you belong with me."

"I know that just as well as you do, but you don't own me, and you can't dictate my life."

"If your life is in jeopardy, then I can, and will, dictate it!"

Her chin thrust out as she finally turned to look at him. "No, you won't. You will talk to me about it, and we will decide together, but you are not going to order me around. I won't have it, especially not in front of your friends."

Liam ground his teeth as he tried to keep a firm hold on his fraying patience. "I will not let you be injured, and if that means I have to tell you what to do, then you are going to do it."

Sera launched to her feet, her hands fisted as she rounded on him. "No, I won't!"

"You're just being obstinate now." He was staggered when her eyes flashed with red.

She couldn't believe he was treating her like this, that he was saying this to her. "I am not being obstinate. I'm telling you that you will not treat me like some possession you can walk all over and tell what to do. I am my own person, Liam, and so help me God if you keep this up, I will go find Beth, and—"

Sera was cut off in mid-tirade as he seized hold of her arms. She started in surprise; she'd never even seen him move. He lifted her, so she was eye-level with him. "I'm telling you right now you don't want to finish that sentence. You will stay away from Beth, and as long as there is any threat to you, you will listen to me!"

"Liam—"

"No!" Torment filled his eyes. "If something were to ever happen to you..."

He broke off as she laid a hand against his cheek. His eyes instantly returned to their brilliant emerald color.

"Nothing is going to happen to me," she vowed. "But you can't treat me like this, Liam. I won't live like that forever." His eyes flashed again as his jaw clenched. "Talk to me, don't order me."

He dropped his head to rest against hers. "Sera, when it comes to this, I can't help but order you around," he admitted with a ragged breath. "I am the one who will protect you and keep you safe. I have to."

Some of Sera's resentment melted as she realized he wasn't trying to be cruel, or unkind to her, he just couldn't bear the thought of losing her. When it came to the issue of her safety, the beast in him was just below the surface, and able to break free at a moment's notice. "All right," she relented. "But could you at least try and talk to me instead of treating me like I'm an idiot."

"You're not an idiot, you're infuriating," he groaned.

Sera frowned at him as he lifted his head to smile at her. "I am not!" she protested.

He lowered her back to the floor. "You're infuriating... aggravating... tempting... and utterly irresistible."

He punctuated each of his words with a kiss. By the time he was done, Sera's anger vanished, and her body burned with desire. She twined her arms around his neck as she smiled seductively and pressed her body against his.

"And you are just as infuriating, aggravating, tempting, and irresistible," she whispered as she brushed her mouth against his.

His lips seared into hers, melting her clear down to her toes as she sighed in contentment. Her fingers stroked the nape of his neck as she opened her mouth to his invasion.

"Hey... oh for God's sake get a room. The party's starting!" Kathleen declared.

Sera pulled reluctantly away to face Kathleen. She stood in the doorway with her hands planted on her hips as she grinned at them. "Hi, Kathleen," Liam greeted.

She shot him a disgruntled look before turning back to Sera. "Well, come on."

"We're coming, we're coming," Sera assured her.

"Sera," Liam growled in her ear.

She frowned at him as she cast a glance out the window. "The sun has set."

His head jerked to the window. "Fuck!"

Sera stroked his cheek in an attempt to soothe him. "It will be all right," she assured him.

"You stay close to me."

"I will," she promised, but the tension in his gaze didn't ease.

"Come on!" Kathleen urged.

Sera turned toward her, but Liam grabbed hold of her arm and pulled her back against his side. Resentment sparked through her again. She rounded on him, but the look in his eyes silenced any further protest. He was angry, but he wasn't mad at her, he was annoyed with himself for not realizing it had become so late. He was also apprehensive. It radiated from him as he held onto her.

She couldn't be angry at him, not when he was looking at her like that. "God, you guys are going to kill each other if you keep this up!" Kathleen took hold of her other arm. "Come on, Sera; you can part with him for a few minutes."

"Just hold on, okay? I'll meet you out there."

Kathleen's eyes darted between them before she gave Liam a scathing look and left. "What is the matter with her?" he asked.

"She thinks you beat me."

"What?" His eyebrows jumped into his hairline.

She grinned as she playfully bumped his hip. "Yeah, she thinks you're too possessive, and you're going to start beating me."

Liam's eyes flashed with humor as the corner of his mouth quirked. "Maybe I should start; you might listen to me then."

Her mouth pursed. "Just try it."

He grinned cockily as he kissed her. "Stay near me, I mean it."

"I will," she promised.

He let go of her arm and followed her out to the packed main room. The room was huge, with massive cathedral ceilings, and about fifty chandeliers hanging from the beams running across it. The bar took up the entire side of the left wall, while the main desk took up half of the right. A massive stone fireplace covered the other half and crackled noisily. A small band was set up on the stage jutting out from the back wall.

There were about a hundred people in the room, but they were all moving around the large space. Kids ran around, dashing by people, and disappearing through the doors leading to the arcade. Longing stabbed through her chest as she watched them go.

Liam squeezed her arm. She forced a smile as she turned to look at him. His eyes were troubled as they searched her face.

"Okay, let's go!" Kathleen clutched her arm and pulled her into the crowd before she could even form a protest.

She glanced over her shoulder at Liam, who was watching her. Sera turned away as Kathleen pulled her along.

LIAM'S EYES were focused upon Sera as she stood with Kathleen at the bar. A young man had approached them and was now leaning entirely too close for his comfort. Liam shifted as annoyance began to rise inside him. Sera's gaze met his, and she smiled at him. He managed a nod in return as his gaze shot pointedly to the man.

"She's not going anywhere with him," Mike informed him.

"I know that," he grated through clenched teeth.

"Then stop looking as if you're going to rip out his throat."

"Speaking of throats," Jack drawled. "I'm hungry."

"We all are," Liam replied coldly.

A group of people dancing by in a conga line momentarily blocked his view of Sera. He watched the line as he picked out the girls who could be possibilities for later. He lifted his gaze to find Sera studying him out of narrowed eyes. It was now his turn to smile sweetly. Her eyes filled with fire as her mouth compressed into a flat line. He had only a second of supreme satisfaction before the guy touched her arm.

"Would you like to dance?" he asked her.

"Oh, no thanks," she replied as she sipped her drink. "I'm sure Kathleen would love to though."

Without thinking she grabbed his arm and propelled him toward Kathleen. She turned back around to find Liam glaring across the dance floor. She wanted to feel satisfaction at his anger, but she didn't. All she felt was the powerful need to go to him, to be with him. She put her drink down and began to wind her way across the floor to him. She paused as the conga line went by with arms and legs kicking in a rush of different directions. She couldn't help but smile and laugh as they shouted and danced along.

Liam's hands settled on her waist, and he pulled her in front of him. She laughed happily as her hands settled upon the chubby woman before her. The music continued to play as they wound their way through the arcade, into the sunroom, and back out to the main floor.

She cast a grin over her shoulder to find Liam smiling down at her. His hands seemed to sear into her waist. The music came to a halt, and the line broke up. Sera whirled into Liam's arms and lifted onto her toes to kiss him.

His grin was cocky and slanted. "I'm hungry." His whispered words sent a mixture of yearning for him, and a craving for blood through her. "So are you, love."

She smiled as she lifted a shoulder. "Maybe."

"For more than one thing," he teased as he rubbed his erect shaft against her provocatively.

Her eyes sparkled as she grinned saucily at him. "Maybe," she teased.

"Well then, I guess I'll have to fulfill both of your hungers."

His nip on her lower lip sent a firestorm of want rushing through her. "Uh huh," she replied dazedly.

He wrapped his arm around her waist and led her off the floor. Sera's lustful haze broke, and she recalled a group of people surrounded them. She cast him a threatening look as he led her over to Mike, and Jack. He'd purposely distracted her and clouded her mind, just as he had deliberately left her in a state of arousal. He chuckled as he kissed her forehead.

"Soon," he promised.

He released his hold on her and turned to survey the crowd. "Where are David and Doug?" she inquired.

"Having fun," Jack replied.

Sera frowned at him as he grinned back at her. "I'll be back," Liam told her.

He turned to leave, but Sera grabbed hold of his arm. "Not a girl," she said quietly.

"Sera..."

Her jaw clenched as a wave of possessiveness washed through her. She didn't even want to think about it. "Not a girl."

His smile was wry with amusement as he brushed her hair back. "Would that upset you?"

She didn't find it at all amusing. "Well I could always go back to that guy at the bar, and see what he's up to."

Liam's smile faded. "Point taken."

"Good." She folded her arms over her chest as she stared crossly at him.

He bent down and brushed a light kiss along her neck before nibbling on her ear. Sera's irritation instantly melted as her body responded to his. "Your wish is my command."

He kissed her on the cheek and melted into the crowd. Sera watched him for a minute before turning back to Jack and Mike. They were both grinning at her knowingly. "Don't," she warned.

They burst into laughter. "I am so glad we get to watch this forever!" Jack cried.

"At least until it happens to you," Sera retorted.

Jack shook his head as he smirked. "I don't think so. I'll run the other way as fast as I can first!"

"I'll be right behind you," Mike said joyfully. "No way am I letting some girl get her hooks into me."

Sera scowled at them as she turned her back to the wall and leaned against it. Kathleen was on the floor dancing with the guy from the bar. Danielle was a few feet away dancing with another man. They were both laughing. Sera felt an answering smile tug at her lips.

"They're having fun."

"Yep," Mike replied absently as his gaze searched the crowded floor.

"What's the matter?"

He cast her a lopsided grin. "Searching for dinner," he replied.

"Oh," she said dully as Jack chuckled.

"Hey guys," Doug appeared at Sera's side with a cute red-haired girl tucked under his arm. "This is Bridgette."

"Hey," they all greeted absently.

"Bridgette's got a room, so we're going to head up there. Come get me if you need me."

Bridgette giggled as she ducked her head shyly. Mike and Jack exchanged knowing glances and grinned; Sera rolled her eyes at them. "And what room would that be?" Jack asked.

"Two twenty-four," Bridgette answered with another giggle.

Doug grinned as he turned and walked away from them. "Why don't we get rooms?" Sera suggested.

"Oh, baby!" Jack cried with a mock raise of his eyebrows. "You're not my type, but thanks for the offer."

Sera snorted as she shook her head. "Any woman who walks is your type."

Jack grinned as he shrugged his shoulders. "True."

"We probably could get rooms," Mike said. "If they have any open. I'll go check."

He moved swiftly through the throng until it swallowed him. Sera studied the crowd impatiently as she waited for Liam to return. Instinctively, she drew within herself to search for him. The knowledge he was feeding slammed into her. Sera pulled immediately back as hunger blasted through her, burned into her veins, and caused her teeth to lengthen.

"Hey, you okay?" Jack demanded worriedly.

Sera shook her head and dropped it into her hands as the pulses within the room beat against her. Sera whimpered as she tried to shut it out.

"Come on." Jack grabbed her arm and began to propel her through the crowd.

Sera kept her head bowed and her hand over her forehead to shield her face. The blazing hunger in her eased as the crowd faded away. She groaned as Jack slid her onto a sofa. She didn't have to look up to know they were back in the sunroom; she recognized the smell of it.

"Feel better?" She nodded but still couldn't bring herself to look at him. "It will get easier."

Sera risked raising her head to find him watching her sympathetically. "When?" she whispered.

"It takes some time, but eventually you can control it with no problem. I promise."

Sera turned her gaze from his to stare at the night. She was still shaking, and there was a fierce burning making its way through her veins. "It hurts."

"You get used to that also."

She turned back to him, but he was no longer looking at her. His pupils dilated as he searched the room. "Jack—"

"Get out of here, Sera!" he shouted. "Now! Go now!"

Sera leapt to her feet as the side door burst open. They spun toward it as cold air blasted into the room on a rush of wind and violent red eyes. Jack leapt forward, only to be flung across the room and slammed into the fireplace. Sera screamed as she lurched toward his lifeless body.

"Jack!" Hands snatched hold of her arms and yanked her backward. "No!"

Her wail broke off when the hands scrambling over her skin, covered her mouth. She thrashed in their grasp, kicking and clawing at the hands pinning her against a massive chest. She knew it wasn't Beth who held her, but one of the other things. She bit deep into his meaty palm; satisfaction filled her as his blood spurted forth. He hissed loudly in her ear as something smashed against her head. Sera was left dazed and disoriented as she went limp in his arms.

Cold air blasted against her skin, she had just started to renew her fight when she was hit again, and the world went black.

CHAPTER TWENTY-TWO

LIAM FROZE in the middle of the crowd. The people dancing bumped and jostled into him, but he didn't notice. He spotted Mike making his way back toward where Liam had left Sera. David was cutting across the floor toward him.

"Excuse me."

Liam ignored the young girl as his eyes shot toward where Sera had been. His heart leapt into his throat as an all-consuming sense of urgency enveloped him. He shoved through the crowd, ignoring the startled cries and angry looks shot his way.

"Where is she?" he demanded.

"She was here with Jack." Mike gave him a look that said he thought Liam had flipped his lid.

"Where is she now?" he spat.

"Hey Liam, calm down..."

He spun away from David and opened himself to her presence. Nothing but darkness encompassed him as the beast burst forth.

"Holy shit!" Mike yelled. "Not here, Liam! Not here!"

He shook off their hands as he shoved his way through the crowd. He could smell her blood. He knocked someone to the ground in his haste. "Hey!" they shouted.

Liam burst out of the crowd as he followed the scent of her blood to the sunroom. "Jack!"

Mike and David shoved past him as they ran to Jack's side. They grabbed hold of his arms and shook him forcefully. Liam stepped out of the shattered windows and into the snowy night. His eyes rapidly scanned the horizon as he searched for any sign of her presence. There was no movement within the shadows of the still forest, but he could still feel her.

"Get Doug!" he yelled over his shoulder before disappearing into the night.

SERA WOKE SLOWLY, her head ached unbelievably, and there was an awful metallic taste in her mouth. Her jaw and cheek were sore, but it was nothing compared to the stabbing pain in her skull. She moaned as she rolled onto her side.

"Sleeping Beauty's awake."

Sera stifled a groan as she recognized the haunting, cold voice. A hand brushed over her forehead and brushed her hair away. She scuttled away from the touch as her eyes flew open. Agony shot through her battered skull as she blinked against the dim light. Beth knelt before her, a small, hate-filled smile on her beautiful, blurry face.

"I see my boys were a little too rough on you. I'm sorry about that."

Sera swallowed as she closed her eyes. The pain was beginning to subside. She put her hands beneath her and shoved herself into a sitting position; a small moan escaped her as she fell backward. Thankfully, a cold wall braced her. She slumped against it, breathing shallowly as she allowed the chill of the wall to ease the pounding in her head.

She opened her eyes again. They were in a small cave with jagged rock walls. A small fire danced in the center of the cave; Beth sat on the other side of it, studying her with a bemused smile. Sera's gaze drifted past her to the long tunnel leading out. Even with her enhanced vision, she couldn't see the end of it.

The three men behind Beth were half hidden in the shadows playing across the walls. Their arms were folded over their chests as they stared at her with reddened eyes. "Can we keep her?" one asked.

"Maybe," Beth replied absently. Sera knew no matter what, Beth would not let her leave this cave alive. She tilted her chin defiantly as she met Beth's hostile gaze. Beth smiled chillingly as her eyes flashed with hatred. "Maybe not."

"She would be fun to play with," another said.

"Oh trust me, boys, we will be playing," Beth assured. "But not yet. First, we have to wait for lover boy."

Fury suffused Sera; it burned through her veins and gave her the strength to move. She climbed unsteadily to her feet, her gaze locked on Beth's as she leaned against the wall. "That's part of the reason why I went back for him, why I changed him. One of the best I ever had. Then, he left me."

"Do you blame him?" Sera managed to grate out.

Beth's eyes flashed as a cruel smile twisted her face. "Then, he found you. I've always heard about the soul mate thing, I personally never believed in it, but I guess it is true. Do you know if you die, he dies? If he dies, you die?"

Beth moved unhurriedly around the fire. "You go insane if you do not immediately die," she continued. "I wonder what happens when you witness the death of the other?"

Some of Sera's defiance melted as a wave of cold terror washed through her. Her heart seemed to stop beating as her chest constricted. She couldn't bear to have anything happen to Liam. Her legs began to tremble, and it was only sheer willpower keeping them beneath her. Beth's eyes were gleaming as she stopped before Sera.

"Maybe I'll just keep you alive, and make him do whatever I want to keep you that way."

"I would rather be dead," Sera stated.

Beth's laugh was chilling as she touched Sera's cheek. Sera glared hatefully down at her as she jerked her face away. "I could probably even force him to make love to me, and make you watch."

The new demon inside her burst instantly free as she lunged forward. Sera managed to hook her fingers into Beth's shirt and claw into her skin as a haze of red clouded her vision. Beth snarled viciously and ripped free of Sera's grasp as hands seized her throat. Sera choked and thrashed as she was hauled against a solid chest.

Beth panted heavily as one of the men cradled her throat within his firm grasp. "You are so lucky I want you alive for this!" Beth spat.

Sera went limp in the man's hold, but he didn't release her. She panted as she tried to think of a way she could get herself out of this mess before Liam arrived. She had no doubt he would come for her, but she couldn't risk losing him, and these monsters were so much stronger than he was, so much crueler.

Her breath froze in her lungs as her head jerked up. "No," she breathed.

Beth flashed a grin as she turned around. "He's here."

Sera kicked and spit as she renewed her struggle. "Stay still, little girl!" her captor grated in her ear. "Or I'll break you like a twig."

"Liam, no!" Sera screamed.

A blast of fury ripped into her skull. Sera went limp as

Liam's presence invaded her mind and soul. She whimpered as panic and wrath chilled her from the inside out. Tears instantly began to slide down her cheeks. He was alone; she knew that. He had come alone, and he was going to die. He couldn't beat them, not alone.

Please go away, she pleaded silently. *Please.*

He didn't go away but appeared within the tunnel of the cave. Her heart leapt into her throat as his gaze fell upon her, red and livid. For a second, his eyes flickered, and the brilliant green of them blazed forth. His eyes returned to a vibrant ruby color as they landed on the man holding her. His face twisted into a furious snarl, and a vein in his forehead jumped forth as his jaw clenched.

"Hello, lover," Beth taunted.

Anger rushed through her as possessiveness swept her like a tsunami. She stiffened in the man's grasp. His hand dug into her neck as his claws pierced her skin. She bit back a cry of agony.

Slowly he turned from her to look at Beth and the other two men. "Beth," he growled.

Beth's smile was taunting as she gracefully moved around the fire. Everything inside him screamed at him to destroy and kill everyone here. It was only the thought of Sera keeping him at bay. If he attacked Beth now, he knew the man holding Sera would kill her.

"Did you come alone? Not smart lover, not smart," Beth continued to taunt as she stopped before him.

He glared at her hatefully, but every sense focused on Sera. Her fear beat at him as she remained unmoving within the man's grasp. Her silent plea for him to leave was the only thought he could register from her.

Beth's eyes sparkled with malice as she took a step forward. "What exactly do you plan to do?" she asked sweetly.

"I plan to kill you," he grated.

Sera couldn't suppress a whimper as the hand dug deeper into her throat. The man holding her lifted her, so her toes barely touched the ground. Liam's eyes flashed violently. The men in the shadows moved slightly forward.

"She'll be dead before you can move," Beth said laughingly. "It makes you mad he's touching her, doesn't it? Holding her? Stroking her?"

Sera whimpered again as the man nuzzled her neck. He seemed to be taking some cue from Beth. "She smells sweet," the man said huskily.

Sera tried to twist her head away, but he held her firmly as he leisurely licked her face. She couldn't see past the red haze clouding her vision as Liam's rage slammed into her skull.

"That really does upset you," Beth whispered. "Think about what they'll do to her when you're gone."

His last thread of control unraveled and he lunged furiously at Beth. She writhed within his grasp, hissing and spitting as he pulled her against him. His hands ripped into her arms, causing her blood to flow.

"Let her go!" he bellowed at the man holding Sera as his hand wrapped around Beth's throat.

The man holding Sera laughed as the other two steadily crept forward. "You're not going to kill her as long as I have this one. We can survive without Beth, can you say the same?"

Liam dug deeper into Beth's throat; he wanted to rip her throat out, destroy her; tear her apart. Sera's eyes were haunting as they fell on him, her terror beat against him.

He took in the air around him. He could sense his friends, they were coming, but they weren't close enough. "If I were you, I would let her go before I rip out your girlfriend's neck," the man holding Sera warned.

Sera's gasp brought his attention back to her. The blood

trickling down her throat was a vibrant splash of red against the paleness of her skin. The sight of it tore at him as it clawed into his gut. His hold on Beth involuntarily tightened, and his fingers dug deeper into her flesh. Beth spat as Sera flung herself backward.

The resounding crack that followed filled her with satisfaction as the brute's nose gave way beneath the force of her skull. He howled and released her as he grabbed his shattered nose. Sera twisted, braced her feet against his legs, and shoved forward. He grabbed her again, but then his grasp slipped, and she plummeted to the cave floor. Her hands and knees stung from the impact, but she launched herself back to her feet.

Liam had only a second to react as the other two rushed toward her. He ripped his hand across Beth's throat. Blood poured across his hand as she gurgled in distress and her hands flew to her torn windpipe. He shoved Beth aside and leapt over the fire as Sera jumped to her feet.

He grasped hold of her arms and pushed her backward as one of them grasped for her. Sera cried out as her back connected with the rock wall. She didn't have time to register anything before Liam was shoved against her. The two monsters were on top of him, clawing and hissing viciously. The one she wounded was recovered and coming at them again.

Sera screamed as one of them slashed at Liam. Blood spurted from his arm and splashed across her face. She struggled to get away so she could help him, but Liam kept her pinned against the wall as they slashed and punched at each other.

Claws tore at her as the one she injured arrived at Liam's side. She cried out as they ripped through her clothes, tore through her skin, and sliced across her ribcage. Liam howled as he grabbed hold of the arm and ripped it back. Claws ripped into the side of his face, slashing him to the cheekbone; he didn't seem to notice as he snapped the arm within his grasp.

A scream echoed through the cavern as the man stumbled back. Liam turned toward the other two, but they were on him. Their teeth snapped as one grasped his neck. Liam clutched the hand as the man tried to rip him away from Sera. He clung to the arm as claws sank deep into his throat.

He seized hold of the man's throat. The man's blood flowed forth beneath his long claws and poured down his arm. The man left jagged tears across his neck as he jerked back. Blinking against the pain suffusing him, Liam drove a fist straight into his nose and knocked him back a few feet.

Behind him, Sera fought to get free, but he couldn't let her out. These men would destroy her if he did. The other man reached behind him and grabbed Sera's arm. Rage tore through him as he swung back with his free arm and forcefully shoved her into the wall. Sera tore free of the grasp.

Her eyes widened as they landed upon the man clinging to Liam. They were going to kill him; she knew it. No matter how fueled he was by fury and love, they were going to kill him. They were too strong and too many. Something tore inside of her, and a primitive force burst free. She launched herself over Liam's back as she swung out ferociously. She caught the one holding him across the lower jaw and sliced him to the bone.

Liam tried to push her back, but she held onto his shoulder, refusing to back down. If he died, then she died, but she was not going down without a fight. Without warning the one holding Liam was ripped away. Sera caught only a glimpse of Mike's twisted face before his back turned. David and Doug were suddenly beside her as they pulled the others away. Jack was holding the throat of the one with the broken arm and shattered nose.

Sera slumped forward; relief flowed through her as Liam

straightened. His eyes were still ablaze as they settled on her. A cry of horror escaped as she stretched a hand out to touch his sliced cheek and torn neck. He took her hand, halting her from touching him.

He released her hand, and it fell limply back to her side. His gaze drifted over her; a snarl curved his mouth as his eyes landed on her torn side. His hands convulsed as he turned away. She knew there would be no reaching him, not now.

Sera slumped against the wall; her head bent as she inhaled a shuddery breath. Her whole body hurt. Her fingers clutched at the ragged wound in her side. Blood coated her fingers, but beneath that, she could feel muscle and bone. Nausea and weakness rolled through her as she slid to the ground, tired and drained. Black swarmed across her eyes, but she forced it back as she lifted her head to gaze dully at Liam.

He was holding Beth above the ground. She struggled weakly in his grasp as blood soaked her shirt. His claws dug deep, and he ripped through flesh and sinew as he tore the life from her. He threw her body aside and turned toward his friends. Their gazes held the same bloodlust he felt as they stood over the remains of the men.

"Liam."

Sera's weak voice dimmed the fury in him as he turned toward her. She lifted her blood-coated hands. His heart froze in his chest when her hands fell to her sides, and she slumped to the floor.

CHAPTER TWENTY-THREE

"I'll get some towels!" Mike yelled.

Liam barely heard him as he strode across the room with Sera in his arms. Her head lolled against his shoulder. Blood seeped through the shirt he had wrapped around her; it now ran down his stomach to wet the edge of his jeans and his skin. Normally, the amount of blood she'd lost wouldn't be a concern, but she was still so new and unsure of her abilities. She could staunch the blood flow on her own, from the inside out, and she had done some of it, but not enough. Her body would do the rest on its own, but Liam wasn't sure if it would happen in time. One thing was for sure, she needed blood, and she needed it now. Unfortunately, although he fed earlier, he was now weak and drained from blood loss himself.

He laid her on the bed and sat beside her as he pulled back the shirt to examine her wounds. Deep claw marks had torn through her flesh to reveal the sharp white of the bone beneath. The marks she'd managed to heal still showed some of the muscle. The wounds in her neck had healed completely, but blood still streaked her skin and wet the collar of her shirt.

"Here."

Liam took the towels Mike offered and pressed them against her side. Sera moaned but remained unconscious. Liam's brow furrowed as Mike hovered anxiously by his side. "She doesn't look so good," he murmured.

"I know that!" Liam retorted. Mike's eyes darted worriedly to him, but he refrained from saying anything else. "She'll be all right as long as we get some blood in her."

Liam brushed her hair back from her brow. Red streaked the ends of it. He desperately hoped it wasn't too late, that she hadn't already slipped past a line he wouldn't be able to cross. He couldn't lose her. The thought tore his heart and soul to shreds. He wouldn't lose her. He couldn't allow it. Blood seeped through the towels to wet his hands again.

"Take these." He gave them to Mike, and he disappeared into the bathroom to get more. Liam examined the wound again. More muscle had formed, but the process seemed to be stalled. He pressed a fresh towel against her side.

"She'll be all right," he whispered.

Mike didn't say anything as he handed over more towels and knelt by Liam's side. He gave him a questioning look before taking hold of her hand. Liam shot him an angry look but didn't say anything.

"I'm sure she will." Mike sounded doubtful as he squeezed Sera's hand and released it.

Liam closed his eyes and bent his head. She was still and cold beneath his touch. He could feel the waning strength within her; feel the tenuous hold she had upon life. Her breath barely caused her chest to rise. "Where are they?" he demanded.

"They'll be here soon."

Liam glanced hopelessly around the small hotel room. A

knock on the door snapped his head around. Mike jumped to his feet and hurried to open it. David, Doug, and Jack came into the room, each pulling someone along with them. There was a dull, glazed look in the eyes of the people as they stood soundlessly in the doorway. Doug shut the door and ushered them further into the room. Liam didn't care two of them were women and Sera would be upset. It didn't matter right now.

He climbed swiftly to his feet. "Hold this," he told Mike.

Mike hurried forward as Liam dragged the first girl into the bathroom.

LIAM CRADLED Sera's head as he pressed her mouth firmly against the slit he made at the base of his throat. She was too weak to feed on her own, too weak to even move. He held her close as the blood trickled down her throat and seeped into her veins. He could feel it healing her wounds as muscle and skin gradually repaired itself.

Even though he could feel her healing, she was still weak and unresponsive. If he wasn't holding her, she would fall back to the bed. He clung to her, praying for her safety, for her life. He had done nothing to deserve her, but if he lost her now, he knew he wouldn't be able to survive it.

Sera please, he sent the desperate plea into her mind through his blood. He felt a small flicker of a response as he continued to plead with her, to wish her to live. Her hands twitched in his lap. He fought back the waves of hope crashing through him. It was too soon to hope, too soon to know if she was truly going to be all right. Please, he pleaded over and over again.

Her mouth twitched on his neck, and she swallowed for

herself. His hands dug into her hair as her teeth pressed against his neck. He turned his head as she bit deep into him. He held her as he allowed her to take whatever she needed, whatever would help her. Her hands twitched again, and then her arms wrapped around his back.

Her mind filtered into his. He could feel her weakness, feel her hunger, and hear the tears she shed. Her love enveloped him in a cocoon, and for the first time in hours, he was confident she would survive. He was unable to get her close enough, unable to feel enough of her as relief filled him.

Eventually, she released her hold on him. Her eyes landed on him as she managed a weak smile. "You're going to be okay," he said.

"Yes," she croaked out.

He lifted her off the bed and carried her into the bathroom. Although she was sated, and her wounds healed, she was still incredibly weak. He set her down on the edge of the tub and stripped the bloodied clothes off her. She watched him in silence, her skin so pale it was nearly translucent, and her eyes shadowed.

Blood streaked across her cheekbones, hair, stomach, and thighs. Dark scratches still marred her side. For the first time, her naked body didn't bring him to instant arousal. Instead, all he felt was a need to care for her, to protect her, and shield her. He shed his clothes, scooped her back up, and held her against his chest as he stepped into the tub. He turned the water on and adjusted the temperature before pulling the tab for the shower. The water hit them with stinging hot needles. She rested her head weakly against his chest as the blood flowed off them. The water ran red for a long time as he gently washed it from her hair and body.

Stepping from the shower, he wrapped her within a towel

and carried her back to the bed. He crawled in beside her and pulled her against his side. She curled against him, her tiny hand clinging to his chest as she drifted to sleep. He stared at the ceiling as she breathed steadily; her body was warm and comforting against his side.

CHAPTER TWENTY-FOUR

Sera tossed the last of her clothes into a box and closed the lid. She was unbelievably tired and so grateful the packing was finally complete. The past few months had seemed to stretch on for years. Her classes had been endless, and she struggled every minute just to get through them. Where once her whole life had been books and good grades, now it took every ounce of strength she had just to sit through classes.

She spent her nights with Liam, but the time apart during the day was torturous. Not to mention the police inquiry into Jacob's disappearance lasted for over a week. Liam had wanted to take her away, but she was determined to stay and face it. If they ran, they would look guilty, and without a body, there was nothing the police could do to any of them. Other than Michelle revealing to the police she told Jacob where Sera was; they had no proof Jacob ever came to see her. Eventually, he was written off as an unsolved disappearance, and the police left them alone, and finally so had Michelle.

Sera was unbelievably grateful they wouldn't be starting their new lives as wanted criminals, on top of the other complications they already had and would always have. Their lives were never going to be normal, but she didn't care. They would always be happy.

She turned to Kathleen who was sitting on her bed. For the first time since the beginning of the school year, Kathleen's side of the room was immaculate.

"I can't believe it's over," Kathleen murmured.

Sera smiled weakly at her, silently thinking the same thing as she slid onto her bed. "Why don't you come with us?" she asked.

Kathleen smiled wanly. "I don't know; Oregon isn't exactly my idea of a happening place."

Sera absently fiddled with the edge of the box. Oregon had never been her idea of a happening place either, but they found a house there that was perfect for all of them. It was a large cabin, on a lake, and surrounded by woods. The nearest neighbor was five miles away, and the town only had a population of three hundred. Most people wouldn't even know they were there, let alone bother them. For the first time, she saw what their powers were capable of as they were used to help acquire the house.

"It's peaceful there," Sera said.

"I guess, but I thought you wanted to get your master's degree?"

Sera didn't know how to tell Kathleen she wouldn't need her master's or any other form of education. She only finished off this year because she had come this far, and stopping mid-semester of her senior year seemed like a waste. Now, she just wanted to hide herself away with Liam and the others. She just wanted to start a new life, to have a home and a family.

"Not anymore."

Kathleen's eyes were questioning as they met Sera's. She didn't say she thought Sera was giving up her hopes and dreams for Liam; she had said it often enough in the past couple of months. Then again, Kathleen didn't know what Sera was now. If their roles were reversed, and it was Kathleen in her position, Sera would be thinking the same thing.

Besides, there was something more, another reason why she had to go, why she wanted nothing but shelter and protection.

"I'll be in California, I'm sure we'll see each other often," Kathleen said.

Sera smiled weakly. "Yeah, I'm sure we will."

Kathleen looked doubtful. "Well, at least I know I'll like my new roommate, but it won't be the same."

"You and Danielle will have fun. Think of all the parties you guys will go to."

"Yeah, all the parties you're going to miss out on," Kathleen replied pointedly.

Sera smiled as she shook her head. "I couldn't party anyway." Kathleen lifted an eyebrow questioningly. "I'm pregnant, Kathleen."

Kathleen's mouth dropped open as she stared at her in surprise. "Sera, are you sure?" Sera smiled as her hand instinctively fluttered to her stomach and the tiny life inside. "How far?"

"Three months."

"How could you not tell me?"

"I wasn't sure until last week."

She couldn't tell her she'd been completely petrified and unsure of what to think or do. Unsure of what exactly was growing inside of her. "Does Liam know?"

"He does."

"What did he say?"

Sera smiled as she recalled his exact reaction. At first, he'd been elated, hugging and kissing her as he yelled happily. Then, reality sank in. The same reality that crashed on her and knocked out the joy, the same reality that robbed her of all the happiness she'd initially felt. David contacted his friends in Pennsylvania, while Sera and Liam sat anxiously by, hoping and praying she wouldn't have to get rid of their baby.

David's friends assured him it was all right, that she wouldn't give birth to a monster and everything would be okay. According to them, her child would be a vampire at birth and would grow until maturity, after that it would age no more. They assured David there was no harm to her or the child and there had been others of their kind born, and they had all been normal, or as normal as they could be.

Sera was still frightened though, and so was Liam. Although, most of his worries centered on her, while hers centered upon the life growing inside her. Their child would have no choice in its life. It would be born into a world of blood and death, and she prayed it wouldn't grow to resent them for it. Prayed David's friends were right, and everything would be fine. She had already grown to love the baby inside her, and she wanted it more than anything, but she was scared.

"He's happy," she finally answered. Which was true, he was happy, he was just frightened something would happen to her, and that fear overshadowed everything else.

"And you?" Kathleen asked.

Sera smiled as her hand stroked her stomach. "I'm very happy." Kathleen studied her intently, obviously not fully believing her. "I'm a little scared; we're both a little scared."

"Well, that's to be expected." Then, Kathleen grinned as she climbed to her feet. "You always wanted a big family. Are you two going to get married?"

Sera bit back a laugh. She had never even thought about a wedding; their relationship went far deeper than marriage. Their relationship was different, stronger, eternal, but of course, Kathleen would think of marriage as the ultimate bond.

"I see you told her," Liam said.

Sera looked up as Liam appeared in the doorway.

"Move." Jack shoved roughly by Liam as he strode into the room. "Like you need a stupid piece of paper," he mumbled as he grabbed boxes off the floor. "You two are sickening enough now."

"Thanks, Jack," Sera replied.

He grinned at her as he shuffled the boxes in his arm. "It's true," he defended.

"Yeah, it is," Mike said.

"So what do you say? Do you want to get married?" Liam asked.

Sera gaped at him. "Liam—"

"I bet you always dreamed of a big wedding, with a cake, and a beautiful white dress."

Now Jack, Mike, Doug, and David were gawking at him. Sera grinned at him. As far as she was concerned they didn't need any vows, they had already made them, but she had always dreamed of a wedding. He strode across the room and knelt before her as he took hold of her hand.

"So, will you marry me?"

His eyes twinkled merrily as he gazed at her. Sera grinned back at him. "Yes."

He smiled as he stood, wrapped his hand around the back of her head, and kissed her. The touch of his lips instantly sent a bolt of lust through her. She pulled back before she could completely lose herself to him. "Oh!" Kathleen cried happily. "We have so much planning to do! We'll need a dress and a caterer, and we're going to need to find a hall! I'm sure Oregon has some beautiful places! We'll have to start looking immediately. Unless you want to wait until after you have the baby, then it will be a winter wedding!"

Kathleen continued to prattle on about the plans.

"Oh for crying out loud!" Mike interrupted. "Could you make these plans on the plane, before we miss it?"

Sera's grin widened as she slid her arms around Liam's neck and kissed him again.

"Oh, congratulations!" Kathleen cried as she threw her arms around them both. "I'm so happy for you!"

Sera laughed as she wrapped her arms around her friend.

EPILOGUE

Sera rested her arms on the railing of the porch as she watched Liam glide across the lawn. Behind him, the lake was bright with the setting sun. The mountains loomed high above it and stretched for miles across the vast sky. She loved the coziness and security their home provided. The warmth enveloping it.

A seductive smile curved his mouth; his eyes sparkled as he caught her watching him. David's friends had been right about everything. Their children were happy and as normal as they could be for not being human. The children didn't fully understand that yet, but one day they would. David was also right about their desire for each other not dimming but growing stronger. Their love was more intense than ever, and it continued to grow every day.

"Mommy!" Ethan cried as he left his father's side. Sera moved to head him off as she was trying to rid him of his habit of running upstairs. In his overwhelming, four-year-old exuberance, he was more than likely going to fall.

He mounted the top step and raced across the porch to her.

His black hair was tousled and windblown as he flung himself into her arms. She scooped him up and held him close as his mischievous green eyes twinkled merrily. He looked so much like his father it was shocking.

"You're not supposed to run up the stairs," she scolded.

He grinned as he flung his arms around her neck, knowing it was enough to get him out of trouble. Liam stepped onto the porch; his head cocked as he studied them. Sera shrugged and grinned; she didn't feel any shame. He shook his head disapprovingly as he smiled and shifted their two-year-old daughter, Isabelle, in his grasp. Her chubby arms wrapped around his neck as she lifted her golden head to smile at Sera.

Liam moved swiftly across the porch as Ethan slid down her leg and bolted through the open sliding glass doors. Isabelle instantly wanted down to follow her brother. Liam set her on her feet so she could toddle through the door after him. "You're a wonderful disciplinarian."

Sera grinned as he braced his arms on the railing behind her. Her hands instantly fluttered to his chest. "I can't refuse you either," she told him.

"Damn right."

His kiss sizzled through her body, causing her to melt as she wrapped her arms around his neck and pressed against him. He pulled her closer, ravishing her mouth as the evidence of his need for her pressed firmly against her belly. Sera moaned softly as she eagerly responded to his kiss.

"It's the middle of the day! Go to your room!" Sera pulled away to grin happily at Jack. He was standing in the open doorway with Mike, Doug, and David by his side. "Did you have to be right about everything?" he demanded of David.

David leaned against the doorframe. "The way you guys are going there's going to be a hundred kids in this house," Mike said.

"Maybe then you guys will move out," Liam replied teasingly.

"Don't count on it. What time do Kathleen and Danielle come in?" Doug inquired.

"Four thirty," Sera answered.

"Why don't you guys pick them up," Liam suggested. The four of them scowled back at him. "Or at least two of you."

"And what would you like the other two of us to do?" David asked with a smirk.

Liam took hold of Sera's hand and pulled her toward the doors. "Watch the kids."

David shook his head as Jack threw his hands up in surrender. "A thousand kids," he mumbled. "I'm going to the airport; these two make me sick."

"I hate being right," David said.

"I'm glad you were," Sera replied with a laugh. "We'll be right back."

"No, we won't."

Liam pulled her through the door and down the hall. Sera laughed as she broke away and raced up the stairs with him on her heels. She had only a moment to realize they were never going to break Ethan's habit of running upstairs if they were his role models before Liam pulled her into his arms and his mouth descended on hers. All rational thought fled from her mind as she was swept away by him.

21 years later

"WHAT IS THAT?" Ian inquired.

Isabelle didn't know, but it radiated through the inside of her, shaking her to the core. Something was off; something wasn't right. It wasn't a scary feeling, but it upset her nonetheless. There was something in those shadows she'd never felt before, something she didn't understand.

"What are you guys talking about?" Delia demanded.

"Isabelle, go inside," Ethan commanded.

Isabelle shot him a nasty look as her jaw clenched and her hands fisted at her sides. She wasn't going anywhere if it meant leaving them alone with whatever the strange presence was. "No."

"Come on." A girl's voice, Jess's, cut through the air.

Isabelle could tell she was pulling on the man's hand beside her, but he wasn't moving.

"Stop."

The command, issued in a deep, husky voice, stopped Jess's movements. It also caused a bolt of amazement, and something else, something she didn't recognize, to jolt through Isabelle.

"Stefan," Jess said impatiently.

Isabelle strained to see through the shadows. Her night vision was exceptional, and she could make out a small, thin girl with light blonde hair standing in front of the car. Her hand was on the arm of the man next to her. Isabelle's gaze sharpened on him. His shoulders were broad, his build large and muscular, and his hair the color of the night surrounding him. The disturbance in the air came from him.

"It's him," Ethan whispered.

"Yes," Aiden agreed, his voice barely audible.

"Huh?" Delia asked.

They all ignored her as they focused their attention on the strange man hidden within the shadows. Isabelle could barely make out the planes of his face and the firm set of his jaw. He looked as cold as concrete, and he was as still as stone. His eyes were the color of onyx and focused on them.

"Come on, Stefan!" Jess pulled on his arm again.

He shrugged off her grasp as the shadows enfolded him within their embrace. Isabelle's heart leapt into her throat. She suddenly knew what was off, what he was.

"Like knows like!" she gasped.

"What?" Delia asked in confusion, as she took a quick step away from Isabelle and her siblings.

"Shit," Ethan's stance became even more rigid as his hands fisted at his sides. Her brothers grouped closer.

"You people are strange," Delia said as her eyes traveled fearfully over them. "I want to see my mom."

"What do we do?" Aiden whispered.

There was a shifting among the shadows, a small bristling as the man moved ever so slightly. "I wouldn't do anything," he informed them coldly.

Jess had called him Stefan, Isabelle remembered as she took an instinctive step closer to her brothers. There was something about his voice, something strange, but not unpleasant as it enveloped her like a warm cloak. It did something inside of her, caused something to stir and shift in a way she'd never experienced.

"Ethan," she whispered fearfully.

Ethan stepped forward to shield her more.

The man, Stefan, laughed faintly as he finally started to move forward. "I'm not going to harm you."

Another shiver slid through Isabelle at the sound of his voice. The shadows parted around him as he moved into the light. Isabelle's breath froze in her lungs; the world seemed to rock on its axis as her eyes locked on him. The angles of his perfectly sculpted face were highlighted by the light playing off his strong face.

His gaze traveled over her brothers before settling on her. His eyes were as black as onyx and just as cold. They penetrated through her, racking her bones as they seemed to steal straight into her soul. He was the only thing she could see and feel.

Everything else disappeared.

Then his gaze moved from hers, breaking the brief connection. Isabelle felt an incredible sense of loss as the breath rushed out of her, and the world slammed into place. With a startled cry, she turned and shoved her way past Aiden and Ian as she fled into the sanctuary of her house.

Read on for a sneak peek from *Destined*, Book 2 in the series. Or purchase now and continue reading:
brendakdavies.com/Dswb

Visit the Erica Stevens/Brenda K. Davies Book Club on Facebook for exclusive giveaways and all things book related. Come join the fun:
brendakdavies.com/ESBKDBookClub

**Stay in touch on updates and new releases from the author by joining the mailing list!
Mailing list for Brenda K. Davies Updates:**
brendakdavies.com/ESBKDNews

SNEAK PEEK
DESTINED, VAMPIRE AWAKENINGS BOOK 2

ETHAN POKED his head around the corner of the alley; his eyes instantly went to the diner across the street again. Light pooled from the streetlights, it spilled across the road and sidewalk, illuminating the cars parked along the road. Light from the diner blazed out of its big, plate glass windows. The woman who had captured his attention was sitting in one of the booths; her blonde head bent over the table as she read through something laying open in front of her. She looked oddly familiar. Biting his lower lip, his brows knit together as he studied her more carefully. He knew he'd seen her somewhere before, he knew her somehow, he just couldn't remember where or how.

He pulled his head back and leaned against the cold stone wall. He closed his eyes, searching his memory for any hint of who she might be. He had been doing the same thing for the last five minutes, and it was proving to be a useless endeavor.

"What are you doing?"

He jumped, his eyes flew open as Mike and Jack stepped out of the shadows of the alley. "Don't do that!" he snapped.

They grinned as they exchanged amused glances. They

knew he hated it when they cloaked their presence from him and popped out of nowhere to try scaring him. It often worked. What aggravated him the most was he couldn't do it to them. He couldn't control his powers as well as they could, and they knew it.

"So, what are you doing?" Mike asked again.

Ethan scowled at them as he glanced around the corner again. "I was looking at that woman in the diner."

"Ah hell," Jack groaned. "Don't tell us you're going to turn into your mother and father!"

"Hardly!" Ethan snorted, the thought alone made his stomach turn. "She looks familiar, but I can't place who she is."

Mike and Jack exchanged a glance before Mike poked his head out of the alley to look. "Where?" Mike asked.

Ethan leaned around him and pointed to the small, pudgy woman in the diner window.

Mike frowned thoughtfully, then his eyes widened in astonishment, and his mouth dropped. "It's Kathleen!"

"What?" Jack demanded, shoving his way past them. "Wow! It is! Crap, is that what we'd look like now?"

"She seems to have aged pretty well," Mike said thoughtfully. "She must be what, forty-seven?"

"How old are you, dumb ass?" Jack retorted sarcastically.

Mike scowled at him before turning his attention back to the diner. "Forty-seven," he muttered.

Jack smiled at him before turning his attention back to the diner. "There you go. Well, I guess she doesn't look bad. I'm just glad we don't look like that. Wrinkles," he said with a shudder.

"Shut up, Jack. Ethan, go over there and talk to her," Mike commanded.

"What?" Ethan demanded as he rounded on him in disbelief.

Mike nodded toward the diner; his short blond hair fell around his face. "Go over there."

Ethan stared at him incredulously. "*You* go over there," he retorted.

Mike and Jack looked at him like he was an idiot.

"We knew Kathleen in college, if she saw the way we look now, she'd probably have a heart attack," Jack explained slowly as if Ethan were dumb.

Ethan suddenly remembered who she was. Kathleen had been his mother's best friend in college, but he hadn't seen her in over fifteen years. He glanced back at the diner in disbelief. "What am *I* going to say to her?"

"Just go over there and see how she's doing. I'm sure your mom would like to know. Now, go on," Mike encouraged.

Ethan scowled at him. "I'm a little too old for you to be ordering around."

"You're not that big yet, now go."

He would have stayed and argued with them, but he knew it was pointless. They always won, and besides, he was more than a little curious to see how she was doing. He left the alley and jogged across the rain-washed street to the diner. The bell above the door rang as he entered, and the smell of human food instantly assaulted his senses.

Wrinkling his nose at the smell, he glanced down the line of booths to the middle-aged blonde sitting in one of them. Her short blonde hair was pulled into a ponytail, and strands of it fell free to curl around her small, heart-shaped face.

He was unable to move as he stared at her. She was not the woman he remembered. This woman had lines around her mouth and eyes, her forehead was creased, and her skin was beginning to sag around her neck and chin. Strands of gray streaked her hair. This is what his mother should look like, he realized with a start. The thought was incredibly sad and more than a little frightening. For the first time, he truly understood his immortality.

"Can I help you?"

Ethan blinked as he was pulled from his reverie by the cute waitress who stepped before him. An admiring gleam lit her brown eyes as she openly surveyed him. He returned her smile without thinking.

She moved a little closer, the menus in her hand brushed against his chest. "Would you like to sit?" she asked.

"Oh, ah no," he replied, casting a glance at Kathleen as he recalled why he was here. "I just came to see someone."

Her mouth pouted as she stepped back. Ethan brushed past her, instantly forgetting her existence as he made his way toward Kathleen. He hadn't seen her since he was ten years old, he highly doubted she would remember him, but he might as well try and talk to her. Besides, Mike and Jack would be pissed if he went back with nothing, and he didn't feel like dealing with the two of them.

"Hi, Kathleen, right?"

She looked up from the newspaper in front of her. Her large blue eyes blinked in surprise as her mouth dropped open. "Liam?" she gasped.

Ethan smiled as he slid into the booth across from her. "No, Liam's my father. I'm Ethan."

A cheerful smile spread over her pretty face. "I'm sorry, it's just... you look just like your father!"

Ethan slid an arm over the back of the booth. "So I've been told."

Kathleen's blue eyes rapidly scanned his face and posture as she shook her head in disbelief. "I can see some of your mother in you though. How is she?" she asked eagerly as she leaned across the table.

Although she'd gained some weight, and her face was aged,

she was much like the Kathleen he recalled. She was energetic, with an easy smile, and an amazing amount of warmth pouring from her.

He felt a stab of sorrow for his parents and their friends. They'd been forced to push Kathleen out of their lives to protect her and themselves. He knew how much it hurt his mother, and from the haunted look in Kathleen's eyes, he could tell it had hurt her too.

"She's doing well."

"Are they still living in Oregon?"

Ethan nodded. "Yes."

"Does she have the big family she always dreamed of?" she asked eagerly.

Ethan snorted as he grinned. *Big* was not the way he would describe the mob that was his family. "Yeah, there are ten of us."

Kathleen chuckled. "Your father must be going insane with so many kids."

"Nah, he likes it. Mike and David swear they're going to keep going until they have a thousand kids. Fortunately, they've decided to take a break for a while."

He bit his bottom lip, stopping himself before he told her they planned to have more later. He wasn't accustomed to speaking with humans, and he knew his comment would have only confused her.

"Honey, that's not a break, its menopause. Trust me, I know."

Ethan couldn't help but laugh. He'd forgotten how blunt, and open, Kathleen was. "I guess so."

"Mike and David are still around?" she blurted.

He nodded as he thought of the asses hiding in the alley across the street. "Yeah, so are Jack and Doug."

"I can't believe it. I don't know how I lost touch with everyone, but I guess as the years go by..." she broke off as she glanced down at the paper before her. "Ah well, such is life. So how about yourself? What have you been up to?"

Ethan bit his bottom lip. How was he supposed to tell this woman he hadn't been doing anything but living with Mike, Jack, Doug, and David in the house they'd built behind his parents' home? He didn't have to be up to anything. He didn't have to do anything but lounge around, enjoy his life, and help keep his unruly brood of brothers and sisters under control. He could do other things; he simply didn't want to.

"Ah, not much," he hedged.

She grinned as she pointed at him. "That's your mother."

"Huh?" he asked in confusion.

"She always used to bite her lip when she felt uncomfortable, or nervous, or when she was deep in thought," she explained with a wistful smile.

"Yeah, she still does."

Kathleen's eyes came back to his. "Well, you have to be up to something. College?"

"I graduated," he lied. He hadn't felt like being bothered to go away to school. His father, mother, and his friends told him he would enjoy the experience, even if he didn't need the education, but he didn't want to go. "I do odd jobs here and there." This was at least true.

Kathleen nodded and took a sip of her water. "I'm sure you'll find your way someday."

"Yeah."

Ethan glanced out the window. Mike and Jack remained hidden within the shadows of the alleyway, but he could see them.

"What about you?" he asked, returning his attention to her. "The last I knew you were going to France, to ah... take pictures?" he recalled.

Kathleen leaned back in the booth. "That was my ex-husband, he was the photographer. My daughters and I went with him."

Ethan barely remembered her daughters, and he couldn't recall their names. He knew one was two years younger than him and closer to his sister, Isabelle. The other was very young the last time he'd seen her.

"I'm actually between jobs right now." Her voice grew distant and thoughtful as her forehead furrowed.

Ethan realized the paper she was reading was opened to the classified section. He frowned as he wondered what it must be like to have to work and worry about how to pay bills, and survive. He was grateful he would never have to know.

"What about your mom and dad?" she asked, pulling him out of his wandering thoughts. "What are they doing now?"

He forced himself not to bite his lip as he met her steady gaze. "Dad's a lawyer," he lied.

"Never thought I'd see that," she said with a rueful smile. "I never thought your dad was the type to settle down, at least not until he met your mom."

He shrugged as his gaze traveled longingly toward the window. He was growing more uncomfortable by the second; he just wanted to be back outside, where he was free. And where Jack and Mike were waiting to bombard him with questions, he realized.

"Well, I thought I would say hi and see how you were doing. I have to get going now," he said.

He was very adept at lying. He should be, he had been doing it his whole life, and he thought nothing of letting them roll off his tongue now.

"Oh yeah," she said quickly. "Of course. Tell everyone I say hi, and tell your mom..." her voice trailed off as her eyes became distant again. "Tell your mom I miss her."

Again, Ethan felt a twinge of sorrow. His mother had given

up her friends, more so than his father. He suddenly understood the wistful look that crossed her face when his dad, David, Doug, Jack, and Mike recalled stories of their younger days in high school and college. Without thinking, Ethan took her hand and squeezed it. She seemed as startled by the gesture as he did. He'd never touched a human being to offer them comfort, but this woman looked so sad he needed to give her some solace.

"I will," he promised.

She patted his hand before releasing it. "Are they still living at the same place?"

"Yes."

She nodded her eyes still sad and distant. "Maybe I'll give her a call."

"I'm sure she would like that."

He turned to leave. "Ethan."

"Yeah?" He paused to look back at her.

"Are they still as in love as they used to be?"

"Even more so," he said honestly.

She beamed at him as tears filled her large eyes. "That's wonderful."

Ethan left before she started to cry. He didn't deal well with humans under normal conditions; he sure didn't know how to handle an emotional one. Not that his sisters didn't get erratically emotional sometimes, but they were stronger and tougher than any human could ever be. He dashed across the street where Mike and Jack almost pounced on him.

"Let's get to the car first," he said briskly. "I'm ready to go home."

They exchanged glances, but they followed him back to the car. Ethan filled them in on the conversation as they left California behind and headed into Oregon.

"For God's sake, Ethan, get up!" Isabelle cried as she tugged at his arm.

Her brother groaned as he stubbornly refused to look at her. "Isabelle, I'm telling you right now, if you don't get out of my room, I'll—"

"You'll what?" she demanded. "Nothing, that's what, now get up!"

Planting her hands on her hips, she scowled at him as he opened one emerald-colored eye to peep up at her.

"What are you doing here anyway? Go back to your own house," he grumbled as he rolled over and buried himself beneath the sheet.

She reached down and ripped the sheet off.

"Hey!" he yelled as he tried to pull the sheet back.

She refused to relent as they were caught in a tug of war she was determined to win. "Ethan Joseph, get out of this bed right now!"

He scowled ferociously at her. She didn't back down as she met his look with one just as ferocious. "What do you want?" he snapped.

"Kyle and Cassidy climbed up a tree; they refuse to come down."

"Get Ian," he grumbled as he finally managed to wrench his sheet back.

She instantly grabbed it again. "Ian is with Mike, David, Doug, Jack, dad, and Aiden, so forget about Aiden too. They got out of bed this morning, unlike *some* people, and went to town to get more wood for the new house."

Ethan groaned as he threw his arm over his eyes. "They're immortal, tell them to jump."

"Ethan!" she cried in exasperation. "They can still break

bones, and what if they accidentally stake themselves on the way down?"

She knew he was trying to stifle a laugh at the image her words conjured. The only thing holding him back from doing so was knowing his brother and sister as well as she did. The possibility of them accidentally staking themselves was good. With a loud groan, he threw the sheet aside and swung his legs out of bed. Isabelle smiled smugly as she stepped back.

He didn't bother to look at her as he tugged on his jeans and a T-shirt. "How do they manage to get themselves into these messes?" he muttered.

"The same way we did."

He groaned as he shook back his tousled hair. "Who dared them to go up the tree?" he grumbled.

"Julian."

"Of course," he groaned.

Isabelle waited for him to slip his sneakers on before heading outdoors. She led the way down the path through the woods before veering off on another path leading further into the forest. They spent many hours playing in these woods as children, and Isabelle knew the trails like the back of her hand.

"Does mom know?" Ethan demanded.

"Like I was going to tell her, she has enough on her mind right now."

"Huh?" Ethan asked tiredly.

Isabelle shook her hair back as she cast a scowl over her shoulder at him. "Never mind," she muttered.

Ethan stuck his tongue out at her. Isabelle forced herself not to laugh as she made a face at him. They may be adults now, but he was the one person who could always bring out her childish side, and she loved that the most about him. She turned down the path leading to the tree house.

The distinct chant of, "Jump! Jump!" drifted to them.

"Ah, hell!" Ethan muttered as he broke into a run.

Isabelle was right on his heels as they burst into a small clearing. Willow and Julian stood at the base of a huge sycamore, looking up into its high, leaf-filled branches as they continued to shout at their younger siblings. Cassidy scooted down a branch, trying to adjust her hold as she started to slide sideways. Kyle, the less daring of the twins, had a death grip on his branch.

"Don't you dare jump!" Ethan bellowed, causing even Isabelle to start.

Willow and Julian spun around to gaze guiltily at them. Cassidy let out a yelp as she jerked in surprise. With horrifying clarity, Isabelle realized Cassidy wasn't going to keep her hold on the branch as she slid perilously. Ethan rushed forward, catching her just before she hit the ground. He grunted under the weight of her tiny body, his knees hitting the ground from the force of the impact.

Isabelle rushed up to them, a little breathless as her heart hammered with dread. Cassidy lay for a moment, her tiny face scrunched up. Then, one dazzling blue eye popped open, and she warily looked up at Ethan. She twisted her head, her long sandy blonde hair covering her face as she looked at the ground just inches beneath her. She turned back and burst into a brilliant grin as she easily hopped out of his arms.

"Thanks!" Cassidy cried.

"Don't mention it," Ethan grumbled, shaking his head as he rose.

"Good catch," Julian said in awe.

Ethan wiped the dirt off the knees of his jeans. "Show off," Isabelle teased. He scowled at her before smiling. She lifted her head to peer through the thick branches at Kyle. "How are you going to get the other one?"

"Think they could both fall out alive?" he asked hopefully

"Do you think a snowball could survive in Hell?" she retorted.

"Yeah, that's what I thought too," he mumbled unhappily.

She slapped him on the back. "When was the last time you climbed a tree?"

His face twisted thoughtfully. "Ten years, maybe."

Kyle was clinging to his branch, his face white as a ghost.

"Jump, Kyle; it's fun!" Cassidy urged her twin.

"Don't you dare jump!" Isabelle yelled at her brother, shooting Cassidy a silencing look.

Cassidy smiled back as she hopped from foot to foot, not the least bit ashamed. "Well, it is!" she protested.

"And if I hadn't caught you?" Ethan demanded.

She shrugged, refusing to be intimidated by her older siblings. "It would hurt, but I heal fast!"

Isabelle shook her head and fought not to laugh as she met Ethan's aggravated gaze. "How do you argue with that?" she inquired.

"Easily," he said before turning back to Cassidy. "Mom and dad would find out what you did."

Cassidy's mouth dropped as she worriedly looked over at Willow and Julian. "We only climbed a tree! There's nothing wrong with that!" she protested.

"After those two dared you!" he snapped, shooting a censuring look at Willow and Julian. They didn't look remotely ashamed as they stared unabashedly back at him.

"Forget it, Ethan, you're fighting a losing battle," Isabelle told him. "Kyle, scoot to the branch below you! It's a pretty clear drop from there."

"I'm scared!" Kyle wailed. "I don't want to let go."

"What kind of immortal is scared to fall from a tree?" Julian taunted.

"The smart kind!" Ethan retorted.

"I think you're going to have to go get him," she told Ethan.

"I'm too old for this crap," he muttered as he angrily tugged on his shaggy black hair.

Isabelle grinned at him, not deterred by his sour expression. "You're only twenty-five; just think how you're going to feel in a hundred years."

He turned away from her and grabbed one of the thick lower branches. Isabelle shaded her eyes against the sun as he climbed to their brother. Kyle slid his small arms around Ethan's neck and climbed onto his back; he clung to him for dear life. Isabelle stifled a laugh at the sound of Ethan's choking. She knew he would be annoyed if he heard her laughing at him, but it took all she had not to. A lot of curses, scratches, and mumbled threats later, he slid safely back to the ground. The minute he hit the ground, Kyle hopped off his back and raced over to join his siblings.

"Not so fast!" Isabelle yelled as they turned to bolt down the path. "There will be no more climbing trees! And if I find out the two of you dare them to do something stupid again, I'm going to tell mom and dad, and you'll be grounded for a month! Understand?"

"Yeah, yeah," Willow and Julian mumbled.

"Don't you yeah, yeah me, or I'll go and tell them right now."

"No don't!" they both yelled. "We'll be good."

"Good, and you two," she continued as she turned to her younger siblings. "I want your promise that if they do dare you to do something, you will *not* do it."

"We promise!" Kyle and Cassidy vowed in unison.

It was a useless promise; it would only be a matter of time before they were back into some mischief or another. "Go," she said wearily.

They turned and bolted down the path, disappearing easily into the woods. "How long do you think it will be before they're in trouble again?" Ethan asked as he absently pulled a twig from his shirt.

"Before they hit the end of the path," Isabelle answered with a small smile.

"Most likely. So, what's going on with mom?"

Isabelle started back down the path. "Nothing really, she's been quiet since you told her about running into her friend Karen last month."

"Kathleen," Ethan corrected.

"Whatever," she replied absently. "Plus, with Aiden going to college this fall, she's a little upset."

"Starting to get empty nest syndrome?"

Isabelle laughed as she pushed against his shoulder. "I don't think this nest will ever be empty."

Ethan grinned back at her. "Not with the two of us here. She was that upset about Kathleen?"

"Yeah, she was," Isabelle replied sadly. "She's been talking about her a lot since then, reminiscing and stuff."

Ethan frowned thoughtfully. "I know Kathleen seemed to miss her."

"Mom feels the same way. Every time she mentions her name, she gets this distant look in her eyes. It's sad."

"Well, there's nothing we can do about it."

"I know," Isabelle whispered.

"Hey, don't get all glum on me now!"

Isabelle grinned at him as she shoved his arm. He smiled as he playfully pushed her back. Out of all her siblings, Ethan was the most like her, and the one she was closest to. Neither of them had much use for the human race, other than food, and Isabelle didn't even bother with them for that.

The idea of actually going out in the world, and living amongst people, didn't appeal to either of them. Unlike the two of them though, Ian was already attending the University of

Oregon, and he loved it. Aiden was thrilled about going away to school in the fall, and although Victoria and Abigail were only fifteen, they were already flipping through college brochures.

However, she and Ethan were content to stay here. Isabelle rarely went out into the world, rarely even left her yard. Ethan went out more than she did, but not nearly as often as The Stooges did (as they referred to Mike, Doug, Jack, and David), or Ian, Aiden, Vicky, and Abby. Isabelle wasn't particularly fond of humans as it was, and the idea of actually living amongst them didn't appeal to her.

She liked her life here, the peace and security it offered. She supposed it was cowardly of her to stay hidden away when there was a huge world she could easily explore. However, she harbored a secret fear, and the possibility of her fear coming true was enough to make her never want to leave.

She glanced over at Ethan to find him smiling, his hands in his pockets, and his black head bowed. "What are you thinking about?" she asked teasingly.

Ethan instantly wiped the grin from his face. "Nothing."

She cocked an elegant eyebrow as she smiled at him slyly. "Girls?"

"Hardly," he retorted.

She laughed as she tossed back her hair. "Don't lie, Ethan, I know you."

He scowled at her as they stepped out of the woods. "And what about you?" he demanded.

She frowned as she looked at him. "What about me?" she retorted.

He grinned at her as he slung his arm around her shoulders. "Boys?" he taunted.

Isabelle laughed as she leaned against his side. "I wouldn't waste my time or my energy."

"Speaking of time and energy," Ethan groaned as a pickup,

laden with wood, pulled into the driveway. Another followed up the hill and parked next to it.

Isabelle started to laugh as she slipped free of his arm. "It's for *our* house," she reminded him.

"Does that mean you're going to help?" he inquired.

"Yeah, right," she replied.

She laughed as she skipped away with Ethan muttering behind her.

∼

Download *Destined* and continue reading:
brendakdavies.com/Dswb

∼

Stay in touch on updates, sales, and new releases by joining to the mailing list:
brendakdavies.com/ESBKDNews

Visit the Erica Stevens/Brenda K. Davies Book Club on Facebook for exclusive giveaways and all things book related. Come join the fun:
brendakdavies.com/ESBKDBookClub

FIND THE AUTHOR

Brenda K. Davies Mailing List:
brendakdavies.com/News

Facebook: brendakdavies.com/BKDfb

Brenda K. Davies Book Club:
brendakdavies.com/BKDBooks

Instagram: brendakdavies.com/BKDInsta
Twitter: brendakdavies.com/BKDTweet
Website: www.brendakdavies.com

ALSO FROM THE AUTHOR

Books written under the pen name Brenda K. Davies

The Vampire Awakenings Series

Awakened (Book 1)

Destined (Book 2)

Untamed (Book 3)

Enraptured (Book 4)

Undone (Book 5)

Fractured (Book 6)

Ravaged (Book 7)

Consumed (Book 8)

Unforeseen (Book 9)

Forsaken (Book 10)

Relentless (Book 11)

Legacy (Book 12)

The Alliance Series

Eternally Bound (Book 1)

Bound by Vengeance (Book 2)

Bound by Darkness (Book 3)

Bound by Passion (Book 4)

Bound by Torment (Book 5)

Bound by Danger (Book 6)

Bound by Deception (Book 7)

Bound by Fate (Book 8)

Bound by Blood (Book 9)

Bound by Love (Book 10)

The Road to Hell Series

Good Intentions (Book 1)

Carved (Book 2)

The Road (Book 3)

Into Hell (Book 4)

Hell on Earth Series

Hell on Earth (Book 1)

Into the Abyss (Book 2)

Kiss of Death (Book 3)

Edge of the Darkness (Book 4)

The Shadow Realms

Shadows of Fire (Book 1)

Shadows of Discovery (Book 2)

Shadows of Betrayal (Book 3)

Shadows of Fury (Book 4)

Shadows of Destiny (Book 5)

Shadows of Light (Book 6)

Wicked Curses (Book 7)

Sinful Curses (Book 8)

Coming 2023

Gilded Curses

Coming 2023

Historical Romance

A Stolen Heart

Books written under the pen name Erica Stevens

The Coven Series

Nightmares (Book 1)

The Maze (Book 2)

Dream Walker (Book 3)

The Captive Series

Captured (Book 1)

Renegade (Book 2)

Refugee (Book 3)

Salvation (Book 4)

Redemption (Book 5)

Broken (The Captive Series Prequel)

Vengeance (Book 6)

Unbound (Book 7)

The Kindred Series

Kindred (Book 1)

Ashes (Book 2)

Kindled (Book 3)

Inferno (Book 4)

Phoenix Rising (Book 5)

The Fire & Ice Series

Frost Burn (Book 1)

Arctic Fire (Book 2)

Scorched Ice (Book 3)

The Ravening Series

The Ravening (Book 1)

Taken Over (Book 2)

Reclamation (Book 3)

The Survivor Chronicles

The Upheaval (Book 1)

The Divide (Book 2)

The Forsaken (Book 3)

The Risen (Book 4)

ABOUT THE AUTHOR

Brenda K. Davies is the USA Today Bestselling author of the Vampire Awakening Series, Alliance Series, Road to Hell Series, Hell on Earth Series, and historical romantic fiction. She also writes under the pen name, Erica Stevens. When not out with friends and family, she can be found at home with her husband, son, dogs, cat, and horse.

Printed by Amazon Italia Logistica S.r.l.
Torrazza Piemonte (TO), Italy